PENGUI
ABOUT

Meena Arora Nayak is a writer and translator. She lives in the Washington DC metropolitan area with her husband and daughter. *About Daddy* is her second novel.

About Daddy

Meena Arora Nayak

PENGUIN BOOKS

Penguin Books India (P) Ltd., 11 Community Centre, Panchsheel Park, New Delhi 110 017, India
Penguin Books Ltd., 27 Wrights Lane, London W8 5TZ, UK
Penguin Putnam Inc., 375 Hudson Street, New York, NY 10014, USA
Penguin Books Australia Ltd., Ringwood, Victoria, Australia
Penguin Books Canada Ltd., 10 Alcorn Avenue, Suite 300, Toronto, Ontario M4V 3B2,Canada
Penguin Books (NZ) Ltd., Cnr Rosedale and Airborne Roads, Albany, Auckland, New Zealand

First published by Penguin Books India 2000

Copyright © Meena Arora Nayak 2000

10 9 8 7 6 5 4 3 2 1

Typeset in *Sabon Roman* by SÜRYA, New Delhi
Printed at Chaman Offset Printers, New Delhi

This is a work of fiction. Names, characters, places and incidents are either the product of
the author's imagination or are used fictitiously and any resemblance to any actual person,
living or dead, events or locales is entirely coincidental.

To Daddy
for his legacy

To Guriya
for accepting

Then from the night-warm soilbed of your heart
you dug the seeds, still green, from which your death
would sprout: your own, your perfect death, the one
that was your whole life's perfect consummation.

—Rilke, 'Requiem for a Friend'

Acknowledgements

I thank my parents for reliving their painful past for me.

I thank the superintendent of Budail jail in Chandigarh for allowing me to experience a moment of prison life.

I thank Manoj Kumar, Balaji and Naam Deo of the Indian BSF for teaching me the metaphors of barbed wire at the Wagah border.

I also thank Jane Chelius for believing in this book, despite everything; Bapsi Sidhwa for appearing like a fairy godmother; Bunty for discovering the magic wand; Professor Larson for reaffirming my writing life; Teji for tirelessly organizing my other lives to accommodate writing; and Karthika and Diya for letting this book flow through their intensities.

And I thank Babu for teaching me the intricate science of kites.

chapter one

Ten thousand volts.

My hand trembles as I reach out to feel the air surrounding galvanized twin walls of steel wire separated by immense fuzz balls of barbed mesh. The air at the border is unassuming, gently crisp in the wake of a cloudy fall day.

'Don't cremate me in India,' Daddy once said to me. 'I cannot ask her to bear the weight of my pyre. I have taken from her enough. But sprinkle my ashes on the border so that my soul can feel the wound I helped inflict as long as it bleeds.'

For a moment I stand and look at this place Daddy has chosen for his soul's unrest. This demarcation charged with enough electricity to light up a whole city or to fry anyone who dares to cross it, this narrow strip of no man's land guarded heavily on both sides by military forces as though to contain all histories of the two countries within it.

On the Indian side, where I stand, the border is secured by an ordinary military post. Disciplined hedges line a tarred road that leads to the outside boundary gate beyond which the city of Amritgarh sprawls in disinterested dailiness. Behind the hedges, on either side of the road, are rows of brick buildings, square and evenly spaced. Closer to me, between the buildings and the barbed wire, is a grove of eucalyptus trees followed by a bridge of gravel on which tourists wander around with cameras around their necks. Unarmed troopers stand by benignly. I watch some people as they wave at a security guard camouflaged in his blind among the trees. Others stand in line to see suspicious shadows illuminated a sickly green in the orbs of night-vision binoculars held by a parka-clad trooper who directs their eyes away from the golden lights that are mounted like imitation suns on top of the steel walls. A few temerarious ones approach the boundary and peer through its barbs at land that stretches familiarly from under their feet across to the other side to Pakistan. 'I helped divide India.' I can hear Daddy's anguish in my head. 'I killed the trust between Hindus and Muslims so that they can never live together in peace again. I hurt her. I cut her up.'

'Hush. Rest in peace now,' I whisper, slipping off my backpack which contains the rosewood box that has Daddy's ashes in it. This is how it all ends, I think: a handful of dust sprinkled on earth, mingling with earth; nothing remaining to tell of an existence. Cradling the backpack in my arms, I wish Daddy had asked me to bury him instead so that I could have visited his grave whenever I wanted. This seems so final. I close my eyes and rock gently, pressing the backpack close to my chest, seeking his embrace one last time. But there's only the weight of the rosewood box against my heart. The rosewood box and my Nikon FG. Seizing the chance to preserve a memory of his last penance, I loosen the beaded string of the bag and reach inside for my camera. There is the fleeting thought that photography might be prohibited here. I look around for signboards, but there are none. I remember my travel agent telling me that this border is not a restricted area any more. However, none of the tourists around me seem to be using their cameras. Instinctively, I begin to inch away from the crowd, stopping at a few yards' distance. Bringing the camera out, I place my backpack on the ground and grope inside it for the film I bought at Baltimore Washington International Airport. One of the rolls, I remember, is 1000 ASA. I don't want to use a slower speed because I am loath to use a flash. It will attract too much attention. Checking the print on the various film boxes, I finally find the one I'm looking for and tear it open. Loading my camera hurriedly, and adjusting it to autofocus, I raise it to my eye. Then I frame a picture around the steel roots stabbing the earth. When I press the shutter, its click sounds loud in my ear. I glance at the main area, but not a single head turns in my direction. Finally, ready to let go, I slip the camera back inside my bag and step closer to the barbed wire. Going down on my knees, I take out the rosewood box and lay it on the ground. 'Goodbye, Daddy,' I whisper.

Suddenly, a piercing whistle shoots through the air. My head jerks up. Picking up the box and backpack, I stand up quickly and turn around. The ground under my feet begins to pound with heavy boots and the air over my head whirls with cyclic sirens. In the main area, tourist pursuits are suspended by loud military voices issuing orders. As I begin to move towards the other people, a cylinder of floodlight descends around me, trapping me like a bug. My body freezes.

'Haath khade karo,' a voice booms out in Hindi. At the back of my mind I translate the words into English: 'Hands raise do,' but I can't seem to put the words together to make sense.

'Haath Khade Karo,' repeats the voice. This time my brain is able to straighten out the order of the words and I want to obey, but it is as though my body has turned to stone. Before me, armed guards like cadets in a drill, begin to line up one by one to form a semicircle at the periphery of light, their heavy guns pointing directly at me. Terror begins to pound in my heart with a hammerhead, threatening to demolish me. With a detached horror, I wait for my body to crumble at my feet.

'Raise your hands—NOW.' Guns are cocked around me, snapping in my head like the fingers of a hypnotist breaking a trance, and every nerve inside me bursts into convulsions. Shaking uncontrollably, I drop my backpack on the ground, and clutching the box to my chest with one hand, raise the other above my head.

'Put the box on the ground and raise your other hand.'

I hold the box closer.

'Put it down.' Feet shuffle as the circle tightens.

My eyes trained on the gun directly in front of me, one hand still raised above my head, I bend and place the box carefully on the ground at my feet. The dark shapes around me move closer. I take a step backwards.

'Stop. Do not move. What is in the box?'

'My father ...' I can feel my lips form the words in Hindi, but no sound comes out.

'What are you doing here?'

'I'm a tourist,' I want to say and begin to translate it aloud, searching desperately for the Hindi word for tourist, but to no avail.

'What is in the box?' I am asked again. The guns draw closer.

'Ashes,' I finally whisper in English.

Ashes ... ashes ... ashes ... The word hisses in the air, sweeping the sound from one mouth to another.

'She says everything will be ashes,' I hear the conclusion.

As if in slow motion, the semicircle of metal around me widens. Beyond it, a stampede breaks out among the tourists. Somewhere in the distance, I hear the crackling of a radio and the words 'bomb squad' reach my ears. Relief sweeps through my inert senses. This isn't about the picture at all, I think. 'No. No, wait,' I call out, reaching for the box. 'You're mistaken. This box is not a bomb.'

'Move away from the box,' I am ordered in Hindi again.

'This box is not a bomb. It has my father's ashes in it.'

'She doesn't understand Hindi,' another voice advises.

A form steps forward into the light and gestures me with his gun to move away from the box. 'Come,' he says in English, his face a mime's shadowless white, his gun starkly black.

Calling upon the syllables of the elusive language, I try to explain in Hindi this time. 'Listen to me. This box has my father's ashes. It's not a bomb.'

Realizing I speak their language, fresh orders are issued.

'If you don't move away from the box this minute, you

will be shot.'

I stumble towards the metal curve, explaining urgently. 'Please, listen to me. You have made a mistake.' Even as I reach within the semicircle, I am seized by numerous hands. Hands rough and curt probe everywhere—my legs, my inner thighs, my waist, my arms, my underarms, my breasts. 'Stop it!' I scream in outrage, wiggling my body to dislodge them. 'Stop it.' I slap away their lingering violations.

'Chalo.' I am pushed forward.

'Where? I'm telling you you're mistaken. That box is not a bomb. Why don't you open it and see?'

The butt of a gun hits the back of my shoulder and I fall to the ground on my hands and knees. My bones jar with the impact and a painful sob breaks through my throat. Hearing a loud gasp within a few feet of me, I raise my eyes and see an old woman extend a palsied hand towards me before she is pulled away by a young man. I am hoisted up by the upper arms and, before I can regain my balance, dragged over the gravel down the paved road towards the brick buildings. Somewhere along the way, I lose a sneaker and my stockinged foot is pulled along the tarmac, its skin snagging and tearing, sparking off trails of agony up my leg. Screaming in pain and anger, I am finally brought to an open door where an armed guard stands at stony attention. He doesn't move a muscle as I am lifted over the doorstep and deposited on the floor of a room harshly bright with fluorescent lights. I lie there on my side for a moment, savouring the reprieve, letting the soothing cold of the cement floor seep in through my cheek. But, before long, I hear heavy footsteps and see two spit-shined, black boots come to a halt near my face.

'Please get up,' a calm voice tells me in English clipped with the staccato of a British accent.

Placing a palm on the floor before me, bracing all my weight on it, I stand up painfully.

He is a big man. He is a colossal man dressed in foliage green. His shoulder is decorated with a number of red and gold stripes. On his long upper lip is a moustache so neatly trimmed and so deeply black, it could be a strip of velvet plastered there. One of his ears is missing; only a stump of cartilage remains.

'What is your name?' he asks, beginning to move towards a green metal desk against the farthest wall of the room, directly across from the door.

Regaining some of my confidence from his voice, I take a deep breath and release it slowly. 'Look, I'm an American tourist,' I say. 'Your men have mistaken my box for a bomb.'

'What is your name?' he asks again, sitting behind his desk.

'Simran. Simran Mehta.'

'Please sit, Miss Mehta.' He indicates the chairs on the other side of the desk. I limp to the matching green metal chairs with jute knit backs and seats, but I don't sit. 'Your men have made a mistake. That box is not a bomb.'

'Please sit. I need to ask you some questions.'

I perch on the edge of a chair.

'What is in the box?'

'My father's ashes.'

'What are you doing here with your father's ashes?'

'He wanted me to scatter them on the border of India and Pakistan.'

'Why?'

Why? What can I say? Because the guilt of his crimes won't let him rest even in death? Because he thought he perpetrated the partition of India and Pakistan?

'Why, Miss Mehta?'

I look down at my hands clenching and unclenching in my lap. 'Because he loved India,' I finally say.

'Yes, but why the border? Why not in the Ganga as is the normal practice?'

'He lived in India before the Partition. That's how he remembered it. As one country.'

'When did he leave India?'

'1946, '47. I'm not sure.'

'What was his name?'

I look up, wondering if they have war tribunals in this country. I'm afraid they might have Daddy's name on a list of war criminals.

'Speak up, Miss Mehta. What was his name?'

'Manohar Mehta,' I say softly, watching his face, but no trace of recognition flashes across it.

'When did he die?'

'September 15th. Two weeks ago.'

'Do you have a death certificate?'

'Yes, but not with me.'

'Where are you staying?'

'At Mayur Mahal hotel.'

'Is the certificate there?'

'No. I didn't bring it with me to India.'

'Do you have any relatives here in India?'

'No.' I shake my head.

'Who else do you have in your family?'

'No one. My mother died five years ago.'

'Ah.' He leans back in his chair, a knowing smile wrinkling the edges of the velvet moustache. 'Alone and on a mission. What else are you carrying, Miss Mehta?' he says as though he has already classified Daddy's ashes as incriminating material.

'What do you mean?' I stand up, forgetting my hurt foot. Pain shoots through the toes, making me lose my balance. Grabbing hold of the back of a chair, I straighten up. 'I'm a tourist,' I say. 'I'm not carrying anything illegal.'

'But you're not just a tourist, are you, Miss Mehta?' He sits up again, folding his hands on the desk, still smiling that I-know-your-secret smile. 'You're on a mission. How long do you plan to be in India?'

'I don't know what you're talking about.' I can hear my voice turn shrill with frustration. 'I've told you why I'm here. All you have to do is open the box and you'll see I'm telling the truth.'

'How long do you plan to be here?' he asks again, the smile disappearing from his face.

'Fifteen days,' I say grudgingly.

'What else is on your agenda?'

'This is ridiculous,' I say, making no effort to conceal the anger that is building inside me. 'Look, I've had just about enough of this. I haven't done anything, yet your men have harassed me and hurt me, and now you're making all these allegations. I'm an American citizen. You can't do this to me. I have half a mind to inform my Consulate about this.' Then, thinking quickly, I add, 'However, if you give me my things and let me return to my hotel, I'll try to forget this happened.'

'I'm afraid I can't do that,' he says calmly. 'I'll have to keep you here overnight.'

'What? You've got to be kidding.' The chair I'm holding tips forward as I lean against it in disbelief. Setting it back in place, I stand without support. 'You can't do that,' I shout at him. 'I haven't done anything. Why don't you open the box and see? All it has are ashes. My father's ashes.'

He gives me a long-suffering look as though waiting for a childish tantrum to exhaust itself.

'This is crazy.' Rage makes my voice tremble, and I can feel my eyes prick with its impotence. For a moment I stand rigidly, urging my body to control its reflexes. Then I take a deep breath and, pulling myself to my full height as best as I can on one foot, say quietly, 'I want to call the American Consulate.'

He looks at me for a second longer, then pushing his chair back, he gets up. 'Your Consulate will be informed,' he says.

'I want to call them right now.'

Ignoring me, he picks up a gold-trimmed military hat from the desk and fits it on his head, straightening the rim with his thumb and forefinger. 'Shamim,' he calls, stepping away from the desk.

'Wait a second!' I scream at him. 'Why are you doing this? I haven't done anything.'

He comes around the desk. 'We have to make inquiries,' he says. Behind me I hear the starchy swish of a sari.

'What inquiries? I'm just a tourist,' I scream, but he

walks away. I turn around to see an androgynous form made
female only by attire, standing behind me. She is flat and
square like a cardboard cut-out. Her hair is cropped close to
her scalp. 'Chalo!' she says, clasping a hand around my
elbow. Her voice is harsh.

'Wait a second.' I pull my arm out of her grip and limp
after the officer, screaming, 'Let me call my Consulate.' The
muzzle of a gun appears in my face. Tears of anger and
frustration finally find release and spill onto my cheeks. I
stand helplessly, watching the one-eared giant step through
the door and disappear into the evening half-light.

'Come,' Shamim grabs my elbow again.

'No,' I cry, trying to pry her fingers off my arm. 'I won't
come. I'm not going to stay here.'

She gestures to two guards with her free hand, and in a
moment, I am grasped by my upper arms again and dragged
from the bright room through a dark corridor to the back of
the building.

Shamim unlocks a barred iron door, and the guards
push me in.

'No!' I scream, getting up hurriedly to beat the door
with my fists. 'You can't do this. You can't keep me here.
Open this door!'

For long moments I shout into the empty corridor till my
anger dissolves into defeated sobs, and I sink to the floor,
turning around to rest my aching back against the bars. A
nauseating smell of stale urine hits my nose. Wiping my eyes
with the back of my hands, I look around. I am in a small,
rectangular cell. Across from me is a barred window through
which a square piece of dark sky hangs like a picture on the
wall. In the dirty yellow light of a bulb hanging from the
centre of the ceiling, I see whitewash peeling off the walls in
patches like scabs, revealing ugly, scarred underskin. The cell
is empty except for a bare wooden chair set under the light,
facing the door. In one far corner I see a large hole cut into
the floor. The cement around it is sticky and discoloured
from unwashed urine stains. I turn my eyes away in revulsion,
willing myself not to vomit. Raising myself painfully, I limp

towards the chair and perch on its edge, turning around to stare helplessly out of the window. My mind is reduced to the single dimension of being trapped in a nightmare.

It starts to rain. I can see heavy drops of water strike the iron bars of the window and shatter into a ricochet of spray. I wonder if the rosewood box containing Daddy's ashes is still lying under suspicion near the barbed border of India and Pakistan. The thought of a bomb squad examining Daddy's fine grey ashes through the large insect eyes of their metal masks brings a fresh sob to my throat. I wish I had opened the box before I placed it on the ground so that the rain could have washed Daddy's ashes away and mingled them with the soil at the border as he had wished.

I sit looking at the window. It allows my vision a square piece of suspended rain. Limping towards it, I raise myself on the toes of my good foot and try to look beyond, but my eyes only reach the level of the sill. Raindrops sprinkle my burning eyes. I wipe the moisture away impatiently. The wooden chair stands a few feet from the window. Lifting its back, I drag it across. Its spindly, square legs rattle along the rough floor. Pulling it to the wall, I climb onto it and look out. In the distance, I can see the border lit up with numerous lights like the site of a carnival—a desolate, ghostly carnival devoid of people. It is hard to imagine that only an hour or so ago it had been swarming with tourists and then with armed men and patrol jeeps. In the golden rain, the boundary looks like melting latticework. Underneath, water washes away soil across the border, from one country to another, a shared alluvium.

'The rain is so forgiving,' Daddy used to say. I remember the first time he told me about rain in India, showing me the scars on his head from one end of the crown to the other like a tiara forever embellished in his scalp.

I must have been about six or seven at that time. Mummy used to work back then and our neighbour, Mrs Ferrier, used to babysit me, taking me and her son, Scott, with her to the various volunteer programmes she was involved in. I remember the time her church group organized a food and blanket drive for the people in Bangladesh who had been ravaged not only by the horrors of war but also by the swollen waters of the Padma. At the meetings I would listen sometimes to stories of starving, shelterless people in this faraway land birthed by India through a war with Pakistan, but with a child's fleeting interest, I would soon forget them in the distractions of the church's playground and Scott's monster trucks. Then one day, Farzana, a new girl in my class, accosted me in the girl's bathroom and called me 'enemy' with the contempt of a racial slur. 'No, I'm not,' I told her, hardly understanding what she meant. 'Yes, you are,' she insisted. 'Indians are our enemies.' She was from Pakistan. Her parents had recently migrated to the United States. 'I'm not Indian, I'm American,' I told her. 'No, you're not. You're Indian; my Mummy said so.' 'No, I'm not,' I shouted and ran out into the corridor. Of course, I knew I was Indian, but only because my parents were. I had never considered being Indian as my own identity.

That day when Mrs Ferrier brought me home, I ran past my mother at the door and up the stairs, to empty out the hall closet. I heard Mummy close the door and call me, but ignoring her, I took out all the sheets and blankets smelling sweetly of the lavender potpourri she kept in the corners of the closet. Then I pulled off the comforters and sheets from my parents' bed and then my own, and stuffed everything into two large trash bags. As I dragged the bags down, my father joined my mother at the foot of the stairs. 'What's in the trash bags, Simi?' my mother asked.

'I'm giving away blankets to the people in Bangladesh.'

'What? Oh, for Ann's church group? Honey, I've already donated some stuff to her.'

I just kept on going.

'Simi, honey, hold on a moment. It's wonderful that you feel so strongly about this, but we've already given as much as we can.'

Going past them, I opened the front door and tried to pull the trash bags over the threshold. One bag caught on a nail and ripped. A corner of my parents' comforter tumbled out.

'Hold, on, hold on.' My mother took the bags from me and lifted them back inside. 'Let's not give away our own bedding. You don't need to do that.'

'I do,' I said, tears filling my eyes.

'Why?'

'Because it won't stop raining.' I brushed off the tears from my eyes, but more kept coming.

My mother took me in her arms and sat down with me on the stairs. 'Hush, baby. You want to tell us what's going on?'

With a loud sob I pulled out of her arms and darted up the stairs to throw myself face down on the bare mattress of my bed. After a moment I felt it sag on one side as my mother sat down beside me.

'What's the matter, Simi?' she asked, her hand caressing my hair.

'I hate the rain.' I sat up sobbing. 'I hate it. It's hurting all those people in the new country India made. I hate it. I hate you. I want to be Indian. Why don't you ever tell me I'm Indian? You're Indian, Daddy's Indian, then how come I'm not?'

My parents just stared at me speechlessly.

'I hate it. I'm nothing. I'm not American, I'm not Hispanic, I'm not from Pakistan, I'm not Indian. What am I?'

'Sure you're Indian.' My mother reached to touch my hair again.

'No, I'm not.' I jerked my head away. 'If I am, then how come you never talk to me about India, how come we never go there to visit, how come we don't speak the language or wear the clothes or talk about it? How come you never talk to me about India? Did you even know that there was a war in India? How come you never told me if I'm Indian? And the people there, they don't even have dry blankets because it won't stop raining. I hate the rain.' I broke down completely then, falling back on the mattress, my sobs vibrating in the hollows between the springs.

My mother pulled me onto her lap. 'Hush, baby. It's

okay. It's okay.'

'Don't hate the rain.' My father spoke for the first time, his voice so strained it was as if he were in physical pain. 'Don't hate the rain,' he said again. 'The rain in India is so forgiving.' I lifted my head and looked at him through a haze of tears. 'Simran,' he said, coming forward and lifting me off Mummy's lap to sit me down on the bed. 'I'm the one you should blame,' he said, sitting beside me. 'I'm the reason we don't visit India. Why we don't talk about it.'

'Why?' I said, wiping the tears away.

He bent his head then so I could see the scars not quite concealed under his thick hair. 'Because I love India here,' he touched two fingers to his head, 'and here.' He touched the same fingers to his heart. 'But I hurt her. I hurt India. I hurt her very badly.' My mother reached across me and placed a hand on his arm.

'It's all right,' he said, covering her hand with his. 'It's all right. She needs to know. You know, don't you?' he asked me, 'that a long time ago India and Pakistan were one country?'

I nodded. 'We learned about that in Asia Week. We also learned about Gandhi.'

'That's right. Mahatma Gandhi helped liberate India through non-violence, but he couldn't stop her people from dividing the country.'

'Why, Daddy?'

'Because some Hindus and Muslims who didn't want to live together any more started killing each other, and the British, who ruled India at that time, divided her into two parts. They gave one part to the Muslims and the other part to the rest of the people. So the people who lived on the wrong side had to leave their homes and go to the side they belonged to. But there were some bad people who couldn't wait for them to leave. They began killing them all.'

'Whose side were you on, Daddy?'

'I don't know. I was a Hindu which meant that I had to be on the Indian side; but I lived with Gajji, my gym teacher, in Lahore which was to be in Pakistan, on the Muslim side.'

'Did the Muslims hurt you, Daddy?' I touched his head.

'Yes. They killed my father, too.' I could see his Adam's apple bob as he swallowed hard. 'But that didn't happen in Lahore. You see, in Lahore, people lived together in peace; they didn't want to be divided. But they were afraid. They knew that the hatred spreading in the rest of the country would soon enter Lahore, too, so the young men in Lahore began to watch out for strangers in their streets. They began to patrol their neighbourhoods with whatever weapons they could find: kitchen knives, axes, staffs, anything. They wanted to protect each other. They were ready to kill anyone who threatened to divide them. You see, they were happy together, the Muslims and Hindus. They trusted each other with their lives.' He became quiet, staring at his hands.

'What happened then, Daddy?' I asked.

He got up and walked to the window. An early moon stuck like a pasted sticker to the cold afterlight of the sky. 'Then Gajji was killed,' he said almost in a whisper.

Mummy got up and went to stand beside Daddy. I saw the knuckles of her hand turn white as she gripped Daddy's shoulder. When he turned to look at her, she shook her head.

A terrible fear rose up my spine. 'What did you do, Daddy?' I asked.

Daddy looked at Mummy for a while, then at me, then turned to look out of the window again. 'What did you do?' I persisted urgently. It was as if I was in the grip of a horror film where, in spite of the terror lurking behind the door, I had to see it opening; I just had to know what lay beyond. Then suddenly with a clarity that shocked me, I knew. 'Did you kill someone, too, Daddy?'

His shoulders rose as he drew a deep breath and held the air in, then slumped. 'I killed a lot of people.' His voice was cold and faraway as if he had entered the realm of the moon. 'I took Gajji's sword and hurt the Muslims in my neighbourhood.'

'No, don't.' My mother had moved to stand between Daddy and me as though by doing so she would prevent his words from reaching me. Daddy turned around and looked straight at me. 'I stood in the middle of the marketplace one day and hacked off innocent people who were only out to shop. I killed ...'

'Enough!' My mother reached to cover his mouth with her hand as if to push the words back in. 'She's too young.'

'I hurt India,' Daddy continued, his voice muffled behind Mummy's hand. 'I killed people who loved me. I killed the trust between Hindus and Muslims so that they would never be able to live together in peace again. I helped divide them forever. I helped divide India. I tore her apart. And I left her bleeding and ran away and I can never go back.'

It seemed to me then that my father was afraid. His fear appeared so tangible, I could feel it in my own throat. I was no longer watching the horror film. I was in it. But strangely enough, my father was not the killer. He was the victim and invisible policemen were chasing him. I was so terrified that they would take him away, I jumped off the bed and ran to him, throwing my arms around his middle to hold him tight.

'You shouldn't have told her that,' I heard my mother say. 'She's too young.'

But I wasn't listening to my parents. I was thinking of ways to protect my father from relentless pursuers, from India whom he had hurt so much. I knew then that I'd never mention this again, ever, to anyone. I knew I'd never even mention the name of India lest the demons of crime and punishment were lurking behind the very syllables. India appeared before me not only as a victim, but as a nemesis; and the crimes my father had committed against her, a terrible secret to lock away in my heart for ever and ever.

I must have whimpered or cried out because my mother loosened my arms from around Daddy's middle and held me against her. 'Hush, baby. It was a long time ago,' she said. 'It's over now. Don't be afraid. Daddy's sorry. He didn't mean to. It was a mistake.'

I turned my head and looked at Daddy from within the fold of Mummy's arms. He sat down on his haunches before me and smiled strangely. 'But the rain,' he said. 'Don't blame the rain. It is forgiving. One day it forgave me and all those other young men like me. There we were one day, out in the street, brandishing our weapons, looking for people to hurt, and it began to rain—hard. It seemed as though the clouds had burst to put out the fire that was burning in our hearts. We all ran for shelter under eaves of houses, trees, anything. We all ran, Hindus, Muslims, all looking for shelter from the rain. And while it poured around us, we looked at each other and we looked away, because we were suddenly ashamed of the evidence of violence in our hands. When it stopped raining, we went home. That day our weapons had been silenced by the rain. And it forgave us all, that rain.'

My mother slept in my bed that night, holding me close as though to protect me from the past, or perhaps the future, because the next day she enrolled me in a Sunday school where I could learn Hindi and regain some of my lost identity.

'What are you doing?'

My foot slips off the edge of the chair and, landing on my bad foot, I crash to the floor, the chair tumbling over me.

'What are you doing?' Shamim asks me again from the door.

Pushing the chair off, I sit up and pull my injured foot onto my lap. I can see the skin over the toes scraped clean, leaving bits of nylon stocking congealed to the flesh underneath. Blood fills under the nail of my big toe and streams off the side onto the sole. Something sharp must have sliced through the quick.

'My foot is bleeding,' I tell her.

'What were you doing at the window?'

'Looking out. It's raining.'

'You can't move the chair around.'

I nod. 'My foot. It's bleeding. Can you get me something for it?' But she has already disappeared. I sit with my foot in my lap, crying softly, feeling a stickiness against my thighs as drops of blood soak through my pants.

Whether I pass out or fall asleep from exhaustion, I

don't know, but I am awakened again by the sensation of something crawling on the toes of my hurt foot. Sometime in my unconscious state, my leg must have slipped from my lap and now lies stretched before me on the floor. I lift my foot with both hands to bring it back to the lap and see a large black ant meandering over the exposed flesh. In horror I flick it off and peer at the floor. An army of ants is skirting around my legs. My eyes follow them to the hole in the corner—single file, head-to-rear, a patrol marching on to battle till they reach me, the enemy, and separate, each one searching for a vantage point of attack. I get up hurriedly, shaking them off my clothes, my skin crawling with the sensation of millions of ugly, black, hairy things.

Stamping my foot to shoo away the ants, I climb onto the chair, bringing my hurt foot onto my lap again. In my mind I can see it oozing with infection from germs carried from the hole. I wish I could tie up the open wounds to protect them from warring bacteria. I look around desperately for some bit of fabric, but other than the clothes on my body there is nothing in the cell. I pull out a corner of my shirt and hold it against the lacerations, but the pressure makes my big toe bleed again, and in a moment, a large stain begins to appear on the cloth. I try to tear off a strip from the front end, but the material has been made to last. Cursing loudly, I try to rip the sleeve by reaching with one hand and pulling it near the seam till I can feel a thread snap. Slowly, my long nails digging into the material, I am able to tear the sleeve free. I bandage it around my foot carefully and begin on the other sleeve till it comes loose as well. I wrap that around too, as tightly as I can. Tomorrow, I promise myself, a doctor, a hot bath and beautiful clothes.

Daddy loved to see me dressed in beautiful new clothes. His favourite activity used to be to take me shopping. 'To make up for the one shirt I owned,' he would say. I remember the last dress he bought me: black chiffon, knee-length, with a scooped neck and little black buttons all down the front—a deceptively simple dress, perfect for any occasion. The first and last time I wore it was at his funeral when

I watched his body encased in a simple wooden coffin,
gliding into the incinerator of a local funeral home. I
returned home with a handful of fine grey dust in a plain
rosewood box. I didn't shed a tear. I was not shocked or
devastated, because his death was familiar to me. I had
watched it follow him like a shadow all my life, and since
Mummy's death, I had seen it eclipse his very existence.

I remember that evening we had been relaxing after
work, watching a stand-up comic on television. I was laughing
half-heartedly at his inane jokes, when suddenly Daddy burst
into loud, uninitiated laughter as though remembering a
timeless joke. I looked at him, surprised at the sound. I had
never heard him laugh so loudly. Then he clutched his chest
and crumpled up on the sofa. I rushed to his side. As I knelt
beside him, reaching to place my own hand over his on his
chest, a gurgling rattle emitted from his mouth as his heart
contracted for the last time, and the remaining air in his
lungs flapped against the lawless muscles of his vocal chords.
The pores of the house inhaled that fearful death rattle
mingled with grotesque laughter, and for days after that,
exhaled it into my silences. I could hear it even in my sleep.
For nights after that I sat in his favourite chair, a black
leather-bound Laz-E-Boy, clutching the rosewood box to my
heart, deafened by the loud breathing of the house echoing
laughter and death rattles. Sleep would come to me sometimes,
and I would nod off on the arm of the chair only to be
awakened again by the echoes. Finally, one night, I pulled
open the drawer where I knew he kept the magic quilt of my
childhood, the beggar's mantle his mother had made for
him, and lay down with it covering my ears. That night I
slept long and hard, my ears made impenetrable by his shield
against death.

chapter two

The door in front of me clangs open, jerking heavily on the rust of its hinges. Three men file in. All three are unarmed and dressed in khaki uniforms, different from the foliage green of the men who arrested me. They have realized their mistake and have come to tell me that I am free to go, I think. Lowering my bandaged foot, I look at them expectantly. They are a motley group. One of them is scrawny and light skinned. The parting in the centre of his oil-slicked black hair is so wide and straight, it shines like a beam of light on his head. The second one is big, with the sagging torso of a weightlifter. His sleeves are rolled up, revealing bulging forearms covered thickly with curly black hair. The third, of medium build, has teeth bucking out of his lips, giving him a perpetual idiot grin. There is a large gap between the two front teeth. As the three come and stand before me, I see the overhead light intensify the menacing shadows on their faces and a fear begins to curl in the pit of my stomach. I sit staring at their faces, one to the other, trying to figure out why they are here.

'We come to ask you who you are working for?' the gap-toothed man finally asks softly in broken English.

'What?' My voice comes out in a parched rasp.

'Who you are working for?' he asks me again, his voice impatient.

'Why are you asking me this?' My throat prickles when I speak. 'I told that other officer, I'm an American tourist,'

I say, sucking saliva from the inside of my mouth to offer my gullet some relief.

'I am asking you question. Who you are working for? Answer.'

'EasyWrite,' I say, feeling the burning in my throat. 'I work for a small desktop publishing company in America called EasyWrite.'

'Pani lao,' my interrogator says to his colleagues. The scrawny one goes out of the cell, closing the door behind him. 'Who else you are working for?' The interrogation continues.

'No one,' I say. 'I keep telling you all that you have made a mistake. I'm just a tourist from America.'

He looks at me quietly for a moment. Then, bringing his face close to mine, he says, spraying me with spittle through the cavernous gap in his teeth, 'I am advising you, if you not cooperate, you will regret.'

'I am cooperating. I'm telling you the truth,' I say, resisting the urge to wipe my face.

'That is to be seen,' he says, his face still close to mine. I lean as far back as I can to dodge another onslaught of flying spittle. 'Why you come here?'

'I already told the other officer that. I came here to scatter my father's ashes on the border.'

'Hmm,' he says, straightening up and moving back a few steps.

The door to the cell opens and the scrawny officer returns with a clear glass tumbler filled with water. He hands it to my interrogator who in turn holds it before my face. As I reach for it, Scott's warning at BWI airport rings in my ears, 'And remember, don't drink the water. It'll kill you.' Swallowing the thirst, I let my hand fall back in my lap again.

'Drink,' the man orders me.

I shake my head. He withdraws his hand and stands looking into the water as though seeking his next question there. 'Why you take photograph of border?' he asks distractedly.

Dread lands like a ton of bricks in my stomach. 'Wh-what photograph?' I stammer.

Suddenly, my face is pelted with water. Sputtering and gasping for breath, I lean so far back in the chair, it almost topples over. 'Why you take photograph of border?' His voice has become loud and belligerent now.

'I . . . I wanted to have a picture of my father's last resting place.'

He steps forward again and the next instant, his palm strikes my cheek, flinging me off the chair. A burning consumes my face as though it has been seared by a hot iron. Nursing my cheek, I lie on the floor, crying in pain and terror.

'Tell truth!' I am told.

'That *is* the truth.' The words flap in my swollen cheek.

I see the weightlifter approach me this time. Whimpering, I cower close to the floor, holding my arms over my face. He bends forward and grabs me by my arm. I scream, trying to break loose. He deposits me on the chair, and walking around, clamps his hands on my shoulders from behind, pinning me to its shaky, wooden back.

'Please,' I cry, wiggling my shoulders to loosen his hold. 'I'm sorry I took a picture, but I didn't know I wasn't allowed. There is no sign.'

I see the third man pull out a pair of handcuffs from his belt and pass them to his colleague behind me who pulls my arms across the chair back and cuffs my wrists tightly. The sides of the chair dig deep into the crooks of my elbows.

'Who you are connected with?' the gap-toothed man asks.

'What do you mean?' I ask bewildered. 'I'm just a tourist.'

He comes towards me again.

'No,' I cry. 'No, please. I don't know what you are talking about. Please believe me.'

'Why you are here in Amritgarh?'

I look at him fearfully. 'My father's ashes . . .'

This time I can see the blow coming; the nerve ends in

my cheek are already braced for it. But the pain, when his open palm strikes, is so intense, that for a moment I think he has ripped the skin off my face. Screams reverberate in the room. They must be mine, because behind me I hear a snickering laugh and the words, 'Saali Amreekan chut ki cheekhen to desi hain.' Someone grabs the hair on the crown of my head and pulls it back. Sobbing in pain, I see buck-teeth only inches away from my face. 'Are you spy?' he asks very softly.

'No,' I wail loudly.

'You are spy,' he declares.

'No.'

He pulls harder on my hair. I cringe in pain. He brings the ball of his hand up hard under my chin. The bones in my face explode, spewing shrapnel into my head. I hear a strange ringing in my ears, and my vision blurs. Inside my mouth, I taste blood, perhaps from having bitten my tongue.

'You are spy,' he says again.

Stunned, I try to focus on his face, but he seems to have grown another head.

'Admit.'

I close my eyes tightly, then open them again. The duplicate head has disappeared.

'Admit. You are spy.'

No, I want to say, but the muscles in my face seem to have settled in painful paralysis. He releases my hair and straightens up. I see him make a gesture to the third man who takes out a piece of paper from a pocket in his shirt and, opening its folds, hands it to my tormentor.

'Sign this.' He waves the paper before my eyes. 'If you sign, we not hurt you.'

I try to focus on the handwritten scrawl.

'Says you admitting you are spy.'

'No.' My lips are able to move again, but I can hardly hear my own voice.

'Sign this,' comes the order, louder this time.

I shake my head warily, watching him, dreading his next move. Hands descend on my shoulders from behind. My breath catching in my throat, I stiffen against the back of the chair. Slowly, spanning over my chest, I feel them inching towards my breasts. I look down in horror. They are like two serpentine monsters matted with thick, curly black hair. As they reach my breasts and grab them, a strangled sob breaks out of my throat. I squirm and wriggle, the sides of the chair scraping against my confined arms. 'No. Stop. Please,' I beg, but the hands tighten around my breasts, kneading, squeezing. Crying noisily, I try to bite at one of the arms. 'Saali Amreekan chut.' I hear a curse over my head, and the hand I had tried to bite shoots to my crotch and cups it tightly. Screams tear out of my throat. 'Stop! Make him stop,' I plead the men in front of me. 'Please make him stop.'

Ugly smiles break upon their faces.

'You sign paper?'

'Yes,' I wail. 'Yes. Just make him stop.'

The hands on my body linger a moment longer before they are removed. I slump in the chair, my body broken with sobs. When the gap-toothed man approaches me with paper and pen, I am prepared to sign. I mean to do it, I really do, but as he halts before my chair, I don't know what instinct of survival prevails, and I swing out my sneakered foot, kicking him in the groin as hard as I can. I see him crumble, clutching his crotch with both hands. Then a fist smashes into the side of my face and I crash to the floor losing consciousness.

The little girl is crying. She's been hurt. She's looking for her Mummy to kiss the pain away. 'Hush now.' It's her Daddy. He's covering her with a ragged old quilt and saying, 'This is a magic quilt. It makes pain disappear. Here now. You lie down and I'll tell you a story about the little boy to whom this quilt belonged.'

I snuggle deeper into the familiar comfort of the quilt and let Daddy tell me the story of the magic quilt again.

'This quilt belonged to a little boy,' he says. 'It's a patchwork quilt made from old pieces of fabric taken from discarded clothing. The boy's mother made it for him when he was four, to protect him from death.

You see, the boy had three sisters and four brothers. But the brothers all died before he was born. They were all struck by a curious fever at the age of four; a gentle fever, never rising above the hundred-degree mark, never totally incapacitating, simmering just under the tender skin, emitting a gentle warmth. For the two older brothers, it lasted for four years. When they were eight, it burst through the skin, raging like a fire for two days before finally consuming their young lives. The younger brothers lived till their sixth year and succumbed to its wrath. The boy's sisters—one, the oldest of all the children and the other, somewhere in between, enviously watched their brothers being pampered and spoiled in sickness. They wondered at the burning rage of the fever and were confused by their brothers' deaths. They lived through the condemned years unscathed.

And then, the boy was born. In the first three years of his life, he was anointed by all the religious orders of the world. His limbs were burdened with numerous amulets and bracelets, and his sleep was guarded by various objects from knives to goat droppings hidden under his pillow to ward off death. His mother spent all her time taking him to holy men in the hope that the curse that threatened her sons could be revoked. When the boy entered his fourth year, a hush fell over his life. It was as though all around him people were holding their breath—his sisters, his mother, the neighbours, the friends he played with. And then it struck. Not the quiet fever of a hundred degrees, but the raging fire of death. For two days he lay on a mat on the mud floor of his two-room hut, fighting with the claimant of his young life. Then a neighbour whispered to his mother about a holy man from the Himalayas on his way to Kanyakumari.

'There's a curse on your male offspring,' he told her. 'A curse from your previous birth—you killed a beggar woman's four-year-old son. Disown your son. He is no longer yours. Make him a beggar, a mendicant who has to beg even for his food. He belongs to no one. Only then will the beggar woman be avenged.'

The boy lay on the mat, the balls of his eyes ascending slowly into the lids, his lips moving in a gibberish conversation with death. His mother sat beside him sewing a quilt, a patchwork quilt that homeless fakirs wear to ward off the vagaries of the weather. Even as patch built up on patch, the fever broke. She lay the colourful quilt on his sweating form, all the time chanting to the bereaved mother from another life, 'Leave him be. He doesn't belong to me. He is a beggar just like you. He has no one to feed him or love him. He is not mine. Like you, I have no son.'

The sweat from his young body soaked the quilt and he opened his eyes, shivering.

'Get up, son,' his mother said. 'Go and beg for your food. Here is a bowl.' She handed him the wooden bowl given to her by the holy man.

For a whole year the boy begged for his food, wearing the incongruous quilt over his shoulders, calling out at each door in the neighbourhood, 'Do you have a few morsels to spare?' He played with the neighbourhood children and quarrelled with them, envious of their marbles, their toys. His mother would not buy him any of his own. In the evening he would knock at the door of the house that had once been his. His mother would open the door a tiny crack and lead him to a mat in the courtyard. All night she would steal furtive glances at him, her love weeping intensely in her bosom. She longed to take him in her arms, but the spectre of her four dead sons was too vivid in her mind. She would hold her arms over her breasts and rock herself, convincing death with a sob caught in her throat, 'He is not mine. He doesn't belong to me.'

On his fifth birthday, she prepared sweetmeats. The three sisters, now between the ages of seven and twelve, put them on large platters and, covering them with colourful scarves, walked to every house in the neighbourhood to share their mother's gratitude. Then she sat her son down on the mat beside her and fed him till he could eat no more. The vigil had come to an end. The boy had survived the beggar woman's curse. And it was all because of this quilt.

Someone is shaking my shoulder. I try to pull the quilt
closer and lose myself in its magic, but the pain in my body
won't let me move. 'Get up,' someone is saying in Hindi. I
try to open my eyes to see who it is, but my eyelids lift only
a fraction. Through slit lids I see two heavy black boots
planted firmly on a cement floor swarming with ants.
Suddenly the events of the night flash before me, and I
huddle closer to the uneven, ant-ridden floor, drawing tightly
into myself. 'Get up,' the guard says again, bending over me.

I cover my face with my arms to ward off the blow.

'Get up and come with me.'

'Where?' Every muscle around my lips twists painfully to
utter that word. I raise my hand to feel my face, realizing
that I am no longer cuffed. My face is hot and swollen with
a dried trail of blood at the corner of my mouth reaching
down my chin and under it.

'Colonel saab wants to see you in the office.'

The ashes, I think. They've examined the box. Hope
pumps energy back into my battered body. I get up hurriedly,
unmindful of the pain, swaying unsteadily on my feet. The
guard tucks his hand under my elbow roughly and walks me
out of the cell to the front office where the one-eared giant
is sitting at his desk littered with things. My things. My
passport, my pocketbook, my Air France ticket, half a dozen
rolls of unused film, the bottle of mineral water I had
purchased from the hotel's restaurant, my compact, my
burnished rose lipstick, and a large green flask I haven't seen
before. My backpack is lying on the floor under the desk.

The colonel nods to the guard who salutes and leaves.
Then, 'Good morning,' he says to me. 'Please sit down.' His
voice is a little husky this morning.

I stumble towards the chair and sit.

'I hope you have rested,' he says, smiling.

I look at him surprised. Can't he see? Doesn't he know?

'Three of your men ... last night ...' My tongue feels
thick, my lips bulbous. My words slur.

He glances at my face for a second before turning his

attention to the objects on his desk. Picking up my passport, he reads, 'Simran Carla Mehta. That's your name?'

'Your men tortured me last night to make me admit to being a spy.'

'Carla. Interesting. Italian, isn't it?' he continues as if I haven't spoken.

'Are you going to release me? Have they examined my box?'

'Yes,' he answers, still smiling. I wonder which question he has answered. 'You're going to release me?' I ask again to make sure.

'I have to ask you some questions,' he says.

'What do you want to know?'

'I asked you if your middle name is Italian.'

'It's Latin American. It was my mother's middle name.'

'Your mother was Mexican?'

'No. Her mother was Latin American and her father was from India.'

'Your father is an American citizen, too, isn't he?'

'My father is dead. I told you. The box,' my voice breaks. 'The box . . .'

'Let's talk about the box later. I want to ask you some other questions.' His voice cracks a little. He clears his throat quietly and, unscrewing the plastic cup from the top of the green flask, fills it with a steaming, golden brew. Taking a short sip, he holds the liquid behind his teeth before allowing it to descend down his gullet. Then he looks at me and smiles again. 'I got caught in the rain last night and woke up with a sore throat. My wife has made me a special tea.' He takes another sip.

The steam rising from the cup makes me realize how cold I am. I can feel goose bumps break out on my bare arms. I rub a hand over one arm, flinching as it touches the bruises.

'Would you like some tea?'

I eye the flask, wondering if his wife's remedy for a sore throat will appeal to me, but the warmth contained in his cup looks so inviting.

I nod.

He presses the buzzer on his desk. A guard appears.

'Chai lao.' He orders the guard to bring tea. 'It begins to get chilly this time of year. We ask our jawans to pull out their parkas at this time.'

I suddenly remember my jacket had been in my knapsack. 'My jacket,' I begin, glancing under the desk.

'Your belongings have been taken care of. They will be returned when you leave.'

'When?'

He ignores my question. 'Tell me, Miss Mehta, why are you in India?'

'My father ... I told you. My father wanted me to scatter his ashes on the border. I've come to India for that. The guard at the entrance told me the border is no longer a restricted area. Look, if I need permission, just tell me where to go. And my box? May I please have it back now?'

He is flipping through the pages of my passport again. 'You are planning to visit Pakistan?'

I nod. 'My father used to live in Lahore. I want to go see it.'

He picks up my backpack from the floor and removes the camera from it. My stomach turns.

'Nikon FG,' he says, turning it around to look at it from every angle. 'Good camera.'

'You probably know I took a picture of the border. I just wanted to have something by which I could remember my father's last resting place. I'm sorry. I didn't know I wasn't allowed. There are no signs.'

'There's a sign near the entrance gate.' He is fiddling with the buttons on my camera. 'I bet this lens takes powerful shots.' He holds the camera up and looks at me through the viewfinder. 'Very revealing.'

'Please,' I plead at the dark glass orb. 'I'm sorry. I didn't notice any sign. I just wanted one picture of Daddy's resting place. It's just for me. I'm not going to show it to anybody.'

'You used 1000 ASA film. That's very light sensitive, isn't it? Very fast?'

I nod.

'You don't need to use a flash with that, right?'

I nod again.

'Why, Miss Mehta? Why didn't you want to use a flash?' His voice has lost some of its smile now.

'I . . . I don't like flash photography.' The excuse sounds lame even to my own ears.

'Perhaps because a flash attracts too much attention?'

'No. No, of course not,' I say quickly. 'It's just that a flash . . . I think it distorts pictures.'

'Ah,' he says as though enlightened. 'Of course.'

'Please, I'm really sorry I took the picture. I should have known better, but I didn't mean any harm. Please, believe me.'

'Here's your tea.' He motions to the guard who has just returned with a cup and saucer rattling on an aluminium tray. He sets the tea before me.

'Please, you must believe me. I haven't come here to . . . to do anything wrong.'

'Drink your tea, Miss Mehta,' he says, laying the camera down on the desk.

I sit for a moment with my eyes closed, willing myself not to cry.

'I hear Americans are very fond of coffee. I'm sorry I can't offer you coffee. The dhaba here only makes tea.'

'It's okay,' I say, opening my eyes and picking up the teacup. Its rough china is deceptively cold against my lips. The steaming hot tea smoulders the cut on my tongue.

'How long are you planning to stay in India?'

'I told you yesterday—fifteen days.'

He laughs. 'Ah yes, so you did. Fifteen days. You can't see India in fifteen days. It's a big country, you know.'

'I know, but I'm not planning to see India. At least not all of it.'

'Then what parts are you planning to see? Only the borders?'

'No, of course not. I only came here because . . . Please, I didn't mean any harm. I'm just a tourist. Please believe me.' I can feel desperation mounting in my throat. 'You can't keep me here for sightseeing. There were so many other people there, visiting the border. What did I do wrong?' Tears burn a stinging trail down my cheeks.

'What did your father do in America?' he asks, leaning back in his chair.

'He was a computer engineer.'

'Did he work for the Government?'

'No. He worked for a private company.'

'What is its name?'

'JMIS.'

'Ah. Even better.'

'What do you mean?'

'Doesn't Jason Myers Information Services specialize in encryption?'

'Yes, but . . . he didn't . . . he wasn't ever involved with espionage, especially against India. He wouldn't have done anything to hurt India. He loved India.' I cover my face with my hands, trying to keep the sobs at bay.

'Then why did he leave?'

'Because he . . . the Partition . . . he . . . I don't know,' I say through my hands. 'I don't know.'

'Those aren't really his ashes, are they?'

My head jerks up. I look at him for a second, letting the meaning of his words sink in.

'Perhaps they were a cover-up.'

'No . . . no,' I say, shaking my head. 'You've got to believe me. My father died two weeks ago. His last wish was that I come to India to scatter his ashes on the border. That's all. I'm not involved with any terrorist group or spy ring. I'm sorry I took that picture. It was stupid of me. Here,' I reach for the camera with a trembling hand. 'I'll give you the roll of film,' I say, turning it upside down to press the rewind button. But when I begin to wind the little arm in the direction of the arrow, it spins on an empty compartment. I pull it out to open the back of the camera. The film is gone.

He sits up and begins putting my belongings in the backpack. 'Our country has very strict laws against any threat to our national security,' he says without looking up.

'But I'm not a threat,' I say, putting the camera down. 'How can I convince you?'

'You can't,' he says, looking at me again. 'I'm afraid I can't let you go yet.' He presses a buzzer on his desk. Within seconds a guard appears at my side.

'Please,' I beg, my hands folded before me. 'Please believe me.'

He waves a hand at the guard who grabs my arm and pulls me out of the chair. 'You've got to believe me,' I cry. 'I'll call home and have someone send me Daddy's death certificate by Federal Express. I'll have the funeral home send me a verification.'

He continues clearing his desk. The guard begins to lead me away. 'Please,' I plead over my shoulder, but the colonel has turned his attention to the black telephone on his desk and is dialling a number on the rotary dial. Crying softly, I let the guard take me back to the cell with the torture chair, the peeing hole, an army of ants, and one square foot of sky.

The gate clangs shut behind me. For a long time I stand with my back against it, sobbing at the accusations, at the imagined crimes committed for the sake of a father, and the unmerciful penance forced upon me for the real crimes committed by that father. For a long time I just stand against the bars and sob. Finally, I sink to the floor, replaying the interrogation in my mind over and over till one question runs into another and Daddy's guilt and my innocence become one.

The readily warming sun pouring in through the little window eventually soothes my aching body to sleep.

chapter three

As the blood-like warmth of the sun begins to drain away from me, I awaken to find myself lying against iron bars. My ribs are clenched between tightening clamps, my head is being pounded with a sledgehammer, my face feels as if it has exploded out of a cannon, and my foot is cold and leaden. My foot. I try to wiggle my toes, but I feel nothing except a dead weight at the end of my leg. Fearfully, I pull the foot up and untie the stiff bandages. The skin feels tight and icy, its cells closed to the warmth of my hands. 'No,' I cry out, slapping the foot as though it is an errant child, but there is only a mild vibration in the capillaries. I stand up and stomp it on the floor. A thin trickle of blood begins to fill the quick of my big toe. Tears of relief pouring down my cheeks, I let myself down on the floor and bring the foot on my lap again to rub my palm against it, warming the frozen vessels.

The sound of the bugle announces the end of another day. I sit listening to it, visualizing the scene narrated by my cab driver about the guards on either side embracing, symbolizing the close of yet another day of peace between the two countries. I have been in custody for twenty-four hours.

'Colonel saab wants to see you.' A guard opens the door and gestures to me with his gun. Limping on one foot, I hobble into the front office again. He is sitting at the desk just as he had been this morning. There are two other men on either side of him. One of them is wearing a black suit and a shocking pink turban. There is a hair net over his thin beard, which is stretched taut against his cheeks and knotted under his chin. The other is a narrow-shouldered man with a moustache so thinly lined it could have been drawn with an eyeliner. He is wearing a khaki uniform similar to the ones my interrogators were wearing the night before.

This time I am not asked to sit. I notice the two guards on either side of me have their guns exposed, their muzzles pointing at me.

'Miss Simran Mehta, this is Magistrate Gurcharan Singh.' The colonel looks towards the man in the turban. 'And this,' he says, referring to the other man, 'is Assistant Superintendent of Police, Subhash Verma. The magistrate will tell you your charges.'

'My charges?' I look at the three inscrutable faces, my blood beginning to turn cold.

'Miss Simran Mehta,' the magistrate begins. 'You are being charged with carrying suspicious equipment at the border. We have found you a threat to our national security.'

I open my mouth to tell them that they are mistaken, but my mouth is dry and something like a bubble of air is bouncing in my throat.

'You will be held in custody at Amritgarh jail till your case can be tried in court. You will be transferred to that jail at 7 a.m. tomorrow morning. Please be ready.'

'This is a mistake,' I finally say, swallowing hard, but something gurgles in my stomach and I feel hysterical laughter rise up my throat. 'Carrying suspicious equipment? Threat to national security?' I laugh shrilly. 'That box has my father's ashes. My dead father's ashes.'

'Your belongings will be kept for you by the police in safe custody till the required time.'

'What required time? How long? You've made a mistake.'

'Ram Singh will take you back to your cell now,' I am told.

I look at the faces before me, blank screens pulled over them, disguising the falsity they have validated. Suddenly my mind clears and snaps to attention.

'Wait,' I raise my hand. 'I'd like to speak with someone. A lawyer, my Consulate. I'm an American citizen. I want to speak to someone in my Consulate. You can't do this to me. I'm innocent and I'll prove it. Let me talk to my Consulate.'

'I'm afraid that is not possible right now. But please be assured that your Consulate will be informed,' the colonel says.

'I need to speak to someone NOW. I've been asking you since yesterday to let me talk to my Consulate. You can't deny me that. I'm an American citizen.'

'We can allow you one phone call. But whom will you call? It's 5:30. The American Consulate closes at 5 p.m. There won't be anyone there to answer your call. Ram Singh, le jao.'

Boots shuffle behind me.

Ignoring the presence of the guard, I continue glaring at the colonel. 'Let me talk to a lawyer then. You can't just apprehend me. I'm an American citizen.'

'This is now a police case,' he informs me. 'It's out of military hands.' He gestures to the officer in khaki who curls a sneering lip at me. 'Do you know a lawyer?' he asks me. 'No, but I'm sure I can find one in the phone book,' I say, suffusing my voice with confidence. He shakes his head in denial. 'The court will refer your case to a lawyer.'

The colonel nods his head at the guard behind me who takes my elbow and tries to steer me away. The guard's touch is surprisingly gentle. I turn to look at him. He is small and grey-haired, and he looks at me kindly. Pulling my arm free from his loose grip, I square my shoulders, and holding my blood-smeared chin high, turn around and walk back to my cell.

A strange sense of relief pervades my being, as though the chase has ended—the chase that began in my sophomore year at high school. I walk to the chair and sit down wearily, remembering Farzana, the girl from Pakistan. She and I were constantly thrown into class projects together. I guess the teachers, assuming our cultural similarities, figured we would be compatible. She and I maintained a polite camaraderie through these projects, until the time we were assigned a project on tundra vegetation. One day I went to her house to pick up some books and she invited me in. I met her grandmother who had just come from Lahore to live with them. She was an old lady with thin grey hair and a face so wrinkled, the skin could have been knife-painted. The right sleeve of her shirt was empty. 'What happened to your grandmother's arm?' I asked Farzana.

'Someone cut it off a long time ago during the Partition riots back home,' she said.

Even at that time I couldn't remember what I said to her then, or how I rushed to her bathroom to be violently sick. All I could remember was seeing Daddy standing in a street hacking at people with his sword over and over again, slicing off heads and arms. Right arms. Farzana's grandmother's arm. I must have walked back home and got into bed, because the next thing I remember is Mummy sitting beside me on the bed, mopping at my brow with a towel, and Daddy bending over me with a concerned look.

'What's the matter, sweetheart? Are you sick? You're completely wet. Look at your hair, it's soaked,' I remember Mummy saying.

Then it was Daddy's hand on my forehead. 'She doesn't have a fever,' he said.

I pulled his hand off and clutched it urgently. I had to tell him. I had to tell him to be careful, but all I could say was, 'I saw her, I saw her.'

'Who, Simi? Who did you see?'

'One of them.' I had to tell him to stay away from Farzana, from her grandmother, to never let her see him. She'd recognize him. I had to tell him, but I couldn't. The doctor came and prescribed a sedative, suggesting I stay home the next day. I woke up the next morning with a sense of foreboding, my mind keenly aware of every passing moment, waiting. Waiting for what I didn't know, but every time the phone rang, my skin pricked with a cold sweat, my breath stuck in my throat. I let Mummy answer all calls.

And then it was she. I was in my room when she called. 'It's Farzana,' I heard Mummy say. I looked around my room frantically for a route to escape, then I flew into the bathroom and turned on the shower. I must have remained locked in that bathroom for over an hour, waiting for the phone to ring again. Finally, exhausted, I slipped into my room, only to bury myself deep in the covers. Later, when I heard Daddy come home, I got up resolutely and went down. I had to tell him about Farzana's grandmother. But how? All evening I sat watching him covertly, afraid of losing him, missing him in my heart, knowing I couldn't tell him, afraid of the consequences if he found out. When the phone rang again, Daddy got up to answer it. 'No, Daddy. Don't answer the phone,' I screamed. Both my parents stared at me as if I had suddenly gone mad.

'Simi, what is it?' Mummy said. 'Have you done something wrong, something at school?'

Daddy moved towards the kitchen to get the phone. I jumped out of the chair and grabbed his arm. 'Please, Daddy, don't answer the phone.' The ringing stopped. My father took me by the arms and sat me down on a chair.

'All right then, Simran, tell us what the matter is. What is it? There's obviously something you're not telling us, something that's scaring you to death.'

I threw myself into his arms and began sobbing. 'Hush,' he soothed me, but the tears would not stop. 'Tell you what,' he said, 'Mummy'll give you another of those pills Dr Perrini prescribed, and you go to bed, and tomorrow we'll talk about it.'

Even as the sedative took effect that night, I promised myself I would take care of Daddy. Groggily, I thought about making my parents move to another city, getting my father to undergo facial cosmetic surgery so no one would recognize him, going to the Indian Embassy and confessing all. My last thought that night was to beg them to put me in jail instead of my father.

I missed that whole week of school. I stopped answering all phone calls during the day, letting my mother tell my friends to stop calling for a while, and in the evening when Daddy came home, I flew to the phone every time it rang so he wouldn't get a chance to answer it. But after that day, Farzana never called. My parents took me to see a psychiatrist. I made up a story of having nightmares in which the school's walls dripped blood and a killer hid in a dark closet ready to grab me.

'Have you been seeing a lot of horror movies?' he asked.

'No,' I said. 'I'm just afraid to go back to school.'

'Is it just your school or do you have nightmares about other schools, too?'

That gave me an idea. Another school. A transfer. No Farzana, no one-armed grandmother ready to accuse Daddy. Daddy's identity safeguarded. But Scott? I was already going steady with him. He was the only reason I hesitated. But I was even willing to sacrifice Scott to protect Daddy.

'No. I never dream about other schools. In fact, I'll be all right if I can go to another school,' I told the psychiatrist.

He told my parents that it was probably just growing pains, or some little incident at school that I had exaggerated in my mind. 'She doesn't seem to be able to forget it, though. Perhaps you might think about talking to the school authorities to get her transferred to another school.' He gave them a letter recommending a change of schools, and I transferred to another high school. I never saw Farzana again. But the nightmare of her grandmother hounding Daddy never really left me. It lay dormant in some fear-ridden space in my mind, recurring every once in a while so I would always know it hadn't given up the chase. And now, perhaps, the chase is finally over.

Sparrows chirping outside my window are a sign that the night has passed. I look at my watch. The time is 8:05 p.m. Recalling that I didn't adjust it to the local time on my arrival, I try to remember what my travel agent told me about the time difference. India is either nine and a half hours ahead or ten and a half, depending on the solstice and America's daylight savings time adjustment. I cannot remember if we lost an hour or gained one this past solstice.

I try to recall the magic words that prevent confusion about
the time. 'Fall backwards spring forward,' I whisper, or is it
the other way around? I can never get that right. So the time
is now either 5:35 a.m. or 6:35 a.m. I walk to the window
and look out. The sky has almost lost the night and looks
more like a 6:30 sky than a 5:30 one. In half an hour I am
going to lose total control of this situation. Battling an
onslaught of panic, I try to draw up a plan of action: a call
to the Consulate, but the Colonel has transferred my case to
the police. I'll have to wait till we get to Amritgarh jail
before making my call. I wonder how long it will take to get
there. What if I arrive before nine? There won't be anyone
at the Consulate to answer my call. Okay then, I'll call a
lawyer. Surely they will have a telephone directory listing
lawyers who are available twenty-four hours. Perhaps, I can
even make a call to Scott. He will be home from work; after
all, it will be late evening in Batonsville. But will they allow
me to make an international call? I can pay them, but my
pocket book is in their possession. No, I decide, just a call
to the Consulate will suffice. After all, I am an American and
the Consulate is there to protect me. My tax dollars ensure
that.

When the bolts slide open, I limp to the door, ready for
it to swing out. Even before Shamim issues the order, I step
outside. As I enter the front office, I notice there is no one
at the desk. 'Wait there,' Shamim says, pointing to the
chairs. 'Colonel saab will be here any minute.'

I stand before the desk, cracking my fingers, looking
around. There is a jawan on duty at the entrance, and Ram
Singh is standing a few feet away from me, his rifle deceptively
idle by his side. I look at the desk to see if my backpack is
still there. The desk is empty except for a newspaper lying
on it, folded neatly in a triple fold as though someone has
singled out an article. I can see that some of the lines in the
article have been underlined in red. Idly, I try to read the
headline upside down, forming each letter in my mind:
BOMB ATTEMPT AT AMRITGARH BORDER FOILED
BY BSF GUARDS. The blood drains out of my body and

back again, pounding into my heart in tight fists of rage. What laws does this land have? Laws that not only force the innocent to accept guilt but authenticate that guilt with the power of the press? Holding myself erect, I steady my breath and summon the resolve of the night before. I must read the article. I must see what other lies are being pinned on me. Training my eyes, I peer at the small print, trying to decode the accusations that follow, but reading each minuscule letter upside down and conjugating it to the next and the next to make a word blurs my vision. Agitated, I take a step forward towards the desk. The idle gun is cocked behind me. My back stiffens. I turn around slowly, allowing myself the time to shape my lips in a disarming smile. 'Woh akhbar dekh loon?' I ask Ram Singh softly if I may look at the newspaper. He shakes his head silently. 'Please, I want to read my horoscope,' I say. He just stands there, his legs a little apart, his hands holding the gun carelessly, but his eyes look at me apologetically. I turn back to the newspaper and, lowering my lids, school my eyes once again. 'This evening at 5:30 p.m. as the flags were lowered at Amritgarh border in the midst of sightseeing tourists, a young lady was detected loitering . . .' There is a sound of footsteps behind me. I straighten up and rub my eyes to wipe out all traces of strain from them.

'We are moving you to Amritgarh jail,' the colonel says, going behind his desk. His face is ruddy from the morning air.

'Colonel,' I say quietly, 'You know I am innocent.'

He is busy straightening out the folds of the newspaper and doesn't even look up. 'Ram Singh,' he says, settling down in his chair. 'Le jao.'

After a bone-shattering drive in a closed police jeep, the midday sun blinds my arrival at Amritgarh jail. But within moments I realize that the colours I see are not behind my eyelids. The entrance of Amritgarh State Jail has been painted by a berserk cubist. Four large triangles in orange, green, white and red form the immense iron square of the

main gate. Two armed guards are on duty at the gate. I
notice that their uniforms, unlike the foliage green of the
colonel's and that of his men, are khaki. I recall the uniforms
of the three men who tortured me and a dread descends
upon me, smothering all hopes of being allowed to contact
anyone. For a desperate second I think about making a run
for it. My eyes dart around the area. There are policemen
everywhere. Some are sitting on benches beside the driveway
like commuters at a bus stop, others are lounging in the
verdant lawns that stretch on either side; their weapons are
lying in the grass beside them like the iguanas I once saw in
a reptile farm, languishing in the sun that never warmed
them. Something glints above the gate. I look up to see a
brick recess with a small hole carved into it. From within,
the dark unblinking eye of a machine gun's muzzle lies in
wait like a predator. With a frustrated sigh, I lean against
the jeep and watch Ram Singh walk up to one of the
policemen on duty with a rifle slung on his shoulder, and a
stapled bunch of papers in his hand. I see the two men
exchange some words before a face-sized window opens out
of the red triangle and a khaki turban above a set of dark
eyes appears. Ram Singh holds up the papers for the eyes to
read. There is a rattle of bolts and a small, narrow door,
cutting out the centres of the red and blue triangles, opens
inwards. Ram Singh signals for me to go in. Dragging little
limping steps, I take my time. He stands by patiently. When
I reach the gate, he takes my elbow and guides me over the
six-inch iron frame. I have to bend my head to step through
the dwarf door. Inside, I see a square enclave locked in by
another iron gate, the same size as the main gate, but this
one is not painted. Its iron grey is decorated with two long,
heavy chains hanging from the top, ending in giant handcuffs.
The air reeks of insecticide.

The odour grows stronger as Ram Singh leads me
through an open door adjacent to the main gate. The room
we enter is large and windowless. It has a big wooden desk
at the far end and a chair pushed away at an angle as though
someone has got up in a hurry. A spotless white towel is

spread on the back of the chair. All along the other three walls, similar chairs, sans towel, line the sides as though awaiting the scene of a grand inquisition. Ram Singh halts in the middle of the room, signalling me to do the same. We stand like that. At attention. Me, with one foot resting against the other, and Ram Singh, on my right, at arm's length, his body erect, one hand resting on his weapon, the other fisted by his side. The minutes tick away. My good leg begins to tire. I look at the empty chairs around me and then at Ram Singh. His eyes are trained directly in front of him at the opposite wall. He is obviously willing to wait his entire lifetime if need be. Keeping an eye on him, I begin to inch towards a chair, when suddenly, the hand that has been resting on the weapon springs to salute smartly. I turn my head to see a tall, handsome man with a salt-and-pepper goatee and grizzly, dark, almost blue-black hair brushed back from a sharp widow's peak, come in through the door behind the desk. He is folding a white towel meticulously, pinching the folds between the pads of his index finger and thumb.

'Khade raho,' he orders me sharply to remain standing. I put my hurt foot on the floor tenderly and shift my weight. He nods at Ram Singh who clicks his heels and leaves the room.

'Do you understand Hindi?' he asks me in immaculate English.

I nod.

'Good,' he says, still in English, and sits in the towel-backed chair. 'Who do you work for?' His fingers play with the switch of a table lamp, creating and erasing a bright yellow pool on the desk.

'I want to call my Consulate,' I say.

He ignores my request. 'You have been sent to me for carrying suspicious equipment.'

'I have been falsely accused. I want to talk to my Consulate.'

'I have received you as a threat to our national security.'

'I am innocent till proven guilty. Or doesn't the Indian

legal system recognize that right?'

'Be quiet,' he says softly, his finger resting on the light switch as though on a trigger. 'Do you know what punishment the Indian legal system enjoins for threatening national security? Death by hanging.'

I purse my lips and look at him defiantly. 'I am an American citizen. I want to talk to my Consulate.'

'Lower your eyes,' he orders. 'As long as you are in my jail, you will observe the discipline of my jail. You have come here as a criminal and will be treated as one. It is the rule in my prison that whosoever appears before me must answer me only when addressed directly, and that too, in a soft voice. Your eyes must not be raised beyond the edge of this desk and your hands must be held behind your back or I will have you shackled and put in solitary confinement for indiscipline.'

My hands hang loosely by my side. I am not afraid of looking directly into his eyes. They are black and hard like marbles glinting coldly in narrow, closely spaced sockets. In his starched, finely ironed khaki uniform, he appears both a hardened criminal and a well-groomed gentleman.

He meets my eyes for a split second before pressing the buzzer on his desk. Immediately, I hear a shuffle of boots at the door.

'You will be kept in solitary till you learn the discipline of this jail. This is a model jail and you will not be allowed to break its rules,' he says. 'Remove your shoes and valuables.'

Staggering on my hurt foot, I bend down and pull off my sneaker. Unstrapping my watch, I pick up my sneaker and place both items on the desk before him.

'Le jao,' he thunders to the guard, pushing the bedraggled shoe off the desk with the point of a pencil.

I am grabbed by the upper arm and hoisted out of the room. 'I want to call my Consulate,' I shout at the officer over my shoulder, and he answers me with a short, contemptuous laugh. The guard drags me to the enclave, then releasing my arm, knocks the giant handcuff on the gate, filling the confined space with a metallic echo. A small door, a twin to the one outside, opens, and I am pushed through it into a fragrant courtyard. Roses? They are everywhere and of all hues, growing in wide, disciplined beds. Men in spotless white clothes are squatting among the bushes, tending to the blooms. They stop and stare at me as I am led limping down the paved lane in the centre to another solid iron gate at the end of the courtyard. The guard accompanying me bangs at the door with his fist. 'Kya hai?' a female voice hails from inside.

'Qaidi,' the guard calls out and another small door opens inwards. I am delivered into the presence of a tall, thin woman dressed in the uniform khaki sari. The guard converses with her for a few minutes while I stand watching. It is hard to tell her age. Except for the sun-deepened lines around her lips and forehead, her face is smooth. Her hair, white and gleaming with oil, is parted in the centre and pulled back in a tight bun. The parting is filled heavily with bright red vermilion. Finally, nodding to the guard, she pulls the door shut and pushing the bolt home, turns to me. 'What is your name?' she asks through betel-juice-reddened lips. Her teeth are brown and corroded.

'Simran,' I say.

'I'm Prema. But you will call me Matinee. I'm the daytime warden. Wait here,' she says, opening the wooden door of a room beside the gate and going in to return a second later with a bunch of keys. 'Come.' She begins to lead me along the high wall. Stretched on the other side of us, I see an open area littered with scattered beds of sickly flowers. 'I have been ordered to keep you in solitary till the order of the Saab Bahadur. That's the Superintendent of the jail. We have to call him that, Saab Bahadur. He likes to be called that. What did you do? Normally we do not put anyone in solitary in the beginning, except, of course, dangerous criminals. What did you do?' She keeps up a flowing monologue in Hindi, not once expecting a reply. 'After the Saab Bahadur orders, you will stay with the others in that barrack.' She points to a large rectangular shack on the far side of the open area. The entire front of the shack is open with two sides of a large double gate swung out on either side of it. Faded pieces of female clothing are spread out on the gate, drying. I can see a couple of women sitting on the ground outside it. 'Come,' Matinee says, walking towards the farthest end of the area where I can see a semicircle of barred cells on a raised, cemented platform. Following her, I climb the single step onto the platform, glancing through the bars of the first cell. An old woman squats just inside the door, the desperation of a doomed creature in her eyes. As I look at her, I am engulfed with acute embarrassment for having to witness the loss of her being, that I have to avert my eyes. I follow Prema, keeping my eyes away from the remaining cells, staring directly in front at the warden's silver-haired bun. Prema stops at the other end of the semicircle and unlocks a cell. 'Go in,' she says. 'This is yours till Saab Bahadur sends his orders.'

I step inside. A rank smell of old, unwashed clothes hits my nose even though the cell seems to be bare except for a threadbare mat on the floor and a dark blanket lying folded in one corner. At a glance, I see a narrow cell divided by a waist-high mud wall with a terracotta urn on it. I step forward and cup my palm around the belly of the urn. It is cool to the touch. Removing the tin bowl covering its mouth, I look inside. Water shimmers in its depths, tantalizing my parched throat and dehydrated body. But Scott's warning is like a guiding angel. Replacing the bowl, I step behind the wall where I see a toilet, a real toilet, built into the floor. Its once white ceramic is yellowed by years of use and lack of cleaning, and pockmarked with a host of flies. I stand facing the bars as Prema locks my door. From where I stand I can see the door of the first cell. The old lady still squats behind the bars, her hands on her knees, the white corner of her sari covering her grey head, her cheeks collapsed against her toothless gums, her lips disappearing inwards, her eyes peering at me with an insane gleam. The cell next to hers seems to be empty. In the third cell I see a body clad in a white sari lying on the floor with her back to the bars. The cell next to that also seems to be empty. The edge of the fifth cell, one cell away from mine, is as far as my eyes can go. From where I am, I am unable to see the barracks, but I can hear laughter and voices. Among those, I am surprised to hear a child's tinkling laugh.

I am still standing at the gate, waving away flies, looking at the barred sunlight growing out of my shadow on the platform before me when a girl in her late teens appears from the direction of the barracks and climbs up to my cell. She is dressed in a tattered but clean white sari. Two braids tied at the ends with bright red string hang down over her slight breasts. 'What's the name?' Her Hindi is rude, but her voice is friendly. I turn my eyes away, feeling no urge to communicate with the inmates.

'My name is Koki,' she says.

'I told you, Koki, don't talk to her. It is Saab Bahadur's order.' The warden appears behind her.

Koki flashes a smile at me and turns away. Suddenly, there is a loud banging at the iron gate. Within minutes the warden is at the gate, opening it to allow in two men wearing kurta-pajamas, carrying tin pails which they line against the wall near the gate. After they leave, the warden locks the door behind them and walks to the cells. I watch her open the door of the first cell, but the old woman just sits there in the open doorway even after she is released. Then slowly, her hands pushing her knees down, she stands up. One of her shoulders is bunched over her back, giving her a lopsided humpback. A sparse, middle-aged woman emerges from the third cell. Her face is very dark, and she has sharp, beady eyes and large bulbous lips. Her shoulder-length hair is untied and well oiled and falls in thin rat's tails down her back. She glances in my direction before swinging her head around and walking away towards the pails. I await the occupant of the other cell, but Matinee tucks the bunch of keys in the waistband of her sari and walks back to the pails, gesturing to the prisoners in front of the barracks.

'And her, and her?' I see a young girl of about five skip towards the cells, pointing at me. She is painfully thin, and the faded red dress on her body hangs loosely from her shoulders to her calves. She has short, unevenly cut black hair parted in the middle and slicked to either side of her face with oil.

'Be quiet. Order nahin hai,' Prema smiles at her.

I watch the child approach unhesitatingly to grip the bars of my cell with one thin hand, a perfect smile on her sunburnt face.

I stand behind the bars, looking at the child, wondering at her presence in the jail. An emaciated young woman appears hastily and takes the child's hand. The little girl grips the bars tighter. Her fingers are pried open, and she is carried away.

I want to withdraw behind the wall of the cell to hide from the shame of captivity, but I stand my ground and watch the women form a single file before the pails, holding out tin plates in their hands. Prema doles out food. Then, filling up two plates, she climbs onto the platform and slides one under the bars of my door and the other under the bars of the cell third from the end.

'Eat,' she calls out to us. I glance sideways at the other occupied cell and see a flash of white as someone picks up the plate. I turn to look at my own food. Inquisitive flies are hovering over its aromas, descending to alight on the burnt chapatis and the greenish puddle of some kind of lentil soup. I get up and flick the flies away but make no effort to pick up the plate. I am determined not to give in to any observances of the system. Waving my hand over the food, I keep my eyes averted, but in spite of me, my stomach begins to growl. I realize I haven't eaten for nearly thirty-six hours. Convincing myself that losing my strength to hunger will serve no purpose, I bend forward and pick up the plate. Taking it to a corner I sit on the mat and begin to eat, breaking small pieces of chapati to dip into the soup. The food is gritty and laced heavily with hot chillies. Barely chewing the food, I swallow whole bits of chapati and am surprised to find my plate empty. My tongue begins to sting from the spices, and I look again at the terracotta urn on top of the partition wall. Then I stand up and look for Matinee. She is sitting in the centre of the compound on a cot, spreading a white paste from a flat, wooden box on a heart-shaped betel leaf, chatting with the woman who had carried the child away.

'Prema,' I call out. She looks up at me, then goes back to her after-lunch paan.

'Matinee,' I call again. She folds the leaf into a perfect triangle and tucking it inside her cheek, walks to the edge of the platform before my cell.

'What is it?' Her voice is a trifle impatient.

'I want water. I can't drink the water from that urn. I need some boiled water.'

'Why?' she asks.

'I can't drink this water. I'll get sick. My stomach is not used to this water,' I try to explain.

She smiles. Her lips, puckered tightly over her teeth to hold the paan in, wrinkle at the corners in amusement. 'You can't get better water than this,' she says, wiping red spittle from the corners of her mouth with a thumb and forefinger.

'I'm really thirsty. I haven't had a drink of water in two days. Can I get some boiled water, please?'

'Ask Saab Bahadur when he comes tomorrow.'

As she leaves, I see the humpbacked woman approach my cell, looking at me with her head cocked to one side. I glance at her and away. She continues to stand and stare at me. Disconcerted by her fixed look, I sit down with my back to the bars.

'Drink the water,' she says softly.

I turn my head to look at her. She points to the urn on the partition wall. 'Drink it.'

I shake my head.

'Don't go to sleep then.'

'Why?'

She climbs onto the platform and in a hushed voice asks me, 'Didn't your mother tell you about the woman who lost her soul in search of water?'

Despite myself, she has my attention. I shake my head.

'Tsk,' she says at the negligence of my mother. 'Listen.

Once, there was a woman who fell asleep thirsty. But her soul would not sleep because of the thirst. So while the woman's body slept, her soul left her body to look for water. On the doorstep of a house, she found a jar with its cover a little askew. When she looked inside the jar, she saw cool sparkling water. Immediately, she slipped inside and began quenching her thirst. She was so thirsty that she drank all night. She was still drinking at dawn when the lady of the house woke up. Seeing her jar uncovered, she replaced the cover on it tightly. Now when the woman's thirst was satisfied, her soul wanted to leave the jar and return to her body. But she couldn't, because the lid was on so tight. She couldn't move it; she was trapped. Her thirst had trapped her.'

A shiver runs down my spine. 'I'm not that thirsty,' I tell her.

All day I sit in my cell staring at the bars shadow outwards and inwards in response to the position of the sun, preparing pleas of help to the American Consulate in my head. My bravado strangled within the confines of the cell by elasticized time, I am now prepared to swallow my pride and cooperate with the Superintendent in the hope that he will allow me to talk to the Consulate or send a letter. I plan a call to Scott to beg him to come to India and rescue me. The whole situation is so unreal that I'm convinced it cannot last. If the American Consulate cannot straighten it out, I reason with myself, my innocence will surely become obvious when I'm tried in court. After all, they don't have any evidence to prove otherwise. In my mind I resolve to make whatever time I have here pass smoothly by complying with the rules so that they don't have anything to hold against me.

As the shadows begin to climb the partition wall to mingle with the dark recesses of my cell, I hear the main gate to the female ward open. I stand up to see a flash of green as Prema spreads a shawl over her shoulders and stands aside to allow a fat lady in the uniform sari to enter. They talk for a minute before Prema steps through the gate. The fat lady closes it behind her. Wondering if this is the night warden, I watch her walk towards the platform and the cells. For someone her size, she has a very light step, as though gravity and her bulk are unrelated. Her short hair is tucked behind her thick ears and a bunch of keys tinkles at her waist as she approaches the cell beside mine. I see her peer in before turning to look at me.

'You are Simran?' Her voice is heavy; almost like a man's.

I nod.

'What did you do?' She reaches above her head to wave away a mosquito. There is a large half-moon stain of sweat under her armpit.

I shake my head. 'Nothing.'

'Hmph! Everybody who comes here says that. But let me tell you that you are here to stay, so you better behave. This is a model jail. We don't want any indiscipline.'

I look at her for a moment before nodding.

'Hmph!' she says again and turns away to step off the platform only to return a few minutes later, holding the old humpback by the arm. I watch her unlock the first cell and lead the old woman inside before closing the door and relocking it. Once again, the humpback settles on the floor just inside the bars, her hands resting on her knees, her eyes gleaming insanely.

Soon there is a knock at the main door and two men carrying pails are let in again. I see the night warden ladle some soup into an empty bucket and cover it up. Then she counts out some chapatis and ties them up in a piece of fabric. Picking up the covered pail and the bundle of chapatis, she disappears inside the warden's room beside the gate to reappear a moment later, empty-handed. I see her walk to the barracks, then to the first cell to release the humpback, then to the other locked cell where an invisible inmate passes her a plate from between the bars, and finally to my cell to stand before me.

'Where is your plate?'

I pick up my plate from the floor and pass it to her from

between the bars. She takes it between her finger and thumb
and flings it back inside the cell. The tin hits the partition
wall sharply and falls to the floor with a clatter.

'Wash it. You think we have servants here to wash your
dirty dishes?'

Quietly I bend, and, picking up the offensive utensil,
wash it with water from the urn, rinsing it over the toilet.
The soup from the morning has dried on it and is hard to
take off. I scrub it with the tips of my fingers before rinsing
it again. Shaking the moisture from it, I take it back to her.
She grabs it impatiently and walks away. A few minutes
later she returns with a little puddle of green lentil soup and
one chapati. The portion is much smaller than what it was
in the morning.

I eye the food for a while before deciding not to eat. I'm
afraid of being assailed by spices and thirst after the meal.
Instead, I lie down on the mat, closing my eyes, waiting for
the impending darkness.

As I sleep that night, the dryness in my throat spreads to
my very cells, begging for water. I wonder if that soul was
ever delivered from its watery death. Some hours later I
awaken from a dream about wandering around looking for
cool, sparkling water. My mind reaching out to my soul, I
stagger to the partition wall. My body already faint from the
first symptoms of dehydration, I grab the urn and remove
the tin bowl covering it. In the light of the compound, the
water twinkles at me. Tilting the urn, I fill the bowl and
place it against my lips to take a sip. At first, the unmoving
muscles of my throat resist the water. Then it spreads,
permeating its coolness in my burning blood. I drink till I
can drink no more. Then taking the bowl, I fling it to the
farthest corner of the cell. Keeping the mouth of the urn
uncovered, and placing the urn close to the mat, I lie down
to sleep, content that I have saved my soul from the water
trap.

Sometime in the middle of the night the foreign bodies
from the water rise in mutiny and I wake up with the day's
meal in my throat. All night I sit by the yellowed ceramic

toilet, retching my tortured insides out.

Around dawn I feel someone shake my shoulder. Hazily, I see the night warden with her nose covered with a corner of her sari. 'What's the matter with you?' she asks.

I let my eyelids drop again and fall into exhausted sleep.

Someone is pulling my eyelids up forcibly. This time I awaken to see Prema bending over me, holding her nose between a thumb and forefinger.

'How are you?' she asks.

'I couldn't let my soul be trapped, so I drank the water,' I explain to her.

'Oh yes, the water. I have talked to Saab Bahadur. He says you will be allowed to boil your own water. Come and lie down on the mat,' she says. I realize I'm stretched out beside the toilet and try to sit up. My chin feels stiff with the crust of vomit and my cell is filled with the stench of regurgitated food. I let Prema help me up and walk me to the mat near the door of the cell. When she leaves, she keeps the door open behind her. I have a string of visitors beginning with the little girl. She wrinkles her nose when she enters. Her mother asks me how I feel. Koki comes, and even the thick-lipped, oily-haired lady makes an appearance. Finally, the humpback waddles in and lays her gnarled hand on my forehead. 'You quenched your thirst,' she says. I am too weak to summon up enough Hindi to respond, so I smile at her to let her know I bear no resentment against her for her advice.

Suddenly Prema appears in a rush, and shooing everyone out, shuts my door. Even as she locks it, there is a clanging on the gate and the Superintendent is let in. He walks all the way around the semicircle and halts before my cell.

'Open it,' he orders the warden. Prema rushes forward to unlock my door. He covers his mouth and nose with a white hand towel as he approaches me.

'Give her a bath,' he tells Matinee. 'Tell her to wash her clothes. This stink could kill a man.' To me he says, 'Prema tells me you need boiled water. This is a model jail. We look after our inmates here and try to fulfil their needs. Some wood will be sent to you every morning to boil water.' He waits, perhaps, for an expression of gratitude from me. I lie, looking at him quietly.

'I am sure you know the result of indiscipline now. Today you will be allowed to stay with the other women in the barracks.'

'I want to send a letter to my Consulate,' I say with as much energy as I can muster.

He looks at me blankly for a moment, then his face breaks into an amused smile. 'We'll see,' he says.

Prema enters my cell, holding a hand over her nose.

'Come,' she says, gesturing me to follow. I stagger behind her to a set of sheet-iron stalls with open tops built behind the barracks against the farthest wall of the compound. Prema hands me a tablet of dirty brown soap and a white and brown chequered piece of fabric. 'Clean yourself and your clothes,' she tells me, pointing to one of the stalls.

I open the door and look inside what is probably a shower room. Fumes of stale urine assail me. Instinctively I take a step backwards.

'Go on, take a bath.' Prema gives me a gentle push.

I step into the stall. My bare toes curl in revulsion as I feel slime coating the floor under my feet. The door is shut behind me. I stand for a moment holding my breath, wondering if I can refuse to bathe, but the idea of water laving my body is too inviting. I turn to throw the towel on top of the door and begin to remove my blood-stained pants and sleeveless shirt. The cold early morning air reaches down and pounces on my exposed body like a hungry carnivore, carving out patches of numbed flesh. Stripping off my shredded stockings, I advance towards the waist-high faucet jutting out of the end wall. My feet still curled, touching the slime-layered floor with only my toes and heels, I turn on the faucet. A heavy blast of cold water splashes against my legs and the blood in my feet pricks like icicles. Trembling uncontrollably, I remove my bra and panties and crouch under the water, gasping as the first blast hits me, the hidden reserves of heat under my skin form a weak buffer.

I wash myself thoroughly, scrubbing the soap vigorously all over, cleaning out the gashes on my foot, rubbing a gentle hand over the stinging bruises on my face. The soap doesn't make any lather, but I can feel a layer of greasy soapiness on my skin that takes a while to wash off. Finally, turning off the water, I use the thin fabric to dry myself, but its thin cotton is soaked almost immediately. Shaking the moisture out of my short hair, I wrap the wet fabric around my body sarong style and squat before the faucet to wash my clothes. But the bloodstains on them are indelible and my fingers hurt from scrubbing them. Giving up, I lay the clothes under the water to allow the soap to rinse out. Then wringing them, I raise myself and tiptoe out of the stall.

Koki calls me from the barracks. I hesitate, looking at the closed door of my cell.

'Go on,' the matinee says. 'Saab Bahadur has allowed you to stay with the other women.'

Still trembling from the cold, I move towards her. I am received by outstretched arms holding a blanket full of holes. Koki wraps me in it and settles me on the mat while the child's mother takes my wet clothes and steps out to hang them on a clothesline stretching from one of the barrack gates to the shrubs growing behind it. My body continues to tremble. Koki brings more blankets, and piling them upon me, begins to rub my hands and feet. I lie down in the comforting warmth, my exhausted body relaxing in sleep.

chapter four

For two days and nights, a fever burns in my body. On the third night I awaken to see a crescent moon hanging like a clipped fingernail in the sky. Around me, inmates covered with blankets lie huddled on the floor and, against the wall, piles of their belongings lean like misshapen dwarfs. As I lie listening to the steady breathing around me, I hear a muffled squeak. Mice. An involuntary tremor passes down my spine and I make to get up, my eyes trying to distinguish the shadows across the floor. The body beside me stirs and the child's mother sits up. She lays her palm on my forehead and smiles at me. 'The fever has broken. How do you feel?' she whispers.

'I saw a mouse over there.'

'There are a few of them.'

I sit up quickly and gather my legs under me.

'Don't worry. They won't bother you. They normally stay in the corners. Go back to sleep. You've been very sick.'

I lie down again hesitantly, my legs gathered close, my eyes trained to the site where I had spotted the rodent. I'm sure it will be impossible to sleep now, but within moments my mind begins to wander in zones of nebulous thought and I drift back to sleep.

For the next week, I concentrate on recovering my health and adjusting to the lack of everyday comforts. My bones ache from sleeping on the floor, and the pleasure of a warm comforter plagues my nights as I lie huddled under my

thin blanket. I crave for those muggy days in Batonsville
when the humidity in the air makes all cosmetic moisturizers
redundant. Most mornings, after my cold bath, the skin on
my face stretches painfully across my cheeks, stinging with
dryness. There are no mirrors in prison so I satisfy myself by
tracing the puffy bruises on my face with my fingertips,
reading them like Braille to tell their shape and colour. I
spend countless hours worrying about infections from the
lack of hygiene, like using my finger and a brash, spicy
powder for my teeth instead of a toothbrush and toothpaste,
using cold water from a rusty, mucus-lined tin can to clean
myself instead of toilet paper, sharing a sliver of brown soap
with six other women. But all these become mere
inconveniences when I get my period for the first time in
prison. When I ask Prema for a box of tampons or sanitary
napkins, she looks at me blankly then goes into her room
and returns with a bundle of dirty, brownish cotton wool.
'Ask Koki to give you a piece of cloth.' Koki takes an old,
threadbare sari from a pile on the floor and tears two wide
strips. She takes the cotton from me and wraps it in one of
the pieces in the fashion of a diaper. 'Here,' she says, digging
in the pile and pulling out my torn stockings. 'I saved this for
you. It'll be more comfortable than a cord. Tie it around
your waist to hold up the two ends.' She also tells me to
throw away the used cotton in the uncovered trash bin
behind the barracks but to wash the fabric so it can be used
again. 'These are yours now,' she says, patting the diaper.
'Wash one and use one.' I take the monstrosities to the
bathroom and stand against the wall and weep, wishing I
could dig a hole in the ground and bury them. In fact, I wish
I could bury my head, too, and not emerge till I am back in
America in my centrally heated, well-equipped Batonsville
home only two blocks away from a drug store and centuries
beyond the unsanitary toilet of the dark ages.

I am nurtured back to health, physically and mentally,
by my co-inmates who now look upon me as one of them.
Koki sits with me for hours in the winter sun, talking to me,
asking me questions about my family, correcting my Hindi,

massaging my foot. Kubrima, the humpback, treats me like
an invalid daughter. At every meal she watches me finger my
food, urging me to eat more. She personally lights the few
logs I am provided every morning to boil water and fills an
urn for me, keeping it in a sunless corner of the courtyard
to cool it. When I brush my teeth, she makes sure I use the
boiled water in case I swallow some while gargling. She
makes a herbal paste from the milk of aloe leaves growing
beside the cells and mud, to spread on the bruises on my face
and the lacerations on my foot. Koki tells me Kubrima
poisoned her daughter and husband thirty years ago with rat
poison to save them from starvation. Even though she took
some of the same poison herself, she somehow survived. The
police broke the bones in her shoulder during interrogation
and they set all wrong, giving her a humpback. Her name is
Janaki Devi, but because of her age and her back, everyone
calls her Kubrima, which means humpbacked mother.

'She completed her sentence seven years ago, but because
of her mental condition, she is kept in captivity for safe
keeping. She's mad. They lock her up just before meals,
because when hunger strikes her, she loses control. The
starving demons of her past make her a mad woman,' Koki
says.

Koki also tells me about the other inmates. The thick-
lipped lady, Fulo, was a member of a gang of robbers. 'We
don't trust her, saali chugalkhor. She is great friends with
Malti, the night warden. She is her spy, always carrying tales
about us to her. Haramzadi. She is the only one who gets a
full portion of food in the evening.'

'Why?'

'Because she is the night warden's chamchi, her stooge.
That bitch, Malti, sells half our food.'

I recall the extra pail and the bundle of chapatis I had
seen Malti smuggle into her room.

Krishna, the little girl's mother, gouged a man's stomach
out with a rake. He had raped her. She was doing fourteen
years out of which she had already completed six. Her
daughter, Hema, was born right here in the barracks of

Amritgarh jail's female ward.

'So Hema will grow up in jail? Why doesn't Krishna let someone else on the outside take care of her—her mother or someone?'

'There is no one. Her family has disowned her. A woman's honour is everything. Her family will never forgive her for losing that.'

'For getting raped? That wasn't her fault.'

Koki shrugs. 'It's always the woman's fault.'

I ask her about her own crime.

'I'm an artist with a blade.'

'What do you mean?'

'My brother and I used to pick pockets. We had a small gang. Most of us have no homes or family, so we got together and formed a family. All day we worked, and in the evening we met in an abandoned railway carriage. It was a living. We made just enough to buy food and some clothes. Nothing fancy. Just enough to cover our bodies. We weren't hurting anyone. We took as much as we needed and then we called it quits for the day. We were happy. But this duniya saala, didn't let us live and be happy. One day I picked a babu's pocket. I didn't know he was a politician's son-in-law. The haramzada leader sent the dogs to sniff us out. They raided the carriage. They didn't find anything. There was nothing to find, but they caught all of us. All except Chami, my brother's friend. He ran away. That chhokra could run. We used to call him Hawa. He was like the wind, here one minute and there the next. The rest of us, Giri, Shalu, my brother and I, we were all thrown in jail.'

'How long are you in for?'

'I don't know. I'm still waiting for my trial. But I've already been here one year. So has my brother. Poor Ramu. He didn't even want to do this in the beginning. I taught him the art. I'm really good. Give me a blade and a pocket full of money and I can make a cut so fine you'd think a heart doctor did it.'

'Where's Ramu?'

'Here. In Amritgarh jail. He's in the male section. I see

him sometimes on Holi and Diwali.'

'And the other woman? The one in the locked cell?'

'She's Sultana. We don't know very much about her because she doesn't talk to any of us. She only came here a few weeks ago. Matinee told us that she killed two young men because they were Hindus. Matinee says she's a terrorist. That's why she's kept locked up. She's dangerous. These saale terrorists are the devil's children. They should be locked up. They, and the leaders. They are children of the same mother. Greedy haramzade. They'll kill anyone to fill their own pockets, saale ma ke chod. For religion, they say when they are among people, and when they are alone, they fuck that same religion. They rape, they loot and live like kings. What religion? There is no religion. It's all politics and personal profit. They're all alike, these Hindu, Musalmaan, terrorists, all of them. Chutiya saale. They don't care about the people. It is only because of them that one community has become thirsty for the other's blood. When I was outside, my friends and I, we used to live like a family. Chami is a Musalmaan. In fact, when we first met him, his mother was alive. He wasn't a thief then. He used to live with his mother in a slum and go to school and everything. His mother used to make paper bags to support him. One day Ramu met him in the street and they became friends. Chami took us to his jhuggi once. His mother fed us daal and roti and told us we could all live there in their home. She didn't care that most of us were Hindus, and we didn't care that they were Musalmaan.'

'So did you live with them?'

'No. She died. Chami told us she was very sick and they didn't have money for a doctor. When she died we took Chami in like a brother.'

That day, walking around in the compound, I feel a gratifying sense of continuum between Daddy's life in this country more than a half century ago and the present. I'm amazed at how human nature sustains. How Koki's friends sound so much like the people Daddy lived with in this country. How powers of love and acceptance among these people seem unaltered over the years. I remember Daddy telling me about his Muslim friend, Amjad, and how his family gathered Daddy in the fold of their love as though he were a long lost son.

The year Daddy survived the beggar woman's curse, plague struck his village, and his mother perished in it. His father gathered his remaining family and his son's death-defying quilt and went to live with his sister in Lahore. Daddy's aunt turned out to be a mean, childless woman who resented her poor clerk husband and hated her unchanging life. The arrival of penniless relatives was right in keeping with her fate. As soon as she took in Daddy and his sisters, she put the girls to work in the house. All day she made them cook and clean and at meals she cursed them all for leaching upon her. So Daddy's father pawned his deceased wife's gold bangles and bought a barber's kit to set up shop under a peepul tree at the corner of the street. He knew his daughters were all growing up faster than bamboo shoots and would soon need dowries for marriage. Daddy, however, dressed in the only shirt he owned, was allowed to go to a local government school six kilometres away. Over the years, his sisters were all married off one by one. When he was eleven, Daddy's father left him.

A beggar used to frequent their street. He was rumoured to be a retired magistrate, and he could well have been one, for he spoke the language of the white sahibs very well. He would sit beside Daddy's father under the peepul tree, lost in meditation, totally without a care. A stray dog bit him once and the wound festered. Daddy and his friends sat and watched the ants climb into the putrefying flesh in his leg. 'They are God's creatures too,' the beggar would say. 'This is God's body. Who am I to interfere?' Sometimes he would pick up mud from the street and rub it into the festering wound. My grandfather would sit with him all day, listening to him, watching him sway with a gentle motion as though a delicate breeze were passing through him. And then miraculously, the beggar's infected wound healed. The boys saw him walking down the street without even a limp. Then one day he was gone, and with him, my grandfather.

Left alone in his aunt's house, Daddy began to bear the brunt of all her frustrations. She started calling upon Daddy to do all the chores and, eventually, more than the chores. In the morning, while everyone snuggled greedily, grabbing the last cozy moments of sleep, she would wake my father up to fetch ashes to scrub the dirty dishes. Daddy would run to the halwai's shop across the street and scoop out ashes from the furnace left overnight to cool. The rush was to get to the furnace before the halwai's servants cleaned it out. If the ashes were not enough, or were too gritty from unburned coal, she would make him run across town to the other halwai's till she had enough. Soon she started waking him up even earlier so he could clean the dishes before he went to school. Then there was the water to be fetched from the community well. Shivering in just his underwear, he would stand in a queue behind women with large buckets or earthenware jars, waiting for his turn at the well. Hauling buckets of water from the well, he would fill the two he had brought along, and carrying one in each hand, his fingers numb from the cold weight, he would bring them back to the house. On days that his aunt washed her hair, he would have to go back to refill the buckets.

Then one day, Daddy's aunt forbade him to go to school. 'I can't afford the fees,' she said. 'Besides, I need someone in the house to help me with all the chores.' Slowly, the food on his plate began to get more and more scarce till his aunt begrudged him every morsel. One evening, towards the end of his frugal meal, faint memories of his patchwork quilt stirred in his mind. A quilt and a plate full of food begged from the neighbours. He got up and ran to the storeroom where his father's meagre belongings had been put away. He searched the room till he found the quilt. It was a little tattered and much too small to be spread across his shoulders, but it was his quilt, nonetheless. He pulled it around his neck, and slipping out of the house, started walking towards the Muslim section of the street. The Hindus, he feared, would know him and would carry tales to his aunt. The first door he knocked on was Amjad's, but he didn't know that, because in all his years of friendship with Amjad, he had never been to his house. He had met Amjad some years ago on the vacant lot in the neighbourhood, where, after school, all the boys used to gather to play. Daddy's favourite game was to watch the kites, his eagle eyes always awaiting that fatal cut which one glass-tinged yarn would inflict on another. Then he would speed towards the path of the kite's rudderless descent and retrieve the prize. There were always others, too, who awaited such booty. And, of course, there was the rightful owner whose sharp flying had initiated the pecha. Swiftness was always the victor, and in that, my father excelled. It was during one such kite race that my father met Amjad.

It was a beautiful kite, not too large to defy the winds, and not too small to fear it. It was a kite that could conquer the skies with its streamlined sides, crafted not with the vanity of a peacock, but for the flight of a sparrow, one half red and one half blue, with a short blue tail like the feather of a blue jay. Amjad's eye was on it as he tightened the spool of his own bigger and heavier yellow kite. He steered towards the soaring blue and red kite. When its owner relaxed the string to allow it more flight, Amjad swooped on it like a vulture. With his nine-thread yarn coated with powdered glass, he severed the other kite clean off its loose spool. For a moment the kite remained at its height then floated towards the ground, disoriented and dislodged. Daddy was already running in the direction he instinctively knew the kite would take. Even before it floated to the ground, Daddy reached for its short, severed lifeline. But as he pulled the string towards him, Amjad grabbed the kite.

'It's mine,' Amjad explained to Daddy. 'It's my kata.'

'But I got it first,' my father declared.

'Let go,' Amjad yanked at the thread. It slipped out of Daddy's hand leaving a fine furrow of red across his palm. He looked at his bleeding palm and, enraged, threw himself on Amjad, grabbing the kite. Breaking its fine wooden bones, he tore the blue and red paper into shreds and tossing it on the ground, spat on it.

'Take it now. It's all yours,' he said.

In a trice Amjad was upon him, beating the living daylights out of him. He was a couple of inches taller than my father and half a dozen pounds heavier. In no time at all he had my father doubled on the ground with a punched stomach, a bloody nose and a cut lip. Then he grabbed the front of my father's only shirt and yanked till the buttons flew open, tearing the overwashed, weak material all down the front.

'That's for the kite,' he said and walked away.

Daddy's aunt gave him a beating with a broom for ruining his school shirt. The next morning, she took one of her husband's old khaki shirts, cut off the cuffs to shorten the arm length, and made him wear that to school.

Amjad's mother heard about the fight and sent her son on a mission of truce to the lot. Amjad gave Daddy a sweetmeat and offered to let him fly his kite that day. Amjad and Daddy became the best of friends, but Daddy never forgave his best friend for ruining the only shirt he owned.

And now there he was at his friend's house, begging for food.

Amjad opened the door a slight crack when Daddy knocked. 'What do you want?' he asked.

Daddy hesitated. How could he tell his friend that he was begging? But the tantalizing smell of freshly-cooked curry and whole-wheat chapatis baked on an open fire would not allow him to leave. He stood at the door, fingering the quilt.

'I can't come to play now,' Amjad said. 'We are going to eat.'

'Amjad, who is it?' A woman's voice called from inside.

'It's my friend,' Amjad called back.

'Tell him to come inside. Don't stand at the door.'

'What do you want?' Amjad asked again.

'Can I come inside?' Amjad opened the door wider.

Daddy stepped inside. The fragrance of food grew stronger. A large woman dressed in a loose salwar-kameez walked into the room. She had clear white skin and kohl-blackened eyes that sparkled with love.   ·

'What is your name, beta?' she asked.

'Manohar.'

'Amjad,' she turned to her son, 'go get your friend some mithai.'

Amjad went inside and in a moment reappeared with a plate full of sweetmeats—colourful barfi, layered brilliantly with silver varaq. Daddy pounced on the plate, grabbing two-three pieces in each hand, stuffing his mouth till little morsels spilled out from the corners.

'Manohar, it is very late. Won't your mother worry about you? It is almost time for dinner. Won't she be waiting for you?'

Daddy shook his head. 'My mother is dead,' he said, flicking the clammy paste of the sweetmeat from the roof of his mouth with his tongue.

'Where have you been for so many days?' Amjad asked. 'I won three kites. Wait. I'll show you.'

'Later, Amjad,' his mother said. 'Beta,' she said, bending down to take Daddy's chin in her hand. 'What is the matter? Why are you out so late? Don't you have someone who will worry about you?'

Daddy drew away, jerking his chin out of her hand. 'No,' he said, staring at the floor. 'No one will worry about me.'

'But you must stay with someone. Who looks after you?' she persisted.

For a moment Daddy continued to stare at the wooden floor scrubbed to a dull sheen, then replied inaudibly. 'I stay with my aunt.'

'Won't she miss you?'

'Yes.' He looked up, his eyes angry, his voice bitter. 'My aunt will miss me. There won't be anyone to clean the dirty dishes after dinner.'

Amjad's mother was silent for a minute. Then her eyes clouded over and she took my father's wrist and pulled him closer to her. A warm smell of spices and fragrant hair oil engulfed Daddy.

'Doesn't she give you anything to eat?'

'A little,' Daddy admitted.

'But not enough.'

Daddy shook his head.

'Tell me the truth, beta. What are you doing on the street at this time?'

Daddy pulled the quilt closer, clutching the edges with both hands. 'I came out to beg for food,' he said, raising his chin in defiance.

Amjad's mother gathered him in her arms, tears smudging the kohl in her eyes. In the circle of her soft bangled arms, his face smothered in her ample bosom, Daddy began to tell his story, his voice choking from the reminder of how a mother's love felt.

'You don't ever have to go back to her house,' Amjad's mother promised him. 'Stay here with us. In the morning you can go to school with Amjad and in the evening you can help his father in the shop just like Amjad does.' Amjad's father owned a small jewellery store.

Amjad's house was larger than his aunt's. It had three storeys with the rooms built in concentric circles, leaving the centre open for a three-levelled skylight. Amjad's father made enough money to afford electricity. There were electric bulbs hanging from thin brown wires in the kitchen and living room. Daddy was relieved that he wouldn't have to spend countless daylight hours cleaning the lentils and rice. But the best surprise was a water pump in the yard outside the house. Even if Amjad's mother made him fill water, at least he wouldn't have to carry it two blocks, let alone wait in line for the other women to get their fill.

Amjad's mother took him in like a son. She had always wanted another child, but after Amjad, she had not been able to conceive. Her husband loved her too much to want to marry again for more children, so they had contented themselves with Amjad. She opened up one of the many unused rooms in the house, dusted it clean and set up a bed for Daddy.

His first night there, Daddy lay on his bed, looking out of the open door at the tender brilliance of the stars. He located the family of three stars that shone one beside the other, bonded even in death. His older sister used to sit him on her lap and tell him the story of Shravan Kumar, the loving son, who had sat his blind parents in two baskets and levering the baskets on a wooden plank, had carried them around on a pilgrimage. When he had been killed accidentally by a hunter, his parents had been so heartbroken that they, too, had given up their lives. God had installed this loving family in his skies where they always shone together— Shravan Kumar in the centre, and his parents on either side. Daddy lay staring at the family till his eyes blurred. Then he searched all over the sky, wondering which star was his mother, for hadn't his sister told him that when good people died, God made them stars so they could be beacons for other people and guide them in goodness? He knew his mother had been the best.

The next morning, he woke up early and went down the stairs to the kitchen. He was searching for the box in which to fetch ashes for the dishes when Amjad's mother came in.

'It's early, child. Couldn't you sleep? Don't worry. It was a new place and an unfamiliar bed. You'll soon get used to it. Then you won't wake up till it is almost time to go to school.'

'Where's the box for the ashes? I must fetch them before the halwai's servant cleans out the furnace.'

'What ashes? Why do you need ashes?' she asked.

'For the dirty dishes.'

'I don't need ashes. I clean my dishes with raw mud and I get mine right here in my yard. And you don't need to get that for me; I will get it when I need it.'

'Then what can I do?'

She looked at Daddy, tears making her eyes sparkle brighter than ever. She sat him down on the mat in the kitchen and said, 'Listen, Manohar, you are my son now, just like Amjad is my son. He doesn't have to help me in the housework and neither do you. Now go to the pump and clean up. There are some neem sticks for your teeth lying on that sill. After that, come back here, and I'll give you something to eat. Then you must get ready for school. I have already talked to Amjad's father. He will buy you the books you need and will send your fees with Amjad.'

'I haven't brought my school shirt,' Daddy stated.

'Don't worry about that. I'll give you something of Amjad's to wear. Now run along. I'm going to wake Amjad up. Even the curses of the rising sun don't awaken him.'

I realize I am standing at the edge of the platform before Sultana's cell. I climb up and call her softly. I want to see the face of terrorism. The inside seems to be empty. She is probably sitting behind the wall. I stand looking for long moments, wondering at her need for such incessant seclusion.

chapter five

Having regained my health, I resume my persistence in wanting to inform the American Consulate. Every morning when the Superintendent comes on his scheduled round, I ask him, 'Have you heard from my Consulate?' This becomes my daily form of greeting. He gives the same answer every morning. 'Your Consulate has been informed.' I wonder if he is telling the truth. One morning I ask him to allow me paper and pen so I can write a letter to the Consulate. 'We'll see,' he says.

'That's not the way to ask these haramzadas for things,' Koki tells me.

'Then how shall I ask?'

'You have to fight for it.'

'What do you mean?'

'Make him take notice of your demand.'

'How?'

'Go on a hunger strike.'

I think about that for a moment before shaking my head. I don't wish to make any waves and anger the authorities. Besides, the Consulate has probably been informed. These things take time. I decide to give it a few more days.

Many more days pass. One day, after Malti has locked the gates and retired to her room, I lie on the mat and look at the high compound wall with its curling hedge of barbed wire all along the top, drawing out a plan of escape by scaling it. I wonder what is on the other side. 'Mine fields,'

Koki tells me. 'There are fields of grain and vegetable, but because some of the male prisoners work in them, they are more heavily guarded than the jail itself.' I give up staring at the wall, directing my eyes instead to the sky above us. I remember Daddy telling me how at sunset, one fire would burn in the Pacific sky and another would burn in the ocean. He would stand on the deck of the *Hai Wangtsing*, the steamer he boarded from Shanghai two days after arriving on a ship from Bombay, and watch that double expanse of sky—a sky above and a sky below, both bleeding blackness into their bellies from the stars that embedded them like shards of glass, and feel a dark comfort at God's own spaces duplicating his life. I look up to see the sky only partially visible, blocked off by the high prison wall. Laying my head down, I weep into my blanket, afraid that for the rest of my life this bit of sky is all I will be able to call my own. My heart craves to see those wide expanses if only to see reflections of Daddy's life in them. I know with a sense of hopelessness that nothing is going to change now. No one from the Consulate will come to rescue me. No one is going to help me prove my innocence. I weep quietly all night.

The flowers at the base of the platform are old and wrinkled even before they emerge from their buds. They are a dirty yellow, as though the soil from the earth has travelled up their shoots and stained them. I can't identify them. Perhaps they are chrysanthemums.

Koki and I are squatting on our haunches one morning, collecting these aged flowers in our laps to make a garland for Hema, when Prema comes to tell me I have a visitor.

I see the flowers in my lap begin to tremble, and I realize that the knees they are laid out on are shaking. In fact, such a trembling erupts in my body it is as though every cell in it is fibrillating. Koki jumps up and, shaking off the petals from her sari, takes my hand and pulls me up. 'Come on,' she says, 'your gorment has sent somebody.'

My steps erratic, I follow Prema out of the small metal gate across the fragrant courtyard through a wooden door adjacent to the large iron gate of the enclave into a small ante-room, the front of which is latticed steel from the waist up. I stand just inside the door, gripping the tremors of my fingers in my fists, looking this side and that of the net.

'Simi,' I hear someone say softly. The familiar voice attaches itself to me like wings.

'Scott?' I whisper, my body a bird as it flies across the room, only to be halted in mid flight by the wire that spreads like a hunter's net.

'Oh, baby ... baby ... baby.' His fingers reach through the triangular lattices of the net, entwining mine. 'I've been so afraid.'

'Scott ...' All the pain, the frustration, the futility of the past two weeks is catalyzed in his dear face. I lean my forehead against the wire and sob loudly, inconsolably.

'Oh baby.' His fingertips reach through the net to feel my tears. 'Sh ... sh ...' he whispers gently. We stand there a long time, just like that.

'How'd you find me?' I finally ask.

'That's not important now. I just did. I had to. Fifteen days and no word from you. I was so worried.'

'They think I was carrying a bomb. Can you imagine Daddy's ashes a bomb?' I try to say flippantly, but my voice breaks. 'I took a picture of the border. They told me I was a threat to their national security.'

'Yes, I heard.'

'From whom?'

'The colonel who arrested you.'

'You met him?'

'Yes, among many others. I've been in India for five days trying to figure out where you were.'

'I bet jail was the first place you looked.' I am so happy and relieved to see Scott, I feel I can even joke about my situation.

'Actually, the second.' he says smiling. 'My first was the local maharajah's harem.'

I look down at my tattered, stained, once white jeans and sleeveless shirt and laugh. 'Dressed like this, the maharajah would have taken me for his state beggar.'

He looks at me then from head to toe. I see my horrible state in his eyes.

'Do I look that bad?'

'No. Oh, no, sweetheart. You look just as beautiful as ever. My Indian princess. But you look so ... so thin. And those bruises on your face. What'd they do to you?'

'I've been sick. I drank bad water. But I'm okay now. Really I am.' I don't mention that horrendous night of torture. 'Tell me, how'd you find me?'

'Remember you were going to call me on the night you arrived? I waited for your call. I waited for a whole week. You should've seen me. I was retrieving messages from my machine from work. I left my cell phone on all the time. It was crazy. I started checking with AT&T to see if the lines to India were clear. I couldn't understand why you hadn't called. Finally, I called your travel agent and got the number of the hotel you were supposed to be staying at. The guy at the hotel told me you'd checked in one day and left, and the following morning the police had arrived and confiscated your luggage. He knew you'd been arrested, but he didn't know for what. I went crazy. I called the Indian Embassy. I called the American Consulate in India. I even went to see Jim, you know, my attorney friend? He's the one who said, "Go to India. See what's going on." So I walked into Debbie's office the next morning and told her I wanted emergency leave for an unspecified period of time. I should've known better. I've said it before and I'll say it again, that woman's a bitch. She gave me all this crap about project deadlines and company policies regarding leave, so I said "fuck you" and cleared out my desk. Then I took the next available flight to India.'

'Scott, I'm sorry. You shouldn't have. I can't believe you quit your job.'

'I'd been telling you for months I would. I'd had it with Debbie and her you-work-for-me-you-have-no-life trip. Besides, I needed a vacation. I'll find something else when we go back. Let's not worry about that now. We've got to figure out a way to get you out of this mess. I've already contacted the US Consulate. They're the ones who helped me locate you. It took me five days. The cops here wouldn't even tell me whether you were in custody.'

'The Superintendent here kept telling me that the Consulate had been informed. I should've guessed.'

'Thank God I found you.' He covers his face with his hands, rubbing the tips of his fingers over his eyelids.

'So what happens now?' I say, sitting down on the only chair on my side of the room.

'I'm going to get you out of here.'

'How? God knows when my trial will be. They haven't even set a date yet. Not that that'll be of any help. No one listens here. Everything seems to be predetermined.'

'Please baby, try not to worry. I'm talking to the Consulate. You're an American. They can't do this to you. I'll make sure of that. I'm meeting with a foreign affairs official at the Consulate today. I'm sure when I come next time, I'll have good news if not your release papers.'

I smile at him, thanking him, loving him with my eyes. He places his palms flat against the net. I place my own against his, absorbing his warmth.

'Time over,' the guard at the door says tonelessly. I curl my fingers through the diamond shapes of the lattice work and grip his for a minute before turning away quickly and walking out of the door, imagining the deep blue irises in his aquarelle eyes contract as they do with emotion.

I go back to the barracks walking on air.

'What happened?' Koki is waiting impatiently near the iron gate when I step in. I throw my arms around her, hugging her, swirling her around in a little jig. 'Koki, oh, Koki. You know who came to see me? Scott, my boyfriend from America.'

'From Amreeka? How did he find out?'

'It's a long story.' I hook her arm in mine and walk back jauntily. 'But he's here now, and he's going to get me out. He's talking to the Consulate. Do you know the Superintendent lied to me? He never informed the American

Consulate. Wait till I see him in the morning. I'll tell him exactly what I think of him.'

Koki stops in her tracks, pulling me to a halt. 'Don't do that. Don't say anything to that haramzada. He'll find a way to stop your Scott. Just be quiet. Don't even tell anyone else here. Prison walls have elephant ears. If that bitch, Fulo, finds out, she'll ruin everything. Just keep mum.'

I take Koki's advice and tell the others only that a friend had come to visit. But silently I begin to bid farewell to everything that has provided me any solace in this place. The pitiful, ageing flowers, the winter sun with its lover's warmth, the crisp evening light clustered with moths, the inmates who bring food every day, the icicle-sharp water, my corner in the barracks, my colourless, rough blanket. I play more games with little Hema and massage Kubrima's back more lovingly. I even help Fulo extract a splinter from her finger. On my evening walk I go a little closer to Sultana's cell and stand outside her bars. One evening I see her feet poking out from behind the wall as she sits on the floor beside the toilet.

'Sultana,' I say softly. Her feet remain motionless.

'Sultana,' I say again. She gathers her feet in. 'Please, can I talk to you?'

A moment later I see her step out from behind the wall. In the soft afterglow of the sunset, her face is the colour of sun-satiated wheat. Her long black hair is loose and hangs down her shoulders like a dark cascading waterfall, offsetting her well-shaped, white-sari-clad figure. She is the epitome of the proverbial Indian woman—beautiful. There is no other word to describe her. But her eyes hardly match the rest of her. They are large and black, but opaque. Cold, like twin pieces of rock.

Now that I have her attention, I don't know what to say. 'How are you?' I ask inanely.

She doesn't answer but continues to pound me with her eyes.

'I . . . I just wondered why you never talk to anyone.'

'Don't you know?' she says. 'You're not allowed to talk to me.' Her voice is low and flat as though her words hover

over a pit of emotion but never dip into it.

'But we never see you either.'

'What's there to see?' she says and walks back into the darkness.

I stand looking at the apparent emptiness of her cell for a while before turning around to head towards the barracks.

A whole week passes before Scott comes to see me again.

'They only have visiting hours once a week,' he explains.

'I know,' I say. 'But I thought the people at the Consulate . . .'

'We're working on it. Apparently, it isn't as easy as I thought it'd be. This country has pretty strict laws about any suspicious activity against their security.'

'What do they mean suspicious activity? Sprinkling a dead father's ashes is suspicious activity?' I can feel tears pricking the insides of my eyes.

'I know. I know, baby. I told Elaine Johnson, the foreign affairs official, about the purpose of your visit. She says you should've obtained permission.'

'Permission? Why? That place is a fucking tourist sight. Hundreds of people visit there every day. They gape at the border like they would at a fucking freak show. *They* don't require permission, and I require permission to pay the greatest homage ever?' I cover my face with my hands, letting the sobs take over.

Scott just sits across from me, waiting for me to calm down.

'Sorry,' I say after a while, wiping the tears away with the back of my hand. 'I'm sorry. I didn't mean to take it out on you. It's just that I thought . . . I hoped . . .'

'I know, baby. I'm sorry, too. But hey, I haven't given up yet. Not by a long shot. I'm going to keep at it till we can clean up this mess. I'll get you out of here if I have to write to the President of the United States, the UN, Amnesty International, whoever. I'll do anything to get you out of here as soon as possible.'

I smile at him and nod. 'Thanks, Scott. I know you're doing your best.'

'You better believe it. Come here.' He gets up, gesturing me to come close to the net. I stand up and approach him. He purses his lips and squeezes them through one of the little steel diamonds. I laugh softly and place my lips on his. He holds his creased lips on mine for a moment, then I feel the lines relax and the tip of his tongue move on the inside moist skin of my lips.

'Oh God, Simi,' he says, moving away and rubbing his mouth to erase the lines of the net imprinted around his mouth. 'I've got to get you out of here.'

Scott's Thursday afternoon visits become the nucleus of my existence as I live the monotony of prison life: waking at the crack of dawn, breathing in lungs full of air to avoid having to inhale the odours of the toilet and bath later, eating lukewarm green soup and gritty chapatis, watering the flowers that never know their prime, playing games with Hema, talking to Koki and the others, eating lukewarm green soup and gritty chapatis, walking around in circles in the evening, retiring behind the bars in the barracks to lie on the mat, looking out at a piece of sky, freezing under the thin blanket in the cold winter night, waking up at dawn . . . days pass like facsimiles of each other.

Sometimes, especially in the evening, when the night warden and Fulo are involved in deep conversation, I walk to Sultana's cell and call her softly. She and I talk a little now, mostly about her life before the murders.

'I was doing my BA in history. I wanted to be a history professor. Initially, I had wanted to be an excavator, but my father didn't approve of my going away to strange places for months in the company of strange men.'

'Tell me about your father,' I ask her once. She gives me that same cold look and turns away. She never talks about her family or the reason she is here. I remember Koki telling me her father died in a fire during a communal riot. I almost envy her her pure bereavement, the utter loss that follows the sudden and unexpected death of a parent. Daddy's death was hardly that. He nurtured its seed within him since the partition of India and Pakistan, but for thirty years my

mother didn't allow the seed to flower. I asked her one day
how she knew it had to be prevented from burgeoning. 'I
knew the very first time I saw him,' she said. She must have
been twelve then. It was the morning after her grandfather
had celebrated the Independence of India with a bonfire in
the backyard where he and his friends had burned heaps and
heaps of files of important-looking papers. 'The last fire of
Gaddar,' they had toasted each other. From as far back as
she could remember, she knew that even though her family
lived in America, they were Indians. She knew that there was
a secret about her grandfather she must not tell anyone—
that the apparently simple son of the soil, a rice farmer, was
really an important official of the Gaddar party, the American
counterpart of any and all Independence revolts in India.

That day she had entered the living room to bid her
grandfather a good morning before going to school. Instead
of reading the Guru Granth Sahib, which he did every
morning, she saw him watching a young man who was
sitting on the floor with his head hanging between his knees.
He was weeping and weeping as though he would not stop.
He held his muscular arms stiffly by his sides, gripping the
floor with his fingers as though unwilling to allow himself
even the comfort of his hands. Mingled with sobs, he was
telling her grandfather a terrible story of a nation on the
brink of division, of death and destruction, of rage and
killing, and then of self-imposed punishment, of exile. When
his sobs were spent, the house grew quiet; there was only the
sound of tears spattering the floor between his knees. 'The
lot of freedom fighters is pain and suffering. Glory comes
only after death.' Words she had heard her grandfather say
many times now finally presented themselves in palpable
form, in the suffering form of the young man on the floor.

'Enough now,' her grandfather said to him, 'all gaddar
ended yesterday. Today you and I will begin to forgive. Get
up.'

The young man just sat there, his head hung low.

'Enough,' her grandfather said again. 'Get up and go to
work. What will the other workers think of you? A grown

man crying.'

He looked up then and pushed his long hair back. She saw his face, strong like a young wrestler's, streaked with grime and tears. 'I can't work here,' he said on a hiccough. 'I've only come to get my quilt.'

'Why can't you work here?'

'Rahematullah . . .' He stuck his face between his legs again.

'Don't worry about him. He's been taken care of. He'll live. Now get up. You're a brave young man. In time you'll forgive yourself. Meantime, learn to make a life for yourself in this country. Now go.'

'My quilt,' he said, looking up again.

Her grandfather picked up a ragged old quilt from the sofa and laid it on his shoulders. 'Here.' Then he held up something else in his hand. It was a worn leather pouch. 'Take this, too,' he said.

Daddy got up and, wiping his face with a corner of the quilt, shook his head. 'Not that,' he said.

Her grandfather pressed the pouch into his hands. 'Take it. You've already paid for it.'

Daddy shook his head once again and, placing the pouch on her grandfather's feet, walked out towards the fields.

For ten years Daddy lived on Mummy's farm in the flatlands of Oakland. Ten years in which he went from being a devastated orphan to a trusted son to Mummy's grandfather. He got his high school diploma and then a bachelor's degree from Berkeley, and became the love of Mummy's life.

With new dreams unfolding on the horizon coupled with Mummy's therapeutic closeness, Daddy gradually drew out of himself to build another life, but he remained as close to his guilt as a word or the evocation of a memory. Bewildered at first at his withdrawal at the mere mention of India, Mummy began to eventually accept his silences, wondering, however, at their depth, assuming that the chatter of life would one day fill them. It wasn't until years later that she realized how bottomless those silent chasms were, and how easily their lives could be consumed in them. Mummy's grandfather passed away and, against her mother's wishes, she married Daddy and moved to Batonsville, Maryland, where Daddy accepted a job as a junior engineer. When Mummy was four months pregnant with me, cosmetic surgery was declared the biggest thing ever to hit the beauty-conscious consumer. One evening Mummy asked Daddy why he didn't have his tattoo erased.

'What tattoo?' he asked.

'The name on your arm—Amjad.'

He looked at the fine strokes of Urdu on his forearm for a long time as if reckoning with the world they belonged to, then quietly left the room. She found him in their bedroom later, retracing Amjad's name with the redhot tip of a knitting needle she had been using to make booties for the baby. On the nightstand was a candle melting perfumed wax and singed skin. 'Oh God, Manohar, stop it!' she screamed. He looked up at her, his face contorted with pain. 'You're right. I forfeited him,' he said simply.

She ran to the cabinet to get a capsule of vitamin E. Breaking it on the blistering name on his arm, she whispered, 'I'm sorry,' and realized how porous his guilt was.

From that day on, Mummy formed a buffer in Daddy's life. No news of Daddy's homeland was allowed to filter into our American home. Conversations about India were taboo. Then, five years ago, Mummy died in a car accident on her way to pick Daddy up from work. Daddy bore her death stoically. Perhaps, too stoically. I never saw him shed a tear. Even when he called me at college to tell me, his voice was measured and detached as if he were passing a sentence—on himself. I arrived home with Scott to see him lying beside Mummy's shroud-covered corpse with his arms folded behind his head, his eyes dry, staring at the ceiling. The house was filled with neighbours and friends, some crying loudly, but he seemed unaware of them. When I entered, he got up and took me in his arms. I lay in them for hours, for days, weeping, clinging to his apparent strength, but between us our grief was our own, unshared even with each other. When my grandparents arrived from San Francisco, he stood before my grandmother without a tear or a word while she beat his chest with her fists, sobbing and blaming him for the death of her daughter. After we cremated Mummy, Daddy bought a gun. I knew then that it was my turn to take over the vigil. I moved back home and re-erected the barriers that had crumbled with Mummy's passing. I began to watch Daddy constantly, because although he seemed to resume his life unaffected, I knew that the silence frozen on his face was Mummy's untimely death, and behind it were the reawakened demons of his past. Even though I kept a tight guard, every once in a while, those demons would escape and seep through the barrage in his heart, corroding the centre. They would make him lie on his bed for hours, his eyes gently shut, his body motionless, as if in death. Sitting beside him, watching the rebellious nerve in his temple, I came to know those demons well. I would take his cold hand in mine sometimes and hold it tightly, afraid to let go. Sometimes, a dam would crumble and an unredemptive flood would pour out of him. I was almost grateful for these outpourings because they provided the sap for the roots of my life. I also realized that what I had seen as fear in him that first time, was really pain, and with every revelation, it was his pain that became my own. And it was that pain I bore more than the pain of his death. I didn't shed a single tear when he passed away. His pain and the promise I made him to alleviate it, weighed too heavily in my heart. My father may be dead to the world, but for me he still thrashes in the throes of death, my bereavement still awaits.

'My father's dead,' I tell Sultana. 'That's why I am here. He wanted me to sprinkle his ashes on the border of India and Pakistan.'

'Ashes,' she says, her chin at an angle, trembling.

chapter six

On Thursday when I enter the ante-room to meet Scott, there is a man with him, standing against the wall on the side, with arms folded over his chest, his hands resting in the nooks of his elbows. He is wearing a pair of blue jeans and a handspun cotton kurta the colour of earth.

'Simi,' Scott says, walking up to the steel lattice and reaching for my fingers through the net. 'I want you to meet Arun. Arun's a journalist. He writes for one of the national dailies.'

'Hi,' I say, looking at Arun. His face, a shade or two deeper than his kurta, is dense. It is as though all of life has converged in it. In comparison, Scott's face becomes that of a fledgling still learning the patterns of life, flagrantly displaying each lesson. I wonder why Scott has brought a journalist to see me.

'Hello, Simran,' he says with a brief smile. 'I've been following your story since the time of your arrest,'

'My arrest? That article—bomb attempt foiled by border security forces—was it yours?'

'Yes.'

'Bomb attempt?' I feel an anger rise in my throat. 'Bomb attempt? Do you know what I was carrying in that box you called a bomb? God, what a shoddy piece of journalism! Where was your proof, mister? Bomb attempt. Really!'

He continues to lean against the wall, showing no apparent reaction to my anger. 'Did you read the article?' he asks quietly.

'No. How could I? I was arrested, remember? For a
bomb attempt. I read the headlines at the risk of my life,' I
say, recalling the gun pointed at my back.

'I've read it, Simi,' Scott says. 'It wasn't as bad as you
think. It mentioned the fact that speculations about whether
that really was a bomb were already being made.'

'I'm sorry about the headline,' the journalist says. 'It was
my editor's. I agree it was misleading.'

'Are you here to get my side of the story?' I ask him,
slightly mollified.

'I don't think that is necessary,' he says.

'I brought Arun to meet you,' Scott says, 'because he
might be able to help us.'

'How? By writing about it from his perspective?' I look
at Arun.

'Things work differently here, Simi. Just listen to what
he has to say.'

Arun moves from the far end of the room and comes to
stand beside Scott. 'I can talk to some people,' he says.

'People who will believe I'm innocent?'

'If that's what you want.'

'What do you mean? If you don't believe I'm innocent,
why are you helping me?' I ask him, searching his face. He
doesn't respond to that and his face is too opaque for me to
read. Or, perhaps, he has mastered the art of reining in all
expression. I wonder if people feel cheated by his reticence—
spending all their words and receiving nothing in return. I
wonder, too, how Scott seems to get along so well with him.

'Of course he believes you are innocent,' Scott says, 'and
he's helping us because he believes the system has wronged
you. He believes in justice.'

'You don't have to manipulate the system to help me,'
I say to Arun. 'I'm innocent. I just want to be able to prove
that.'

'We'll let due process prove your innocence,' he says.

'Due process? There's a girl in here who's been waiting
for a trial date for two years. Obviously due process has no
time limits here.'

'That's where Arun comes in.' Scott sounds so trusting. Scott trusts too easily. That is one of our perennial battles. I'm more wary of people and worry constantly about them taking advantage of Scott's simplicity and faith in humanity, his unquestioning trust in his fellow men. 'In fact,' Scott continues, 'That is what I came to tell you today. Arun has put me in touch with a very good lawyer. His name's A. Mathur. Don't ask me what the "A" stands for. I read it on his nameplate. It's twelve letters long. Anyway, Mr Mathur says that with the help of the people Arun knows he will not only be able to get an early trial date, but will also be able to have most of the charges dropped.'

As I listen to Scott and Arun plan my freedom, I realize how unrelated it seems to my innocence or guilt. I ask myself if I would let anyone help me in this way if I were really guilty. I think about Daddy's guilt and his ashes condemned to a lifetime of penance, and I have the answer. I wish I had the luxury of refusing Arun's help, but I know enough of the system now to realize that without his assistance, I might never be able to convince anyone of my innocence. I turn towards Arun and ask him, 'What do you want me to do?'

'Nothing yet. Just keep quiet about this whole thing. I'll take care of the rest.'

I nod my head. 'Thank you,' I say, and suddenly, I'm weary of this whole mess. 'Scott,' I lay my hands flat on the net. 'I think I'm going to go back inside now.'

'Oh, baby,' Scott comes closer to the net and puts his palms against mine. 'Don't sound so low. We'll find a way out of this mess. I promise.' He bends his head and presses a kiss on the ball of my left hand.

'I'll meet you outside, Scott.' I look up to see Arun walk out of the room in long strides.

'Do you think it is wise to involve him?' I ask Scott. 'He might complicate matters. A media person's association with my case might lead them to believe I am politically involved in this country's problems. Can you imagine what kind of sentence I'll get then?'

'I think you're wrong, baby. He really might be able to

pull this off. He looks very sure of himself and totally in control, doesn't he?'

I don't answer. 'How many articles has he done on my case?' I say instead. 'You said he's been following my story ever since I got arrested.'

'Just two. You know about the first one. The second one said something about your visit to India being a pilgrimage.'

'You're kidding. How'd he find out?'

'I think he spoke with the cabby who took you to the border.'

I try to remember my stunted conversation in Hindi with the cab driver. 'Scott, don't tell him about Daddy.'

Scott nods and takes his leave. 'Let me go and talk to him some more. I'll see you next week. I've told the lawyer to come and see you. I think he might be able to get you out on bail.'

I caress his hand with the tips of my fingers. 'I can't wait. I miss you so much.'

'I know, honey. I miss you, too. We've got to get you out of here.'

Koki is waiting for me by the door as usual. 'So?' she asks the usual question.

'So, nothing,' I say. 'No change. The American government still does not want to get involved, but Scott brought a man with him today. An Indian. A journalist. His name's Arun. He claims he can help me.'

'That's great news. These newspaperwallahs have a lot of power. You wait and see, he will get you out.'

On the following Tuesday, two days before Scott's visit, Mr A. Mathur, the lawyer Scott mentioned, comes to see me. Matinee takes me to a small room with a table in the centre and two chairs on either side of it. Mr Mathur is already seated at the table when I enter. He's a middle-aged man with thinning hair and large bugs-eye glasses pushed all the way up his nose. He is dressed in a wrinkled dark brown suit. He stands up when I enter, and after introducing himself, sits down again. Then pulling his bulging briefcase onto his lap, he snaps it open. He speaks to me in English, stressing each word as though he has learnt it not as a spoken language but as a medium in which educational books are written. His unpretentious manner, the way he looks, surprise me. Somehow I cannot imagine him deviating from the straight path of justice to suit his or anyone's purpose. I wonder if I misinterpreted the nature of the journalist's help.

'Now, describe to me again in detail, everything that occurred when you visited the border,' Mr Mathur asks.

I settle in the chair across from him and relate the events in as much detail as I can remember. He listens patiently without interrupting, peering at me closely all the time with his magnified eyes.

'Hm,' he says when I finish. And nothing else.

'What do you think?' I ask him.

'We have a case,' he says quietly.

'You can prove my innocence?'

'I am certain.'

'Without manipulating the law, you can prove my innocence?'

He sits up straight and pushes his glasses further up his nose till his eyelashes and eyebrows all become part of the magnification. Then, clearing his throat he says, 'I have great respect for the law, Miss Mehta. I agreed to take your case only because Arun convinced me you have been wrongfully accused. And now, after talking to you, I am certain.'

That bit about Arun's belief in my innocence catches in my throat like an accusation. I chide myself for having been so abrasive towards him and for doubting his integrity. Promising myself to make it up to him, I turn to Mr Mathur and apologize. 'I didn't mean to offend you,' I tell him. 'Please forgive me if I have. It's just that when I talked to Arun, he made it sound as though strings would have to be pulled to win the case.'

'Oh, yes, Arun will have to pull those strings, as you say, but not to win the case. That is my job. He will only help to hasten the process and to ensure that all the evidence is presented accurately.'

Relief spreads inside me like a smile. 'Will we have to go to trial?' I ask my lawyer.

'Yes. I'm afraid so. A case has been filed.'

'How soon can we go to trial then?'

'I can have you released on bail today, but that would not be advisable.'

'Why not?'

'If I have you released on bail, they will delay your trial date. But if you continue to reside in this prison, I can press them for an early trial.'

'How early?'

'A fortnight, a month.'

'And if I'm out on bail, how long will it take?'

'Who knows? Six months, a year, perhaps more? You see, you are not habituated to such living conditions. You are feeling emotional stress here. I will tell them that. But if you are released on bail, you will be comfortable again.'

I nod, although I'm not sure why they would worry about the comforts of a criminal. After all, isn't that what punishment is all about—deprivation?

'Do you think you can continue to stay here for a little more time?'

I think of my days in the ward and of the stars hidden behind the prison wall. 'I don't know. I feel so ... so helpless here, so trapped.'

'Are you being mistreated?'

'Not more than the others.'

'I know it must be very difficult. You must be in great discomfort here because you are not used to such conditions, but do you think you can tolerate it for a little while longer?'

'I'm not sure.'

'Take some days to think about it. If you want to be released on bail, I can start proceedings immediately, but I want you to think about it first, because if you leave on bail, you may be detained in this town for a long time.'

'When will I see you again?'

'On Friday. That will give you a chance to talk to Mr Ferrier, too. Give me your decision then. In the meantime, I will begin work on your case. Look after yourself,' he says, smiling distractedly and shutting his briefcase. I wonder why he had opened it. He hasn't touched the contents inside.

I return to the ward, debating how much I really hate this place—enough that I want out immediately, or not so much that I can bear to stay a few more weeks? A sharp stone jabs my foot as I step through the gate. With a cry of pain, I lift my foot to look at it. A discolouration of skin on the back of my toes is the only evidence of the earlier bruises, thanks wholly to Kubrima's herbal ministrations, but the sole of my foot is now hard and crusted with dirt filling the dry cracks on the heel. For days, on Koki's goading, I have been asking the Superintendent to allow me shoes or some sort of footwear, but to no effect. As I rub the painful spot, I wonder what my pedicurist back home would say if she saw my feet now. Lisa Chang is a sweet little Oriental girl who smiles all the time but hardly speaks a word of English. Suddenly, I can't wait to have clean, well-pedicured feet again, skin soft and pink, with the nails painted bright red like the colour of Lisa Chang's lipstick. I want out immediately. I want bail. I can hardly wait to see Mr Mathur again to tell him that.

The next day, soon after lunch, I see Matinee walk to Sultana's cell and order her out. In the quiet sunlight outside the bars, Sultana looks even more volatile. Her eyes are congealed with suppressed fury. Her slight shoulders dare the world to call her guilty. Her small form appears ready to spring. I am sitting in the sun playing jackstones with Hema, as Sultana is led to the heavy iron door. In my distraction, the pebbles tumble from my hand.

'Out, out!' Hema shouts excitedly, collecting the jacks eagerly in her small hands.

'Where is she going?' I get up and ask Matinee.

'Saab Bahadur wants to see her.'

'Why?'

'I don't know.'

Sultana does not return for two hours and when she does, her shoulders are slumped, her eyes are downcast and her steps are sluggish. In that one meeting she has been reduced to a criminal. Matinee leads her to her cell and locks her up again.

I watch from a distance for a while, waiting for Matinee to lie down for her nap. As soon as she does, I walk to Sultana's cell and call her name softly. She does not appear.

'Are you all right?' I put my lips close to the bars and whisper into the cell. There is no answer from within.

Late that night, long after we have curled up under our blankets, as I rock myself to sleep, indulging in my nightly fantasy of lying with my head on Scott's bare shoulder, twirling the hair on his chest with my fingers, watching David Letterman against the backdrop of a simulated New York skyline, I hear a faint creak. In the quiet of the night, my ears prick on hearing soft whispers. Someone walks across the platform in front of the cells. I lie still, waiting. I hear footsteps going towards the main gate and wonder what the night warden is doing walking around at this time. Normally, she sleeps jealously, snapping viciously at whoever dares to awaken her. I hear some more whispers. Curiosity gets the better of me and, slipping out from under the blanket, I walk to the corner of the barracks from where the main gate is visible through the bars. I am surprised to see Sultana's slight form facing the heavier one of the warden's. Wondering where she is going at this time of the night, I look up at the sky to determine the time. The moon is high and almost over the compound. It must be close to midnight. I see Malti open the smaller gate and lead Sultana out. In a moment she returns and, shutting the gate, pulls out a chair from her room to settle down in it. I stand at the bars for a long time. I can see her head nod to one side as she falls asleep. A cold draft makes me shiver, so I go back to the mat and pull out my blanket. Wrapping it around me, I sit down facing the bars, keeping the iron gate within sight.

I must have nodded off because I am awakened by the sound of a key turning in the lock. My eyes dart to the main gate. Once again the smaller gate opens and Sultana is pushed through it. She falls to the ground lying prone. A

balled-up white sari follows her. I see the warden shake her
shoulder urgently. Slowly, Sultana raises herself from the
ground. In the light of the moon, I see her blouse is hanging
open over her naked breasts, and just over her thighs, a stain
is spreading wide on the thin material of her petticoat. I
know it is blood. The warden picks up the sari and taking
Sultana's arm, tries to steer her towards the cell, but Sultana
pulls her arm away and losing her balance, falls back on the
ground. I can't bear it any more. Dropping my blanket, I
stand up and rattle the bars. 'Sultana,' I call out.

Malti pulls Sultana up by the arm and begins to drag her
across the compound.

'Sultana,' I call out again, loudly, rattling the bars
harder. By now the others are up, too.

'What's the matter?' Koki comes to stand beside me.

'Sultana. I think she's been raped.'

'Hai Ram!' All the other women are standing at the bars
now.

I rattle them again, loudly. 'Matinee Malti, what's the
matter with her?' I call out to the warden.

She pays no heed to me and continues to drag Sultana
to the cell. Once she has her locked up, she comes to the
barracks and unlocks the gate.

'What have you done to her?' I face her as she enters.

'Shut up, haramzadi,' she screams at me and grabbing
my hair, pulls me out. 'I'm going to lock you up for
indiscipline. Tomorrow morning I will report you to Saab
Bahadur.' Still holding me by the hair, she drags me over the
platform to the cell at the end of the semicircle. As we
approach Sultana's cell, I yank my hair out of her fingers
and grab the bars of Sultana's cell.

'Sultana,' I call out again, sobbing.

Once again I am grabbed by the hair and pushed
towards my old cell to be thrown on the floor.

As she swings the gate shut, I get up and throw myself
against the bars. 'You bitch! How could you do it? How
could you have her raped? Have you no shame? What kind
of a woman are you?'

Malti opens the door of my cell again and, stepping inside, hits me across my face with the flat of her hand. I am flung on the floor. 'Shut your mouth, bitch,' she says and hurrying out of the cell, turns the key.

'Sultana,' I call again, crawling to the door and reaching out through the bars towards Sultana's tattered figure.

I see Malti walk towards the barracks and warn the others not to move or utter a word till further orders. I sit looking at the milky whiteness of the moon, seeing the widening stain on Sultana's petticoat in its centre like a large hole, knowing she must have been raped repeatedly to be bleeding so much, abhorring the system that could allow this to happen.

As the first light of the sun strikes the top of the forty-foot wall, the main door clangs at the change of guard and Prema replaces the night warden.

'Prema,' I call out as soon as I hear the door close behind her.

She hurries towards my cell. 'Malti told me you broke the discipline at night so she had to lock you up. That won't do, Simran. The Saab Bahadur will be angry.'

'Prema,' I say urgently, 'listen to me, please.'

'I have to leave you in here till the Saab Bahadur comes. You can talk to him.'

'Please, listen to me. I don't care if you keep me locked up. Go and see Sultana, please.'

'You are not allowed to talk to Sultana. You know that.'

'Prema, please listen. Last night Malti took Sultana out and when she returned, she was . . . she had blood all over her. Please go and see her.'

Prema looks towards Sultana's cell and, nodding at me, hurries towards it. I walk to the corner and strain my neck to look as far as I am able. My left eye feels painfully swollen from Malti's slap. I hear Prema call out to Sultana from the bars several times before she finally unlocks the door and goes in.

Minutes later, she appears with Sultana who has a blanket wrapped around her body. Her bare legs stick out under it, and she is holding a bundle of white clothes in front of her. I see them walk towards the stalls. A while later Sultana returns to her cell, her body still covered with the blanket, her hair hanging wet down her back, the white bundle darkening the blanket with moisture.

Prema doesn't respond to my calls any more. She busies herself with the breakfast pails once they arrive, then sits on the cot in the centre, having Krishna oil her hair.

The Superintendent comes on his daily round sometime after breakfast. 'I warned you about the discipline in my jail,' he says, the inevitable white towel held in his hand like a child's handkerchief. 'Malti filed a report against you about your behaviour last night. Tsk. And you were doing so well. I'm afraid this will not reflect well in your trial.'

'Do you know what happened in this ward last night?' I ask him, looking at him urgently.

'Quiet,' he says. 'Lower your eyes.'

'Do you know that Sultana was raped last night?'

'Be quiet, woman. Have you gone mad? This is a woman's ward. How can anyone get raped here?'

'She was taken out of here at night.'

'I don't want to hear another word from you, or I will make sure you never leave this cell.' With that he strides away.

Koki sidles up to my cell after he leaves. 'How are you?' she asks.

'How is Sultana?' I ask her.

'I don't know. Poor girl. That bitch Malti told us she's having her monthly.'

'No,' I whisper persistently. 'No. You saw her last night.'

'Yes. We all did. We know what happened, but Malti told us last night that she is having her monthly and warned us against spreading rumours.'

'Malti is a liar.'

'Koki.' Prema is now sitting facing my cell. 'Get away from her or I'll lock you up, too.'

I give Koki a gentle push. 'Go. We'll talk later.'

I am not allowed to see Scott that day when he visits; I am being punished. Helplessly, I watch the sun move across the sky as the day completes its course. Sultana does not appear at her bars all day. Just before dinner, Prema leaves for the night and Malti enters. On her round across the ward, she stops before my cell and stands looking at me. 'Don't ever mess with me again,' she says. I stare back at her.

'Lower your eyes, haramzadi,' she says through her teeth. I continue to stare at her. Slapping the bars of my cell threateningly, she walks away.

I am allowed back in the barracks after twenty-four hours. I sit between the women, narrating the events of that night.

'She eats money,' Krishna says. 'There used to be a young woman here some months ago, Bimla. Now she is in another jail. She was in for murder. What a pretty girl. One night Malti sent her out, too, and when she brought her back, Bimla had lost all her beauty. The light in her face went out. Who knows what animals Malti delivered her to?'

'Can't we do something about it?'

Kubrima cackles with laughter. 'They will break your shoulders,' she says.

'Who do you think will believe us? We are women with the weaknesses of women. Saab Bahadur is convinced that the stain on Sultana's clothes was from the blood of her monthly. Every time something like this happens, they hide the truth behind our frailties,' Krishna says.

'We've got to do something,' I say, cracking my fingers in frustration.

When Mr Mathur comes to see me the next day, I tell him I have changed my mind about bail.

'Why?' he asks.

'I've thought about what you said regarding trial. I think I would rather have an early trial than wait for a late one.' I don't tell him the real reason for not wanting to leave this place yet. The truth is I'm not sure there is a reason for my change of mind. I know only that Sultana has been raped and I can't leave.

'That is good,' Mr Mathur says, patting my hand on the table. 'Now I can proceed with the case.'

On the following Thursday I am allowed to receive Scott again. I'm glad to see that Arun is with him. I'm glad because I know he is the right person to talk to about Sultana.

'What'd you do?' Scott says as soon as I approach the steel net. 'I missed seeing you last week. And Mr Mathur told me you refused to come out on bail. What's going on, Simi?'

'If you lose control now and anger the prison authorities, we may not be able to accomplish anything. We were told you broke the discipline. What did you do?' Arun's voice is admonishing, but I also detect a faint curiosity filter through. That is all the catalyst I need.

'Do you know what's happening in here?' I ask the two men before me. 'Rape. One of the women in my ward was raped last week.'

'Oh, my God! How? Who did it?' Scott is horrified. His eyes open a fraction of an inch wider, the whites of his eyes drowning the aquarelle.

'How do you know?' Arun asks quietly.

'I saw her. The night warden took her out in the dead of night. When she returned, her blouse was hanging open and she had this huge stain of blood on the front of her petticoat.'

'Are you sure she was raped?' Arun asks.

'Of course I'm sure,' I snap at him. Despite my resolve to not let him irk me, I can feel my hackles rise. I can't believe he can even question this. I face him like an adversary. 'You think I'd make up something like this? You sound like the Superintendent here who refuses to believe us. Or perhaps, he chooses not to believe us. I was so glad to see you today because I thought you'd be able to help. It appears to me that I was wrong. You—you reporters would rather make up stories about imagined threats to your national security, but when it comes to stark realities like custodial rape, you shut your eyes and ears. Do you even care about what's happening to people in institutions like these? Do you ever write about them?'

'Why don't you?'

'Why don't I what?'

'Why don't you write about it?'

'What?'

'You know the victim. You have access to her story, and you obviously feel very strongly about it. I think you should write about it. I'll talk to my editor about using it in our weekend section.'

'You can't be serious?'

'No, no, Arun. I don't think Simi should get involved in anything as radical as that,' Scott says. 'She'll only hurt her case. You're the one who said she mustn't do anything to attract attention.'

'No, wait, Scott. I think I would like to bring this to light. I've been feeling so frustrated about this whole business. They shouldn't be allowed to get away with this. I want to report this. I want to file a case against that bitch, Malti, and the bastards who raped Sultana.'

'You can't,' Arun says. 'Only Sultana can file a case. Ask her. If she agrees, I'll help her. In the meantime, shall I arrange for paper and pen?' I look up into his eyes and am startled to see a burgeoning there, and a warmth. A warmth of the earth's womb, a warmth not reaching out but converging inwards, nurturing something newly born in his own being. I am even more astonished when a strange yearning rises in my heart, and for some reason, I feel bereft. A shiver passes through my body.

'Yes,' I tell him.

Some mornings later, Prema hands me a sheaf of papers and a brand new pencil sharpened to needlepoint. 'Saab Bahadur says you like to draw pictures. What kind of pictures do you draw?'

'Pictures? Oh, yes. I'm an artist. I draw all kinds of pictures. Sceneries, people—all kinds.'

'Really? Will you draw a picture of me?'

'Sure,' I say, trying to recall the instructions from my high school art classes.

I make portraits of everyone in the ward. We stick them up on the walls with pieces of chapati made sticky with water. I wonder when I will be able to put the paper and pencil to real use and have Sultana's consent about filing a report. Every time I approach Sultana's cell, I am warned by the wardens. Her cell is guarded day and night now.

Another week passes.

On Thursday morning, I take longer at my bath, washing my hair which is almost shoulder length now, smoothing out the wrinkles in my white cotton sari which was given to me a few days ago because my pants and shirt were in shreds, borrowing a mirror from Prema to see the effects of my toilet. Isn't it strange how you never really remember what your own face looks like? Apart from the definitive marks or blemishes, the main contours of your own face never become a part of your memory. Every time you want to recall what you look like, you have to depend on either a photograph or a mirror to ascertain the ensemble of your features and then memory acts affronted, behaving as though it has known all along. This morning when I borrow Prema's mirror and look at my face for the first time in weeks, my memory is hardly affronted. In fact, it takes new notes. It is a face I hardly know. It is much thinner than I ever remember seeing it, even thinner than that time in my freshman year when I went on a crash diet to attain the emaciation of a supermodel. The planes of my face stand out sharply under the taut skin. My eyes, my best feature, large and liquid brown with long, naturally curling lashes, now dominate my face. There is a glint in them as though a ray of sunlight is connecting with the heart of a teardrop. I can't remember whether this is the way they always looked, but I do remember thinking that brown eyes compared to aquarelle blue were kind of boring. I must have been madly in love with aquarelle blue eyes. I reach behind my head and pull up my hair, stretching the skin around my eyes till they tilt like an Oriental's and, dropping my chin down as far as it will go, I make a face at myself. I am still madly in love with aquarelle blue eyes, I tell my distorted reflection, ignoring the flutter in my heart, a flutter resulting from the craving for a certain warmth not directed towards me.

'Scott is coming today?' Koki asks, seeing me standing in the sun, comb-drying my hair.

'Uhm,' I nod.

'Is it a special day?'

'No. Why do you ask?'

'Oh, just that I've never seen you take so long over yourself before.'

'No. No special day. He's my boyfriend. I want to look nice for him.'

All morning I continue to push away a breathlessness, so that by the time the summon comes, I am a light-headed wreck.

'Simran,' Prema calls out. 'Go on. Your visitor is here.'

Straightening the pleats of my sari, I walk towards the visitors' room. Scott is standing in his usual place in the centre of the room before the net, smiling. My eyes dart around. Suddenly my lungs feel heavy with air and I can breathe normally again.

'Hi, sweetheart. You look beautiful.'

'Thank you,' I say, advancing towards him to stand before the net. 'How are you?'

'Bushed. I was up half the night with stomach cramps and half a dozen trips to the john. It must've been something I ate. I've been so careful about my food here. For your sake I can't afford to get sick.'

'Scott, I'm so sorry. Have you seen a doctor? Are you better now?'

'Yes, a little. But listen, I haven't come here to talk to you about my physical infirmities. I have good news. Arun thinks we might've made a breakthrough.'

'Oh really? Where is he?'

'Who? Arun? He's out of town on a story. He'll be back in a couple of days.'

'What kind of breakthrough?'

'Mr Mathur says he's been talking to the police and it seems that they have no real proof of your involvement in espionage. He says he's almost certain he'll be able to have the charges dropped.'

'Of course there is no proof. Not unless they plant evidence and frame me.'

'No, I don't think there's any likelihood of that. Why would they do that? What purpose would it serve?'

'None to my knowledge. Forget it. I was just speculating. I'm glad, though, that Mr Mathur was able to establish that. When does he think my trial will be?'

'He can't say exactly. But roughly in a month or so. Hang in there. We'll get you out of here yet.'

'I can't wait.'

'Are you still considering writing that article for Arun?'

'Not if I get Sultana to file a report.'

'I wish you wouldn't get involved in all this. You haven't told Mr Mathur about it, have you? You should. It could jeopardize everything.'

'I've got to do this, Scott,' I tell him, promising myself to somehow talk to Sultana that very day.

My main concern is how to get close to her. Even if I am able to have them put me in the cell, I will be a whole cell away from her. I will never be able to talk to her through two walls and an eight-foot room. After lunch I mention the problem to Koki. 'I'll figure out a way,' she promises. 'Let me think about it.'

Two more days pass. In the afternoon, during Prema's nap, I walk to Sultana's cell and talk to her invisible presence. I talk about nothing in particular. About my life in America, my relationship with Scott and how we've known each other since pre-school, how our friendship developed into love—not a crazy passionate love, but a sedate, comforting love, my dreams of a future with Scott. Safe subjects, subjects that will soothe a heart. I don't ask her anything about herself and she doesn't appear from behind the partition, but I know somehow, that she's listening.

On the third afternoon, as Koki sits on a cot in the

compound, teaching Hema and me a Hindi song, I feel a
drop of water on my nose. I look up at the sky thick with
clouds. 'I think it's going to rain today,' I tell Koki. 'You
know, this will be my second rain here. I always imagined
rain in India. My father used to talk about the romance of
it. But this is hardly how I imagined it—in a jail.'

Koki puts her arm around my shoulders. 'Do you still
want to talk to Sultana?'

'Of course.' I look at her. 'But I don't know how I can
manage it.'

'Meet me inside the barracks in five minutes,' she tells
me.

Keeping an eye on Prema who is lying on the cot
chewing her after-lunch paan and snoozing, I watch Koki
walk towards the shrubs behind the barracks. When I see her
return, I enter the barracks. She hands me a short, thick
twig.

'Hide it in your sari,' she advises.

I slip it inside the waistband of my sari quickly, pulling
the material over it to hide it from view. The stick jabs into
my thighs. 'What's it for?' I ask Koki.

'There's a crack in the ceiling of your cell. Let's hope it
rains all night. We'll do something at night so that bitch,
Malti, sends you to your cell. See if you can cut out a large
crack in the ceiling so that it begins to leak. If there's enough
water, Prema will put you in the other cell.'

'What if I can't cut the ceiling at all with this tiny stick?'

'Then we'll try something else.'

'How will I make Malti lock me up?'

'Leave that to me. I'll tell you at dinner. Just follow my
lead. That bitch hates you. She'll use the smallest excuse to
discipline you.'

At dinner that evening, as we file before the pails and
Malti doles out our portions, Koki sighs loudly and, looking
directly at me, says, 'How I hate this food. I wish I didn't
have to eat it.'

Taking my cue from her, I exclaim loudly how the food
stinks. 'I refuse to eat this horrible food day after day. I am

sick of this place. I'm not going to eat till the standard of our food is improved.' Goaded by my own bravado, I take my plate and dump it on the ground at Malti's feet. The others look at me as warily as if I were standing at the edge of a precipice ready to jump.

'Arre, haramzadi,' Malti steps away surprised. 'What do you mean you won't eat this food? If you don't want to eat, you can go hungry. This is a prison, not your motherfucking father's home.'

'You take the name of my father, you ... you bitch. Don't mention my father's name or else.'

'Or else what?' She tucks the corner of her sari into her waistband and faces me belligerently.

'Or else ... I'll pull your tongue out.'

She smacks me soundly across the mouth. 'Haramzadi, you'll pull my tongue out? I'll show you.' She grabs my arm and begins to pull me across the compound to the cell. 'The bitch thinks this is her father's house. Won't eat the food? One day in the cell without food will teach you whose house this is.' She drags me inside the cell and deposits me behind bars. 'Stay hungry. You won't get any food tonight and we'll see what you think of this food in the morning.'

I watch her walk back to the food pails. Koki has taken her plate and is sitting on the cot near the platform, chewing contentedly. I smile at her and begin walking from one end of the cell to the other, looking up at the ceiling to spot the crack Koki mentioned. Outside, a slow drizzle begins to fall, and the inmates scuttle away inside the ward. I see Koki and Krishna pick up the cot between them and carry it to the warden's room. Even as they emerge, the rain becomes heavier. Folding their arms over their heads, they dash towards the barracks. Once again I look up at the ceiling and, sure enough, hear a 'tip, tip'. Water is dripping somewhere onto the mat, but in the darkness I cannot see the source. Going down on my hands and knees, I pass a hand over the mat till I feel the wet spot, then, planting my feet on it, I stand up. In a moment, a drop of water plonks on my head, its coldness splashing against my scalp. Taking the tin bowl from the urn, I place it on my head, and removing myself from under it, lower my arm till the bowl is on the floor. Soon I hear its bottom ring with a metallic drip. I sit down behind the bars, waiting for night to fall and Malti to retire. The rain becomes a fluid drum roll on the platform outside my cell, and inside, the tin bowl begins to lose its ring in the accumulated water. I sit watching Malti with her ample body gathered under a black tent-like umbrella, making her last round before retiring for the night. As soon as the pool of light on the ground before her room vanishes, I climb up on the partition wall. Standing on my toes and stretching my arm to its full length, I am able to just about reach the wetness in the ceiling. Exploring it with my fingertips, I detect a thin line of moisture about six inches long with a soft and pulpy epicentre. I am pleasantly surprised to discover that the ceiling is made of packed mud and not cement as I had thought. Drawing the twig out from the waistband of my sari, I begin to dig into the crack. At first all I can do is scrape at the whitewashed mud, because I am positioned too precariously to administer a hard thrust. But slowly I am able to cut away at it. I have no idea how long I dig, but as soon as I feel rainwater trickle down the twig onto my arm and right into my armpit, I climb off the wall and sit down for a while to rest. My arm feels leaden and numb, but the steady trickle filling up the tin bowl urges me on, and I climb back onto the wall again. I widen the hole till I am able to slip first an index finger through it, and finally, the tips of all five fingers held together. The rain is pouring in now like a weak showerhead. Satisfied at last, I jump off the wall, my feet squelching in the water that has overflowed from the bowl onto the mat. Stepping behind the partition, I place one end of the twig under my foot and try to crack it in the middle, but the soggy piece of wood bends over, unwilling to snap. Slipping it back inside my waistband with its dampness resting against my legs, I lie down on the mat as far away from the leak as possible, praying for the rain to continue through the night.

By the time Prema arrives the next morning in a tight

blue raincoat, I am sitting at the corner of the toilet. The front of the cell is a large puddle.

'Tsk,' Prema says as she approaches my cell. 'It seems the roof is leaking. The rain must have opened a crack.'

I wade through the half-inch layer of water and come to stand at the bars. 'It's a river in here.'

'Again you break the discipline,' she tells me. 'This is not good, Simran. You're a good girl except for these bouts of insanity. What is this about the food?'

'Oh, Matinee, I'm so sorry. I lost my head last night. Actually, I had a fight with my . . .' I pretend coyness, '. . . you know who, and I was telling Koki about it last night and I got so upset. I don't really have any complaints about the food.'

She smiles at me from under the droplets of water clinging to the edge of her triangular blue hood. 'I have to keep you in here for twenty-four hours. Malti is making a report to give to Saab Bahadur.'

'I understand,' I say. 'But please, can you put me in another cell? There's no place here even to sit, and my blanket is soaked. I spent the whole night by the toilet.'

She stands looking at the flow of water for a moment. 'Let me talk to Saab Bahadur,' she says and leaves. A little while later she opens the door of my cell and I dash across to the cell beside Sultana's. Grateful to the rain for confining the others to the barracks, I sit beside the toilet, pounding gently on the wall, matching my knocks to the rain's rhythm till I hear a responding thump. With quick, successive knocks along the wall, I lead Sultana to the front of the cell to the bars and call her name softly.

'I'm here,' her voice floats out in a whisper.

I laugh softly at my ingenuity. 'Sultana, I've wanted to talk to you for so long. How are you?' I ask her.

There is a silence and then her reply, 'Still alive.'

'Were you raped?'

A long silence follows that question.

'Sultana?' I say urgently.

'Yes,' she says softly.

It's my turn to be quiet now. I don't know what to say.
All along I have known what her answer will be, but now
in the face of it, all the words of solace I want to offer
become the language of a powerless tribe. 'I knew,' I say
finally. 'Malti told everyone you were having your period,
but I knew. I saw you that night.'

I hear her laugh—a strange empty sound.

'Who did it?' I ask.

'Four policemen. They took me to the interrogation
room.'

'Was the Superintendent one of them?'

'No. I don't think he knew. When I went to his office in
the morning, a guard gave me this look . . . .'

'Why did you let Malti take you out at night?'

'She told me the Superintendent had called a special
interrogation session.'

'You can't let them get away with this.'

'What difference does it make?'

'Sultana, you've got to report this. I'll report it for you.
Just give me your consent. I've got a friend, a journalist, who
can help you. He'll help you fight this.'

She laughs again, the same hollow sound as if she were
pushing out a foreign breath from her body.

'Sultana, listen to me. You have to report them.'

'It's over. I'll forget about it. I have other things to
remember.'

'But think about the others. They can do this again to
someone else. You can help stop them.'

She's quiet for so long after that, I think she has moved
away.

'Sultana,' I whisper. When there is no answer, I press my
lips close to the bars and call out her name but she still does
not respond. 'Sultana?' I raise my voice a little and am
surprised at how the sound rents the sheets of rain. Warily,
I look towards the barracks, expecting Prema to emerge.
Sultana has probably covered her ears with the silences of
her cell again. I sit, leaning a shoulder against the bars,
holding my hand out limply, watching it bounce with the

impact of the raindrops. 'Sultana?' I try again just one more time. Then, frustrated, I shake the moisture from my hand and withdraw it within the folds of my sari.

'It's over,' she says, her voice so close to the bars, it is as though she has her lips pressed to the space between them.

'You don't want to file a report?'

'No.'

'Okay, but we can still talk about other things, right?'

'Yes,' she says.

All day we sit side by side near the wall, our foreheads resting against the bars, whispering. When we hear a footstep, we stop and move away.

'What did you do?' I ask her. 'Koki told me you are a terrorist.'

'Perhaps,' she says. 'They killed my father, my neighbours. They ruined my brother's life.'

'What happened?'

She's quiet again. This time I don't press her.

'I killed two men,' she finally says. 'Two Hindu men. They were murderers. The men who burnt my house, they were part of that group. I wish I had managed to kill all of them.'

'Why did they burn your house?'

'Because we are Musalmaan.'

'My father told me about the partition of India and Pakistan and about the enmity between the two communities, but I thought, I hoped, that had ended with the Partition. Back home in America, once in a while, we used to hear about communal riots in India, but I always tried not to believe the American media, especially about affairs in India. They tend to exaggerate situations.'

'It's no exaggeration. It's true. I used to live in this section of town called Karim Gali. It is mainly a Hindu section. At one time I believe, before the Partition, it used to be predominantly Musalmaan, but most of the families went over to Pakistan. Over the years, others moved away to different sections of town because of the pressure from the

Hindus. Every time there was tension between the two
communities in any part of the country, the Hindus in Karim
Gali made us suffer. The shopkeepers were rude to us. The
boys called us names. They started fights with us on the
street and threatened us. It was hard to live there, so people
moved to other Musalmaan areas to get away from all of
this. Now there are only five Musalmaan houses in Karim
Gali and those, too, have been burnt.'

'That's so sad. My father used to tell me how at one
time, before the Partition, the Hindus and Muslims lived like
one community. In fact, my father was adopted by a Muslim
family, his friend's family, and they respected my father's
religion even though they were strict Muslims themselves. I
remember Daddy telling me how one day he asked his
friend's father if he could accompany them to the mosque,
and the reply was, "No, son, you are a Hindu. I don't want
to dishonour your parents by taking you to a mosque."
Daddy was too young to understand what his friend's father
meant and he was very upset. Then something really funny
happened. His friend, who was a few years older than
Daddy, thought he was wiser. He tried to explain the
difference in religions to Daddy. He told my father, "You
cannot go to the mosque with us because your mother forgot
to cut your skin." Daddy wouldn't believe him, so his friend
told him to untie his pajamas and they compared penises and
Daddy finally saw the skin of contention between religions.
But he still couldn't understand what the big deal was. It was
only a little flap of skin. He couldn't figure out why that
made him so different from his friend. You see, my father's
own religion was lost in his memory. It was buried under the
memories of his mother who died when he was five. He
remembered the fragrance of incense sticks she used to light
before a shiny black stone representing Shiva, and Krishna,
to him, was a picture of a young prince holding a flute,
dressed up in gaudy clothes. He knew these were gods, but
for him they were so abstract. What was real for him were
the festivals like Holi, Diwali and Id. And everyone in the
locality, Hindu and Muslim, joined in the festivities. He

knew they were somehow associated with religion. For him, though, the only religion they were associated with was the religion of celebration. So he was sure that there was another religion where you could be both a Hindu and a Muslim and enjoy all the festivals. So he told his friend's father that he was a Hindu and a Muslim. The old man was so overwhelmed by his logic, tears came to his eyes and he kissed him on the forehead and said, "May Allah teach your spirit of human brotherhood to all men in this country." '

'Human brotherhood,' Sultana says bitterly. 'I don't think people even know the meaning of that now. All they know is anger and hatred. To the Hindus, we Musalmaans are all terrorists trained by Pakistan. They hate us and they hate the idea that we are Indians just like them. My father ...' She's silent for a moment. I hear a muffled sob as though she is holding a corner of her sari over her mouth and then she speaks again, her voice unfiltered. 'My father was a school teacher. He used to organize camps for his students and talk to them about secularism. Young Gandhians, he used to call them. He loved his students, Hindu and Musalmaan alike. He taught them to love this country.'

'He sounds like my father's gym teacher, Gajji Pahalwan.'

'In his school?'

'No, he owned a gym, an akhara, I think you call it. He believed in the land as mother, and he used to tell his students, "Her milk will nourish you and provide you the strength you need to build your body. But you have to milch her bosom to reach the source of nourishment." He used to have a two-acre field beside his gym and he made all his initiates start by tilling that land. Most of the students dropped out in the first week because their parents couldn't understand the connection between tilling land and developing bodies. They thought Gajji just wanted his field tilled free of cost. Gajji, of course, knew different. He knew that by manoeuvring his two-oxen tiller, their young bodies would develop muscle power that no amount of exercise could achieve. But more than that, he knew that once the students ate the food they helped grow, their little minds would fill

with such a sense of pride and achievement, it would make
them winners. My father, however, knew that Gajji had a
secret motive behind this cooperative farming. He told me
that Gajji had already tasted the salt of Mother India's tears
in his food, and he knew it wouldn't be long before other
patriot hearts tasted the saline.'

As I talk about Gajji, I can see him clearly in my mind.
Daddy used to describe him so well: A tall, bald man,
reaching almost up to six feet. He had spent twenty-five of
his forty years empowering his limbs so they could squeeze
the strength out of an elephant, and an equal number of
years cultivating a thick, handlebar moustache, the twirl of
which shot quivers of fear into an opponent's heart. But his
eyes, cow's eyes, brown and moist, divulged the secrets of his
soft heart. He hadn't lost a single fight in his life, but he had
never seriously injured any of his opponents either. Gajanan,
or Gajji Pahalwan as he was called, was the city's most
formidable wrestler. It was an honour for any young man to
be accepted as his disciple. Amjad was already his student,
because his father believed it was important to develop not
just minds, but also bodies. So the first Sunday after his
adoption, Daddy was taken to the akhara with Amjad. I
remember Daddy telling me about his first impressions of
Gajji's gym. All around him he saw muscular bodies rubbed
down with mustard oil, gleaming golden, defying the sun
with their brilliance. Immediately, he started visualizing his
own skeletal limbs covered with hard flesh and taut muscles
and his thin chest filled out and broadened with invincible
confidence. He realized then, the vocation of his young life:
he wanted to be a pahalwan.

'So, did Gajji reveal his secret motive to his students?'
Sultana's voice pulls me out of Gajji's akhara.

'Yes. As a matter of fact, he did. The day Mahatma
Gandhi laid the foundation of the Quit India movement,
Gajji pasted a newspaper cutting of him on the akhara wall.
He used to have a framed picture of Hanuman, the monkey
god. It used to hang on that wall, and all the students had
to bow before him before starting exercises. Not for any

religious reason, but only because he is supposed to be the legendary master wrestler. Anyway, that day when Gajji took down Hanuman's picture and put up Gandhiji's, a lot of his students quit. You see, the Muslim League was already in operation by then, and it was sending musclemen to their communities to make sure Muslims realized the need for Pakistan. Gajji was a Hindu, and people were afraid the League would hurt their sons in his akhara. Amjad's parents were afraid, too, and they withdrew Daddy and Amjad. But Daddy started spending most of his time at the akhara. He would tell Amjad to cover for him and slip out of the house. Hardly any of Gajji's students exercised now. The fire had somehow gone out of pahalwani, but it had been replaced by a new zeal. The students now spent their time huddled around Gajji, listening to him talk of patriotism and freedom. Gajji's words filled them with such anger against the British and the Muslim League that they would threaten destruction. "We'll burn the firangis and the Muslim League with them," they'd say, but Gajji believed in Gandhiji's non-violence. He would point to the picture on the wall and shake his head. Gajji was a true Indian, Daddy used to say, a true patriot.'

'Unfortunately, all the Gajjis of the world are either dead or being killed,' Sultana says. 'There's no one to stop the violence any more. My father tried, but they killed him. They couldn't believe he loved this country. All they cared about was that he was a Musalmaan. As if being a Musalmaan excluded him from being Indian or human. Musalmaans, too, have families—people they love, children who will be orphaned if they die. My neighbour, Ghulam bhai, his wife was pregnant. She died in that fire. She wasn't a Pakistani spy. She was only a wife and would have been a mother. Khala, she's seventy years old. She's lived in this country all her life, and before that, her parents, too. This is her country, not Pakistan. But they didn't spare her. Her son and daughter-in-law died in that fire. They had just got married. They hadn't harmed any Hindus. They just wanted to live and be with each other and look after their old mother. Fatima baji, she has three little children. Her husband's body was burnt so badly she couldn't even recognize him. What had Fatima baji ever done to a Hindu? What had her children ever done? And Iftekhar, my brother, my poor brother . . .' her voice becomes heavy. She's quiet for a moment, and then I hear her weeping quietly.

There is a slant to the rain now as though the sky or maybe the earth has tilted. I sit unflinching as its incline drenches me.

'Iftekhar,' I hear Sultana's voice again, soft, lost in memories. 'He loved cricket. He played for his school and was in his college team. He was really good. He used to lie awake at night, staring at the ceiling with this strange smile on his lips. Once I asked him what he was thinking. He looked at me and said, "Baji, one day I'll be a great batsman like Gavaskar. You wait and see, baji. You'll see me on television winning the Man of the Match trophy and you'll tell all your friends, that's my brother. Iftekhar Khan is my brother." He'll never be able to play again. How can he play? He doesn't have hands any more. That fire took his hands. He lost his hands trying to save our father.' She's quiet again. When she continues, her voice is heavy with pain. 'What had he ever done to a Hindu? Nothing. He was so gentle he wouldn't even hurt a fly. When he was little, he used to turn his eyes away every time we crossed a butcher's shop. But they didn't care about him. Bastards.' Her pain turns to rage. 'You know, when I found the man who burnt my house, he was sitting in the canteen drinking tea and laughing. He was laughing. Only a few hours after he had killed five people, he was enjoying a cup of tea and laughing. If I could kill him again, I would.'

'How did you find him?' I ask her.

'I had seen his face when he threw a lighted torch on the roof of my house. I had run outside at the smell of smoke and I saw flames coming out of Khala's house, then suddenly I saw this man run out from the field behind our house. In the blaze I saw his face and recognized him. He used to go to my college. He was much senior, but I had seen him rally in the Hindu youth group. After the ambulance took Abu

and Iftekhar, I hid a large knife under my shawl and went
to college with it. I was going to search for him all over
campus for as many days as it took. But I was lucky. When
I reached college, it was early morning and classes hadn't
started yet, but the canteen was open, so I went in, and there
he was, sitting with two other members of this group,
laughing and talking and drinking tea. I walked up to him
and smiled at him. He saw me smiling and began combing
his hair. He didn't even know who I was. He thought I was
just a girl giving him bhav and his head swelled with that.
I went behind his chair and pulled the knife out from under
my shawl. I sliced his neck from ear to ear. When I finished,
I turned to the others. One boy got up and ran away,
screaming. I let him be, but the other one just sat there, his
eyeballs almost falling out of their sockets, his mouth open.
I drove the knife right into his mouth. It was so easy. I
hadn't thought about how I would do it, but it was so easy.
They say it is easy to hate. It is. Very easy.'

It is so quiet when she stops talking, in spite of the rain.
I lean my back against the wall and close my eyes. In the
silence I hear Daddy talk about hate and how it strikes one
right behind the senses like the eye of a tornado, swirling in
the blood, snatching away all sane thought. Behind my eyes
I see Daddy, his hair wild around his head, his eyes glazed,
blood dripping from his sword as he avenges the death of his
father, the death of Gajji and most of all, the death of his
own humanity. And around him bodies fall soundlessly,
their limbs severed, their heads sliced off.

I remember Daddy telling me about the time communal
hatred started smouldering in Lahore, and Amjad's father
tracked Daddy's father down in the city of Nanowal and
sent him there to protect him from it. How was he to know
that the first embers had already nestled in Daddy's heart,
and he would return ignited?

Lahore was simmering in its January chill on the day of
his return. People eyed strangers with fear. They grew wary
of their own neighbours and doubted the reassuring words
of their friends. Division of the country was imminent.

Resigned faces seemed to ask only one last question: who would get Lahore?

Daddy took a tonga to Macchiwada to Amjad's house. There was a shiny brass lock on the door. The neighbours told him Amjad and his parents had left the city and gone to Rawalpindi to be with relatives during these troubled times.

Daddy pulled his shirt's collar around his neck and walked over to Gajji's akhara. The gym was empty. The field behind it was parched and ungiving. Daddy knocked on the door of Gajji's two-room quarters.

Gajji peeped out hesitantly.

'It's Manohar.' Gajji threw the door wide open. 'My son. Come in.'

He took him into his arms, kissing his forehead, standing back to look at him as though looking at a prodigal son. Then he sat him on the mat and placed a tumbler of milk before him, topping it with a thick layer of malai.

'I heard about Nanowal. It was the wrong time for you to go. I'm sure Amjad's father didn't know of the trouble brewing in that town when he sent you.'

Daddy was silent.

'But I'm glad to see you back safe.'

Daddy could not say a word for fear that if he did, the blood of Nanowal might pour out of his mouth.

'Amjad and his family have gone away to Rawalpindi, I think. If they had known you were returning, they would have waited. Why didn't you write and tell them you were coming?'

There was more silence.

'I heard you went to see your father,' Gajji continued. 'Did you find him? How is he?'

'Gajji Pahalwan, I want to train in your akhara.'

'The akhara is closed. The Musalmaan students stopped coming. I cannot run a Hindu akhara. Besides, I don't train any more.'

'How do you live?'

'I drive a tonga. Lala Ratanlal rents it to me. I pick it up from his house every morning and return it every evening. It's a living.'

'Open your akhara again, Gajji Pahalwan. Let the Musalmaans go, saale haramzade. Let them form their own akhara in Pakistan. Why are you concerned with them, Gajji? We'll show them what we are made of.'

'Be quiet, Manohar.' Gajji stood up. 'Has everything I have taught you come to this? Remember this man?' He pointed to Mahatma Gandhi's picture on the wall, now frayed at the edges and grey with dust and grime. 'Remember this mat where we swore to keep the motherland united? How can you talk about ripping apart your own mother?'

'They killed my father, Gajji Pahalwan. They call us kafirs. If they think we are such a threat to their Islam, let's wipe them out and show them we can do more than threaten.'

'Bachche, don't talk like that. This will pass. We'll be friends again and brothers again. It is only this bad air the firangis are spreading. Once they leave, we will be together again.'

'No, Gajji. We will never be together. Haven't you heard, Hindustan will definitely be divided; Pakistan will come to be?'

Daddy started to train with a mission. He wanted to be prepared even though he wasn't sure what he was preparing for. But he knew instinctively that when the time came, he would know. Under Gajji's reluctant tutelage, he began exercising rigorously, pumping weights, curling, doing bench presses and push-ups from dawn till dusk. The body Daddy had dreamed about in his childhood daydreams began to build in nightmarish anticipation. He was a tall boy. With the muscles filling out in his expectant body, he became a powerful man. He let his hair grow long till it hung in loose ringlets over his shoulders, giving him the appearance of a rebel fakir. He was finally a wrestler, but there were no opponents left to fight in the ring.

The time he had been training for came. The fires that had been burning sporadically in Lahore spread to

Macchiwada. One of the three Hindu houses in the locality—
Shambhunath's—was set on fire one morning. Daddy, who
now lived with Gajji, was working in the field when he saw
an ugly cloud of grey smoke rise into the sky with flashes of
red and ochre renting its nimbus heart.

'Gajji, come quickly,' he called running towards the
smoke.

'Help me! Help me!' A female voice writhed in the
flames.

Three strange men stood before the house with spears.
'Pray that you die in the fire, kafir's wife, because what
awaits outside is worse,' one of them said. The others
laughed. Daddy flung himself at them.

The Muslims of the locality extricated Daddy and rushed
him, bleeding, into a neighbour's house. By the time Gajji
arrived, they had already bandaged his speared arms.

'Gajji, take Manohar and go. Go to the other side. Leave
Lahore. They won't let you live here,' they advised Gajji. But
Gajji wouldn't leave.

One morning as Daddy worked in the gym, his ears
caught the sound of hooves pounding the street. Wondering
why Gajji was home so early with the tonga, Daddy stepped
out. The tonga rushed towards him as though its horse were
being chased by the devil. And there was Gajji, his decapitated
body sitting in the driver's seat soaked with his blood, his
hands still holding the reins. His head sat staring between his
thighs.

Grabbing the horse's reins, Daddy tied them to a post.
Leaving Gajji in the tonga, he ran into the house for the
ancestral sword he knew Gajji kept in a trunk. Pulling it out
of its sheath, he ran back to the tonga and, tenderly releasing
the reins from Gajji's blood-soaked fingers, separated the
horse from the carriage. Swinging onto the horse's back, he
galloped down the street, his long hair flowing wildly
around his powerful shoulders, the sword gleaming like
liquid silver in his hand. Brandishing the weapon over his
head, he entered the busy marketplace. People were out
buying supplies for the day. They cowered before him as he

jumped off the horse and advanced towards them, a terrible
fire burning in his eyes. Severed limbs, decapitated heads fell
around him like windfall fruit. Reeling bodies collapsed at
his feet. With every blow, blood vessels burst, squirting his
face, his hands, his body.

Smeared in Muslim blood, he ran down the streets,
striking anyone who came in the way. He ran towards
Amjad's house. Breaking open the lock with one swift swing
of the bloody sword, he rushed in and out to the backyard.
He climbed down the dry well where Amjad's father had
hidden his wealth in a chest. He missed his footing on the
last notches and slipped the rest of the way to fall on it.
Breaking it open, he stuffed the front of his blood-soaked
shirt with bags of gold coins and ornaments. Then he ran
back into the house up to his room. The chest that had his
quilt was still sitting in the corner. He yanked the lid open
and grabbed the quilt. A piece of red fabric fell to the floor,
its folds opening out to reveal an amulet stone crushed into
bits. He didn't realize that the amulet was the one Amjad's
mother had secured from a Pir for his safety and its smashed
state was the manifestation of the holy man's clairvoyance.
Without a second glance at it, Daddy flew out of the room,
the house, back to Gajji's where he flung himself down in
the freshly-ploughed field. The soil from the field stuck to his
bloodied clothes and body, covering the evidence of his deed.

Later, he washed himself at the water pump and cut
down a tree to build a pyre for Gajji on the field. He tried
to put the severed head against the body to cremate Gajji in
one piece, but the head would not stay; it kept rolling to one
side.

'Gajji, they divided it,' he said brokenly and built
another pyre for the head. With each pyre he lit, he set both
Hindustan and Pakistan aflame. Then he walked away.
Bombay harbour was far away from Lahore, and America
was even farther.

'They're right. I am a terrorist,' Sultana says quietly.

'How long are you in for?' I ask her.

'I don't know. My trial is in two days.'

The next day when Matinee comes to release me, I beg
her to leave me inside. 'Please, I can't sleep in the barracks.
Why can't you leave me here?'

She looks at me surprised. 'Order nahin hai,' she says,
taking my hand and pulling me outside. I watch Sultana
from across the platform after that. She sits with the blanket
over her knees, following me with her eyes.

Two days later, Sultana leaves the jail for her trial, never
to return. She is sentenced to vigorous life imprisonment for
terrorist activities and first degree murder of two young
Hindu males and is transferred to the maximum-security
central prison.

That day I sit alone in a far corner of the barracks and
write about ethnic cleansing through communal bloodbaths.
I write about Gajji and Sultana's father, individuals who
forge paths of communal harmony in this labyrinth of
hatred. I write about Daddy and Sultana, youth lost in blind
rage and revenge. I write about India, the country my father
lamented in his dreams and loved in his death. And I write
about myself, an unwilling participant forced into the midst
of it all and now hopelessly involved. That night, lying under
the blanket, I see Daddy's horrifying image replaced by
Sultana's. The gory pantomime never ends.

chapter seven

Arun comes to visit me alone the following Thursday. As I enter the ante-room, I see him standing at the entrance, waiting for me. I hesitate for a moment, because I'm not sure how to receive him without the buffer of Scott's presence.

'Hello, Simran,' he says as soon as he sees me. 'How is everything?'

'Okay,' I say levelly, walking up to the net. 'Where's Scott?'

'He's in Delhi, talking to some Consulate official. I just came to tell you that.'

'Thank you.'

While getting dressed this morning, I had had so many conversations with him in my mind: Sultana and the injustice of her sentence, the issues I dealt with in the article I wrote, the two pages I have rolled up tightly and hidden in the waistband of my sari. But now, alone with him, even plain, cordial sentences seem to be fractured. So I stand before the steel lattice, my fingertips tracing its diamond-shaped netting, trying to find words that constitute beginnings, wondering if I should go back inside. After all, it seems he has come only to deliver a message. He, too, stands silent, his hands digging deep into the pockets of his kurta, another earth-coloured affair, this time, the parched hue of rain-thirsty soil. If there is a formula to start conversations, he doesn't seem to know it either. This realization suddenly dawns on me and it leaves me surprised. It also makes my sentences whole again.

'Will you stay for a while?' I ask. 'I have thirty minutes of visiting time. I would hate to forgo that just because Scott hasn't come.'

He removes his hands from his pockets and pulls up a chair to sit down. 'How is your friend?' he asks. 'You know, after I left here I remembered who she is. Isn't she the one who killed two members of the Hindu youth group at the University?'

'Yes. Sultana. Of course, the papers must have covered her story. Did they also mention why she killed those men? They were arsonists. They destroyed a bunch of Muslim homes in Sultana's neighbourhood. Her father and a lot of her neighbours died in that fire.'

'Yes. I think some of the papers did mention that fact.'

'Some of the papers? So for the others, she was just a cold-blooded Muslim terrorist? Did your paper cover that story?'

'Yes.' Suddenly he leans back in the chair, looks up at me and smiles. This is the first time I have seen him do so. He is beautiful when he smiles. 'I didn't cover that story, okay? So don't go blaming me for another shoddy piece of journalism.' I stand looking at him for a moment, realizing that something imperceptible has displaced something in me. Pulling up the chair on my side, I sit down.

'I'm sorry I said that,' I say quietly.

'Actually,' he continues, his voice serious again, 'our paper covered the arson, too, in a related column. It was a pretty sad affair. We had photographs and everything.'

'Sultana was sentenced on Tuesday to life in prison,' I tell him, leaning closer to the net to experience whatever it is that might burgeon in his eyes.

'That's too bad. But it was expected.'

There's only resignation there and nothing else, an old acceptance of life. It's his profession, I think. He's seen too much. The thought saddens me. I lean back in my chair with a sigh. 'I wish I could do something for her,' I say.

'Were you able to convince her to file a case against her rapists?'

'No. She said it didn't matter. She said she would forget. She had other things to remember.'

'That's a shame,' he says.

'I've written the article, if you are still interested.'

'Of course I am. Where is it? Do you have it with you?'

'Yes.' Moving the front folds of my sari a little, I extract the roll of papers from my waistband and push it through the net. Arun takes the other end and pulls the roll through.

'What happened to custodial rape?' he asks after reading the whole article.

'It's in there.'

'This is a fine piece of writing, but passé. No one talks about communal peace any more. No one wants to read about it. It's an old, threadbare story. Now, custodial rape—there's a story that can make people sit up and read.'

His words shatter something inside me—a hope conceived, perhaps, the same instant as my promise made to Daddy—a hope to negate the terrible promise.

'This is what I wanted to write,' I say, extending a hand to take back the papers. Don't print this if you don't want to, but this is the story I want to tell. In fact, this is the reason I'm in India.' As soon as I say the words, I wish I could take them back. Now, after what he has just said, I don't want him to know about Daddy. 'Never mind,' I say quickly. 'You wouldn't understand.'

'Actually, I do. Scott told me.'

'Oh.' I wonder what had compelled Scott to break his promise to me.

'In fact, I'm glad you brought that up. If we can claim you as a freedom fighter's daughter, I'm sure your case will be looked at in a totally different light.'

'No. Never.' Daddy, a freedom fighter and Sultana, in prison for murder? 'Leave my father out of this,' I tell him.

'You're the one who mentioned him. Anyway, it was just a thought.'

'Forget it. May I have my article back?' I say, extending a hand again.

He folds the papers in half and puts them in the pocket

of his kurta. 'I'll see what I can do,' he says.

My article appears in that week's weekend section of *The Herald* under the pseudonym, Samir Singh. It is printed exactly as I have written it, with no changes whatsoever. Prema brings it to me that Saturday morning saying, 'Saab Bahadur's orders.'

A few mornings later, the Superintendent informs me that my trial date has been set for 9 a.m. the following Friday, a week away. I am sitting on the ground massaging Kubrima's shoulder when he tells me. I continue massaging her shoulder. Koki, who is standing a few feet away, hears the news and comes to sit beside me.

'They won't be able to prove a thing,' she whispers to me.

I shake my head. 'It doesn't matter.'

That afternoon, Mr Mathur comes to visit me with some documents to sign. 'Remember, you will plead not guilty,' he advises me. 'We have been talking to the officer who booked you and to the magistrate. It seems they have seen the error of this arrest. We might be able to have the charges against you dropped. Act like an innocent American tourist. Do not say anything about this country that might be taken as interest. I know you have had an article published in a newspaper under a different name.'

'Oh, you know about that?'

'Yes. I found out. Why did you not inform me? As your lawyer, I need to know such things. I would have advised you against such a move. My only hope is that the magistrate has not heard about it. If he has—I will have to wait and see what happens.'

'I know you'll do your best,' I say, smiling at him.

On the morning of the trial, Koki helps me wash my hair and straighten out the pleats of my sari. She is unusually quiet.

'Koki, what's the matter?'

She shakes her head. 'I love you like a sister,' she says, hugging me tightly.

'I love you too, Koki. Don't worry about me. I'll be all right.'

'God bless you.' Kubrima places her knotty hand on my head as I sit on the cot waiting for the summons. Krishna sits beside me, smiling nervously. Hema sits in my lap braiding my hair. She has just recently learned to braid and spends all her time braiding anything that can be divided into three strands. I hug her tightly and place a gentle kiss on her temple. She wiggles out of my embrace and complains that I have spoilt her braid.

Finally, there is a clanging on the door and Prema advances towards me, smiling through lips gleaming red with betel juice. 'Come,' she says. 'Don't talk a lot in front of the judge, beti, and keep your eyes lowered.'

The trial takes place in the Superintendent's office and involves three men: the magistrate, the Superintendent and the one-eared giant. When I enter the insecticide sprayed room, all three men are already seated in a row behind the Superintendent's desk with him in the middle. When a guard deposits me before them, six eyes bore holes into me. I look away nervously. In one chair against the wall, my lawyer sits, dressed in his usual brown suit with his briefcase open on his knees. I look at him and attempt a smile. He pushes his glasses up on his nose and looks down at his papers, ignoring my plea. I stand in the centre of the room, my bare toes curling on the cold floor, my hands behind my back, my eyes level with the edge of the Saab Bahadur's desk.

The magistrate begins to talk in a courtroom voice. 'Miss Simran Mehta, we have reviewed the circumstances of your arrest and have had the evidence found on the scene examined thoroughly. It appears that the equipment found on your person is not incriminating. For lack of further evidence, all charges against you are being dropped.'

My eyes dart to his face and then to my lawyer's. He is smiling softly into his papers.

'You are hereby acquitted, but there is one condition. You are to leave this country within seventy-two hours.' He writes something on a file before him. All three men look directly at me, silently.

I look at their faces, one to the other: the colonel with

his large face and a missing ear, the magistrate with a tightly
glued beard and pink turban, and finally, Saab Bahadur, the
Superintendent of this jail with his goatee dyed in theatrical
strands of pepper and salt. Hard-to-forget faces, but faces
that give no sign of their power to rule lives as they have
mine for three months.

The Superintendent picks up a brown bag from his desk
and holds it out to me along with some papers. 'Here,' he
says. 'You can pick up the rest of your belongings from the
storeroom, our malkhana, any time.'

I open the flap of the bag and see my sneaker and watch
in it. Taking out my watch, I look at the time. It is 2:30 a.m.
in America. I turn towards Mr Mathur who is now standing
with his briefcase in one hand. 'What time is it?' I ask him.

He looks at me surprised, then turns his wrist up. 'It's
10:05.'

'Thanks,' I say, adjusting the hands in my watch to
Indian time and strapping it on.

Mr Mathur shakes hands with the three men and guides
me out of the door.

'Congratulations,' he says to me once we are outside in
the enclave. The little door in the main gate is thrown open
by a guard and I step out where the expanse of sunlight
engulfs me.

'Simi.' Scott is standing a few feet from the gate with his
arms wide open. I rush into them. 'God, am I happy to see
you! You're free! We did it.' I look up from over Scott's
shoulder directly into Arun's eyes. He is standing as I first
saw him, in blue jeans and the earth colour kurta, his arms
across his chest, leaning against the front of a white car,
looking as though he belongs intimately to his world. As
though the breeze which flips the corners of his kurta and
settles them back on his legs again, and the sun whose
provocation causes the lines around his eyes to deepen, are
personal interactions. As once before, I feel strangely bereft.

'Congratulations,' he says, holding his hand out.

Still in Scott's embrace, I reach out a hand and take his.
It is warm and dry, the tips of his fingers a little rough as

they grip the back of my hand. I had half expected his hand to be cold, its warmth directed away from the skin, a warmth that can't be shared.

Mr Mathur walks past us to his car, smiling benignly. 'I will see you later,' he tells Scott. 'Hotel Shiraz, right? 7 p.m.? I will be there.'

'What's at 7 p.m. at Hotel Shiraz?' I ask.

'A celebration,' Scott says, hugging me close. 'We're going to celebrate your release. He's a smart lawyer, that Mathur.'

'Shall we go?' Arun says, sliding into the driver's seat of his car. 'I'm sure Simran wants to get as far away as possible from this place as quickly as possible.'

Scott walks me to the car with his arm still around me. He opens the door for me and I slide into the back seat. I watch him get into the passenger seat beside Arun, chattering excitedly about Mr Mathur and his wheelings and dealings with the police. Arun and I are quiet all the way to the luxury hotel where Scott is staying.

'I'll see you at seven,' Arun says, dropping us off in front of the hotel.

Scott checks me into a room next to his. 'Take a long bath, sweetheart. Then you and I are going out to paint this town red.'

'But my luggage? They're holding it for me at the police station. We should go and pick it up.'

'We'll go. But first I want you to get out of that horrible white thing.'

I walk into the bathroom, still holding the papers and the brown bag containing my sneaker. Opening the bag, I look inside. It looks so forlorn and hapless lying on its side at the bottom of the bag, its sole crusty with dirt, severed without its twin. Folding the top of the bag over and over till it tightens around the sneaker, I bend and lay it in the empty trash can. Then I turn to the papers. They contain a list of each item in my luggage. Not bothering to go down the list, I place it on the marble washstand and begin to unwind the folds of my sari. As I remove my tattered underwear, I notice the fluffy white mats scattered on the tiled floor of the bathroom. Enjoying their feel around my calloused feet, I push the shower curtains aside and turn on the hot water faucet, tentatively passing my finger through the water to test the temperature. It warms against my skin and turns hot. Slowly, I turn the cold water faucet till the heat around my finger becomes a gentle warmth. Securing the plug, I let the water fill the bathtub, standing beside it, watching the rippling depression under the faucet. When I step into it and lower myself, the water cradles my body. I lie down, resting my head against the rim. Closing my eyes, I gather the past three months in my mind and begin to channel them out into the laving water, but then I imagine the pores of my skin soaking back everything they expel. I get up hurriedly and, stepping out of the tub, pull the plug. The water gurgles slowly as it disappears down the drain. When the tub is empty again, I step back in and, turning the cold water faucets all the way, stand directly under its lashing torrent. From head to toe, the water beats the outer layers of my skin, demanding I let go of what I hold inside— the frustration at the system, the knowledge of its machinations, the anger at its blatant violations against its victims. I will it all to disappear down the drain where it accumulates in a mini whirlpool, sucked in by the black hole that can contain all without spewing it back. The water beats relentlessly, but my mind, tenaciously clinging to the pain of a father's unending death, will not let go. My legs give way under the onslaught of the water and I slide down to sit on the ceramic floor of the tub, my legs crossed before me. I lay my head back against the wall, letting the water plaster my breasts against my ribs till they disappear, till I can feel its drumming against my very heart before it collects in a little pool in my cupped lap and seeps through the crevices of my legs.

I sit under the shower till my skin begins to hurt. My body staggering from the torture, I get up and with a shaky hand, turn the faucet off, smiling bleakly at having depleted the hotel's water supply and to no effect. The impressions of the last three months are rooted too deep to surrender to a water torture.

Scott enters the bathroom as I step out of the tub, a thick white towel in a turban around my hair. 'Having fun?' he asks.

I smile at him weakly and nod my head.

'Good.' He holds out a glass full of shimmering liquid. 'Here. Thought you might like some bubbly.' I take the glass and sip a little of the champagne. He bends and places a kiss on my nipple.

'You're cold. What'd you do? Take a cold shower? You don't need to. I'm available. We don't have to go out. We can just stay here all day or the entire seventy-two hours. What do you say?'

I look at Scott as he stands smiling at me, the tiny lines beside his eyes like little stalks tied together at the corners, presenting bouquets that are his aquarelle blue eyes, the smooth skin on his cheeks bunching under them like two red clown spots. He seems so happy. Seeing him like this, I silently resolve to indulge his mood.

'I've been confined long enough,' I say smiling. 'Let's go out.' I place the glass on the counter top, watching the bright studio lights reflect deeply in the iridescent liquid. Towelling my hair, I run my fingers through its length and switch on the hairdryer to get rid of the extra moisture. Then wrapping a large fluffy white towel around me, I pad out of the bathroom.

'Close your eyes, close your eyes,' Scott motions, coming towards me. Standing still, I close my eyes obediently. I feel his hand under my elbow as he guides me towards one end of the room. He releases me for a moment and I hear the click of a door opening. 'Okay. Open them now.' I raise my eyelids and find myself staring directly into a closet.

'Ta ra,' he says, sweeping his arms dramatically in the air like a magician.

There are two outfits hanging in the closet, still wrapped in their protective plastic. I step closer and gently pull off the wrap from the first one. It is a two-piece outfit in fine cotton

with a knee-length skirt and a sleeveless blouse, pink and
soft as cherry blossoms. The border of the skirt and the jewel
neckline of the blouse are intricately embroidered with white
thread. Buds of the same pattern are strewn over the rest of
the fabric. 'Chikan,' Scott says from behind me. I turn to
look at him. 'The sales lady at the store told me that's what
the embroidery work is called,' he says. 'Don't ask me why.
It certainly bears no relation to . . .' his face fills with mirth
as he folds his hands in his armpits and flaps them like a
squawking chicken. I smile and turn to the other outfit. 'And
this dazzling ensemble of mirrors . . .' Scott says, reaching
forward and tearing off the plastic, '. . . is simply called
mirror work.' It's beautiful. There must be a thousand, tiny
round mirrors sewn into ruby red flowers on the black
ankle-length skirt and the bodice of the blouse.

'I hope they fit. I told the lady at the store that you are
a perfect eight. She was a little doubtful about size. They use
different measuring standards here. And here,' he points to
two pairs of pumps on the floor of the closet—a white pair
and a black pair. 'I think they're your size. We'll exchange
them if they're not; the store is just around the corner.' Then
he reaches for a shelf above and hands me two purses, white
and black, and two sets of bras and panties, also a black and
a white. 'Sorry, I couldn't get you something out of Victoria's
Secret, but these are pretty, aren't they—lace and everything?
I love them.'

'I bet you do,' I say smiling. 'But you didn't have to buy
me a new wardrobe. I'm going to get my luggage today.'

'Sure, we'll get your luggage. But what're you going to
wear out of here? A sheet? Because, my beautiful young
lady, I'm not allowing you to wear that ugly white thing
they gave you in prison.'

I smile and turn away.

'And that's not all. You're going to be totally pampered
today. I've made an appointment for you at the hotel's
beauty shop for 1 p.m. So in . . .' he looks at his watch,
'exactly twenty-five minutes and ten seconds I'll escort you
downstairs to the beauty parlour. So, my darling, if you'll

kindly get dressed, I've ordered food.'

Carrying the pink-and-white outfit along with the accessories, I go back into the bathroom. The blouse hangs a little loose around the shoulders and waist. They should advertise prison life as a weight loss programme, I think, smiling to myself in the mirror. As I look at myself in my brand new outfit, a phrase Daddy used to use pops into my mind: 'post-war excesses'. Every time we had an argument serious enough to be called a war, he would buy me a new outfit to appease me. 'Like my parachute shirt,' he would say. He told me how after World War II, the markets in Lahore were flooded with war leftovers. Posters of Hitler's face meeting a large fist symbolizing the allied armies; ankle-high, stiff-leathered, black army boots in monstrous sizes that required wads of newspapers and cotton in the toe area to fit ordinary people; tear-proof, milk-white parachute fabric made in England that one could buy cheap—cheaper than the cotton spun in India's mills and taxed by the British government. It was every child's dream to own at least one piece of clothing made out of parachute fabric. Amjad and Daddy both owned snow-white parachute shirts. Post-war excesses—to help erase the memory of war.

I certainly feel like a war-weary veteran, except, I'm not sure I want the memory of this particular war to be erased so easily. Besides, this war is hardly over for me. Turning away from the mirror, I bend and pick up the white sari I had dropped on the floor earlier. Walking to the trash can, I retrieve my sneaker and wrap it up in the sari. Holding the bundle close to my chest, I step into the bedroom. Scott is sitting on a chair, removing covers from the dishes in the food tray that the room service must have delivered. 'What's that?' he asks. I walk to the closet and put the bundle on the top shelf. 'You've got to learn to let go, Simi.' Scott has guessed the contents of the bundle. 'Don't bring that back with you. You're carrying enough baggage as it is.'

I shut the doors of the closet and take a deep breath. After I release it, I'm ready for Scott again. I turn around stylishly and walk slowly towards him. 'How do I look?' I ask brightly.

'Beautiful. Just beautiful. Just as I imagined you would.' It never seizes to amaze me how easily we assume each other's mood, even at a moment's notice.

I slip into the seat opposite him. 'Let's eat,' I say, 'I'm starving.'

There's tomato soup, chicken sandwiches, a potato salad, baked beans and two slices of pie. 'Good old American food,' he says. 'I bet you craved this every day.'

'Actually, I got to like the chapatis and lentils they gave us.'

'Maybe you can have that for your wedding breakfast,' he jokes. 'We can ask the jail's kitchen to cater it.'

After lunch, he escorts me to the beauty salon in the lobby of the hotel. The lady who receives us is dressed in tight blue jeans and a black tank top that balloons over her large bosom. Her lips are coloured a Chinese red, as are her long fingernails. She runs her fingers through my hair and asks me how I want it cut.

I look at my hair in the mirror. It has grown several inches and hangs just below my shoulders. I remember the short pageboy style I had for more than three years. 'Just trim it, please,' I tell the lady.

'Sure,' she says. 'You have beautiful hair.'

After two hours in the salon I feel just as beautiful as Scott's compliment. My face, glowing after a mud pack, is subtly made up with a soft pink lipstick and black mascara; my hands are manicured, the nails painted a shell pink; my feet are soft and creamed, the heels scrubbed clean of crusted, dead skin; my hair is shampooed and styled, curling softly around my shoulders. The salon lady also puts together a make-up kit for me—a bottle of foundation, its shade matched against the inside of my wrist, two cigarette-thin sticks of pink and ruby-red lipstick, a four-inch kohl pencil, a slender case of the blackest black mascara and two tones of powder rouge pressed in the double basin of a plastic case. With my emergency public face tucked securely in my little white purse, I am suitably geared to re-enter the world.

Taking my arm in his, flamboyantly, Scott walks me out of the hotel.

'Are we going to get my luggage?' I ask.

'Plenty of time for that. I've something more important to do. The hotel manager told me the diamond market in this city is spectacular.'

'Two days,' I say. 'We have two days to see this country and you want to see diamonds. Are you thinking about going into the diamond business?'

'You could say that,' he says, tucking my hand in the crook of his arm, his expression curiously blank. I'm afraid he has been in Arun's company too long.

We take a cab to Hira Mandi, the diamond market. Weaving its way through traffic, honking a jagged path in it, our cab stops at a narrow intersection and the driver informs us that Hira Mandi is just ahead of us and that we will have to walk there.

'Why can't you take us?' Scott asks in broken Hindi.

'I can,' he says. 'But it will be easier for you to walk.'

We get out of the cab and after paying the driver, begin to walk in the direction he has pointed. Within moments we are in a narrow street, pressed against a shop window, trying to avoid being run over by a large white vintage Mercedes. There are people everywhere, people and bicycles and rickshaws and cows and scooters and motorcycles and little three-wheel contraptions that run on noisy engines. There are some cars, too—old, beaten up misshapen vehicles along with the occasional shiny, brand new, international model. But it doesn't seem to matter what one is driving, because all these vehicles that hog so much of the narrow street are reduced to incongruity, their pace no faster than a snail's, their persistent honking only adding to the din. I can see why our cab driver advised us to walk. Lining the two sides of the street are elaborate glass doors decorated with brass knobs and flashy signs. Some of the doors even have liveried doormen standing outside on doorsteps. Large women in brightly coloured silk saris and jewellery—mostly diamonds and gold—are wandering in and out of these doors, talking excitedly with their companions.

'Come on,' Scott says, opening the glass door of the store we have our backs pressed against. 'What better place to begin than here?'

Bright lights shine on sparkling glass counters. More women in silk and diamonds sit in red, leather-bound chairs across from smiling salesmen, fingering pieces of jewellery, holding them against their skin and seeking out mirrors. A blast of cold air from an air conditioner hits me and I can feel the goose bumps rise on my arms.

'This way, please.' We are guided into empty chairs at a counter by a young man dressed in a pin-striped, three-piece suit.

'What can I show you today?' he asks, stepping behind the counter.

'We would like to look at some rings,' Scott says nonchalantly.

I turn to look at him sharply, but he is looking down through the glass at an array the salesman is laying out.

'Yes,' Scott says. 'May we see those, please? Simi, what do you think?' he asks as though merely weighing the merits of Pepsi against those of Coke.

'Huh?' I look at the rings in the showcase glittering like millions of pieces of glass in a kaleidoscope. 'They're nice.'

The young man lifts the glass lid and takes out the two rings Scott has pointed out.

Scott requests to see a few more and seeks my approval. Finally, he shakes his head and, thanking the young man, leads me out of the store.

'Scott, are you . . . are you proposing to me?'

He turns towards me in the street and stands holding my hands, his face solemn. 'Simi, will you marry me?'

A ringing starts up behind me. I pull my hands out of Scott's and turn my head to see a little boy on an adult women's bike, standing with his feet planted on the ground on either side of the pedals, pressing the bell on his handlebars. As I look at him, he puckers up his lips and blows a loud kiss towards me. 'Yeh sadak hai,' he calls out, telling me with a mischievous wink, that this is a public road. Then wheeling his bike in between us, he climbs onto the saddle and rides away, swaying precariously. Scott and I come close together again.

'Why are you asking me today?' I say.

'I don't want to lose you to some messed up system again. If we had been married when your father died, I would never have let you come to India on your own, and this . . . this mess could have been avoided.'

'My knight in shining armour,' I say softly.

'So, will you? Marry me?'

'Yes. Yes, Scott, I'll marry you.'

We hunt for a ring in half a dozen more stores. My eyes dazzled with the brilliance of numerous diamonds, the goose bumps permanent fixtures on my arms, we finally find the ring. It is a beautiful cluster of four quarter-carat diamonds in the shape of a flower with a large ruby in its heart. Scott slips it on my finger and places a soft kiss on it. 'You're mine,' he says, softly.

The salesman, smiling from ear to ear, orders Thums Up. 'Congratulations,' he says. 'It is a good engagement ring.' The diamond buttons on his white kurta glint in the light.

Scott buys matching ruby earrings and we rush back to the hotel, realizing we are late for the celebration party. I shake off my white pumps and get out of my new outfit. I quickly douche my face with cold water, looking longingly at the shower, knowing there is no time for it. Wiping off the morning's grime, I open my new kit and apply a fresh coat of mascara, lining my eyes with a deep sixties line. Scrubbing off the pink lipstick with a tissue and shaping my lips with ruby red, I run a comb through my hair and let it swing around my shoulders. Then I step into the black underwear and the black mirror-work dress. Finally, clipping on the ruby earrings, I am ready. Scott has changed too, from his morning's blue jeans and brown cotton shirt, to a dark suit with a crisp white shirt and a red tie. He looks dashing, like an eager young executive out on a power date. I put my

hand on his arm, my ring shining brilliantly against his dark
sleeve, and step out of the room ready for a celebration.

The bar and restaurant of Hotel Shiraz are dimly lit with
candle-bulb chandeliers. The greater part of the floor is
arranged with dinner tables, and the far corner of it is a
dance floor with a live band, which, as we enter, is playing
an old film song. Scott and I are met by the maître d' who
leads us to a table towards the back of the restaurant. Mr
Mathur and Arun are already sitting at a table when we
arrive. Arun is still wearing the jeans he wore this morning,
although he has changed his kurta for a white and green
check button-down shirt. This is the first time I have seen
him wearing something other than earth colours and kurtas.
He looks different—less a son of the soil. Mr Mathur is
wearing his signature brown suit. I wonder whether it is the
same one he had on this morning and on all the other
mornings in prison, or if he owns fifty such suits. There is
a blonde lady in a wide-necked, ivory peasant blouse and a
brightly coloured skirt in an Indian print sitting at the table.
She is a little overweight, or 'all cuddles, no bones' as Scott
would say. I am suddenly aware of my own sharply-
emphasized bones.

Both men stand as we approach. 'Welcome, welcome,'
Mr Mathur says genially.

'Simi, let me introduce you to Elaine Johnson,' Scott
says, stepping forward. 'Elaine is with the American
Consulate.'

I shake hands with her. She smiles. She has on a frosted
pink lipstick that makes her look almost lipless.

'Simran, I'm glad this mess has been cleared up,' she
says, the frost on her lips making their ends squish together.
'I'm sorry the Consulate couldn't do more. But in these
situations the State Department can't get involved.'

I nod. 'It's okay. I understand.'

'It's unfortunate that people who travel to these Third
World countries never prepare themselves for the problems
they could be faced with. Even intsy-wintsy problems can
prove dangerous here. You really should have got permission,

you know. These people don't trust us Americans.'

I nod again, slipping into the chair beside Arun's. I hate her, and not an intsy-wintsy bit either. God, what an attitude! No wonder they didn't trust Americans here.

Mr Mathur gestures to a passing waiter. 'What will you drink?' he asks.

'Beer,' Scott says. 'A glass of red wine, please.' I say.

'We have more than one thing to celebrate,' Scott says, taking my hand and lifting it to display the ring. 'Simi and I got engaged this afternoon.'

'Congratulations,' Mr Mathur rises and comes around to pat Scott on the back. 'Well done. Well done,' he says. Then, turning to me, he places a paternal hand of blessing on my head. 'Be happy, beti.' The muscles in my throat tighten. I get up and give him a hug. 'Thank you for everything,' I say.

Miss Elaine Johnson adds her congratulations.

Arun reaches over and shakes Scott's hand.

Amidst all this handshaking and back patting, the waiter delivers our drinks. I slip back into the chair beside Arun and pick up my glass of wine. Mr Mathur begins to advise Scott on our departure and what we should expect from the police and immigration authorities. Feeling Arun's eyes on me, I turn to look at him, but his sight seems to be trained on something behind me. I turn away, sure that he had averted his eyes to avoid mine. I know I could not have mistaken a look that touched me so intensely. I don't know what Arun expects from this, our last meeting. I don't know what I expect. Daddy used to say the people we meet in this life are debts from a past birth. The amount of debt establishes the extent of the relationship. I don't know whether Arun owes me something from another life or I him, or whether that debt has been paid off. I know only that I will own the memory of him for a long time.

I reach out and lightly touch the back of his hand on the table. I feel a muscle under his skin jump, then his hand stiffens as the pads of his fingers press into the table top. His eyes look straight at me. 'I won't forget you,' I say softly, wishing it weren't so dark in the restaurant. I want to see if

I have engendered revelations on his face.

He nods and turns his face away again.

'If you ever come to the US,' Scott is saying to Mr Mathur, 'please stay with us; and you, too, Arun.'   .

The band begins to play a current hit that seems only faintly familiar now. Mr Mathur sees an acquaintance a couple of tables away and excuses himself to go say hello.

'Dance, sweetheart?' Scott gets up, extending his hand to me.

I turn my head to look at the dance floor where a number of couples are already moving to the beat of the music. Suddenly, I don't see the dancers any more. Before my eyes I see Kubrima waddling across the room, her weary steps throwing the music out of sync, the hump on her back an incongruous protrusion.

'Sweetheart, what do you say? Would you like to dance?'

I turn towards him. 'No. Later, perhaps. I feel a little tired. Why don't you ask Miss Johnson?'

'Are you all right?' He takes my hand and gently massages the back of my wrist with his thumb.

'Oh, yes. I'm just a little tired. All that running around ... I'm fine, really. Ask Miss Johnson to dance.'

He looks at me one last time with concern, then turns towards Elaine Johnson. Soon I see them join in with the other couples, Miss Johnson's boobs bouncing unashamedly close to Scott's chest.

I search again for Kubrima in the crowd.

'So, you're leaving tomorrow?' My heart sinks, leaden. Here it is, the end-saying I was hoping he would leave unsaid.

I nod my head without looking at him.

'I'm sure you can't wait to get back to America, back to your safe life?' he says.

'Actually,' I say watching the dance floor. 'I wish I didn't have to leave so soon.'

'Then don't.'

'What do you mean?' I turn to look at him. 'You know the court order. I have to leave the country within seventy-two hours.'

'You can stay.'

'How?'

'There are ways.'

'What ways?'

'That's a good band out there.' Scott returns with Miss Johnson.

Arun finishes his drink and stands up. 'I have to go. I have to get an early start tomorrow. I'm driving to Delhi to cover a story.'

In a frenzy I try to decide whether I want to explore the hope that was borne by his words. But Scott is already extending his hand to him, saying, 'I want to thank you again for all you've done, Arun. We couldn't have done this without you. Thank you.' And Arun is already pumping Scott's hand, smiling, saying, 'Don't mention it.' And then he's turning towards me to say, 'Have a good life.' And before I can say anything, before I can even catch my breath, he's left the room.

'Scott, may I have that dance now, please?' is all I can finally say.

He springs up and takes my hand. 'I thought you'd never ask.'

We dance every dance after that. Miss Johnson and Mr Mathur each bid farewell in their turn and leave sometime during the night. I order many more glasses of wine. My mind numbed by the alcohol, I let my feet follow Scott's rhythm. When we finally take a cab to the hotel, the first light of the morning sun is touching the sky. In the cab, a patch filters in through the window and sits on Scott's shoulder. I lay my head on that patch and fall asleep. I awaken at the entrance of the hotel only long enough to step out of the cab and go through the double doors to the elevator, then once again, I lay my head on his shoulder and close my eyes. He guides me to his room and lays me on the bed, slipping off my shoes and helping me out of my dress.

chapter eight

Some hours later, I awaken to the sound of a deafening rattle. Then there's silence. Then, Scott's voice penetrates through my head. 'Damned lock. I should have got it fixed.'

I raise myself. A pain splits my skull. 'Awhh.'

'That bad, hm?' Scott is standing at the table, fiddling with the lock on his suitcase. He seems to have been up for hours because the back of his light grey pants and blue shirt are creased as though he has been sitting for a long time with his back against something.

'My head,' I whisper.

'Yes. One too many glasses of wine. The price of freedom. I've ordered coffee. It'll be here soon. Lie down a bit. I'll try not to make any loud noises.'

I lay my throbbing head back on the pillow and close my eyes. I can hear Scott move in the bathroom as though he were wearing horses' hooves, although I know he's probably tiptoeing. Thankfully, room service arrives with coffee soon after. Sipping his coffee, Scott tells me he has already been to the airline office to confirm our tickets for the following day. Our flight is at 10:35 a.m.

'One day. We have one day. What would you like to do?'

'I've got to get my luggage and Daddy's ashes. What am I going to do now, Scott? I can't go back to the border with them.'

'Why not? We'll get permission. Heck, we'll even get

them to accompany us, so they can see for themselves. We'll go and see Elaine and ask her what to do, whom to talk to. We'll play it by the rules this time.'

For no reason at all, my eyes begin to fill with tears.

'Poor baby.' Scott replaces his cup on the table and puts an arm around me.

'Isn't it ironic that I was imprisoned for Daddy's ashes?'

'Hm, but you know what, fucked up though it was, and though I don't ever, repeat, ever want us to be in this shit again, I think we saw an India no tourist will get the opportunity to see. We saw the inside of the machine.'

'Yes, but people save up for months to visit the exotic east and look what we did. I wanted us to visit India, but not like this. I'm sorry, Scott.'

'Hey, we can still see the sights. We have the time.'

'You know, Scott, I don't think I can ever see the sights in India now. They will feel so ... so touristy.'

'Okay, no sights. Maybe, we can do some more shopping later on; that is, if you feel up to it. We can go souvenir shopping. Folks back home will be expecting something.'

I nod my assent.

I shower and put on my pink-and-white chikan outfit again. Scott checks the money in his wallet. I pick up the list of my belongings and we step out of the room. When our cab arrives at the police station, I see familiar khaki uniforms, and a sudden fear assails me. Scott gets out of the cab, but I find myself unable to move.

'Come on,' Scott says, holding the door open for me.

'Scott, I ... Please, can you get the stuff? I'd like to just sit here in the cab.'

'Is something wrong?' he asks.

'No, not really. It's just that all those policemen ...'

Scott bends and pokes his head in. 'Simi, they can't hurt you any more. You've been acquitted. Now, come on.'

When I still don't make a move to get out, he takes the papers from my hand and begins to close the door.

'Wait,' I say, reaching for the handle. 'I'll come. This is ridiculous. I can't believe I'm afraid of uniforms now.'

'Atta girl,' he says, holding the door open.

The inside of the station is crowded. There are people sitting everywhere: on the benches lined against the wall, on the floor, beside the big wooden desk at the far end where a harrowed-looking police officer is talking to an old man in ragged clothes. As I approach the desk, a policeman steps in front of me.

'Yes?' he says.

I present him the papers. He reads the two sheets for a long time, then looks at me from head to toe. 'Saab busy,' he says in English, returning the papers to me. 'Please wait.'

Scott and I move back towards the entrance and stand against the wall beside a policeman holding up a drunk.

'It's like a doctor's office,' Scott whispers to me.

The old man sitting beside the desk gets up and holds his folded hands before him. I see his jaw tremble. Then he bends over and attempts to touch the officer's feet, banging his head on the desk in the process.

'Achha, achha, dekhenge,' the officer assures him, waving him away.

Next, a little boy about ten or twelve is dragged by a policeman before the officer. One side of the boy's head is bleeding profusely. There is an exchange between the officer and policeman who then slaps the boy across the face a number of times. Loud wails fill the station. I flinch and turn my eyes away.

'Let's wait outside,' Scott says to me.

I shake my head. 'We'll miss our turn.'

Together we watch as the officer at the desk reviews the cases. People cry before him. They wring their hands and touch his feet. They sit talking solemnly. They rile against the apparent ambivalence of the police. The officer sits at his desk, the same tired expression on his face, writing in a file before him like an angel at God's court filling out good and bad deeds in the ledgers of people's lives.

Finally it's my turn. Walking up to the desk, I hand over the papers to the officer. He gives them a quick glance then turns to look at me and Scott thoroughly.

'Ramesh,' he calls. 'Take them to the malkhana.' He scribbles his signature on the form and gives it back to me. Scott and I follow the short, squat policeman called Ramesh to another room situated at the back of the station. 'Wait here,' he says and, unlocking the door, goes in to return some time later, dragging one of my bags. The locks on the suitcase seem to have been broken and the lid fits awkwardly as clothes hang out the sides, their corners trailing on the dirty floor. Depositing the bag on the floor at my feet, he goes back in to get the rest of my luggage: the garment bag which is half open with a corner of my favourite blue silk dress caught in the zipper, and my backpack which flops emptily on the floor.

'Please sign,' Ramesh says, holding out a paper clipped onto a board. I take the board from him and look at the long list of tick-marked items.

'Hold on,' Scott says. 'Check the luggage first, Simi.'

Ignoring the larger bags, I bend and pick up the backpack. All it holds is my pocket book, a hairbrush, a lipstick and the bottle of mineral water. I go down on my knees and begin looking through the rest of my luggage. The fragrance of Pantene rises from the suitcase as I open it. Clothes lie crumpled and bedraggled. The bottle of shampoo lies on its side with its snap-cap open, staining the white cotton shirt I had paid eighty-five dollars for. Pushing the clothes aside, I search frantically all over, in the corners, under the clothes, everywhere. Then throwing the lid back on, I turn and try to free the garment bag's zipper. 'Here, let me,' Scott says, taking it from me.

'No. Leave it, Scott. It doesn't matter. I can see there's nothing else in it.'

'Is everything there?'

'It's not here, Scott. Daddy's ...' my chin begins to tremble. 'Daddy's ashes ... the box ... that's missing. They haven't returned Daddy's ashes.'

'Is everything else there?'

I nod. 'I guess so. Except my camera.'

'Can you check your list one more time?' Scott asks the

policeman. 'There was a camera and a box.'

'One minute.' The man goes back inside and returns with the camera in his hands, inspecting it as if it were merchandise he is going to purchase. 'No box,' he says, handing over the camera to Scott.

'Please, can you check your list again?' Scott says.

'No sir. That is all. My record not showing anything else.'

'They didn't even put it on the record. They've taken it.' I flop on the floor amidst my scattered belongings.

'There was a wooden box,' Scott tells the man. 'That's missing. How can we find it? Can we speak to somebody about it?'

He shakes his head. 'Everything here.'

'Come on, Simi,' Scott says, slinging the camera around his neck and reaching down to adjust the lid on the suitcase. 'Come on. We'll talk to the officer outside.'

'I can't take this.' I slap the bag away. 'I don't want it. It's so violated.'

'Are you sure?'

'Yes, I don't want any of it. They can keep it. There's only one thing I want . . .'

Bending down, Scott retrieves my pocket book from the backpack and opens it to reveal the top edges of my credit cards lined neatly in their black leather pockets. He pulls a flap aside and shows me the wad of Indian currency I had exchanged at the airport. 'You want to count this?' he asks me.

I shake my head.

Taking my purse from under my arm, he slips the pocket book inside and grabs my arm. 'Come on. Let's talk to that guy outside about the box.'

I get up and begin to follow Scott down the passageway, angry tears burning in my eyes.

'Wait,' the policeman calls behind us. 'You sign here.' He gestures to me with the clipboard.

I turn back and scribble my name at the bottom of the form. Suddenly he draws closer to me and, looking up and down the passageway, asks in a conspiratorial tone, 'You wanting to sell camera?'

I look at him, my anger suspended for a moment.

'You wanting to sell camera?' he says again, his face close to mine, his beady eyes gleaming.

Something breaks inside me then, and I smack his insensitive face away. 'You can have the fucking camera,' I scream at him. 'I don't want it.' I run towards Scott and try to pull it off from around his neck.

'Simi, stop it. Have you gone crazy?'

'Give the fucking camera to him, Scott. I don't want it.'

'Stop it, Simi. Let him be. Let's go and talk to that man outside.'

Realizing I am still holding the clipboard in my hand, I turn and fling it to the floor. It slides over the smooth surface and comes to rest near the policeman's feet.

The officer at the desk pulls out a file and tells us the box cannot be returned because it is part of police evidence.

'But they didn't find any evidence,' I scream at him. 'That isn't evidence, it's my father's ashes.'

'I'm sorry,' he says, closing the file. 'There's nothing I can do.'

'What do you mean there's nothing you can do? Who can do something then? You can't just keep my box.'

'Next,' the officer calls out, turning his face away from me.

'Wait a second,' I move closer to his desk and lean over to command his attention again. 'I want my box. Who can I talk to? Your superior officer?'

'Simi, come on.' Scott takes my elbow and tries to pull me away. 'There's nothing else you can do here.'

The officer looks at me for a second before turning his eyes away again and gesturing to a policeman standing a few feet away. 'Next case,' he says.

'Fuck you,' I say, banging my hand on his desk. 'I've just about had it with this fucking system. Everything is so screwed up around here.'

'Madam,' he says, standing up behind his desk. 'I must

warn you that if you don't leave this station now I will have you taken into custody.'

'No, no,' Scott says pulling at my elbow. 'We're leaving. She's just upset. That box had her father's ashes. Come on, Simi.' He steers me towards the exit. 'Are you crazy? You want to go back into that shit-hole again?' he says to me once we are outside.

I stand for a moment with my eyes closed, trying to rent through the opaque rage clouding my mind.

'Let's get out of here.' Scott hooks a hand in the crook of my arm.

I pull away from him impatiently, needing to concentrate on clearing my thoughts.

'Why don't you talk to the lawyer, Mathur?' Scott says. 'He'll know what to do.'

Hope sweeps away the nimbus in my mind. I turn to look at Scott gratefully. 'Do you have his telephone number?' I ask him.

He pulls out his wallet and plucks out a folded piece of paper. 'Here they are—our lifelines in India.' He opens out the paper and gives it to me. It has three numbers written on it: Elaine Johnson's, Arun's and Mathur's.

'I've got to find a payphone,' I say, clutching the paper tightly.

'I think I saw one at the end of this block,' Scott says. I begin to hurry along the busy sidewalk, skirting around hawkers, elbowing my way past people standing in groups, talking and laughing, my eyes darting across stores to spot a telephone kiosk.

'There it is.' Scott points towards a store window with large letters painted in red on the glass front. Sonu's Telecom STD, ISO, PCO.

I hesitate before it.

Scott steps up and pushes open the rickety, wooden door. A string of little brass bells hanging on the knob tinkles as we enter. There are a number of people sitting around on chairs, some holding diaries and pens in their laps, others reading newspapers. One side of the room is

taken up by an aluminium desk on which I see two telephones
in use, one by a balding man in a dirty beige dressing gown
and the other by an obese woman in a pink chiffon sari and
henna-red hair. She is talking shrilly into the receiver,
drowning out the voice of the gentleman who is attempting
to block out her voice by sticking an index finger in one ear
while pressing the receiver to the other. There is a young
man sitting behind the desk dressed in a tee shirt so snug,
that the sewed on Nike patch on his breast appears like a
scar. He is leaning forward, peering intently at the neon
digits that change rapidly on the black meter as the minutes
tick away. As we approach the desk, he looks up and asks,
'Local or STD?'

'What . . .?' I begin.

'Local,' Scott answers, obviously familiar with this coded
language. 'But there, inside,' he says, pointing to a narrow
glass door creating a kiosk-like triangular booth against a
corner in which I see a young woman clad in blue jeans and
a red silk kurta with her back to us, talking on the phone.

Scott and I stand by the desk, waiting. As soon as the
woman in the kiosk steps out, Scott makes a move to enter
it. A man sitting across waves his newspaper at us. 'Wait for
turn,' he says, getting up.

'Please,' Scott folds his hands before the man in an
Indian gesture of entreaty. 'Emergency. Two minutes. Please.'

With a condescending look, the man waves to us again
and settles back in the chair.

There's hardly enough room for the two of us in the
narrow cell. I stand pressed between Scott's side and the
glass door as he takes the piece of paper from my hand and
begins punching in the numbers.

I can hear a click when the line connects and then a faint
double ring as the sound spills through the space between
Scott's ear and the receiver. Finally I hear another click and
a voice uttering a monosyllable.

'Mr Mathur?' Scott says.

A monosyllabic response.

'Hi, this is Scott Ferrier.'

I hear a garble then, like the distorted sounds of a phone conversation in a cartoon show.

'No,' Scott finally responds. 'We need your help again. Here, why don't you talk to Simi?' He hands me the receiver, steadying the cradle as the green curls of the wire stretch, taut.

'Mr Mathur,' I say. 'I'm so glad we caught you.'

'Oh, I do not go home till after seven. How can I help you, Miss Mehta?'

I relate the events at the police station, my voice shaking as I tell him about my conversation with the officer in charge. 'They won't return Daddy's ashes,' I say. 'They told me the box is evidence.'

I hear Mr Mathur sigh on the other end. 'I'm sorry,' he says. 'But it is true. If the police confiscate something as evidence they are within legal bounds to keep it.'

'But that was false evidence. You know what that box contains.' I can feel my throat constricting. 'They know what that box has. They acquitted me because they know.'

'That is true,' he says. 'The problem is, the case involved national security.'

'But I was acquitted.' I can hear the shrill note in my voice. Scott hears it, too, because I feel him squeeze my shoulder.

'I can understand your frustration,' Mr Mathur is saying into my ear. 'You are a very brave girl. I have ...'

'Mr Mathur,' I cut him short. 'There must be something you can do. You have to help me. Please.'

'We can file a case,' he says.

'I don't have time to file a case. I only have this evening in the country, remember? I have to leave by tomorrow.'

He's quiet for a moment. I can almost hear his mind scroll through his law books. Then he speaks again. 'I am going to give you Ved Sharma's number. He's the Inspector General of Police. Telephone him and tell him you are my client. Explain your situation to him.' I hear papers being shuffled in the background. 'Ah. Here it is, Sharma's number.'

'Hold on,' I say. 'Let me find a pen.' I turn to Scott who

is already opening the door of the kiosk to borrow a pen from someone outside.

'Mr Mathur, what shall I say to him?' I ask while Scott is gone.

'Tell him everything. He should be familiar with your case, but explain to him about your deportation order and your father's ashes. Let him hear your pain, Miss Mehta. The IG is a family man. Perhaps he will relent.'

Scott returns with a red refill of a ballpoint pen and, holding the paper with the telephone numbers against the wall, waits to add another.

'I'm ready for the number now,' I tell Mr Mathur.

As he says each digit, I call it out loud, and Scott writes it on the paper with the refill held between the tips of his index finger and thumb. The digits come out all shaky and squiggly, tracing out each little imperfection in the wall.

'Ring him now,' Mr Mathur says. 'He will be at home at this time. Best of luck.'

'Thank you,' I say softly.

'Beti,' he says. 'If he refuses, don't lose heart. I will file a case. It might take a little time, but I can bring you back to this country to receive your father's ashes.'

'Thank you,' I say again. 'I'll let you know.' I press the disconnect button and stand with my hand hovering over the dial. My mind is totally blank. I can't recall even the first digit of the IG's telephone number. Silently, Scott holds the paper before my eyes.

My call is answered almost immediately by a servile male voice. 'Hello,' I say. 'Could I speak with Mr Sharma, please?'

'Who is speaking, saab?' I am asked in Hindi.

'My name is Simran.' Unwittingly, I begin in English then revert to Hindi. 'Mr Sharma doesn't know me, but I need to speak with him. My name is Simran Mehta. Tell him my lawyer, Mr Mathur, asked me to call.'

'One minute. I will check if saab is available.' I hear a faint clatter as he places the receiver on a wooden surface. A ghostly hum begins to filter through the pores of my ears, the sound, hypnotic. The minutes tick by. 'This is Sharma,' a whisky-gruff voice shatters the lull.

It takes me a second to readjust to the change.

'Hello?' he says impatiently.

'Mr Sharma.' My voice sounds thin and scratchy. I clear my throat and swallow. 'My name is Simran Mehta. I ... I'm Mr Mathur's client. He gave me your number. I'm sorry to bother you at home, but I had no other option.'

He waits for me to continue.

'I ...' I begin, wondering how to explain the shambles of my visit to India to this formless voice. 'I need your help,' I say.

The silence on the other end continues.

'I don't know if you are familiar with my case,' I begin hesitantly. 'I was arrested about three months ago at the border and put in Amritgarh jail. I had a box. I was carrying my father's ashes in that. He ... my father ... it was his last wish that I scatter his ashes on the border. The security guards at the border thought I was carrying a bomb or something. However, two days ago I was acquitted. They said the arrest was a mistake. The Superintendent of the jail told me to pick up my luggage from the police station. I got all my belongings back, but they refuse to return the box that has my father's ashes in it.' Suddenly, it all comes pouring out in a rush. 'I was very upset, so I talked to Mr Mathur, my lawyer, and he said you would help me. I want my father's ashes back. The court said I have to leave this country within seventy-two hours, but ... Can you ...? Please, I need your help. I can't leave my father's ashes behind. Please, can you help me?

'I know the case,' he says.

'Oh,' I say, a little irritated at him for not having said so earlier. 'Then you know that the box they claim to be evidence, has only my father's ashes in it. Besides, the court did say that I was wrongly arrested.'

'Oh, no, Miss Mehta. The court did not say that. You were arrested for suspicious activity at the border. There was never any doubt about that.'

'But I was acquitted.'

'Only because we saw no reason to keep you further.'

At the back of my mind I can feel a familiar fury begin to creep up again. My fingers tighten on the receiver and the muscles in my wrist clench. 'Mr Sharma, I spent three months in your jail. Don't you think that is a bit harsh for just a suspicion, especially when I was innocent all along?'

Scott puts restraining fingers around my battling wrist, as though to contain the anger in the nucleus of the pulse.

Slowly, I let my fingers relax, surrendering their tension to Scott's wise hand.

'We have strict procedures against any threats to our national security,' the Inspector General of Police is saying.

I take a deep breath. 'I understand,' I say as quietly as I can. 'I've put it behind me now. But please, could you have them return my father's ashes? I'm sorry for any suspicion I might have caused. I just want my father's ashes, and I'll leave India. Please, can you help me?'

'Make an appointment to see me in my office tomorrow. I do not discuss cases on the telephone.'

'Tomorrow? I'm leaving the country tomorrow. My flight is at 10:30 in the morning. I can come to your office any time before eight. Is that all right?'

'Miss Mehta.' I detect a trace of amusement in his voice. 'Offices here don't open till 9 a.m.'

'But that's impossible.' This time it is panic that makes me grip the receiver tightly. 'I have to get to the airport around nine.'

'I'm sorry, there's nothing I can do then.'

'Please, can't you make an exception in my case and see me early tomorrow or even tonight? I can come to your house.'

'I'm busy tonight and I do not go to the office before nine.'

'Please, Mr Sharma. What can I do? How can I leave the country without my father's ashes?'

'I'm sorry, Miss Mehta. Goodbye.'

'Wait a minute,' I say urgently. 'You've got to help me.'

'I'm sorry,' he says again.

'I can't leave without my father's ashes.'

'It will be wise to follow the court order.'

'Mr Sharma ...'

'Goodbye, Miss Mehta.'

'No. Wait a minute.'

The phone is put down, severing all hope. I stand holding the receiver to my ear, my mind filling with the unyielding buzz of the dial tone.

Scott takes the receiver from my hand and replaces it on the cradle. I turn to look at him dumbly. Without a word he gathers me in his arms. I bury my face in his chest, wanting to let myself go, but I seem to have been utterly defeated. I seem to have exhausted my stock of emotive release. Dry-eyed, I can only manage to hold onto Scott abstractedly, the camera he is still wearing around his neck pressing into my chest. I wonder why I had borne Daddy's death just so.

Someone raps on the glass door of the kiosk, then pulls it open. 'Please, if conversation is finished, please vacate the booth.' Without lifting my head, I let Scott lead me out and seat me on a chair while he pays for the calls. All around me I see customers looking at me, their faces sympathetic. I wonder how they can tell. I wonder, if I were to see my own face, would it reveal my grief to me? Perhaps if I had looked in a mirror when Daddy died, I wouldn't be carrying his whole life inside of me. It would have wept out of me.

Scott raises me off the chair and leads me out of the store. 'We could call Elaine and Arun, and see if they can help,' he says.

I shake my head. 'It's no use.'

'What did Mr Mathur say?'

'He'll file a case.'

'He's a good lawyer. He'll win. I have faith in him.'

'It might take years.'

'You know, that might be for the best. You need to come home with me and take it easy for a while. You know, get over this. You're in no shape to fight the system here. Take it easy for a while, and by the time Mr Mathur has the ashes, we can come back and take care of this business. Right now, you need to come home.'

I don't respond to that. I don't know how to respond. I don't know what I want to do. Silently, I start walking down the street. Scott falls into step beside me. It is already late in the afternoon and the sun has expended its entire warmth. A stiff breeze presses against my body. I draw in my shoulders and hold my bare arms over my chest to ward it off.

'Here.' Scott whisks off his light jacket and spreads it over my shoulders. 'Perhaps we should go back to the police station and get a jacket from your luggage.'

I shake my head. 'I'd rather freeze.'

Scott pulls the lapels of the jacket closer around my neck. 'I should have bought you some more clothes.'

Holding the sides of the jacket closed with my arms crossed over it, I continue walking down the sidewalk, oblivious to the shoulders that jostle me, blind to the colourful displays hawkers call my attention to.

'Do you feel up to some shopping?' Scott asks.

I shake my head.

'Where are we going?'

'Karim Gali,' I say.

'What's that?'

'Sultana's house.'

'Why are we going there?'

'I'm going to see her brother.'

'Why?'

I shrug my shoulders. 'I promised her.'

'Are you sure you feel up to it? You should really go back to the hotel. You've had a harrowing day.'

I hunch my shoulders under the jacket. 'You go back if you want to. I'm going to Karim Gali.'

He walks silently beside me for some time. Every once in while I lose him in the crowd, but he reappears moments later, clutching the camera before him like a compass.

'Do you know where it is?'

I shake my head.

He looks at his watch and then at the sky.

'It's getting late Simi, perhaps we . . .'

'I'm going, Scott,' I say, shaking my head at a hawker thrusting a pair of figurines of an Indian bride and groom in my face.

'I was only going to suggest we find him tomorrow morning. Our flight isn't till 10:30. We can go there early.'

'I want to go now.'

'Simi, it's getting late. I promise you we'll go in the morning. Besides, you've had a long day. Let's go back to the hotel now and spend a cozy evening together. I haven't had one of those with you in months.' He puts his arm around my shoulders and draws me into a sideways hug.

I shrug his arm away. 'You go on back to the hotel if you want to. I'm going to Karim Gali.'

'You know, Simi, the trouble with you is that you're too damned bull-headed.'

I continue walking, as does he.

'Do you have any idea how long this might take? For heaven's sake, Simi, give it a rest. We don't know a damned thing about this place. And it isn't as though we know where his house is. We could be out searching all night and then who's to say we'll find him? Maybe he doesn't live there any more. Maybe he left. Maybe he's gone far, far away. We don't have a clue, Simi. I refuse to go on a wild goose chase.'

'Go back to the hotel, Scott,' I tell him again. 'I can do this on my own. In fact, I'd rather do it on my own.'

He's silent for a while, walking alongside of me. A young man in a flashy red shirt appears from amidst a group of snickering young men and, walking directly towards me, deliberately brushes his arm against my breasts.

'What the hell?' Scott puts his arm back on my shoulder and draws me to him protectively. 'This is worse than 14th Ave. I can't leave you alone on these streets.'

'I can take care of myself,' I say, not attempting to push his arm away this time.

'Do you have any idea where this place is?' he finally asks.

'Yes,' I say. 'I know the name of the street.'

'Oh right, as though streets are easy to find in this place. Come on, Simi, be sensible; let's do this in the morning.'

I see a cab coming up the road and, skirting around a man arguing with a hawker about the price of a watch, I run to the edge of the road, flailing my arms up and down to get the driver's attention. The cab passes within a few feet of me and speeds away. I see the back seat is occupied by two women. I continue to stand there, looking up the street. In the rush of traffic, it is hard to tell a cab from other vehicles. I step closer to the road and try to flag down a couple more cabs, but they all seem to be occupied.

'Come on.' Scott takes my arm. 'I think there's a cab stand near that intersection.'

I let him guide me to the stand. He is right. There are a number of black cars with yellow tops with 'For Hire' across their meters parked in the corner of the street. A couple of men are standing leaning against one vehicle, gazing hazily through cigarette smoke at the evening rush. As we approach, one of them disengages himself from his lazy pursuit and clearing his throat, spits a blob of phlegm on the road near his feet. Then he saunters over to us.

'Yes, saab?'

'Karim Gali,' I say. 'Will you take us?'

He shakes his head and walks back to his companions. I watch him say something to them. All the others shake their heads in unison.

I look at them in surprise. 'Aren't you available?' I ask them.

They shake their heads again. I turn to look at their vehicles with the 'For Hire' sign turned up on their meters, then back at them.

'We don't want to go to that area at this time,' one of them volunteers.

'What did he say?' Scott asks. I translate for him and begin walking towards the sidewalk again. Scott joins me. We try to hail a few more cabs on the street, but as soon as the drivers hear our destination, they shake their heads and drive on, sometimes taking other passengers.

The sun has disappeared behind a row of tall shabby buildings, and the evening sky swallows the last speck of its light. Large neon signs and fluorescent lights begin to flash around us as stores prepare for evening business, their owners lighting incense sticks to welcome the evening. I quicken my steps and continue walking down the sidewalk.

'Simi, give it up, please. You'll never get a cab this late. You heard what those drivers told you. It's not safe at this time. Please, Simi, let's go back to the hotel. We'll look for Sultana's brother tomorrow.'

I step down onto the road in the path of a cycle rickshaw. The driver skids to a halt.

'Karim Gali,' I tell him.

He considers my destination for a while.

'Jaoge?' I ask him if he will take us.

'Ten rupees extra.'

'Okay.' I turn around to look for Scott. He is standing at the side of the road with his hands dug deep in his pockets, the camera jutting out of his stomach like a monstrous growth.

'Coming?' I ask him.

He looks at me for a moment before nodding.

The red synthetic seat of the rickshaw is narrow and tilts downwards, making us slide off every time the thin wheels hit a pothole. Planting our feet firmly on the floor of the carriage and clinging to its sides, Scott and I join the mad rush of traffic. After numerous busy roads, the rickshaw veers off on a deserted, badly lit, side street. The smell of open sewers follows us all the way to another street where the road becomes unpaved and stony. On one side of the street we can see small mortar houses nursing dim lights within them, and on the other, the sheet metal of closed store shutters, some of them with garish writing on them. As we come to the end of the street, a faint phosphoric smell of old fire pervades the air.

The rickshaw driver pulls his brakes at the corner.

'Karim Gali,' he says. 'Where do you want to go?'

I look around. Across from where we sit, I can see a

couple of houses bounded by some collapsed shapes on one end, and a vacant lot on the other. In the midst of the houses I can detect some lights, dull and flickering and smudged.

'Stop right here,' I tell the driver and step off the rickshaw.

Scott pays the driver. 'Will you wait?'

The driver looks at him blankly.

'Ask him if he'll wait, Simi. If Sultana's brother is not here, we'll go back in his rickshaw.'

I ask him in Hindi if he will wait.

He shakes his head. 'Nahin, saab.' He explains to me the danger of lurking in this area.

'What did he say?' Scott asks me.

'He won't wait. It isn't safe for him. He's scared.'

Scott gives me a murderous look. 'So what'll we do if he isn't here? I don't think there's anyone here. See how deserted it is?' He turns back to the driver. 'Fifty rupees,' he says, pulling out a bill and waving it before his face.

'Nahin, saab,' the driver shakes his head.

'Hundred.' He peels another bill and presses it in the driver's hand. The man hesitates, eyeing the bill lying in his palm.

'Please, bhai. Bus paanch minute.' I plead with him to allow us only five minutes.

He looks at the bill one more time, then pulling out a small wad of dirty bills from a pocket under his sweater, arranges the fresh crisp one at the end and slips it back.

'Paanch minute,' he says, wheeling his rickshaw into the shadow of a shutter.

Scott and I walk hurriedly across the street. The smell of burnt debris grows stronger as we cross the crumbled structure of a house and stop before the first house still standing.

For some reason I find myself tiptoeing as though afraid that one heavy step might dislodge the fire-hollowed structures around me, bringing them crashing to the ground. Outside the first house, I stand wondering where to knock, because a makeshift piece of illuminated burlap hangs where a door must have been. Inside, I hear the sound of a baby crying.

'Hello,' I say softly, my lips close to the fabric. Suddenly the baby stops crying and the house grows very silent.

'Hello,' I say again. Silence follows.

'I'm looking for Iftekhar. Do you know him?'

Nothing, not a word, not a sound comes from the house. I can hear my own heart beat. Scott comes up behind me and whispers to me to try the other light.

I tiptoe to the house which has a brand new plywood door attached to a blackened jamb with shiny hinges that glint in the moonlight. I knock on the door gently.

'Who is it?' I hear a man ask immediately, almost from right behind, as though he has been awaiting my knock.

'I'm looking for Iftekhar,' I say.

'Who are you?'

'I am a friend of his sister's.'

'Iftekhar doesn't live here any more.'

I stand looking at the closed door for a moment before turning around to face Scott.

'What did he say?' Scott asks me.

'Iftekhar does not live here any more.'

'Ask him if he knows his whereabouts.'

I turn around and ask that of the voice.

There is silence for a moment after which I hear a bolt slide open and a moment later, the door begins to open outwards. I take a few steps back.

A big man with a full beard and a hurricane lantern in his hand is standing at the door.

'Why do you want to know?'

'I . . . I have a message for him from his sister, Sultana. Do you know where I can find him?'

He raises his lantern to look closely at me and then at Scott.

'No,' he says. 'I have no idea.'

I can see he is not telling me the truth, and he makes no effort to hide that fact.

'Please,' I say. 'It's really important.'

He shakes his head.

'Which house is Sultana's?' I ask.

He points to the ruin at the beginning of the row.

I stand staring at a dark pile of rubble before turning away. Behind me the light withdraws inside, and the door closes.

Scott is rubbing his hands over his arms. 'God, this is eerie.' I walk past him to the other end of the row where four walls still support a mortar roof. There is a large tin sheet covering the entrance, hiding a resident from sight. Tentatively, I rap on the sheet with my knuckles. A shrill sound vibrates through it. I step up closer to the entrance, pricking my ears to catch any signs of life. I think I hear the scrape of slippers. Then, nothing.

'Iftekhar?' I call out, my lips against the space between the door jamb and the tin sheet. 'Iftekhar?' There is total silence.

'Let's go, Simi. I hate to leave the rickshaw driver alone for so long. There's obviously no one here.'

'Iftekhar?' I call one last time before turning away, my shoulders sagging under Scott's cotton jacket. Scott takes my arm as we walk back to the street. The rickshaw is still where we left it in the shadows of the store shutters, but we can't see the driver anywhere. Standing in the middle of the street, we look up and down.

'Hello?' Scott says urgently. 'Hello?'

The driver emerges from behind the rickshaw where he has been squatting between his vehicle and a shutter.

Without a word, he turns his rickshaw around and waits for us to climb on.

'Imperial Hotel,' Scott tells him, easing himself in beside me. I gather myself in a corner of the small seat, one hand in my lap, the other gripping the front of Scott's jacket over my breasts. After a while, Scott covers my hand with his own and gives a gentle squeeze. 'I'm sorry,' he says.

'He's there,' I say.

'How do you know? No one answered the door.'

'He's there.'

We ride back to the hotel in silence. Neither of us utters another word, silently acknowledging the demons lurking in the shadows of Karim Gali.

chapter nine

'Are you sure you'll be okay?' Scott asks me for the fifth time since we have entered the hotel. 'Maybe you should sleep in my room today.' I shake my head. 'I'll be fine,' I say.

'I'll tell you what I'll do. I'll leave the key to my room here. That way, if you need me at night, you can just let yourself in.'

'If you wish,' I say, stepping out of my dress and laying it on a chair.

'Let me go and open my door, and I'll bring the key back.'

By the time he returns, I'm lying in bed. He places the key on the bedside table and bends to kiss me gently on the lips. 'Sleep, Simi. Tomorrow, all this won't seem so hopeless.' I close my eyes.

After Scott leaves, I lie in bed for hours unable to sleep. In my mind I keep hearing the click at the end of my conversation with the IG like a verdict, the tone of the disconnected line, a death sentence. I push the sound away, concentrating instead, on the sight of Karim Gali. I replay the scrape of slippers on a bare floor. I'm sure someone was in that house. Could it have been Iftekhar? I try to piece together Sultana's account of the fire and the number of people that live in Karim Gali. I think I have already seen Ghulam bhai, and the baby crying was probably Fatima's child. The only other people who remain are old Khala and Iftekhar. Sultana told me theirs was the last house to be burnt, and by that time, all the residents were awake and were probably able to put out the flames. So the rubble Ghulam Rasul pointed at is probably not from Sultana's house at all. That can only mean that the house with the tin sheet is Sultana's. In fact, I am almost certain it is, and I know I have to go back. I wonder if Scott will agree to return to Karim Gali in the morning. After all, it won't be as fearful in the light of day. But our flight is at 10:30 a.m., and we'll probably have to leave for the airport at least an hour and a half before check-in. There won't be any time unless we go very early in the morning, at about 5 a.m.; only then can we make it back in time. I get out of bed and squaring my shoulders, prepare to discuss my plan with Scott. But all of a sudden, I am too exhausted for another argument. Deciding to go there on my own, I climb back into my bed. Checking my watch, I unstrap it and put it on the bedside table. The time is 12:05. I lie back on the pillow, staring at its radium digits glow in the dark. Slowly, I drift off to sleep only to awaken suddenly an hour later: 1 a.m. After that, I sleep and awaken every hour on the hour, like clockwork. Finally, at 5 a.m., I get up quietly.

The room is still illuminated by the warm, gentle light of the bedside lamp. Splashing cold water in my eyes and brushing my teeth, I slip into the pink dress again. Wishing I hadn't abandoned my entire luggage so impulsively, I spread Scott's cotton jacket on my shoulders and look down at my bare legs with a frown, knowing it will be freezing outside at this time. Then I remember my sari. I grab the key to Scott's room and let myself out into the corridor. His room is very dark, as I expected, all the curtains drawn tightly against the outside lights. I can tell he's sleeping soundly by the way his snore rumbles softly in his throat. I step inside and search for the light switch by the door, knowing that Scott will not awaken. He's like that; protecting himself from the tiniest of lights at the brink of sleep, but once in its depth, he sleeps brave-hearted. Opening the closet near the door, I take the white bundle from the top shelf, and letting myself out of the room, shut the door gently behind me.

Back in my own room, I slip out of the dress and tie the sari, grateful to Koki for having taught me the art, winding the folds back and forth in my hand to make perfect pleats in seconds. Stepping into my white pumps, I strap on my watch and pick up my white purse, making sure it has my pocket book. Then, turning the key softly, I walk to the elevator. There is a bright-eyed young man at the reception desk who wishes me a perky good morning as I approach him. I leave a message for Scott and the keys to both our rooms, requesting that they be sent up with his coffee. 'I had to go back. I'll be here before 9 a.m. Please don't worry,' I write in the note.

The doorman gets me a cab. Slipping some notes in his hand I smile at him and thank him, recalling the nightmare of hailing a cab the night before. 'Karim Gali,' I tell the cab driver, settling myself in the back seat. 'Karim Gali?' The driver gives me a puzzled look. At my confirming nod, he starts the engine and backs out of the driveway.

This early in the morning, the streets of Amritgarh are miraculously deserted. Except for the occasional milkman zooming by with large milk containers tied to the belly of his motorcycle and blanketed forms sitting behind kerosene stoves boiling eggs, there doesn't seem to be anyone about. In the absence of the camouflaging crowds, the garbage on the streets becomes more evident. It is strewn everywhere. Stray pieces of paper, buoyant with the acceleration of wheels, drift to the ground in slow motion.

The sky is gaining transparency by the time we reach the highway. The headlights of passing vehicles glow only in their own centres now, their brilliance redundant on the road before them. Once again, we leave the wider roads and enter the narrow street lined with houses on one side and stores with closed shutters on the other, their graffiti more garish in the light of the early morning. No lights appear from under closed doors now, and the smell of sewage is dulled by the freshness of the day.

As the cab slows down, I turn my head away from the shutters and look ahead. Before me I can see a large mound

of broken bricks with edges frayed and black as though they
are overbaked rejects in a kiln. But scattered around the
mound is evidence of charred households: pieces of half-
burnt furniture, misshapen pans, a lidless trunk full of ashes
amongst which is a shimmering piece of red fabric with its
sequins still intact, the sole of a black patent leather pump
with a tenacious heel buried in the debris, and beside the
mound, three houses, their once white walls a mosaic of
soot, their apertures covered with burlap and brown plywood.

Unlike the rickshaw, the cab drives right up to the site
of arson.

'Where do you want to go?' the driver asks me.

'There.' I point to the third house at the end, the one
beside the vacant lot. As we drive up, I see a little boy in a
maroon sweater reaching below his knees, running in circles
on the road before the houses. The sleeves of the sweater are
much too long for his little arms and flap over his hands like
a dog's ears. A young woman with a wide face and hair
pulled back in a hurriedly-tied knot on her head is fanning
a coal fire in an angeethi. A young girl, probably about six
or seven, sits beside her, squinting from the smoke of the
fire, holding a wailing baby in her lap. As the cab approaches,
the little boy comes to a halt and stands staring at it, his
circles forgotten, his arms hanging limp on either side of
him, the empty sleeves almost touching the ground. 'Bus,' I
tell the driver. 'Stop here.'

He turns the engine off.

As I open the door to step out, I see a gangly youth
squatting on the side of the road, scooping toothpowder
with a finger from a bottle and rubbing it on his teeth.

'How much?' I ask the driver.

'One hundred and seventy-five rupees,' he says.

'Will you wait?' I ask him. 'I have to go back.'

'How long?' he asks.

'Not long. Fifteen-twenty minutes. I'll give you waiting
charges.'

He nods his head.

I close the door and turn to meet the residents of Karim

Gali. The little boy comes running up to me and stops a few feet away to stand and watch. I smile at him and hold my hand out. He scampers away, smiling shyly.

I turn around and begin walking towards the young man. He still squats beside a water pump, the middle finger of his right hand suspended in his mouth, spittle clinging to his chin. As I draw closer, he gets up hurriedly and swings the long handle of the pump, holding his face under the torrent of water that gushes out of the spout. Drying his face on the front ends of his shirt, he faces me, pushing his arms behind his back. He is very skinny, with very black hair as straight as Sultana's, tousled around his wide forehead. His eyes are large and stark black, the same colour as Sultana's, but whereas Sultana's are stony and opaque, his stare back at me with a transparency. He is wearing dirty white pajamas and a tight shirt buttoned over his thin chest.

'Iftekhar?' I ask, as I walk up to him.

A guarded look enters his eyes, but he nods his head.

'I'm Simran Mehta,' I say in Hindi. 'Sultana, your sister, is my friend. I knew her in Amritgarh jail.'

He looks at me—at my dirty, white wrinkled sari. 'From Amreeka?' he says with disbelief.

'My clothes are with the police,' I say by way of explanation. 'They gave me this sari in prison.'

His lips lift at the corners hesitantly. 'Sultana baji told me about you.'

'You met Sultana?'

He nods. 'I took the bus to the Central Jail and went to meet her.'

'How is she?'

His eyes reflect deep shadows under his lashes. 'She's all right.'

'I promised Sultana I would come to see you if and when I got out of jail.'

'When did you get out?'

'Three days ago.' I feel a tug on my sari and look down to see the little boy holding it through a sleeve, smiling up at me. Beside him I see the young woman who was lighting the fire, looking at me with interest. The baby is now on her hip and quiet. Behind her the little girl is standing looking at my white pumps which peep out from under the sari.

'Baji,' the young man turns towards her. 'This is Simran baji. Remember I told you Sultana baji had a friend in jail from Amreeka?'

Fatima's interest in me becomes greater. She comes closer and looks at me openly. 'Salaam walaikum,' she says. 'How are you?'

'I'm fine,' I say, smiling some more.

'Ifti, take her inside the house. I'll bring tea.'

'Oh, that's not necessary,' I say, although the idea of tea sounds wonderful.

'Please, come.' Iftekhar turns around towards the open entrance of his house. The tin sheet has been moved to rest alongside a wall. My eyes fall upon his arms still held behind his back. The sleeves of the shirt are rolled up to the elbows and I see what were once his forearms. They are now mere bones covered with patches of black scabs, pealing in places to reveal a thin layer of baby pink skin. His left hand has no fingers. All that remains are black and pink stubs around the palm; and on the right hand, only the middle finger and the thumb remain.

Swallowing hard, I step in through the door. The little boy takes my hand shyly and falls into step beside me.

'They burnt my house,' Sultana had told me. I see it now. Across from where I stand, there is a gaping hole in the wall that must have been the door to the second room where Sultana's father was trapped. The far corner of the room has crumbled, and light pours in from the jagged opening. The floor of the room is layered thickly with ashes and is littered with scorched rafters, broken bricks, useless furniture and books burnt to their spines.

'Please come,' Iftekhar gestures to me. I look around the room we are in. Except for the black imprint of flames on the walls, it is spotless. On one end is a table with charred edges and a brightly painted green chair with a back frame but no back. There is a kerosene stove on the table and a couple of pans and various dishes. Against the other wall is a cot covered with a white sheet and a thin quilt in a brown and green pattern. A rope is tied across the room from one end to the other on which neatly folded clothes hang.

'Sit, baji,' Iftekhar says, pulling the chair out by sticking his arm under the back frame of the chair and resting its weight on his stump. I perch on its edge and lift the little boy onto my lap. He leans back for a second before clambering off and climbing onto Iftekhar's.

'Sultana used to talk a lot about you,' I tell Iftekhar.

The muscles around his smile tremble as though stiff from lack of use.

'She told me you've just started college. That must be exciting?'

'I don't go to college any more.'

'Why?'

He looks down at his arms held across the boy's chest. 'I can't take notes any more. I can't write.'

'Oh,' I say. That's all—'oh'. Silently I chide myself for not being able to say more, but lately, words—simple words, words of sympathy—have been fading from my memory, as though their usefulness has expired.

'I am learning to work with them. I can do a lot of work now. I can make my own food, although Khala doesn't let me. She stays here with me most of the day and treats me like a child. She doesn't let me do anything. You know what I really want to learn to do again?' His eyes suddenly become animated.

I smile at him encouragingly.

'I want to play cricket. I can hold the bat already, and look, let me show you,' he says excitedly. Pushing the boy off his lap, he falls on his elbows and knees before the cot and slides under it. When he straightens up, there is a red ball held tightly between his finger and thumb. 'Watch,' he says, taking position with one arm flung out and the other held stiffly by his side.

'I've already learnt to spin it.' He turns towards the open entrance and begins to raise the arm behind him to swing the ball, but even before he can bring it around, the ball slips out and falls to the floor with a dull thud. He stands looking at it for a moment, his body still poised to throw a perfect spin ball. The little boy ambles off the bed and retrieves the ball, holding it out to the star cricketer. Shaking his head at the boy, Iftekhar sits back on the cot, his face turned away from me, his arms hidden behind his back again.

Just then, Fatima enters holding the rims of two steaming cups with the pads of her fingertips. One of the cups has a handle missing, and she holds that out to me, extending the other towards Iftekhar, waiting for him to hook his finger in the handle before letting it go.

'How long are you going to be in India?' she asks me, rubbing the tips of her fingers together.

'Not long.'

'You didn't like our country?' she says, sitting down on the cot beside Iftekhar. 'I don't blame you. These harami policemen will catch the people they're not supposed to and won't even touch the real criminals.'

'The men who did this,' I make a wide gesture to encompass the destruction. 'Were they ever caught? I mean the rest of them.'

'Caught?' she laughs mirthlessly. 'The police didn't even look for them. They arrested Sultana for killing two of them and closed the file. We are Musalmaan, behen. This is not our country. The police are not concerned about what happens to us. They don't care about our dead relatives— Ifti's Abu, Ghulam bhai's wife and unborn child, Khala's son and daughter-in-law, my husband.' She lifts one end of her shirt and wipes the corners of her eyes with it. 'No, sister, the police here only catch those they want to, and the rest is all politics. We don't count as citizens, except, of course, when it is time to ask for votes.'

'Enough said, Fatima,' I look up to see the big man I talked to the night before, standing at the door.

'Please forgive me. I didn't recognize you last night. It is hard to trust people at night.'

I shake my head. 'It's all right. I can understand.'

'Baji, this is Ghulam Rasul bhai. He lives next door.'
Iftekhar introduces us.

'Salaam walaikum,' he says, a smile dissecting the hair
around his mouth into a big moustache and a heavy beard,
revealing a thick lower lip and stained, uneven teeth. 'Your
taxi driver is asking how long you're going to be.'

'Oh,' I say, getting up. 'I forgot all about him.' I look
around at the victims in the room. Suddenly, I see them as
inheritors of Daddy's legacy. These could have been the very
same people in Lahore, the people Daddy massacred in his
mindless rage. There are so many apologies I want to offer
them, so many amends I want to make. How can I leave
now? 'If I let him go, will I get a cab back to the hotel?' I
ask.

Ghulam Rasul nods his head. 'Of course. Pardesi in the
next street is a taxi driver. I can call him. He doesn't leave
his house till 10 a.m.'

'Thank you,' I say and step out of the house. Ghulam
Rasul comes with me.

'Why did this happen?' I ask him, walking towards the
cab.

'Who knows,' he says. 'There was a time when we used
to blame the politicians for spreading hatred. But the truth
is, it has never really been politics. Old enmities have come
alive again. It is like 1947 again. Back then, my parents
decided to stay in India after the Partition. They believed this
was their land, their soil. I'm glad they're not alive to see
this. This country doesn't seem ours any more. It just doesn't
seem ours.' He shakes his head as though at the loss of a
civilization.

We walk to where the cab driver is standing against the
side of his car, smoking a thin brown bidi.

'How long will you be?' he asks me, dropping the bidi
on the ground and crushing its smouldering tip with his toe.

'I don't know,' I say. 'You can go if you want to.'

'I'll wait. I just want to know how much longer you will
be.'

'I don't know. Thirty minutes, maybe.'

He nods. 'I'll wait.'

I turn back towards Iftekhar's house.

Fatima is no longer in the room. Instead, an old woman is sitting on the bed beside Iftekhar, rubbing the corner of her white dupatta softly on his arms.

'Baji,' Iftekhar looks up when I enter, 'this is Khala.'

Looking at her, I am reminded of Kubrima, except that her back seems to be bent from pain other than physical.

I smile at her.

'How are you, beti?' she asks me. 'You are Sultana's friend?'

I nod. 'I was in Amritgarh jail for three months. I met Sultana there.'

'You were also in jail?'

I nod.

'What did you do?'

'Baji didn't do anything, Khala. Police kept her in jail on false charges.'

'These policemen,' she says. 'Do they ever catch any real criminals? How did you get out?'

'My lawyer proved that I was innocent.'

'That's good. They appointed a lawyer for Sultana, but he was also one of them, a friend of theirs. He didn't even have a case for Sultana. Not that she needed a case. She only did what the police should have done. But the police don't care. After all, their houses were not burnt to the ground. Their children were not burnt to death. My children were sleeping peacefully. My son had only been married a week. I didn't want to disturb him and his wife. When I heard the commotion outside, I stepped out and I saw this huge flame engulfing one side of my house. I screamed, "Fire! Fire!" Then I turned back inside to warn my son. But even before I could reach the door, that side of the house collapsed before my eyes. That was the end. Nothing was left. Nothing.' Her old eyes fill with tears that spill onto her weathered cheeks. Water collects in the folds of skin making them glisten like strips of cellophane. 'I found the bodies of my children in the rubble. Allah!' She brushes the water out of her eyes with the tips of her fingers. 'There is no justice.'

I walk to the cot and sit beside her, tentatively putting my arm around her bent shoulders.

It is quiet in the room.

'When are you going back to Amreeka, baji?' Iftekhar finally asks.

'Today,'

All eyes turn to me.

'I have a court order,' I explain. 'I have to leave the country. They will not allow me to stay.'

'Will you come back to India to visit?' Iftekhar asks.

'I don't know. I don't think I will be allowed to visit.'

For a minute, there is a remembered desperation in his eyes. Then, he looks away.

'I had to come and see you,' I say softly. 'I'm sorry.' My throat has begun to hurt from the lump that is lodged there. 'I'm sorry about all this. I wish there was something I could do.' How does one apologize for the murder of loved ones, for the betrayal of one's own, for being the daughter of a man who poisoned the very soil meant to nurture? 'I'm sorry,' I say again, getting up.

I bid farewell to everyone and step out of the house. They follow me out the door—Khala, Fatima with the baby on her hip, the boy holding the corner of her shirt, the little girl trailing behind, Ghulam Rasul bhai and Iftekhar, his arms behind his back once again.

'Khuda hafiz, baji,' Iftekhar says, his black eyes mirrors now, of sibling memories. 'Remember me like a brother.'

I step inside the cab and direct the driver to go back to the hotel. I don't look back at the survivors of Karim Gali, the survivors of a madman's rage, who have been unable to salvage their future from it. I close my eyes and replay Iftekhar's words in my mind. 'God protect you, sister. Remember me like a brother.' Daddy had a brother, too; a brother whose name he stole to save his own life. I remember him telling me about that day, when amidst the noise and hoopla of a fair in their vacant lot, Amjad and he vowed to be brothers till eternity. Walking arm in arm, eating clouds of pink cotton candy, they discovered the tattoo man. Amjad walked up to him, and for one paise, the last of his allowance for the fair, got 'Manohar' tattooed on his forearm. Daddy watched the sharp point of the tattoo needle buzz just inside the surface of skin on Amjad's forearm. Fascinated, he watched his name appear in blood in the wake of the needle, and as the grizzled old man wiped off the blood with a dirty rag, he saw fine strokes of Urdu emerge in a shimmering blue. Not wishing to be any less than his newly-found brother, Daddy, too, subjected his forearm to the needle, squeezing his eyes shut as the sharp pain floated against his pale skin. His tattoo read 'Amjad'. Grinning valiantly, holding hands, they walked home and proudly displayed their arms to Amjad's mother. That day, Amjad's mother prostrated herself in prayer seven times instead of five, to ensure that nothing would come between the love of her two sons.

The sun is so clear when I step out of the cab, I can look directly at it without flinching. I know that later the sunlight will blur its circumference and scorch all eyes that dare to look upon it, but for the moment, I tilt my head and let its purity fill my vision. 'Daddy,' I whisper, 'I know your guilt now.' I know that I cannot leave this country till I have delivered his ashes to the penance he craved. I also know I cannot abandon him to an eternity of that penance. I know I cannot leave now, because I am my father's daughter.

chapter ten

Scott is pacing up and down in his room when I enter. He is dressed in a neatly ironed beige linen suit. His luggage is stacked near the door.

'Do you know what time it is? And why are you dressed like that?' he says looking at my sari.

I look at my watch. It is 9:03.

I see my key lying on the bedside table. Picking it up, I turn to go to my room.

'Where were you?' he asks.

'I told you in my note. I went back to see Iftekhar,' I reply from the door, not turning around.

'Oh.'

I step out and walk next door. I hear his footsteps behind me.

'How is he?'

I remember the shadows haunting Iftekhar's face, those mirror-black eyes reflecting only shadows of memories, those arms, crippled stalks; the hands, obscene pink-and-black buds. I remember the cricket ball falling to the ground like a leaden dream. How can I tell him how he is? How can I describe the lives in Karim Gali? Words have died in my throat like aborted embryos. If I open my mouth to speak now, I will only spew their blood.

'Did you find him?'

'Yes,' I say, opening the door and going in. He follows me. 'He was in his house in Karim Gali.'

'How is he?'

'I don't know.' I proceed towards the bathroom.

'What do you mean? You did see him, didn't you?'

'I saw him,'

'And?'

I turn to face him. 'Scott, I'm not going back to the US.'

'Come again?'

'I'm staying here. I'm not going back to the US with you.'

He just stands there with his mouth open.

'I can't go back. Please try to understand. How can I go back? I can't abandon Daddy's ashes in some police lab. I have to fulfil his last wish. There's blood on his soul, Scott. I need to help him atone for that. How can I go back? I can't leave him here and go back to the US. I won't be able to live with myself. I'll stay here till Mr Mathur can figure out a way to get his ashes back.'

'You don't know what you're saying.' He walks to the bed jerkily as if his legs have withdrawn their support, but he doesn't sit down. 'What your father did and suffered half a century ago, is over now. He's not responsible for what is happening in this country. And you are certainly not responsible either. You have your own life to live back in America with me. Mr Mathur said he will contact you when he gets the ashes back. You can't do anything before that. Let him take care of things. I'm not asking you to abandon your father's ashes. But there's nothing you can do here. Don't you see that? Besides, even if you could do something, you can't stay. You have a court order, remember?'

'I'm not going,' I say walking to him. I take the tickets out of his hand, separate the one that has my name on it and tear it into shreds. The little pieces float to the ground. 'I'm not going.'

'You're crazy!' He bends before me and collects the little pieces in his cupped palm. 'Now look what you've done.'

'You go, Scott,' I say, thrusting his ticket in his face.

'Simi.' He takes my shoulders and shakes me. 'What's the matter with you? You can't stay. Don't you understand that? The Indian Government doesn't want you here. If you stay, you'll be doing so illegally. Haven't you been in enough trouble already?'

I shrug his hands off my shoulders. 'So be it,' I say.

'What do you mean?'

'So, I'll be living illegally. I can deal with that. But I can't leave this country. At least, not yet.'

'I won't let you. You're my fiancée and I want you with me in America.' He walks to the phone. 'I'm calling the bell boy.'

'I'm not going, Scott, and you can't make me.'

'Okay.' He hangs up the receiver without dialling. 'Let's suppose for a moment, that you don't go. Where'll you stay? You can't stay here at the hotel. The police will be looking for you.'

'I'll stay with Iftekhar. No one will look for me in that burnt street. The police are too embarrassed to look that way.'

'That's crazy. If you think I'm going to let you wander around in the slums here, exposed to God only knows what forms of terrorism and danger, you're mistaken.' He picks up the receiver again and punches a number. I walk to him and press the disconnect button. I want him to look at me, into my eyes, and understand why I must do this. 'Don't you see?' I say, peering into his face. 'That's exactly why I have to stay—amidst the terrorism and danger, because that's what Daddy created. I want to help undo some of what he started. I want to stay here and and renew the bonds he broke. I want to stay with Iftekhar and help him use his hands again. I want to watch him play cricket again. I want Daddy to stop weeping inside me, Scott. I want to help him find peace.'

He replaces the receiver and leans against the table, his arms crossed over his chest. 'Exactly what did you see in Sultana's house? What happened to you?'

'I saw what Daddy did,' I say almost in a whisper. 'I saw what he started. You should have seen Iftekhar's burnt arms, Khala's grief. She lost her son and daughter-in-law in the fire. These are the very people Daddy hurt, Scott. You should have seen them.'

He reaches to take my face in his hands, his thumbs wiping at tears that I am not even aware have spilled onto my cheeks. 'Get a grip, Simi,' he says softly. 'What you saw has nothing to do with your father. That was over fifty years ago. Come back home with me. There's nothing you can do here. This country's current problems are not of your father's making. You need to realize this and get on with your life. As soon as we get back, we'll set a wedding date.'

I take his wrists and remove his hands from around my face. 'I can't, Scott. I'm sorry.'

'What do you mean you can't? You're wearing my ring. With that ring I thought we made a commitment. I won't let you back out of it. You've got to come back with me.'

I look at the ring on my finger for a long time. With its fine cluster of diamonds shining brilliantly around the large ruby, it looks like a glittering island of blood. Slipping it off my finger, I put it on the table behind him.

'I'm sorry you feel this way, Scott. Go back to the US. I have to stay here till I can get Daddy's ashes. I hope one day, you'll understand why.'

I turn away from him and walk to the door. Opening it, I turn to look at him. He is staring at the ring over his shoulder. Quietly, I close the door behind me and hurry to the elevator.

When I step out on the first floor, I see two policemen standing in the foyer, talking to the man behind the reception desk. My heart begins to pound. I know they are here to ensure I obey the court order. Willing myself to remain calm, I proceed to the main door.

'Madam?'

I stop, my hand on the curved brass handle of the glass door.

'When are you leaving for the airport?'

I turn around slowly to look at the policeman who is now standing a few feet from me, tapping his baton on his heavy black boot.

'In about ten or fifteen minutes. Scott, my fiancé, he's packing. As soon as he's done, we'll leave.'

He looks me up and down, taking note of my bedraggled sari now probably spotted with soot. 'Are you ready?' he asks.

'Of course,' I say, straightening my shoulders.

He tilts his head to one side and looks at me. I look him straight in the eye.

'Where are you going now?'

'Nowhere. Just out for a breath of fresh air for the last time. I love the morning air here. It's so refreshing. It smells so much of ... of India.' He smiles proudly as though he is the owner of the air.

'I'll be back in a few minutes. And we'll leave as soon as my fiancé comes down.'

He nods. I smile. We stand looking at each other for a moment. Then I turn towards the door again, and pushing open the heavy glass doors deliberately, step out.

'One moment, madam.'

I stop mid-step.

'I've got your passport. It will be handed over to you at the airport.'

I nod and go down the two wide stairs. When I look back, he is still standing at the door behind the clear glass, watching me. I smile again and lift my hand in a farewell gesture. Then with slow, nonchalant steps, I walk to the side of the hotel where the garden is located, full of the fragrance and colour of pink and white roses, gladioli, pansies. The cab stand is on the other side, across the driveway. After a few moments of wandering among the flowers, I wonder if it is safe to walk across. I glance towards the main doors of the hotel to see if a khaki uniform is still there, but from where I stand, my eyes go only as far as the gleaming brass border of the door. Frustrated, I look around for another way out. Far at the other end of the garden, I can see a driveway that might not be visible from the door. Walking through the blooms again, I reach what appears to be a service road leading to the main highway. I look at my watch to see that five minutes have already passed since I spoke with the policeman. In another five or ten minutes he will begin to wonder. I look up and down the road for a cab. I see one coming up, but it's already occupied.

Wondering what I will do if I can't get out of here in time, I begin to walk hurriedly away from the hotel. Fortunately, the second cab I hail is not only vacant but the driver also agrees to take me to Karim Gali. I get in the passenger seat as he lowers the meter with a clank. 'Please hurry,' I tell him.

Iftekhar is obviously surprised to see me again. He is in his father's room shovelling debris into a pile when I walk through the doorless entrance of his house and call his name. The shovel falls from his two-digit hand onto the black pile, scattering clouds of soot. Waving his arms before his face and spitting out ashes, he turns around. A fine film of black layers his face.

'Baji, what are you doing here? I thought you were going to Amreeka.'

I shake my head. 'I'm not going, Iftekhar. I want to stay. I want to stay here with you.'

His eyes open so wide, his eyeballs hang suspended for a moment. Then he rushes out of the room, calling, 'Khala, Fatima baji.'

In a moment Fatima comes out of her house with the baby on her hip. 'Did you leave something behind?' she asks me with a smile.

'No.' Iftekhar does not give me a chance to reply. 'Simran baji is not going back to Amreeka. She has come to stay with me.'

The smile disappears from Fatima's face. 'But you were going to leave today. I thought you had an order from the court.'

I nod and smile at her, urging her to understand. 'I don't want to go to America. I want to stay in India.'

'But the order from the court?'

'I'm going to ignore that.'

'They'll come looking for you,' she says. 'There'll be

more trouble for us.'

'Please, Fatima,' I say. 'Please understand. I want to help. All this,' I gesture towards the debris. 'I want to do something to help.'

'We don't need your help,' she says. 'Go back to Amreeka where you belong. We don't want more trouble.'

I look helplessly from her to Iftekhar who is standing to one side, a frown cutting furrows of soot on his forehead.

'I promise I won't be any trouble. No one knows I'm here.'

'The policewallahs are haramzadas. They'll find out where you are and they'll come and hassle us. Go back, Simran. That's the only way you can help us.'

'We'll hide her,' Iftekhar pleads. 'Besides, who will look for a lady like her in these burnt heaps of rubble?'

'They'll look. And they'll create more trouble.'

'Fatima baji, we can't continue to be afraid of the police. Besides, what can they do to us now that hasn't already been done?'

Fatima clutches the child on her hip closer. 'Please go back to Amreeka, Simran.'

'Fatima . . .' We hear Khala's voice from the entrance as she comes waddling in only to stop at the sight of me.

I walk around Fatima and go to the old lady. 'Khala, I've come back. I want to stay here with you all. I don't want to go back to America. I belong here. Can I please stay here with you?'

She opens her arms and I let my head rest on her sagging bosom. 'Beti, you're welcome. We'll think Sultana has come back to us.'

'Khala, it isn't as simple as that,' Fatima says from behind us. 'She's got a court order against her. If she doesn't leave today, the police will look for her. Sooner or later they'll come here, too. It'll only be more police trouble for us.'

'Oh hush, beti,' Khala says. 'Let the police go to jahannum. We can take care of our own. And Simran is our own. She is Sultana's friend.'

I look at Iftekhar. His smile is unashamedly full of expectations. I know I have done the right thing.

'We'll ask Ghulam bhai,' Fatima says, turning away to go back to her house. 'But I'm telling you this is not good.'

'I'll ask him when he comes in the evening,' Iftekhar says quickly, smiling—an expression he seems to have relearned. 'Come, baji, he says. 'Come, sit down.' I turn to look at Fatima's stiff back, then at Khala's encouraging smile and finally at Iftekhar's happy face.

'I was clearing out the rubble from Abu's room. Please sit.' He sticks his left arm in the back of the green chair and lifts it out. I sit down, watching his back move amidst the rubble of wooden beams and furniture through the hole in the room, aware that in a little while, Scott's plane will leave for the United States. I think about my empty house back home and the laughter and death rattle echoing in the silence. Perhaps I could have sold the house and gone to live with Scott in his spacious, jacuzzi-equipped condominium on the seventh floor of a high rise. I have a glimpse of what life could be with Scott: an ideal couple of the nineties, successful in our careers, moving steadily towards a higher tax bracket, saving to buy a luxury home in the suburbs, purchasing boxed relaxation in ClubMed, vacationing in Europe and partying with the politically correct. But then there would also be glorious mornings of waking up in Scott's arms, reading the *Washington Post* in bed, fighting over the sections. There would be relaxed evenings of watching foreign films on television with a paper strip taped to the bottom of the screen to block off the subtitles. There would also be endless nights of love making, reading sex manuals from all over the world, experiencing ecstasies the Chinese way, the African way, the Eskimo way. I sigh, rubbing a slow finger around the skin where only this morning there was a band of glowing diamonds bonding me to him. What had I done? I had thrown away a love and a future to enter this life of fear and hiding in a country that is foreign to me, in a place where I am jeopardizing not only my life but also the lives of these kind, gentle people. And for what? I am not

even sure why I have done this except that I am my father's
daughter.

'Don't mind Fatima baji.' Iftekhar is pushing a blackened
chair with his foot towards the growing pile. 'She is just
afraid. The policewallahs hassled her a lot when she came
back from her parents' house after the fire. They tried to
blame her for the arson. Her parents didn't approve of her
marriage to Ikram bhai. Her parents are very rich, and
Ikram bhai was only a tailor. So she ran away with him. Her
parents didn't speak to her for two years. Then when
Zubeda was born, they came here to see their granddaughter
and accepted Fatima baji back into the family. One of her
brothers still doesn't talk to her. When the arson happened
in her absence, the police found out about her past and her
family's animosity towards her husband. They tried to prove
that it was her family that had avenged themselves by
burning her house and killing her husband. She doesn't like
the police. Don't blame her.'

'Iftekhar,' I say softly. 'Perhaps I shouldn't have come
here. I don't want to jeopardize your lives any further.'

Iftekhar leaves the chair near the pile and comes out of
the room. The layer of soot from this morning has now
thickened into a fine mask on his face, clinging to his hair
and eyebrows and the fuzz on his chin. The front of his shirt
is one big patch of black. 'Baji,' he says, squatting on his
haunches before me. 'I am so happy that you have come to
stay with me. Perhaps I won't be so lonely any more. It is
almost as though Sultana baji is here. We'll take care of the
police. Don't you worry. We'll talk to Ghulam bhai. He'll
help you. Please don't worry.'

I bend down and place a kiss on his cheek, tasting ashes.
'Sultana is lucky to have a brother like you.'

'Do you have any brothers or sisters back in Amreeka?'

I shake my head. 'No, I'm an only child. I missed having
brothers and sisters. I would have loved to have a brother
like you.'

'But I am your brother. From today, please think of me
as a brother.'

Tears prick the corners of my eyes. 'Thank you,' I say softly, 'brother.'

He smiles, his teeth very white in his face, and stands up. 'I had better get some work done. Ghulam bhai says he will help me build this room again. But first I've got to clear out this rubble.'

'Let me help you,' I say, standing up.

'No, no, that's not necessary. You sit.'

'I want to help. I better help you clean it up, especially now that I have to live here.' I smile to let him know it is a joke.

'But your clothes?'

'This,' I say, looking down at my sari. 'You know, I've worn this every day for the past three months. It's time for me to let it go.'

Together, we go about clearing out some of the mess in the room. I pick out the big pieces of burnt furniture, clothing, et cetera, and Iftekhar shovels the little pieces into one pile.

Every once in a while, I see him pull out something from the rubble and rub it on his shirt to look at it wistfully before dropping it on the floor with the others. I wonder how many childhood memories lie hidden under the sooty mountain.

Sometime in the middle of the afternoon, we hear Fatima calling us from the front room.

Iftekhar is wiping off ashes from a fabric lampshade painted in evening colours, of a lake with a single boat on the horizon. The top had probably shown a sky with a moon and stars at one time; now, it is a jagged, charred crown.

'Iftekhar, food is ready,' I hear Fatima say.

'Baji? Simran baji . . .?'

'I've made some for her, too. Come on before it gets cold.'

Iftekhar comes back in. 'Come baji, let us go wash up, Khala and Fatima baji have cooked lunch.'

To my surprise, I realize I'm ravenous. It must be the work. I follow Iftekhar out to the hand pump on the street and let him pump water while I lather my arms and face with the astringent soap he provides and then wash them under the water. Then I move the pump for Iftekhar to do the same. A faint rubbery smell emanates from my arms when I use the towel hanging on a line beside the pump. I look down at my once white sari now blackened with soot. Iftekhar's shirt has fared no better. Smiling in companionship, we proceed to Fatima's house to eat.

Khala and the two children are sitting on a mat before the angeethi Fatima had been lighting this morning. The baby is asleep on a blanket on the floor a little distance away. Fatima is rolling out round balls of flour into large round chapatis and laying them on the cast iron hot plate on the fire. Within moments, the thinned flour fills with air and puffs up. Fatima takes hold of one end and flips it over expertly, twirling it gently with a balled piece of cloth. I remember my mother making chapatis. When I was little, I used to watch her in the kitchen, begging her to let me do some. She even asked one of our Indian friends visiting home to bring back a toy rolling pin and plate so I could roll out my own. As I grew older, I lost interest in making chapatis, delighting only in their taste, so the little red toys had been banished to the kitchen of my doll house, stacked away somewhere in the basement.

Fatima feeds us in silence. Iftekhar and Amjad keep up a lively play and tease as they eat, with Iftekhar stealing pieces of chapati or meat from Amjad's plate and pretending innocence, till Zubeda, unable to hide her giggles, bursts into laughter and Amjad lets out one big wail—'Ifti took it.' Fatima puts a whole chapati on his plate and some more meat to soothe him.

'Do you have any other clothes?' Fatima says looking at my sari as she pours water on my hands outside the house to help me wash off the traces of food.

I shake my head. 'I left them at the police station. I've got to buy some more.'

'If you don't mind wearing salwar-kameez, you can borrow some of mine.'

I look at her surprised.

She wants me to pick out a salwar suit from a tin trunk in her room which has a number of brightly-coloured gold and silver laced dupattas and some salwars folded in one corner along with matching kurtas. 'Please, just give me one that you don't wear any more.'

She pulls out a shimmering green salwar-kameez and a matching dupatta with a thin gold border.

'Oh no. That's beautiful. I couldn't take that.'

'Take it,' she says. 'My husband made this for me when I was younger. I could fit into it before Amjad was born, but now . . .' she gestures towards her waist. 'Besides, I can only wear widow's colours now.'

I shake my head, unable to accept her clothes.

'Take them,' she says, laying them on my shoulder.

I pull the clothes down from my shoulder and thank her quietly. Carrying them back to Iftekhar's house, I ask him to go out for a moment. He steps out, pushing the tin sheet into place over the entrance. I quickly untie the sari and step out of the petticoat. Then pulling on the salwar, I tie the cord. It reaches just over the ankles, a little shorter than it should be, but I love the feel of its cool material against my legs. Except for a little space at the waist, the kurta fits comfortably, too. Then I lay the dupatta on my shoulders. It smells of mothballs and of a musty, cheap perfume. Walking with short, hesitant steps, I open the door of the room and step out.

'Baji, you look beautiful,' Iftekhar says. I look down at the green silk and watch the mid-morning sun glimmer in the material as it would on the still waters of a lake. 'Thank you,' I say to him and proceed towards Fatima's house. She is sitting on the cot, the baby at her breast. Khala is clearing the kitchen. They both look up when I enter.

'Ikramu used to make beautiful clothes,' Khala says softly.

I see Fatima's chin quiver as she attempts to smile at me. 'It looks beautiful on you. I have a few more suits that Ghulam bhai saved from the fire. You can wear those.

They're of no use to me now.'

'Thank you,' I tell her simply.

I'm sitting on the floor of Fatima's house in the half light of dusk, learning the words of an Urdu nursery rhyme from Zubeda, when we hear the sound of wheels on the gravel in front of the house. Amjad is sitting beside me, uttering intermittent words of the rhyme. Khala is rolling the beads of her rosary and patting the baby's head, lulling him to sleep. Iftekhar has gone to buy milk for the children. Fatima is outside, washing clothes at the hand pump.

'That sounds like Ghulam Rasul's bicycle,' Khala says, wrapping her beads in a piece of white fabric. 'But you stay here. Let me go out and make sure.'

All day, the fear of being tracked down has hardly entered my mind. And now, suddenly, I'm scared. I watch as Khala lifts the burlap hanging from the entrance and steps out, letting the thick curtain fall back into place. I hear soft voices outside before Ghulam Rasul bhai enters with Khala behind him.

'Welcome back,' he says.

'I don't know if I've done the right thing, Ghulam bhai.'

'There'll be trouble, of course. But we'll take care of it. Don't you worry. This is your home. This is your land as much as it is ours. You did the right thing by staying.'

I smile at him gratefully. 'Fatima thinks the police will bother you all because of me.'

'I'm sure they will, once they trace you here. But that might not be for a long time. Don't worry. We'll take care of you.'

'Thank you.'

'There's only one thing,' he looks at me uncomfortably.

'What is it, Ghulam bhai? Please, tell me.'

'Well, Khala told me you've come to stay with Iftekhar. He's a grown boy now. It does not seem right for you to stay alone with him.'

'But he's like my brother,' I say quickly.

'Sure, of course. But even then. Listen, Simran, why don't you stay here with Fatima? Khala says she'll move to

Iftekhar's house. What do you say, Khala?'

Khala nods her white head. 'That will be the right thing.'

I nod. 'Of course, that will be all right. I'm sorry I've disrupted your lives like this.'

'No, you haven't. We're happy to have you here,' Ghulam Rasul says.

'Let me tell Fatima,' Khala says, leaving the room.

As soon as she leaves, Ghulam Rasul steps closer to me. 'You'll have to be very careful. Don't go out of the house. If you need to buy anything, send Iftekhar. No one must see you here. I'll tell everyone else to be careful about what they say to people. These are not good times. You can't trust anyone.'

That night when Fatima and I are making a bed for me on the floor, Khala walks to a settee in a corner covered with a brown bedspread. She removes the cover to reveal a blackened trunk dented in places, and opens it. 'This trunk is the only thing that the fire didn't burn,' she says. 'It is from my daughter-in-law's dowry.' She rubs a loving hand along its sides. 'Tarannum. She used to have a beautiful voice. Sitting out there in their room, I would hear her sing to my son. Songs from the talkies. Beautiful songs of love— "Saath jeeyenge, saath marenge (Together we will live, together we shall die)." Allah loved her voice too, and heard the words.' She sighs deeply and brings out a brand new white sheet from the trunk. When Fatima and I open it to spread it on the makeshift bed, acrid fumes of smoke unfurl from its folds and pervade the room.

Lying on the floor, inhaling the miasma of their lives, staring at the white ceiling emblazoned with flags of soot, I finally allow my mind to let down the barriers against thoughts of Scott. He must be flying over the Atlantic now, almost home. I wonder if I will ever see him again. In my heart there is a pain as though a portion of it has been gnawed out, and every breath of air I breathe in worries the exposed nerves.

Scott and I have known each other since pre-school. We used to do everything together—from playing with his trucks in the sandbox to my reading spicy portions of a Harlequin romance to him in my room, forcing him to stay and listen, with the promise that I would do with him, all the things that the heroine of the novel did with her man. We exchanged our first real kiss after that, arranging our bodies on the bed with me on top, pretending Scott had pulled me down in a frenzy of passion. I remember sticking my chewing gum to my palate so it wouldn't interfere with the kiss, but when I opened my mouth to allow him to do all the things they did with tongues in the book, the gum dislodged and fell into his mouth. 'Yuk,' Scott said, spitting it out. We began to laugh then. I can still remember how Scott's body shook under me and my body moved with his motion. I think I fell in love with him then.

In our second year of high school, when fear of Farzana's grandmother forced me to transfer to another school, we started seeing other people, but the time we continued to spend together amounted to a whole lot more than we spent with our dates. Not so much because we were passionately in love, but because we had so much fun together, we didn't want it to stop. After high school, we both chose the same college, supporting each other through the tough days of transition. After one semester at college, we began to date other people again, still fitting in dates with each other on a regular basis. We were comfortable with the arrangement till the time Scott met Emily, the quintessential bimbo—a blonde, blue-eyed girl with breasts that spilled out like sun-softened butter over her low-cut dresses. We decided to stop dating each other then; or rather, he decided and I deluded myself into the spirit of buddyhood, sleeping on tear-soaked pillows and feigning interest in his recounts of dates with Emily. Until one day, sitting in the tavern at school, twirling fibres of pizza cheese around our tongues, Scott told me Emily couldn't understand his removing the slices of pepperoni from the pizza. 'She says, what's the use of ordering a pepperoni pizza if all I'm going to eat is a cheese pizza?'

'You should have told her you like the smell of pepperoni in your cheese, not the actual pepperoni,' I told him. He looked at me for a moment. He looked at me differently, like he was seeing me for the first time.

'She doesn't understand why I spot toothpaste on my brush instead of spreading it in a straight line,' he said, looking directly into my eyes.

'You should have told her it's because you hate it to slither off.'

'She doesn't understand why the first thing I do when I French kiss is probe her palate with my tongue.'

'You should have told her it's because you're checking for hidden gum that might plop into your mouth.'

He began to laugh then, soft shouts of elation as if he had just made a great discovery, and I began to laugh with him. When we recovered, he took my hand in his and asked me if I could stop being his friend.

'What do you mean?'

'I'd like you to be my girlfriend,' he said.

'Why?' I asked him, wanting to hear an answer I knew he wouldn't give, but prepared to accept his offer anyway.

He shrugged his shoulders. 'You're the only one who understands me.'

I sighed and said yes.

'She doesn't understand why I yell "Oh Enlightened One" every time I have an orgasm,' he said suddenly.

I scrolled his life in my mind hurriedly to make a connection, but I didn't get a single clue. 'Gotcha,' he said. 'You don't know because I don't know either, but I like the sound of it, and you've never heard me yell anything, because you and I, we've never done it.'

We became lovers then, in our freshman year at college, and he yelled, 'Oh Enlightened One' every time we had sex, and together we started reading about Zen Buddhism.

We continued going steady through college and through graduate school. When I moved back home to be with Daddy after Mummy's death, we called each other almost every day. He came home for weekends and holidays, and we spent every second together. Even though we never fell passionately in love, we had passionate sex, and we enjoyed it like we enjoyed everything that we did together, and we knew somehow that we would end up marrying each other, because we couldn't bear having to explain the idiosyncrasies of our lives.

If only I could have explained Daddy's guilt to him, I think, wishing that he could have fit into this groove as comfortably as he had in all the others in my life. I close my eyes, knowing that from now on, I will miss him as long as I live.

The following day I slip into life at Karim Gali. After my morning ablutions at the hand pump, I help Fatima cook breakfast for the others. Then I go over to Iftekhar's house and we resume work in his father's room.

'His bed used to be right here.' Iftekhar points to a spot. 'I brought a stray puppy home once. I must have been ten then, or maybe eleven, I'm not sure. But I remember we were having final exams at school. It was my science paper the next day, but I was so taken with the puppy that I played with it all day and all evening. Abu kept telling me to study, but I wouldn't listen. Finally, he got so upset that he took the puppy to his room and said that I wouldn't get him back till the exams were over. That night, he put a loose string around the puppy's neck and tied it to his bedpost right here; you know, so the puppy wouldn't wander off at night. By the next morning, the puppy was dead—strangled. It had twirled around the post till the string tightened into a noose. Abu was so upset, he carried it to the lot behind our house and dug a grave to bury it. But I was so angry with Abu that I didn't talk to him for days. You know, I think I never quite forgave him for killing that puppy. Then when I saw him in the flames, I had to tell him that I forgave him; that I loved him. I tried to beat the fire out around him, yelling at him, trying to wake him up. Such a deep sleep. He never used to sleep so deeply. When he finally awoke, my hands . . .' He looks down at the stubs of his fingers. 'And I couldn't even save him. The beam from the door fell on him. "Get out of here, Ifti," he kept saying. Ghulam bhai pulled me out just in time.' He sits down on his haunches in the space where his father's cot used to be, his face buried in the burnt flesh of his arms, his shoulders shaking. Gently, I lower myself beside him and, laying an arm around him, let him weep. After a while, he sniffs and cleans his nose on the sleeve of his shirt. A blotch of black transfers to the tip of it. I reach out and clean it with my green dupatta edged with gold. We rise quietly and get back to work.

Sitting with everyone in Fatima's house after the meal that evening, we hear the scraping shuffle of a rickshaw coming up Karim Gali and stop in front of the houses. Ghulam Rasul gets up and tiptoes towards the burlap curtain. I watch his shadow loom big against the fabric as he lifts it to look outside. We all watch him quietly, our breaths held as though by mutual consent. 'Ammi,' Amjad says softly. Immediately, Fatima's hand shoots out to cover his mouth. 'Sh. Be quiet.'

'Simran,' Ghulam Rasul bhai whispers, 'Come here.'

I get up and tiptoe to stand beside him, peering out through the side of the curtain. In the street below, I see a rickshaw and moonlight shining on a blonde head. Even before he gets off the rickshaw and turns towards the houses, I know.

'Scott,' I call and rush out into the street, my arms flailing in the air. 'Oh, Scott. What are you doing here? I thought you would be in Batonsville by now.'

I fall into his arms and cling to him. He folds his arms around me. 'Don't ever leave me again,' he whispers.

I draw back. 'Why are you here, Scott?'

He looks up and down the street hurriedly, then towards the rickshaw driver. 'What do you think?' I hear him say.

'I don't know . . . that shout of excitement. Take her inside. I'll check around,' the rickshaw driver replies in perfect English in a voice I know. I walk to the front of the rickshaw and look into the face of the driver to see deep brown eyes and a bushy moustache. There is a dirty piece of fabric tied haphazardly around the forehead, covering his hair, and on his body there is a tattered shirt. White, mud-stained pajamas are tied around his ankles with pieces of cord. On his feet he is wearing dirt-crusted leather sandals.

'Arun?' I whisper in wonderment.

He nods. 'Go inside. Scott, take her inside.'

I lead Scott into Fatima's house and introduce him as a very close friend from America. Then I seat him on the cot and bombard him with questions. Khala, Ghulam Rasul, Iftekhar, Fatima, they all look on with a tolerant look on their faces as we talk rapidly in English.

'What are you doing here? Why didn't you leave?'

'I couldn't. The police, they were waiting for me in the hotel's lobby. As soon as they saw me, they pounced on me and demanded to know where you were.'

'You didn't . . .'

'Of course I didn't tell them. That's why we had to come the way we did, Arun in disguise as my rickshawallah. I told those police guys I wanted to go on a ride in the rickshaw to see the city. They followed me halfway but Arun obviously knows this city better than they do. He took such short cuts, I thought we were in a maze. We lost them somewhere between here and the main road.'

'But didn't they recognize Arun?'

Scott chuckled. 'Apparently not. I'd called Arun about you earlier. We had to warn you that they are looking for you everywhere. I think they talked to the cabby who brought you here yesterday. They'll probably be here looking for you soon. But there was no way of getting the message to you except personally. So Arun told me he'd get a rickshaw and meet me at the corner of the hotel at 8 p.m. I thought he'd be riding the rickshaw, you know, as a passenger. I didn't know he'd be driving it, so when I stood at the corner, the two cops only a few feet from me, this rickshaw driver stops beside me and says, "Saab, you want to go?" in this really pidgin English. I almost said no, but when I looked at him and he winked, I knew it was Arun.'

'Was he angry?'

'Who? Arun? You know, actually he didn't seem the least bit surprised when I told him about your decision.'

'And you? Are you still angry with me?'

'Not any more. This is sort of fun. Scary, but fun.' He chuckles excitedly like a little boy on a great adventure.

'Scott,' I lay my head on his shoulder. 'You're crazy. You know that?'

He chuckles again and straightens up to pull something out of his pocket. In a moment his hand appears with my engagement ring gleaming in his palm. 'Simi,' he says, solemnly. 'Now that we're together again, will you consider being engaged to me again?'

'I don't know. I mean, you're not here of your own free will. I mean, those policemen detained you. Otherwise, you would have been in the good old US of A by now. And you would have been better off that way, believe me.'

'Whoa, hold on. What makes you so sure I would have been better off? I love you. I wouldn't have gone back to the US without you. You surprised me yesterday with your sudden decision of wanting to stay here. It took me a few minutes to get used to the idea, but I wasn't going to take that plane without you. I don't have to go. My visa is valid for three months.'

'Oh, Scott,' I say, watching the irises darken in his aquarelle eyes. 'I love you, and yes, I would like to be engaged to you again,' I say, holding out my ring finger to him.

Picking up the ring, he slips it back on my finger. Its cool weight feels, oh, so comforting. I place my head back on his shoulder and smile happily at our audience. They all sit with soft smiles on their faces, not understanding our conversation, yet comprehending the entire scene.

Arun walks in with Ghulam Rasul following him.

'It appears we are safe for the moment,' he says, then realizing the love flowing in the room, he halts at the door. 'What's going on?' he asks in Hindi.

'They got engaged,' Khala says before any of us can answer.

'Again?' Arun mutters under his breath in English. He squats beside Khala and extending his hands to the fire, turns towards me. 'We've got to get you out of here. They'll find you here. They've already talked to the taxi driver who brought you here yesterday.'

I nod. 'I don't want to endanger the lives of these wonderful people, but where can I go?'

'Are you serious about staying on in India?'

I nod.

'You know that you might have to wait years before Mathur can win the case.'

'I have no other choice.' I wonder if Scott has told him about how I intend to use the time.

'You do,' Arun says. 'I was discussing this with Scott. In this country, bribery works better than the legal system.'

'What do you mean?'

'Oh, only that it is easy to find people who will do anything for a price. Even steal a particular box full of ashes from a police godown. Scott was telling me how a policeman wanted to buy your Nikon camera. If you don't mind losing that, we can use it as an effective bribe.'

'Can you really do that?'

He nods. 'But first, we have to make sure you are safe. It'll take me some time to find the ideal official who will do the deed. Till that time, you've got to stay away from the police.'

'Where can I go?'

He extends his hands to the fire and holds them over the smouldering coals. 'I have a place in mind,' he says. Fiery haloes glow in the crevices between his fingers.

chapter eleven

His name is Kalida. Actually, his name is Kalinath Bandopadhyay. People call him Kalida, 'da' being the suffix people from Bengal confer upon anyone deserving the respect of an elder brother. Kalida is in his early fifties. At least, that's the age of some of the deep lines on his face. His actual age may be several years less or more. He is a fragile man, as fine-boned as a hand-crafted porcelain doll. His thin face is covered with a shaggy salt-and-pepper beard, unlike his hair, which is almost entirely grey, parted in the middle and tucked neatly behind his ears to fall almost to his shoulders. One of his hands lies in lifelong repose against his belly, a victim of a homemade bomb during his exploits in the Naxalite movement in Bengal—a communist effort to liberate the masses from the yoke of feudal lords.

Kalida is a peace activist. He runs an organization called CCPH—Citizens for Communal Peace and Harmony. Arun reveres him like an elder brother. It is to Kalida that Arun takes me. But he doesn't tell me about him right away.

Dressed in Fatima's green salwar-kameez with a large, tent-like black burkha covering me, I sit in Arun's rickshaw early the next morning and ride through the streets of Amritgarh, peering out through the fine cotton netting over my eyes. No suspicious eyebrows are raised at a Muslim woman in purdah sitting in a rickshaw driven by a filthy, ragged rickshaw driver, pedalling strenuously to the bus station. Abandoning his rickshaw in the rickshaw stand of the station, Arun picks up the cotton bag lying at my feet containing the three salwar suits Fatima has given me, and positioning me in a corner beside a closed stall, walks to the ticket window to stand in line. I have no idea where I am headed. Arun does not tell me. 'Trust me,' he says. I do.

Engulfed by my burkha, I stand secluded from the crowds swarming around me. Even this early in the morning, the bus station is like a carnival, with fruit sellers, news-stands, juice machines, makeshift cafés and carts full of peanuts. Travellers weighed down with luggage stand around, awaiting buses to far and near destinations, waving away flies and peering hopefully at conductors calling out bus routes. Wide-eyed children pull away from their mothers to create temporary playgrounds around jostling feet. An old beggar, his feet bound heavily with newspapers and rags, rattles some coins in a tin container as he meanders around people.

Soon Arun and I board a bus which already seems full. I stay right behind him as he checks the assigned numbers on his tickets against the backs of seats. Our seats are occupied by a frail woman and a little boy. The skin on the woman's face is thin and dark with a deep shadow of wrinkles just under the surface, as though even the softness of wrinkles would mar the hard symmetry of her life. Her head is covered with a white malmal dupatta which clings to her oiled hair as though glued to it. Beside her sits a little boy, his hair knotted on top of his head and covered with a square red rag with one edge hanging over the middle of his forehead like a bloody gash. 'Mai, you are sitting on the wrong seats,' Arun says, stepping into the narrow aisle.

The woman looks at Arun with a pleading smile, allowing the lines around her lips to reveal themselves. Opening a knot at the end of her dupatta, she removes some crumpled bills and pushes them towards Arun. 'Bhaiji, can you buy me two tickets for Jhakher? I don't know which window to go to.' Arun turns to look at me. I nod from under my heavy covering.

'Achha,' he says, taking the money. 'I'll buy you the

tickets, but you have to get up. I want to seat my wife before I go.' The woman gathers a bag from under the seat and gets up hurriedly, pulling the boy by his arm. I slide in as she moves into the aisle, and occupy the seat by the window. I can feel the boy's eyes on me as his thin frame is jostled uncontrollably by the passengers moving to and fro in the aisle. Reaching from under the burkha, the bangles Fatima has lent me jangling on my arm, I reach for the boy's hand, urging him to sit beside me. He resists for a moment before his mother nudges him and he reclaims his seat, sitting on the edge of it, looking straight ahead. As Arun leaves the bus, the woman moves to a window, and she and I follow him with our eyes as he elbows his way through the crowd to stand in line again. A few minutes later, he reappears with two tickets in his hand. He helps the woman and boy find their seats before returning to sit beside me. 'So far so good,' he says settling back into the narrow space.

A few minutes later, the driver's door opens and a big, turbaned man climbs onto the seat, tooting his horn once before gunning the engine. I hear a sharp whistle behind me from the conductor and we begin to move, edging out of the station with endless manoeuvres in reverse and first gear, backwards and forward, backwards and forward, missing the shanks of several buses by mere inches, till we are finally on the road. I reach out and open the window beside me, looking out at life on the streets of Amritgarh yet again; this time, through the grey haze of diesel smoke. Beside me, Arun, dressed like a rickshawallah, reads a crumpled Hindi newspaper.

We ride in silence like a newly-married couple, avoiding any conversation, verbal or visual, a little shy in each other's company, a little embarrassed in public. The bus rumbles on, heavy with its overload of passengers, first through the streets of Amritgarh and then on the highway. Suddenly it veers to one side and my hand shoots out from under the burkha to grasp the rail of the seat before me. Just as suddenly, Arun's hand covers mine on the rail. My breath catches. I turn towards him, seeking out his eyes in the

crocheted web of his face. Gently, he unclasps my hand from
the rail and holding it with one hand, reaches with the
fingers of the other to remove my ring.

I pull my hand away. 'I'm sorry,' he bends and whispers
in my ear. 'Diamonds on the hand of a rickshawallah's
wife?' Taking my hand again, he slides the ring off and
drops it in the pocket on his chest. Patting the pocket, he
looks at me and smiles. 'I'll keep it safe,' he says, softly. I
turn away and gaze out of the window again, acutely aware
of the bareness of my finger, but knowing that it is as
necessary as my burning my prison sari in Karim Gali's
vacant lot and giving my pocket book to Scott to take back
to the hotel. I persuaded Ghulam bhai to use most of the
money in it to rebuild Karim Gali, keeping a few hundred
rupees for myself wadded up securely at the bottom of the
bag I have borrowed from Fatima. My watch, I gave to
Fatima as a gift.

'Jhakher,' the conductor calls out loudly as the bus pulls
up before a roadside eating place. I watch the old woman
gather her belongings quickly and push through standing
passengers to get off the bus, the boy following on her heels.
'We're almost there now,' Arun tells me. We are waiting for
the driver to return when I see a policeman board the bus.
The broad metal buckle of his belt is cutting into a bloated
belly, and a thick baton is swinging in his hand. I see him
moving down the aisle, stepping over the luggage on the
floor, squeezing his belly past passengers in the aisle,
advancing directly towards me. Clutching my hands tightly
in my lap, I turn my head away, watching him from the
corner of my eyes. Beside me I can feel Arun tense as he
picks up his paper again and smoothening out the folds,
holds it before his face. For a moment the policeman's hand
rests on the rail of our seat as he waits for a young man to
step aside before proceeding down the aisle to the rear of the
bus. Arun continues his pretence of reading the paper.

A few minutes after we have been on the road again, the
bus stops and Arun gets up.

'Chalo,' he tells me loudly in Hindi to move, pulling out

my bag from under the seat. He makes his way to the front, deliberately avoiding the rear exit even though that is closer to us. Gathering the folds of my burkha around me, I follow him, descending the bus even as the conductor blows his whistle.

There is a lone cart on the side of the road, with peanuts heaped around a little clay pot holding a smouldering piece of wood. A man leans against it smoking the stub of a bidi.

He watches us as we get off and skirt around his cart to walk along the narrow lane running through lush fields.

'Now are you going to tell me where we are?' I ask Arun.

'This is still Jhakher,' he says.

'What's in Jhakher?'

'Kalida.'

'Who's Kalida?'

'You'll see.'

'Arun,' I say exasperated. 'Why can't you tell me? At least I'll be able to prepare myself.'

'You don't have to prepare yourself for Kalida,' he says, walking at a steady pace.

The black sandals Fatima has lent me are a size too small. Their criss-cross design over my toes begins to bite into my flesh, and I start to lag behind.

'Come on,' Arun says, holding the strap of my bag on his shoulder and peeling off his moustache. He reaches up and pulls off his turban and shaking his hair free, combs it back with his fingers. 'It isn't too far now.' The cultivation ends and the path winds, entering a wooded area, and suddenly before us is a clearing with a peepul tree in the centre with its branches spread wide like a layered green cloud. Across the clearing is a large hut made of baked mud, on a low plateau. The entrance to the hut is wide and open with a roped bamboo door pushed against a wall. I follow Arun into the clearing towards the peepul tree under which I can see a little man with grey hair holding a clay figurine in the palm of one hand and caressing it with his fingertips, shaping and reshaping its yielding flesh. He doesn't look up as we approach. Arun and I stand watching him for a while, then Arun finally breaks the silence and says, 'Kalida?'

He looks up then. Eyes, onyx black and keen like freshly-sharpened blades, peer at us from sunken sockets. 'Oh, Arun. Come, come,' he says, laying the figurine in a wooden work tray carefully. Arun bends forward and touches his feet, then squats at the foot of a thick root that is growing like a knotted appendage of the earth. He begins to talk to Kalida in a language I don't understand but know is Bengali because of friends from that community I have back in the US. I hear my name mentioned and Kalida looks my way. He doesn't smile, but a warmth emanates from his face as if he is directing all the energies that build a smile towards me.

I lower myself to the ground a little away from where they sit.

'You can take off your burkha now,' Arun says. 'You're safe here.'

I stand up again and untie the strings of the garment. Removing the headpiece, I smoothen my hair down into its braid self-consciously.

Arun and Kalida continue talking. I sit for a while watching their lips move in rounded intonations of words that make no sense to me. Then I turn to look at the figurine lying on its back in the tray. It is a six-inch figure of a woman with ridiculously large breasts and nipples as big and round as jelly beans. Four arms are growing from her sides. I reach out and pick her up when suddenly Kalida stops talking and takes the figurine from my fingers. 'It is not finished,' he says softly in English. 'Shurajit,' he calls out, turning his head towards the hut. Within moments, a young man dressed in a rough cotton kurta-pajama comes hurrying out towards us. His black hair is like a clown's shaggy wig.

'Take this inside.' Kalida gestures towards the work tray.

I watch the young man carry the tray inside, feeling like a little child who has been admonished for touching a fragile object d'art. After a moment I get up and begin to wander about the compound.

Arun finds me amidst the trees sometime later.

'I'm leaving now, Simran.'

Panic grips me. 'Why? Where are you going?'

'I've got to get back to work.'

'But you can't leave me here alone.'

'What do you mean, alone? I'm leaving you with Kalida.'

'Kalida? You can't just leave me. What will I do here? Make clay figurines of big breasted women with four arms?'

'They're miniatures of Durga, the goddess.'

'Oh.'

'You can help Kalida and the other peace activists run this organization while you wait for your father's ashes.'

'Is that what he does? Is he a peace activist?'

'Uhm. He's head of the CCPH—Citizens for Communal Peace and Harmony. It's a very well-known organization, in both the Hindu and Muslim communities. It's really like an umbrella organization for other, smaller units. And Kalida—he's one of the most respected men in Amritgarh. You're safe from the police here. No one will look for an illegal alien in Kalida's house.'

'Arun, I don't know if Scott told you, but while I'm waiting, I want to help people like Sultana's brother.'

'Yes, he told me. But you know you can't stay with Iftekhar. The CCPH is like a liaison between people like Iftekhar and the government. It helps people like him by making sure their voice is heard. That's one of the reasons I brought you here.'

Wondering if I will be satisfied staying on the periphery of hurting lives, I begin to ask him to tell me a little more about the organization. But he holds up his hand. 'You'll find out more about CCPH by living here,' he says. 'I've got to go now. Kalida will take care of you.'

I stand watching his receding back through the branches of trees as long as I can, feeling the strange emptiness in my heart that follows farewells. Then I walk back to the peepul. Kalida is no longer sitting amidst its roots. I turn towards the open door of the hut, peering through the sun-dazzled entrance to see if he is inside. He is sitting on a mat in front of a low writing desk. My bag is lying beside him. Behind him, the wall is lined with books stacked together on crude wooden shelves built from the floor to mid-wall. As I enter, he turns around to look at me. 'Will you work with us?' he asks in English.

I nod half-heartedly, not quite sure what he expects of me.

'Good,' he says. 'Then you must accept this as your home as long as you live here.'

I stand looking at him, composing words of gratitude in my mind, but before I can utter them, he says, 'Go to the kitchen over there and ask Shurajit where the broom is. The courtyard needs cleaning.'

All thank-yous freeze on my lips and I look at him surprised. But having dismissed me thus, he has already turned back to the papers on his desk. Seething with resentment, I turn in the direction he has pointed and enter the kitchen. It is a small room alternately stripped with sun and shade. Narrow apertures are cut all along the east wall through which sunlight pours in thick beams as though from a projector. Revealed at the end of one beam, I see Shurajit squatting before a kerosene stove stirring something in a pot. Smoke from the stove and the pot rises, mingles and diffuses in the particles of light. Shurajit looks towards me as I open the door.

'Where's the broom?' I ask him in Hindi.

He smiles and points to a corner where a handful of long yellowish grass lies tied together with a piece of string.

I pick it up and walk out of the room, pausing near Kalida's desk for a moment where he continues to work, unmindful of my presence. Throwing my head back and holding the broom stiffly by my side, I step down into the courtyard. The ground looks clean and dirtless, but bending from the waist, I begin to sweep with short jerky strokes. Clouds of dust rise like smoke from a dragon's mouth and swirl close to the ground from which Shurajit suddenly materializes like an apparition. 'Sprinkle some water to calm the dust,' he says, pouring water from a glass into his cupped palm and sprinkling it around in a sanctifying circle. The dust settles on the packed mud like some great animal whose wrath has been contained.

'Come,' Shurajit says. 'I have made you some tea.'

I pick up the broom and follow him into the kitchen. Dropping it back into its corner, I choose a beam of sunlight close to him and sit down under its radiance.

'Here,' Shurajit says, balling a rag in his hand and lifting a pot to pour thick golden tea into a china mug.

'Kalida asked you to sweep the courtyard,' he makes a statement.

I nod.

'Trust Kalida,' he says, smiling. 'He knows I swept it this morning. Don't be upset with Kalida. Cleaning the house is the first job he assigns to anyone who comes here. He just wants you to know this isn't a guesthouse. That's his way of telling you that the work has to be shared. It's sort of symbolic of everyone working together for the country. You know, like a kind of brotherhood.'

'What do you do?'

'You mean here or in my profession?'

'Both.' I am surprised that he has a profession other than the work in this commune.

'Well, here I'm cook, domestic help, legal advisor and Kalida's personal assistant all rolled in one, but otherwise, I'm a lawyer.'

'A lawyer? You mean you actually practise law?'

'Sure. Although most of my clients don't pay—in monetary terms that is. Most of them are poor farmers or menial workers. I fight their cases for them and they bring me grain or vegetables or jute baskets or banana-leaf platters or shoes or whatever they can manage. One woman even knitted me a sweater. Her husband died without writing a will and his relatives claimed the acre of land he had owned. I'm pretty successful, really.'

I look at him then. I mean, really look at him closely. With his smooth brown skin and shock of unruly hair, he hardly looks old enough to be in college, let alone a graduate from law school. Besides, a wrinkled cotton kurta-pajama and dirty fingernails somehow don't fit my image of a successful lawyer.

'So, where are you from? You've got a strange foreign accent.'

'Oh. Sorry—about the accent, I mean. I'm from around here.'

'Amritgarh?'

I nod.

He stares at me deliberately, then laughs. 'It's okay. You don't have to tell me. The fact that you're here to help the cause is enough. The rest is your personal business.'

I smile at him gratefully.

'Drink your tea,' he says, pointing towards the steaming mug. 'I don't know how much sugar you take, but I put in two spoons.'

'It's all right. I've learnt to appreciate really sweet tea in India.'

'Aha, so you're not from India. I thought as much,' he teases me.

'Oops,' I say smiling. 'You're right. I'm not from India. I'm American.'

'You've come all the way from America to help CCPH? Wow.'

'Well, not really,' I say, picking up the mug full of tea and taking a tentative sip. 'But I'm happy to be here.'

'Let's hope you can still say that after a few days. It's a pretty rough life, especially for someone who is used to the luxuries of America.'

'I don't think I'll have a problem.'

'That's the spirit,' he says, putting the larger pot back on the stove. 'Actually, it isn't that bad. We eat three full meals, we have a roof over our heads, we have clothes to wear. What else can one ask for? And if we have a problem, we go to Bishan. He's our problem solver. Actually, he's our handyman. No, wait a minute. He's our printer—or is that, publisher? Let's just say, he's everything else that I'm not.

He's also Kalida's driver. And most of all, he makes sure we live comfortable lives.'

'How many others live here?' I ask him.

'That's it. Bishan, Kalida, I, and now you. Most of the time it's just us, but during a rally or demonstration, we get truckloads of guest-activists who help in the organization. It's like a wedding party then. You think you can handle more than a hundred people? You'll have to be our official hostess, considering you're the only woman resident of this house—along with Bishan, of course, who isn't any less than a woman on Sundays when he washes his hair. You won't believe, his hair is down to here.' He touches the back of his thighs.

I laugh. 'I think I'm going to enjoy being the hostess here. And now I think it's about time the hostess helped with the other chores. What can I do?'

'You can take this tea to Kalida,' he says, pouring some more of the brew into another mug. 'I've already prepared lunch, but you can help me make dinner later on.'

'Okay,' I say, getting up with Kalida's tea in my hand.

'Oh, didi,' he says, as I reach the door. 'We all wash our own dishes here.' He indicates the empty tea mug.

Embarrassment makes my cheeks feel warm. 'Of course. I'm sorry,' I say, coming back and, putting Kalida's mug back on the floor, I pick up my own empty one to wash it from the water contained in large urns standing in a corner under a faucet.

'It gives you the freedom to spit in your dishes if you want to,' he says, looking at me with a twinkle in his eyes.

'Excuse me?'

'If you know you have to wash your own dishes, you won't refrain from spitting in them if it pleases you.'

'Sure,' I say laughing, 'just don't give me your mug next time. Washed or not, I'd hate to drink out of something you've spit in.'

I pick up Kalida's tea and leave the kitchen.

Kalida is still sitting at his low desk, writing with a gold-topped fountain pen. 'Kalida, tea,' I say, approaching him.

'Ah,' he screws the top back on his pen and taking the mug from me, says, 'Sit,' patting the floor beside him. 'I am composing an agenda for a peace rally we are having on 6th December to observe the fifth anniversary of the demolition of the Babri Masjid. Arun told me you were engaged in desktop publishing in America. We don't have a computer, but there is an old printing press in the room at the back. Bishan runs it for us. You can help him. Here, look at this.' He hands me a legal pad with a full handwritten page of beautiful penmanship, the letters flowing gracefully across in calligraphic cursive.

'I heard about this back home,' I say, reading the speech. 'The American media covered it in some detail.' In fact, Daddy's last wish was the consequence of this very incident. The news of the demolition and the subsequent riots pervaded so much of the news media that I was unable to keep it from him. It was like blood oozing from multiple wounds on a body. I could only stem so many. I didn't let him listen to any news or read any newspapers covering world events for days, but how was I to know that every avenue of communication was suspect? One day he received a letter in the mail from a local Hindu organization asking all Hindus to unite and support the demolition by donating money for the erection of a temple in its stead. He crumpled the letter and threw it in the trash. But deep in the night, I felt his presence by my bedside. Hovering over a dream realm, I felt him take my hand from where it lay limp in sleep on the comforter, and sit holding it for a long time. Then I heard him whisper, 'I didn't deserve you. I thought you were sent to us to compensate your mother for me. I loved you because I loved her, but you brought hope into my life. Will you be my hope in death, too?' Instinctively, my fingers tightened around his, afraid. 'No,' he said. 'Don't worry about me. I'm fine. I won't do anything crazy. I just want you to promise me something. Promise me, that after I die, you will take my ashes to India and scatter them on the border of India and Pakistan.' Then he brought my hand to his lips. A single teardrop accompanied that kiss. When he left my room, I fell asleep again, his words no more than a memory of a dream. But that teardrop emblazoned my skin. It was as indelible as the tattoo he wore on his forearm. Unwittingly, Arun had delivered me into the very heart of that promise.

'My English is not very good,' Kalida says. 'Correct it if there are mistakes. In fact, you can be our official proofreader.'

I read the speech carefully again, grateful now for being allowed to help. He gives me another paper, and I read that as well, inserting a punctuation mark here, correcting a preposition there. I fall into the pattern of work as naturally as though I have been doing it for years, intuitively editing Kalida's words to his liking. We spend the morning in happy camaraderie, Kalida making the agenda for the rally, the manifesto, the speeches, and I, proofreading, making small changes here and there, mostly reading them aloud to give him a sense of how they will sound to an audience.

Shurajit calls us for lunch around midday, informing us that Bishan has gone to town and will not be joining us.

'I made maachh and bhaath,' he tells Kalida. 'Bishan won't be here to object to a Bengali meal.'

'Aha,' Kalida says, rubbing his hand on his stomach like an excited child. I see the black points of his eyes gleam. 'We should send Bishan away more often.'

'Bishan is a Punjabi and likes his chapatis at lunch. He is not fond of fish and rice,' Shurajit explains to me.

We eat in the kitchen, sitting close together on the floor, our forms throwing the tangential beams awry. Shurajit shows me how to remove the long, needle-like bones from the fish before mixing it with the rice, and talks about the government's latest measures to curb terrorist activity in the area.

'You have to separate the smaller bones carefully with your tongue as you eat,' Kalida says, 'otherwise they will lodge in your throat like thorns.'

After lunch, Kalida retires to a room beside the kitchen, closing the door behind him.

'Come,' Shurajit says, picking up my bag from where it

is lying beside Kalida's desk. 'I'll show you to your room.'
He takes me to the only other room in the house. It is on the
other side, right across from Kalida's.

'Where do you sleep?' I ask him.

'Bishan and I sleep in this main room.' In a corner, I see
two mattresses piled one on top of the other and beside
them, rows of thick fabric-bound law books sitting on the
floor. Near the books, there is a stack of colourful paperbacks.

'Bishan reads cheap detective novels,' Shurajit says
pointing to the stack. 'In his other life he is Sherlock
Holmes.'

The room he takes me to is big and bare with a wide
window in one wall. Through it I can see the grove of trees.
Under it there is a mattress on the floor with a folded white
quilt on the pillow. On the opposite wall I see a large poster,
the entire upper half of which is a black sky with a red sun
in a corner. Under the sky, there are hordes of dark figures
disappearing into the horizon. Etched across the figures is a
poem in Hindi.

'What does it say?' I ask Shurajit.

'You can't read Hindi?'

'I can, sort of. I learnt it a long time ago, but I haven't
used it much. When I was in ... recently, a friend tried to
teach it to me again.' I remember Koki acting the teacher in
prison, writing sentences in mud with the end of a stick and
testing Hema and me on our knowledge of Hindi. 'Wait.
Let's see if I can remember.' I piece the letters together
slowly, looking towards Shurajit for help. Finally, I am able
to read the first line: Chale chalo dilon mein ghaav leke bhi
chale chalo. 'Move on, move on, even with wounded hearts,
move on.' I translate it into English.

'That's very good,' Shurajit says. 'I won't tell you what
the rest of it says. You read it yourself. When you're done
with this one, we'll put up another poster in your room so
you can practise your Hindi. Consider this a continuation of
your lessons.'

He places my bag beside the mattress. 'Do you want to
rest a little?' he asks me.

I shake my head. 'I've never been able to sleep in the afternoon. What are you going to do? Can I help you?'

'Sure. I'm going to start dinner pretty soon. I like to cook it while the light is still good and the kitchen is warm. At night that room becomes a freezer.'

'I'll help,' I say, following him out of the room. He shows me how to knead flour for chapatis and together we cut little florets of cauliflower to make a vegetable curry. I help him refill the urns from the faucet when the water supply comes on. We talk a little about Kalida and the CCPH.

'After an incidence of violence, organizations such as ours seem such an apology. Sometimes I wonder if we have any meaning at all. All we can provide is a catharsis for everyone but the victims, with our patriotic speeches of nationalism, our rallies, our demonstrations. But we can't seem to touch the victims. We can't reach their hearts. We can only make sure the government compensates them for their losses. Ten thousand rupees for a life, five thousand for a bread-earning limb. Sometimes it all seems so useless, and every day the violence escalates.'

'But at least you care. As long as people like you and Bishan and Kalida exist, there's always hope.' There has to be, otherwise . . . how will Daddy ever rest in peace, I think.

'Oh, good things happen, too. Sometimes we are able to talk to people and curb potential violence. We try to diffuse volatile situations. We mediate between the people and rash government measures. We organize protests. Sometimes we are effective. That's why I've stayed here so long. Kalida has taught me a lot. He's made me care.'

As the sun falls through the grove of trees, melting like liquid gold into the leaves, Shurajit shows me around the compound, walking among the trees, pointing out the ones that bear fruit and the ones that don't. A rustle of leaves on the path leading up from the fields indicates the arrival of a visitor. Instinctively, I step behind Shurajit.

'It's probably Bishan,' he says, sensing my fear.

A man in a large black turban, with shoulders carved out from the side of a mountain, appears among the trees.

'This is Bishan?' I whisper to Shurajit, recalling the effeminate picture he had drawn of the man.

'This is Bishan,' he says loudly.

Shurajit makes the introductions and Bishan joins his hands before me.

'Satsriakal,' he says. 'Welcome to CCPH.'

'She's going to invade your territory,' Shurajit warns him. 'Kalida wants her to help you run the press.'

Big white teeth flash in Bishan's bearded face. 'Welcome, welcome,' he says.

We walk back to the house together where Kalida is sitting on the stairs waiting for us.

'Ah, Bishan,' he says. 'I want to show Simran the press. She's going to help you run it.'

We walk together behind the hut to a shack almost hidden from view by large shrubs.

It is like the cave of a dinosaur filled with the odours of the monster's staple diet—old ink and musty paper. The printing press looks as old as the history of printing.

'This machine . . .' I begin. 'I don't think . . . I'm not sure I can help with this machine. It seems ancient. Does it work?'

'Bishan can make it purr,' Kalida says.

I look at Bishan who is standing with a shoulder against the machine, smiling from ear to ear. He walks around the machine as if circumambulating a deity, then comes to stand against its flank. 'It works,' he says.

'He'll show you how it works,' Kalida assures me. I approach the monstrous contraption warily, reaching out my hand to touch its well-greased joints.

'Here.' Bishan walks to a switch and turns it on. A low rumble begins as if from the throat of the earth and fills the air around us.

'No, no,' Kalida shakes his hand at Bishan. 'Tomorrow, tomorrow. Don't use electricity at this time. See, it is dark now. People need electricity to light their homes. Come,' he says to me. 'Tomorrow, in the light of the sun, Bishan will show you the working of his machine.'

As we walk out of the room, Kalida tells me that they use electricity sparingly, completing all work in the light of the day. After dinner Shurajit produces a kerosene lamp and shows me to the bathroom. 'There's no connection there,' he explains, gesturing me to follow him through the front room, out of the hut, to an outhouse around the back with two doors. After handing me a piece of soap and a thin towel, he leaves. I push in one of the doors tentatively, expecting the odours of the prison toilets to hit my nose, but a soft deodorizing smell emanates from it. I hold the lamp out to see a ceramic seat embedded in the ground. Pulling the door shut, I turn my attention to the other section where there is a large iron tub shimmering with water. The floor of the bathroom is cemented and dry under my feet.

I squat before the tub and splash icy water on my face, remembering to brace my nerves for the knots of numbness that form under my skin. Holding the towel over my face to transmit the warmth of my hands, I wait for the knots to melt away, then I pick up the lamp and walk back to the hut. An owl hoots in a tree somewhere above me.

'Owls can foresee dissolution,' I remember Kubrima saying, while she flung stones at the owl who had come to sit on the prison wall one evening. Daddy had a portent of dissolution living in his house. He owned a pet white owl, Oma, who ate rodents. Having lived in a cage all his life, the owl was unfamiliar with the ways of his tribe. His instincts must have dulled, too, because he could never kill the rodent himself. In the beginning, when Daddy first got him from the pet shop, he would release a mouse into Oma's closet-sized cage, but Oma would just sit on his perch blinking his big, transparent eyelids at the petrified rodent. Sometimes, in a flurry of feathers, he would pounce on his prey only to release him a moment later, bewildered at the life that still thrashed in him. Finally, Daddy started filling a tub of water to drown the mouse before placing it in Oma's claws. For hours after that, the house would stink of dead rats. My mother finally persuaded Daddy to donate Oma to the local zoo.

I hurry away towards the hut, the hooting an echo behind me.

That night I dream about Daddy and Scott and Oma. Scott is sitting in Daddy's Laz-E-Boy holding Oma in his hands and singing the silly rhyme he had concocted for him when he was a kid:

> There is an owl called Oma
> who lives his life in a coma.
> He can't hunt for food
> 'coz he thinks killing rats is rude.
> Wise old stupid owl Oma.

Slowly Scott's fingers inch up to Oma's neck and he begins to squeeze. I see Oma's head drop to one side and hang over Scott's hand. Loud wails break out of Scott's throat and his tears splash onto Oma's white feathers. Slowly, still crying, Scott brings Oma up to his chest and presses his lifeless head into his shoulder. Then suddenly, Oma is Daddy. The head that lolls against Scott's shoulder is Daddy's and the sounds of Scott's wails are now the laughter and rattles in my house. Scott is dry-eyed again. He lifts Daddy's head from his chest and removing himself from the chair, lays Daddy's form down gently on the seat and gestures me to follow him outside to the backyard. I walk behind him to the sliding door and look back at the chair. Daddy is now sitting in the Laz-E-Boy smiling such a pure smile, happiness floods my heart and I skip into the backyard behind Scott. A hole has been dug there and the loamy fragrance of fresh mud fills my senses. Scott has dead Oma in his arms again. He kneels before the hole and lays him inside. Together, we shovel the mud back into the hole with our hands, smiling and laughing like little children, chanting Oma's rhyme over and over again.

I awaken the next morning with a feeling of well-being only to see a large red sun in a black sky and people, hundreds of them, thousands, moving on relentlessly. I lie staring at the poster, feeling like an alien inside my skin. Something in me seems to be at odds with this place.

Something doesn't seem to belong. Desperately, I try to recall the first line in the poem and repeat it to myself. Chale chalo dilon mein ghaav leke bhi chale chalo. Move on move on, I urge myself, even with wounded hearts, move on. I try to read the next line but the foreign alphabet evades me. I trace and retrace the letters in my brain, and in some far away corner I can even decipher the shapes, but it is as though a veil has dropped over them, and I can only guess at their actual sounds. Again and again I try, my heart pounding in fear. Just one line, I tell myself, let me read just one line, as though by doing so I will be able to join those crowds. 'Chalo . . .' I read and slowly the rest of the line becomes clear to me. Lahu luhan paon leke bhi chale chalo. Move on even with bloodied feet, move on.

I rise then and open out the doors of my room.

Kalida is walking in the grove of trees when I step out for my morning ablutions.

'Good morning,' I call out to him. He stops and turns around, looking at me as though expecting something. I stand outside the bathroom, holding a towel and a bottle of toothpowder, wondering. After a moment he nods and moves away. I push open the door of the bathroom, still wondering what he had expected.

When I emerge again, Kalida is walking towards the compound where he is met by Bishan. I watch the proud Sikh bend and touch Kalida's feet with his hands. Kalida places a flat palm on his back briefly. Then together they climb the two stairs and disappear inside. Gathering up my towel, I spread it quickly on the branches of the peepul and hurry inside to seek out Kalida. I find him sitting on the kitchen floor beside Shurajit, drinking a cup of tea. Walking in resolutely, I stop before him and bending, touch his bare feet with both my hands. I feel the gentle touch of his hand on my hair and when I look up again, there is a twinkle lodged deep in his night black eyes. 'Thakur mongol korey,' he says softly. I'm not sure what that means, but I like the benevolent sound of it.

'Didi, tea?' Shurajit asks.

I nod and sit down beside Kalida on the mat, watching Shurajit pour out tea from a pot into a mug.

'I hope this isn't yours,' I tell him.

'I don't know,' he says. 'It could be. They all look alike.'

Laughing, I inspect the cup and raise it to my lips.

'Bishan will print out our handouts today,' Kalida tells me. 'See if you can learn to operate the machine. But first, you must help Shurajit in the kitchen. Serve your stomach before you serve the world,' he says smiling.

I help Shurajit prepare a simple meal of chapatis and potatoes and boil some more tea on the wood fire he has lit beside the kerosene stove. I call Bishan and Kalida into the kitchen once we are done, and we eat together on the floor, discussing the events of the rally as easily as if we are planning a project at work.

Days of routine follow. Every morning, I welcome the shaft of sunlight into my room and decipher yet another line of the poem. Three times a day I help Shurajit prepare meals, using the time in between to help Bishan with the printing press. After my initial fear of the monster, I become very comfortable with it. Following Bishan's instructions carefully, I am able to typeset the letters, spread black ink and place paper against its gigantic stomach to print out sheet after sheet of handouts. We print not only handouts, but also posters, and a thin volume of the aftermath of the demolition of Babri Masjid, collecting facts and statistics from newspapers and reports from other organizations. In the early evening, while the sun affords us its last light, I sit with Kalida and proofread his speeches. Sometimes I sit with the others, and while Kalida talks about literature, art, world affairs, the weather, food, et cetera, we make placards of old pieces of cardboard with swabs of cotton dipped in paint. I discover that Kalida is extremely well read and can quote passages as easily from Nietzsche as from the Bhagavad Gita and the Quran.

'He never went to school,' Shurajit tells me one day, sniffing at the onions he is chopping on the board. 'He read his first two books when he was sixteen. First, *Das Kapital*, then the *Red Book*, and then he joined the Naxalites.'

'From literature to violence. Naturally.'

Shurajit laughs. 'He hurt his hand there. A homemade bomb exploded in his hand.'

'Is that what convinced him to change allegiance?'

'No, the government did. He went to jail and came out a different man.'

'Quite a man.'

He nods. 'The last of the best.'

chapter twelve

A few days before the sixth of December, men and women wearing cotton on their bodies and earnest looks on their faces begin to visit the compound.

'Other activists and members of other organizations,' Shurajit tells me. 'This is going to be the largest peace rally this city has seen.'

They talk for hours, grouped together in the front room with Kalida. Most of them leave as evening descends, but some of the men stay. The front room looks like an impromptu hospital with mattresses Shurajit brings out of a large tin trunk, lined corner to corner on the floor. Shurajit and I spend a lot more time in the kitchen now. I resent that. I want to be out there with the others, listening to their plans, sharing the process of peace. I voice my resentment to Shurajit once.

'You are sharing in the process. We all are. In whatever way we can. Don't you think food is as important to man as peace? Maybe, even more. You, Miss Simran Mehta, are involved most of all, because you are the hostess under whose auspices this rally will take off, and whose badly cooked food will sustain the demonstrators.'

'I don't serve badly cooked food,' I say, making a face at him, kneading dough for chapatis with an expertise that would make anyone envious.

The morning of the rally, I emerge from my room, victorious. I have read the last line of the poem. Shurajit is standing outside my door with a newspaper-wrapped bundle in his hands.

'I was just going to knock,' he says.

'With the shade that remains in your heart, move on, move on,' I tell him, translating the line still ringing in my mind.

'Okay,' he says. 'But you'll need to be dressed right to move on, move on. Here. I've got you the clothes in which you can move on.'

'What's this?' I ask, taking the bundle and ripping off the newspaper. Inside is a white cotton sari along with a blouse and petticoat. There is also a pair of blue and white rubber flip-flops.

'Bishan bought these in town yesterday. You probably don't want to go to the rally in a shimmering green suit with golden embroidery. It isn't a wedding, you know.'

At the sight of the white sari, my hands begin to tremble. I am back in prison again and Prema is standing outside the bathroom with a newspaper bundle in her arms containing the prisoner's white sari to replace the clothes from my world, rags though they were. 'Thanks, Shurajit. Tell Bishan I said thanks,' I say, running towards the grove where I know Kalida must surely be.

'Kalida, I can't go to the rally,' I say out of breath.

'It is your decision.'

'I want to go, but the police. I mean, Arun must have told you about my status.'

'Yes. It is sad. Our laws have fettered you. This is your home.' His arm encompasses the acres spread behind him where the trees rustle in free-spirited abandon as the morning breeze tickles their branches. 'You should be free here.' With his long hair bejewelled with dewdrops from the trees, his white dhoti and kurta pure from receiving the first sun, he appears to me like a bestower of boons, boons that promise eternal freedom.

I bend down and smear my forehead with the dust from his feet. He touches my head and says, 'In my house you are safe.'

Feeling strangely at peace I walk back into the house, the white sari clutched to my chest like a shield.

Silently, I help Shurajit prepare a quick breakfast of salted chapatis and tea, not explaining to him why I cannot go, saying only, that crowds make me nervous.

After the last of the activists have gone, I take a leisurely bath and wash my hair. On an impulse, I decide to wear the white sari. Pulling it out of the newspaper wrap, I drape it around me. Then throwing a corner of it over my shoulder and measuring it down to the back of my knees, I make a flowing pallu. Wondering if Shurajit keeps a mirror hidden somewhere, I wander into the front room. As I look behind stacks of books, my ears pick up a low drone in the distance. Stepping out into the courtyard, I stand still, trying to identify the sound. It seems to get louder, a rising crescendo in the air. Suddenly, I know what it is. It is a motorcycle coming up the path leading to the compound. Visions of a khaki uniform riding that motorcycle catapult me into action. I run back inside the cottage and pull the door shut. But there is no bolt on the inside. Desperately I look for a stick or cane to stick into the handles, but outside I hear the vehicle slowing down, its rapid expulsion of air petering out into a slow phut-phut like bullets being fired successively. My heart echoing the motorcycle's engine, I tiptoe away from the main room to my own, where I know the bolt is intact. I hear someone push open the door of the main room even as I slip the bolt home in my own. I run to the window and push it open, thinking of jumping out and hiding in the grove of trees. When I hear footsteps crossing the main room, I try to swing one leg over the window frame but the sari is in the way. I grip the jamb and try to hike myself up when I hear someone call out my name, the voice familiar. 'Simran?' I hear again, this time almost outside my door. 'Are you in there? It's me—Arun.' Relief breaks out on my forehead and upper lip. On shaky legs, I walk to the door and open it. He is standing just outside, stark white socks peeping out from under the cuffs of his jeans, the fingers of his right hand curled around the rolled top of a large brown paper bag. Now that the fear has ceased, I can feel my chest pulse with its aftermath. I stand before him unable to speak. His eyes skim over my face, pausing on each feature, then blinking, onto the next, then blinking again, like the cold eye of a camera taking snapshots of my eyes, my nose, my lips ... Even as I look at him looking at me, I see him change as though the very core of his being has cracked. Emotions hopscotch on his face with such fluidity, I stand hypnotized. Slowly, ever so slowly, like a shoot raising its head towards light, he raises his left hand and brings it to my face. My eyes follow its path. Reaching with the index finger, he touches my upper lip. A sweat bead explodes, smearing wet fire on my skin. 'I didn't mean to scare you,' he says softly. I continue standing, staring, feeling. His eyelids drop, only for a second, but long enough for him to collect himself. When he opens his eyes again, the Arun I know is back. I am suddenly deafened by my own breathing. Had I been holding my breath these past few seconds?

'I have something for you.' He extends the paper bag towards me.

'What is it?' I take the bag from him and begin to unroll the top to look inside. A faint incinerated smell fills my senses. The paper bag is a quarter full with a familiar, greyish powder. My hands begin to shake. 'Are these ...?' My mouth feels dry.

'Yes,' he says. 'Your father's ashes.'

I try to roll the top of the bag shut again, but my hands are trembling so much I'm afraid I'm going to drop the bag.

'Here,' he says, trying to take it from me. 'Let me put it away.' But I can't seem to let go. I bring the bag close to my chest and fold my arms over it. I can feel tremors pass through my arms.

'Why don't you sit down?' He takes one elbow and leads me to the mattress inside. I lower myself carefully and sit with knees drawn up, holding the bag on my lap, my arms still around it. 'I'm sorry,' I say on a jerky laugh. 'I think it's delayed shock.'

He stands before me looking down. I want him to sit

beside me. I want him to take me in his arms. I want to put
my head in the curve of his neck where it descends to meet
his shoulder. I want him to absorb the tremors that are
flowing through my body. I want his comfort, but I can't ask
him, not when he's standing there guarding his own core
jealously, unwilling to let it alchemize with anything or
anyone. I wonder if the first few moments of revelation had
been a distortion of my fear, or an illusion stemming from
my relief.

After a few minutes, I feel my body settle into its steady
rhythms again. 'I'm all right now,' I say, putting the bag on
the mattress beside me. 'How did you ...? Was is it the
camera?' I ask.

'Yes, the camera did the trick. Sorry I couldn't get the
box. My man emptied out the ashes in this bag. This way no
one will ever discover they are missing. There is a rosewood
box still sitting in a police godown.'

'Thank you,' I say.

'Am I forgiven?'

I look up at him sharply, hopefully, but nothing on his
face has changed. 'For what?' I ask.

'For writing that first article about you?'

I shake my head. 'No. I'll never forgive you for that.'

He looks at me. I can see faint surprise in his eyes.
'That's fine,' he says. 'At least we'll have that between us.'

I don't want him to do this. I don't want him to make
inferences from behind that face. I shake my head again and
stand up. 'Would you like some tea?'

'Sure.' He waits for me to lead him out of the room to
the kitchen. I can feel his presence behind my back like
static. Outside the main room, I see his shoes lying
haphazardly on the first step, one shoe turned over on its
face. What was it Daddy used to read in shoes placed this
way? A desire unfulfilled? I bend and straighten the shoe,
laying it beside its twin, face up.

Once in the kitchen, I light the kerosene stove and
measuring out two cups of water from the urn into a pan,
put it on the fire.

Arun finds a spot under one of the sunbeams and settles down cross-legged, his jeans pulling taut over his thighs. I look away. Except for the sound of the hungry flame lapping up the kerosene, there's silence.

'I have to scatter them on the border,' I say after a while.

'You will. I'll find someone else to bribe. Hold on to them for a while till I find somebody.'

More silence follows. I can feel his eyes on me now. Then he asks quietly, 'Why the border?'

'He wanted it that way.'

'I know. Scott told me. But why the border?'

I watch tongues of blue flame lick at the bottom of the pan, leaving soot-black stains in their wake. 'He felt he caused the division. He hurt a lot of people, and then he ran away. He never stopped feeling guilty about that. All his life he felt guilty, and the worst part was, he couldn't come back. The pain was too vivid.'

'And you want him to continue feeling the pain even in death?'

I look at him then. There's genuine concern there. Not the density, not the starkness of emotion, but a genuine desire to understand.

'It's not what I want that matters. It was his last wish,' I say. 'I have to fulfil it.'

'What do you want? Do you want him to suffer endlessly?'

I feel suddenly angry at his interference. 'I have to do what he wanted. His soul needs the penance. You don't know what he did.'

'I have an idea, Scott told me. But what he did was almost fifty years ago. Don't you think he has suffered enough? I don't know how much you make a man pay for his crimes in your country, but here in India, we believe that after death a man should be allowed peace. We absolve him of all his sins when he departs. That is why all ashes are scattered in the Ganga. We believe her waters liberate a person from all guilt. Don't you think your father deserves that?'

I get up and reach out for the sugar and tea leaves.

Setting them near the stove, I move towards the windows and sit directly under one, my back leaning against it. A shaft of light, slanting in through the aperture, passes over my head and pours onto a spot just before me. 'You know, when I was released from jail I went to see Sultana's brother,' I say, watching the particles of dust suspended helplessly in the shaft. 'Remember Sultana? The girl who was raped in jail? Remember her story?' I look at him.

He nods.

'Remember what happened to her brother and her neighbours? And all in the name of communal violence. My father started that.'

'Perhaps. But those times were treacherous. Thousands turned murderers overnight. The whole nation turned violent. Your father was no different. But what those misguided people started at that time is not an excuse for what is happening now. Those people are not to be blamed for today's problems. Let me tell you about today's India. It might be a reflection of 1947, but believe me, it is a false reflection. What is happening today has nothing to do with what happened in 1947. What your father did was over after the Partition. Today, it is all politics. And believe me, your father had no hand in today's politics.'

'But innocent people are getting hurt. How can one not feel the pain?'

'Yes. Unfortunately, people are getting hurt. But this is a problem that stems from within our system. It isn't because someone killed someone else; and it's not going to go away by wiping a few tears, or feeling the pain.'

'How can you say that?' His callousness hurts. 'You're the one who brought me here to CCPH.'

'Don't get me wrong. I understand why you had to stay back for your father's ashes, but to believe that your father is responsible and that consequently you are, too, is foolishness. Your guilt is self-imposed, Simran. It'll destroy you like it did your father. If you feel you have to help, by all means stay on, but only because you care, not because you feel responsible. And for heaven's sake, lay your father to rest, because until you do, you'll never have a life of your own. Give yourself your life, and give your father the peace all Hindus achieve. He deserves it. If you love him, you'll do this for him.'

The water in the pan begins to boil; I can hear it gurgling madly. I move to the stove and busy myself adding sugar and tea, watching the crushed black leaves bleed into the water. Then I uncover a pan of milk, measure out half a cup of it and pour it in. The black suddenly turns a light gold. I let it boil one time, then folding a rag around my hand, lift the pan off the stove. I sieve the tea into a cup and nudge it towards Arun. I cover the remaining tea in the pan with a plate and turn off the stove. A faint smell of burnt kerosene pervades the kitchen.

'Excuse me,' I say, getting up.

'Aren't you going to have some?' he asks.

Without answering, I walk out of the kitchen, skirting around the cottage to go into the grove. The sun is deep among the trees. I walk through patches of sunlight and shade to the end of the grove where I know the fruit trees are. Here, the sun is lying full-bodied on the ground, the leafless trees in temporary death, unable to absorb any more of its heat, their branches already brittle like those of a corpse on a pyre. Under my feet I feel the soft crunch of dry leaves, remains of the trees, scattered on the soil that nurtured them. Behind me I hear another set of footsteps, treading warily as though on sanctified ground. 'Simran? I'm sorry. I had no right to say that.'

I continue walking. He falls into step beside me. He's wearing his shoes now.

'You know, winter used to be my father's favourite season. He loved the winter sun. He had chairs placed strategically in his den to catch every shifting ray of the winter sun. On sunny Sundays, he would move from one chair to another, playing musical chairs all day so as not to miss a single moment of its warmth. Every Sunday Mummy would pack our meals in a basket, and we would have a picnic in his den. He would sit in the sun, cutting fruits and

vegetables in floral designs—carrot rounds with sheared
edges like the petals of a daisy, apples with centres carved
like roses. He would arrange the fruity flowers on a platter
and sprinkle salt and red chilli powder on them, squeezing
lime juice to moisten the spices. He loved raw vegetables and
fruits soaked in red chilli powder—lots of chilli powder.
Every time I popped one in my mouth, I would hang my
tongue out like a sweating puppy and he would laugh,
placing a pinch of salt on my tongue to take away the sting.
And later, hiccoughs would inevitably constrict my throat.
He would then shove whole teaspoonfuls of sugar in my
mouth. "My salt and sugar baby," he would call me. I used
to think he called me that because of the salt and sugar he
placed on my tongue, but it wasn't. Many years later, he
told me it was because I was born from the sweetness of
Mummy's love and the salt of his tears.

'One Sunday morning I remember I woke up a little
earlier than usual and went to his den. He was sitting in the
east corner chair, leaning back, his head resting against the
wall, his eyes only half open, his body still. The sun was
shining directly at him, into him, into his very core. His skin
was like parchment, brilliant with its reflection. I thought
about going and sitting at his feet, but when I looked down,
I saw sunlight growing there as though flowering out of his
body like the branches of a willow and taking root again at
his feet. He looked so peaceful, so at one with himself and
the sun, I turned around quietly and left. I wanted that peace
to continue, but I knew it was only an illusion. Even in
happy times there was always a mistiness. Except for that
one time, I never saw him at peace. You don't know how
desperately I wanted that peace to be his for always. I loved
him. I loved him despite everything.'

'You should see the Ganga in the winter. People say it
has been sullied by washing the sins of people for thousands
of years. But the winter sun still glimmers in it as brightly as
ever. Haridwar is only a four-hour drive from Amritgarh.
Buses go there all day.'

I turn to look at him then. Somewhere along this sun-drenched grove, his face has dissolved into a wondrous transparency. Such tenderness caresses me, I almost weep from the touch of it, or, perhaps, it is only the memory of Daddy that threatens me with tears.

'Your tea must have gone cold by now,' I say, looking away.

'That's okay, I've got to be going anyway. I have to catch the rally.'

'You were supposed to be there, weren't you?'

He nods.

'Thank you,' I say.

'It's being attended by so many people, I won't be missed for a while.'

'It's a big event, isn't it?'

'The biggest this city has ever seen. Everyone is showing up. Peace rallies have become a fashion in this country. Society hostesses like to boast about them at their dinner parties. Filmstars use them to embark on political careers.'

'Do they help? I mean, the rallies?'

'Sometimes. It's a way of creating awareness among people who would not normally spend a single moment thinking about the situation.'

'You know, after I've taken care of the ashes, I think I would like to stay on for a while.'

He turns to look at me. 'What about Scott?'

Guilt descends on me. I haven't thought about him even once this afternoon.

'How is Scott?' I ask. 'When can I see him?'

'He's fine. The police have lifted their round-the-clock watch over him. I told him to start being seen with someone else to mislead the police into believing he has lost interest in you. He's started hanging around with Elaine Johnson.'

I can't prevent the frown that settles between my eyebrows.

'Don't worry. Your fiancé is not straying. It was my suggestion to divert attention from you.'

'When can I see him?'

'Soon. He'll be in Delhi for a while. I persuaded him to

take advantage of his visit here and see some of the country instead of sitting in his hotel room, moping about you and your problems. Besides, if the police are still watching him, they'll lose your scent. I'll bring him here when he returns in a week or so. Or perhaps you can get into your Muslim disguise and I can take you to him. He's going to be·staying at a different hotel when he returns. He said he can't afford to continue living at the Imperial. He'll probably stay at the Palace Hotel. It's pretty good. Not in the five-star league, but pretty good.'

'Poor Scott, I've put him through so much.'

'He'll get over it,' he says.

Talking about Scott has wrenched me from the sun, Daddy and Arun.

We walk back to the kitchen in silence where the sunbeams have moved back to glide vertical against the wall. I light the kerosene stove again and pour Arun's tea in the pan and reheat it.

He takes off his shoes once more and sits on the bare floor away from me, his face reticent.

'Why do you do that?' I ask impulsively.

'What?'

'Hide yourself behind your face.'

'What are you talking about?'

'No really, Arun, you've got an uncanny way of hiding all your emotions. When I used to see you in jail, looking so self-contained and indifferent, I used to feel so cheated.'

He doesn't respond. He just sits there looking at me, yet not looking.

The tea boils over. Instinctively, I reach out and pick up the pan and immediately drop it with a cry. My fingers are on fire. Tea spills all over the stove causing the flames to splutter and die, filling the kitchen with a sweet acrid smell of kerosene and burnt tea. Arun grabs my wrist and plunges my hand into the urn full of water. He holds it there. I try to pull it out a number of times, but he keeps a tight grip, counting ek beda tare, do beda tare, all the way upto sixty and then starting from one again.

'What are you doing?' I ask, laughing.

'Keeping your finger in cold water for three minutes. My mother taught me that.'

'Back where I come from, we count one mississippi two mississippi.'

'My mother used to say beda tare; it means, may your ship sail. Every time she was angry with me and my sister, instead of using abusive language, she would yell blessings. We started using her angry blessings as filler words.'

When he finally draws my hand out, it is pale and vulnerable, its cells moist and exposed. He turns it around and peers at it. There is a white streak running across the tips of two fingers.

'The pain will escape in a blister,' Arun says, taking my other hand and cradling my burnt hand in it.

'I'm sorry about the tea. Let me make you another cup.'

'No,' he says. 'I'd better be going. The rally will be over pretty soon. I should at least show my face.'

'When will Kalida and the others be back?'

'Probably around six. Once the sun sets, people seek other entertainment.'

'What time is it now?'

He turns his wrist and looks at his watch. 'About five.'

'I'd better start dinner,' I say. 'I hardly have any time.'

It's a simple statement, a mundane statement—'I hardly have any time'—yet it suddenly unmasks him, arresting his face in an emotion as raw and defenceless as a newly-delivered stab wound.

'Twenty hours,' I think I hear him say.

'I'm sorry? What was that?' And it's over. His face sets in mortar. Thick, opaque, impenetrable.

'I have to leave.' His voice has hardened, too, as if the mortar has slithered down his throat. 'I'll see you sometime,' he says, turning away. I watch his feet as he leaves the kitchen, each heel landing on the floor squarely followed by the ball, the tender instep curling away from the impact.

In a few moments I hear the motorcycle being gunned, then the engine picks up the rhythm as it moves out of the courtyard, towards the path to the main road. I hear its sound become a hum in the air. I try to close my ears to it. But strangely enough, it begins to grow louder. I shake my head to throw off the sound, but it's very close. It's in the courtyard again. I get up hurriedly and run outside. He's sitting astride his motorcycle, a black helmet covering his head, its visor shading his eyes. He's got one foot on the ground to steady the machine as it vibrates impatiently between his legs.

I don't want to see him again or to talk to him. I want to begin missing him. I want to have enough time between his absence and the arrival of the others to think about him and nestle him within me.

He pulls out a packet from a bag tied to the side of the machine and gestures to me.

'Give these to Kalida. Tell him these are his tickets for Kashmir.'

As soon as I take the packet from him, he puts the machine in gear. This time I stay outside till the cacophony of the nesting birds drowns his visit out.

Kalida, Shurajit and Bishan return soon after. I welcome them home with a hot meal. We sit in the kitchen and eat. I don't need to ask if the rally has been successful. I can see the satisfaction in the faces before me. They talk about the attendance at the rally, about the verve and motivation of the attendees. Kalida smiles. 'Peace cannot be won by rallies alone, but it's a step forward.'

When we retire to our room, I pick up the bag containing Daddy's ashes and stand with it for a moment, thinking about Arun and the sun glimmering in the Ganga. I put the paper bag in the satchel I borrowed from Fatima and lay it gently against the wall close to the mattress. Then I begin to pull out the pleats of my sari to prepare for bed. Suddenly I remember Kalida's tickets still sitting in the kitchen. Stuffing the pleats back into the waistband of my petticoat, I tiptoe into the front room, but Shurajit and Bishan are not in bed yet. Stepping outside, I go into the kitchen and retrieve the packet to take it to Kalida. I knock gently at his closed door. I think I hear him say, 'Come in.' When I push the door open, I almost topple a hurricane lantern placed near the entrance. There is no electric light in the room.

Hundreds of shadows of hundreds of Durgas surround me. In one hand she holds a sword, in the other, a conch shell; the third is raised in benediction, and in the fourth is a trident gorging the belly of a miniature monster under her feet, each figurine a nucleus of violence.

'Such wrath,' I hear Kalida's voice from a corner.

I turn my head in the direction of his voice. He is sitting on the floor in the far corner, his back against the wall, facing the Durgas, casting hardly any shadow of his own. He is so effaced by the looming shadows, it is as though his very presence had been consumed by them.

He holds his hand out to me.

Hurriedly, afraid he might disappear before my very eyes, I go and kneel before him.

'The second principle is violence,' he says.

I look at his face. His eyes are closed and it seems as though all the contours from his face have been erased. He is only a voice.

'It comes. Later it comes. Peace. But first, violence. There is no other way.'

'The principle for what, Kalida?' I whisper.

'Creation,' he says. 'The Puranas list the process of creation.'

'What is the first principle?'

'Quiescence. Void. And from that, chaos, the battle of the forces of good with those of evil, and then creation, peace. My father used to make Durga figurines for Durga Puja. The Devi in her natural form—no clothes, no weapons, just her hands in readiness for the violence to come. Those who bought her put weapons in her hands and prepared her to slay Mahishasur, the monster, the force of darkness. In my father's house, both Mahishasur and the Devi resided together, quiescent.'

He opens his eyes, and slowly the lines on his face return, settling into familiar grooves. He becomes quiet. His eyes close again, and his head falls back against the wall. For a long time I sit looking at him, then thinking he has fallen asleep, I put the packet beside him.

'Soon I will go to Kashmir.'

'That is what I came to tell you. Arun asked me to give you the tickets.'

He does not open his eyes again. I rise and letting myself out quietly, walk to my room with the poster of the red sun, the black sky and hordes of dark figures walking into a broad horizon of peace—or is it violence? I'm not sure any more. Even the once-read and comprehended words of the poem become a blur in the descending darkness. I lie down with my back to Daddy's ashes.

That night I am woken by the sound of a terrible rumbling in the earth. I place my palm flat against the floor, but the rumble does not enter my cells. I realize it is a sound that does not rise out of the earth, but hangs suspended somewhere in between. For a long time I lie listening to the steady roar, then almost lulled by it, I fall asleep again.

The next morning when we are all sitting under our guardian beams, eating breakfast, I ask the others if they heard a rumble the night before. Bishan looks up startled, then turns to Kalida.

'Bishan was running the press,' Kalida tells me.

'Oh,' I say, wondering what happened to his resolve not to use electricity at night.

'He was printing out some material I have to take with me to Kashmir.'

'Why didn't you wake me? I could have helped you.'

'It's all right,' Bishan says. 'It was late.'

Kalida leaves for Kashmir after three days. Bishan and I print out a lot of material for him during the day, and sometimes at night I can hear Bishan run the machine again. I think about getting up to help him, but something in Kalida's manner when I broached the subject the other day tells me that he does not want me to help Bishan at night. On the morning Kalida leaves, walking down the path between the fields to take a bus to Amritgarh, I get the broom from the kitchen and, as part of my daily chores, begin sweeping the courtyard. Suddenly, Shurajit comes running out of the kitchen.

'Stop. Don't sweep yet.'

I stop and look at him.

'Kalida just left. Wait a while before you sweep the ground.'

'Why?'

'It's a bad omen.'

'Why?'

'I don't know. My mother used to tell me that it is a bad omen for the person who has left. As though you are sweeping his presence away.'

I laugh, but put the broom down. 'That's only a superstition, Shurajit.'

He looks at me sheepishly before turning away to the kitchen to return with a steel urn full of water which he places carefully between the roots of the peepul, a talisman to ensure Kalida's safe return.

'I'm making Bishan's favourite food today. Alu paranthas. Have you ever eaten them?' he asks me.

'Yes.' I follow him back to the kitchen. 'My mother used to make them. They're delicious.'

'Bishan loves them. All Punjabis do. Your mother was Punjabi?'

'No. I don't know. She could have been. My grandfather left India a long time ago. She was born in America. I never asked her where in India her father was from.'

'Your father was born in America, too?'

'No. He was born in a village near Lahore.'

'Aha, so you are Punjabi. Bishan's parents used to live in Lahore before the Partition. Bishan wants to visit Lahore one day, but he's going to wait till he can go there without a passport.'

'Without a passport? How can he do that?'

'Who knows? One day, perhaps . . .' His words trail off and he begins to peel the soft boiled potatoes with his fingers.

'You mean India might sign a treaty with Pakistan for

unrestricted travel or something?'

He looks at me confused, as though trying to recall a conversation from a long time ago. Then, shaking his head at his apparent loss of memory, he asks, 'Have your parents ever visited Lahore?'

'My parents are dead.'

'That's sad. Do you have any brothers and sisters?'

'None. What about you? Do you have any family?'

'Yes,' he says. 'My mother lives in a village near Calcutta. I visit her sometimes. I also have a little sister. Well, she's hardly little any more. She's almost twenty. I'm looking for a husband for her. Do you know anyone who's a Bengali Brahmin, has a secure job and a fat bank balance? Oh, and is also very good looking? Actually, the ability to keep her happy is the only important criterion.'

'How about Bishan?'

He laughs. 'I've already considered him even though he doesn't fit any of the above criteria, except perhaps, the last. Besides, Bishan's heart belongs to someone else. She lives in Amritgarh. He goes to see her sometimes.'

'That must be hard. Why doesn't she come and live with him here?'

Shurajit laughs again. 'She can't. She's a schoolteacher. She can't leave her job. Someone has to make the money. Bishan surely doesn't.'

'Why? Doesn't the organization pay anything?'

He shakes his head. 'This is not a job.'

'Bishan could open his own press when he marries her.'

'Marries who?' Bishan says behind me.

I turn and laugh. 'We were talking about your girlfriend.'

He turns a deep red and glowers at Shurajit. 'I don't want to get married yet. There is a lot of work to be done here.'

We clean the rooms, sweeping and scrubbing every nook and corner. We wash all the sheets and then the blankets at a faucet behind the kitchen. Shurajit beats them with a heavy wooden stick shaped like a narrow cricket bat and I rinse them out in three different buckets full of water, one after the other, till the water in the last bucket is clear of residual soap. Bishan ties a rope from the peepul to a post dug into the soft ground behind the kitchen and hangs them out to dry where they billow out like clouds hovering close to the earth. Later we fold them together and carry them inside. Exhausted from our day of cleaning, we settle down on the stairs to watch the sky change colour before our eyes. The evening air is cold and I pull my dupatta around me like a shawl. Bishan goes in for a moment and returns with a blanket. Taking it from him gratefully, I drape it over my shoulders. Shurajit takes one end of it and sneaks his arm in. I laugh and release some more of it. Soon the three of us are huddled together on the stairs of the hut, snuggling under a single blanket, exchanging life stories, sharing histories. I find out Shurajit has been with the CCPH for about five years. He had heard Kalida speak at a peace conference in his college when he was still a student of law, and had been so overwhelmed that he had decided right then to join his team of activists. 'And you?' I ask Bishan. Bishan looks at me, then takes a corner of the blanket and covers his face with it, holding it with a hand over the eyes. Shurajit taps my hand lightly to gain my attention. When I turn to look at him, he shakes his head, and I realize that Bishan's life, too, is not to be mentioned, because it too, conceals wounds that are forbidden to heal. I reach out and cover Bishan's hand on the blanket with my own.

'If Kalida hadn't brought me here, I would have torn him limb by limb.' His voice is so cold, despite the blanket covering his face, it cuts right through me.

'Who?' I ask softly.

'There was someone. A haramzada policewallah—used to think every Sikh is a terrorist. Finished off every single Sikh male in the village.'

A deep silence settles upon us when he stops speaking. A raucous bird suddenly calls. Bishan wipes his eyes with the corner of the blanket and removes it from his face. 'Let it go.' He shakes his head. 'Another time.' He turns to look at me, his lips attempting a smile. 'You—how did you end up here in Amritgarh, working for the CCPH?'

Quietly, I tell them about my visit to India, my prison term, Daddy's ashes in my satchel and how they were confiscated to lie derelict for months in some police lab, and my absconding to hide here in Jhakher. 'Haramzade!' Bishan spits out. Shurajit puts an arm around me and brings my head to rest on his shoulder. 'Arun did right in bringing you here.' Bishan stands up. 'Don't you worry, sister,' he says in English, 'that India where brother take care of sister still alive. Here brother can give even life for sister. Do not worry.' He goes inside again and returns with a bottle in his hand. 'Tonight with my new sister, I start new year.' He takes a swig from the bottle.

A new year. The last day of 1997. The first day of 1998. I have lost track of time completely. How irrelevant dates seem now, how unidentifiable the days, like breathing—one breath similar to the next and the next. How can you number them individually, except of course, for those you miss when your heart skips a beat or those you use half a dozen in a second and feel grateful that life is not measured by the breaths you take. But you know that each day, like each breath, is absolutely necessary to your life.

I try to remember how I spent last New Year's Eve. A memory, as though nestled at the bottom of a champagne glass, sends up flashes in bubbles. Margaret West's basement, enlarged reproductions of paintings by Georgia O'Keeffe on the walls, of petal soft vaginas in pastel shades; the smell of bean dip in my nose from the spill on Scott's white shirt just under his chin where my head rested while we danced; and then the sonorous sounds of the grandfather clock ringing in the new year—the very clock Margaret West bought for $4995 at an auction and talked about for weeks till we couldn't hear another stroke of a pendulum without wanting to scream, 'Shut up, Margaret West.' One, two, three . . . twelve strokes. We stood still and patiently heard them all. The champagne went flat soon after, and the New Year's resolution of not spending another penny on tacky pieces of clothing that I stacked away in my closet and never wore, lasted but a month. I look down at Fatima's bright pink salwar-kameez with puffed sleeves and golden stars embroidered all over the front and smile. This would surely have been one piece of clothing tucked away in the farthest corner of my closet. I look around, wanting to impress every second of this New Year's Eve upon my mind so that whatever happens to me for the rest of the year, I will know how it all began. I look at the peepul before us, spread like an old woman protecting her brood, and the moon glinting on the steel urn between its roots, awaiting Kalida's return. I look at the jagged shapes of trees in the grove, breaking the symmetry of the dark horizon. I turn to look at Shurajit beside me, a corner of the blanket covering his clown's head, his arm still around my shoulders in brotherly affection, and at Bishan, gaining his warmth from the bottle, humming a lilting tune under his breath. Slowly, he begins to sing the words. The lyrics are unfamiliar to me—something about desire becoming insane in our hearts but what remains to be tested is the strength in our arms. I know that this New Year's I will resolve to fulfil that very same insane desire.

Shurajit takes the bottle from Bishan and waving it before my eyes, challenges me. 'This is village liquor. It's very potent. Would you like to try some?' I nod my head and take a swig. The liquor burns in my throat like a small fire before coursing in a red-hot streak down my gullet, to settle like embers around my heart.

'Wooh.' I shake my head as I feel its vapours rise to my head.

Shurajit and Bishan laugh as they pass the bottle between them, joining their voices in song. Soon the two voices are raised in volume, shouting the lyrics to the dark woods beyond. Suddenly the sky bursts into a million points of light that float down into oblivion after a second of brilliance. The air is rent with yells far away, in another land. 'Twelve o'clock.' Bishan breaks the rhythm of the song for a moment and raising his bottle to the skies, shouts 'Happy New Year', before picking up the melody again.

I hear the hollow drone of a motorcycle engine and

blocking out the song, prick my ears to the sound. It is coming from the path that leads up to the compound, nearer and nearer even as I listen. I grab Shurajit's arm. He stops singing immediately. Both Shurajit and Bishan get up.

'Go inside,' Shurajit whispers to me. Bishan squares his shoulders and steps into the clearing with his large arms held over his chest.

I tiptoe towards the house and step inside, pulling the door shut, knowing in my heart who it is, but cautious just in case. In a moment I see the motorcycle appear over the incline and come to a growling halt in the clearing. The rider removes the helmet from his head and I can see my heart didn't lie. I fling open the door and run towards the figure.

His arms receive me warmly, tightening around me for a moment. 'Hey, you seem happy to see me.'

I disengage myself from his arms in embarrassment and smile up at him. 'Happy New Year, Arun.'

'You guys seem to be enjoying yourselves here. Mind if I join you?' he asks Bishan and Shurajit. They settle back on the stairs and pass him the half-empty bottle.

'Here's to peace in the new year,' he says, raising the bottle and taking a swig.

I bend down and retrieving the blanket, sit down in one corner. Arun passes the bottle to me.

'This is crazy stuff,' I tell him. 'Beats anything I've ever drunk.'

'And drunk you'll be before you know it,' he warns me.

'What are you doing here?' I ask him.

'I came to see you.'

I look at him, feeling drunk already. I turn my head away in confusion.

'Kalida asked me to check on you.'

'Oh,' I say, disappointed. 'When will he return from Kashmir?'

'In a week's time.'

'If everything goes as planned,' Shurajit says.

'He will come,' Bishan says, giving Shurajit a strange, stony-eyed look.

'What's he doing in Kashmir?'

Bishan and Shurajit avoid my eyes as I look from one to the other.

'Oh, this and that,' Arun finally says.

'Are there members of CCPH in Kashmir?'

'No,' Arun says. 'But he's trying to establish a branch there. Right now, he's gone there to talk to the leaders of Jamat-e-Islami and the Student's Islamic Movement. There have been reports about a lot of activity in Pakistan occupied Kashmir. We're afraid of the chaos the two parties backed by the PoK government may cause.'

'So Kalida is going to bring the cause of peace to them?'

'Something like that. Although it's probably a lost cause. The situation has gone way beyond finding solutions through talks.'

'Is he safe?' A tremendous fear suddenly rises in my heart as if the hall of souls in heaven is empty and Kalida is the last surviving soul. If he perished, it would be the end of life on earth. 'What if something happens to him?'

An uncomfortable silence settles over us as the men around me push their own dark thoughts away, to prevent them from reaching out to answer my question.

'It is late,' Bishan says, putting the bottle down and getting up. 'I must sleep. Amardeep has a holiday tomorrow. She will wait for me early in the morning.'

'I'm ready for bed too.' Shurajit gets up. 'Arun, will you stay the night? I'll make you a bed.'

Arun nods.

Arun and I sit on with the length of the stair between us.

'He's going to be all right. Right?' I ask softly.

Arun nods again. 'Don't worry.' He looks at me with such gentleness in his eyes, the smile I give him trembles at the corners. Suddenly, he shivers. 'Want to share my blanket?' I ask. He nods and slides closer to me, taking the corner of the blanket I offer and pulling it over his shoulders.

'I'm sure you've never spent New Year's Eve like this, sitting on a cold stair, sharing an old blanket.'

'No,' I say. 'But from now on I think this is how I'm

going to spend every New Year's.'

'Promise?' he says, moving closer into the blanket till his warm leg presses against mine. One side of me, the side that is pleasured by his, is so warm that I am acutely aware of the cold jealously creeping up the other.

I stretch my feet till my toes touch his legs crossed at the ankles. 'God, it's freezing.'

'Why don't we go inside?'

'Okay,' I say, snuggling closer to his side, my toes moving the cuffs of his pants up a little to rest between his bare legs. His spiky hairs sneak between my toes and tickle the tender crevices.

For a long time we just sit there, not speaking or breathing. There is such turmoil within me, I'm afraid it will transfer itself to the very earth I sit on.

'Simran?' he whispers.

'Hm?'

'Let's go inside.'

I nod. But we continue sitting, our forms trembling with the cold and something else, except my toes which are very warm now. Lucky toes.

'You know what?' Arun says after a while. 'My arse is frozen.'

I laugh and pull my feet out. 'Let's go inside.'

We get up. I hold the blanket around me and we tiptoe inside. Bishan and Shurajit are fast asleep on the floor in one corner of the room, wrapped in their sun-fragrant blankets. A deep snore, perhaps Bishan's, reverberates in the room. Beside them is a bare mattress with a blanket folded on one end, waiting for Arun.

Going around the empty mattress, I walk to my room and swinging open the door, step inside. He stands at the door looking fixedly at my mattress, his hands clenched in the pockets of his jeans, digging deep, as though bearing down upon his weight to prevent himself from being drawn into the room.

'Arun?' I say softly.

His eyes jump to my face, and my legs begin to melt at

the knees from the heat in them. I extend my hand to him—perhaps, only to support myself.

'Goodnight, Simran,' he says and turning abruptly, walks quickly to the room with the extra mattress. Somehow I manage to walk to my own mattress and lowering myself on it, pull the blanket over my head, trying to block out everything. But when another burst of fireworks flashes in the sky, I know my window lights up with its brilliance.

The next morning when I emerge from my room, I find Arun sitting under the peepul tree, smoothing a hand back and forth over a gnarly root. His eyes are downcast, watching his hand as if he is involved in some deep therapy.

'Hi.' I lower myself beside him. The sun is hazy this morning. Perhaps the smoke from the fireworks last night has smudged its rays.

'We've got to talk,' he says.

I nod.

He digs for something in the breast pocket of his shirt.

'Here,' he says, holding Scott's ring out to me. 'I think you'd better wear this now.'

I sit staring at the ring for long minutes. Then, taking it from his hand, I fold my fist around it.

'I'm sorry,' he says.

The cluster of diamonds and rubies digs into the flesh of my palm.

'Scott really loves you.'

'How is he?' I say, swallowing.

'He's fine. He's still in Delhi. He called me yesterday and told me to wish you a Happy New Year and to tell you that he really misses you. He'll return by the end of the week. I'll see what the police situation is. Then, perhaps, I'll take you to see him.'

I nod.

'He's a fine man. You deserve someone like him.'

I open my palm and look at the ring again. The skin around it is a dull red as though the ruby has bled.

'Well, I'll see you soon. I've got to go.' He gets up and stands for a moment looking down at me, making no attempt to hide the need in his eyes.

I nod and look away towards the trees. I cannot bear to see his face so exposed.

When I hear footsteps moving away from the peepul, I call his name. He stops.

I walk up to him. 'The last time you were here you said something about twenty hours. What did you mean?'

He takes a deep breath and looks far away into the trees. 'I thought if I could spend twenty hours with you it would be enough.'

'Enough for what?'

He doesn't answer, just continues looking at the trees.

'You still owe me some hours,' I say and turn around. Behind me I hear silence. Without looking back I walk towards the kitchen. I finish making tea before I hear the revving of the motorcycle engine and a drone of reverberating sound. Slowly I get up and walk to my room. Pulling out the green dupatta from my bag, I take one corner of it and tie the ring in it. I know I will never wear it again.

chapter thirteen

The news of the bombing of the school bus in Karachi precedes Kalida's arrival. One morning I see Shurajit sitting before a steaming pot, reading an article in the newspaper intently. As soon as he sees me enter, he folds the paper and slips it between some pots.

'What were you reading?' I ask.

'Nothing of importance,' he says, not meeting my eyes. 'Just some article.'

'About what?'

'A school bus was bombed in Karachi.'

'That's terrible. Was anybody hurt?'

He's quiet for a while, pouring tea for me. 'There were twenty-two children on board.'

'Good God! You know, this is what I don't understand about terrorists. Why do they have to hurt ordinary citizens—innocent children at that? Their fight isn't with children.'

Shurajit gets up hurriedly and leaves the kitchen. I pull out the paper from where he has hidden it and read the headlines: BOMB BLAST IN SCHOOL BUS KILLS 22 CHILDREN AND DRIVER. JIYE SIND SUSPECTED.

Kalida returns two days later. One evening, sitting on the stairs watching the sun set, I see him walking up the wooded path. A bag is slung over his shoulder. His hair is tied back from his forehead; the lines on his face are more austere; his eyes are deep dark pieces of coal, combustible at the first hint of flame.

I run to him and, taking the bag from his shoulder, bend to touch the dust of his feet to my forehead. He places his palm flat on my back and takes a deep breath. 'Thakur mongol korey,' he says.

'How are you, Kalida?' I ask him, straightening up.

He looks at the trees in the distance as though the question has come from them. 'I wish the children had been spared.'

'You're talking about the school bus in Karachi? I read about that. When will all this end, Kalida? When will the healing begin?'

'There can be no healing. More will follow,' he says, as an ordinance already written.

'I wish there was a way in which we could stop all this.'

'Shivratri is in two weeks. Religious fervour will be high. Come, there's a lot of work to be done.'

Bishan and Shurajit meet him in the courtyard. Each touches his feet in reverence. He blesses them and prepares for his bath.

A few days later, I am walking in the grove one afternoon when I see a young boy running up the path to the compound.

'Kalida,' he pants, bending over double to regain some of his breath.

I run inside and call Kalida who is sitting at the desk in the front room, filling the syringe-back of his pen with black ink. 'There's a boy here to see you. He seems to be very agitated.'

Kalida gets up and gathering up the loose corner of his dhoti, rushes out.

'Kalida,'—the boy's voice is a little more composed— 'Janki Das. They killed him and his family. Come quickly, Kalida.'

'Bishan, Shurajit, come with me.' Kalida begins to run towards the path. I join the others, not even thinking about the wisdom of my action.

Down by the peanut stand, we await a bus or any form of transportation. An Ambassador coming up the road stops beside us and a man with a bulging belly hardly concealed by a starched white kurta with gold buttons, steps out. He folds his hands before Kalida. 'Can I give you a ride?' he asks.

Kalida nods and we bundle in at the back.

'Is everything all right?' the man asks, turning around to look at Kalida.

'I think Janki Das and his family have been killed. I just got the news.'

'Oho. That is terrible.' He instructs the driver to step on it, directing him to go to Krishan Nagar.

'We were afraid of something like this,' he continues. 'With the Shivratri procession only a few weeks away and the trouble in Kashmir, we were afraid of this.'

'Who's he?' I whisper to Shurajit.

'He owns a couple of diamond stores in Hira Mandi. He's a member of a Hindu organization, but he donates regularly to our cause.'

The Ambassador speeds through the streets of Amritgarh, honking incessantly at the traffic, squeezing through tight spaces, turning into the narrow streets of a residential area and coming to a halt behind a dozen police vehicles and a rapidly increasing crowd. 'Saab, the police will only let the press or police vehicles through. I can't go any further,' the driver informs the man.

'That's all right,' Kalida says, opening the door on his side and getting out quickly. As I step out behind the boy, a police officer appears, waving the driver of our car away. Instinctively, I step behind Shurajit. Kalida rushes into the crowd, elbowing his way through. Bishan follows. As Shurajit begins to do the same, I grab his kurta from behind. He covers my hand with his own. Slowly we turn around and begin walking in the direction from which we have come.

'I'm sorry. I feel so selfish. I mean, all those people there, dead, and I'm worried about being discovered. I'm sorry. Perhaps, if I'd worn my sari ... I feel so exposed in this outfit. We left in such a hurry I didn't even pick up the dupatta. I could have covered my face with it.'

Shurajit squeezes my hand as we continue to walk around the corner, away from the crowd, away from the police cars and away from death, without so much as a glimpse at its face. Behind us a lone voice rises tentatively from the pit of the crowd: 'Musalmaan tu jaag zara (Oh Muslim awaken),' followed by another voice, a little stronger, a little surer: 'Zulmi shaitan ko maar gira (Kill the cruel oppressor).' A hum, as though arising from the rays of a magnetic flux, greets the lone voices and then more voices join in till the air is rent with remorseless admission of the deed. Shurajit and I keep walking. Suddenly, a car stops beside us. Shurajit comes around to stand between me and the vehicle, taking my hand in his again. A window winds down on the passenger side and Arun's face looks out.

'What are you doing here?' he asks me.

'I'm taking her back,' Shurajit says. 'The news came as such a shock, she just ran along with the rest of us.'

'Get in,' Arun tells us.

'Are you going to take us to Jhakher?' I ask him.

'Not if you don't want to go.'

'I don't, but the police?'

'I don't think they'll notice. Just remember to keep your head away from the windows. We're going in there.'

Shurajit and I climb into the back seat. The PRESS sticker flashes big on the windscreen. I duck my head as we pass policemen standing at the outer edges of the crowd, holding back the thrust of people with heavy bamboo staffs. Arun's colleague stops the car just on the inside of the crowd, squeezes in between two other press vehicles and comes to a halt behind an ambulance. He gets out, gesturing to Arun.

'Are you going to stay with her?' Shurajit asks him. Arun nods and Shurajit gets out of the car, too. 'I'll be back soon,' he says to me. 'Just stay inside the car and keep your head down. You think you'll be all right?'

I nod. Arun slides over to the driver's seat and sits for a moment looking at me in the rear-view mirror. I notice a fine web of red weariness in the whites of his eyes, as if he hasn't been sleeping well.

'I'll be all right,' I say, looking away. 'You can go if you want to.'

'Yes,' he says, but continues sitting there, running a hand through his hair.

'Who was Janki Das?' I ask after a while.

'He was the head of the temple committee.'

'Why did they kill him?'

'He was planning to take the Shivratri procession through a Muslim section.'

'Why? Didn't he know it would upset the Muslims?'

'He was a bastard,' he says with more than warranted anger.

I look in the rear-view mirror in surprise. I can tell in his eyes that the anger is directed at something within himself. Pushing back his hair with both hands, he finally opens the door and, without saying a word to me, walks into the crowd. I follow his back to a group gathered in front of a large house. As he draws near, some people step aside and I see on the ground before them, two bodies covered in white sheets smattered a bright red. Such a rich colour, the colour of blood. Then the circle closes around the sight. I turn my head to look towards Janki Das's house and see Kalida sitting on the doorstep holding the prone figure of a little girl to his chest. Long black braids with blue ribbons tied in neat bows at the ends hang over his arm. The front of his white kurta gets smeared with blood as he cradles her in his lap. I see his shoulders shake and in between slogans I hear sobs, compulsive, wrenched from the very heart of grief. Some people remove the girl from his arm and lay her on the ground beside the other two corpses. Then they pull a white sheet over her that spreads way past her little legs. In a moment, a bright red begins to bud in the centre of the sheet. The sobs rise now, like a ground swell, drowning out the slogans. Kalida falls back against the door, his head leaning against the door jamb, one arm open-palmed, lying on his legs and the other, listless against his stomach. Arun comes to sit beside him, putting his arm around him and drawing his head to his shoulder. Policemen emerge from the house and behind them, an old woman comes out beating her sagging breasts and wailing. She stands at the door, pounding the jamb with her forehead. Bishan goes to her and holds her against his big chest.

Suddenly, a man from the crowd breaks free of the bamboo staffs and stands facing the people. 'My Hindu brothers, if the Musalmaan in this country think they can put fear in our hearts with this cruelty, they are mistaken. This is a land of Hindus and we will not let the stooges of Pakistan take it over. Janki Dasji has gone, but the Shivratri juloos will be, and it will pass through Islam Market just as he had planned.'

Such a commotion follows this statement, I'm afraid the whole crowd is going to self-destruct before my eyes.

'If the Musalmaan think they can get away with these murders, let me inform them that Hindus are no cowards. We can respond in kind. If there has to be bloodshed, so be it. Let me warn them that rivers of blood will flow before we let them dictate to us in our own country.'

I look towards the policemen, expecting them to push this man back into the fold of the crowd, but he continues to persist unrestrained.

I look towards Kalida, urging him with my mind to rise and put a stop to this talk of violence, but he seems too engulfed in his own grief.

'My Hindu brothers, the time has come for revenge.' There is loud applause from the crowd. 'Show them, my brothers, that Hindus are not eunuchs.' A war-like yell breaks out as if the revenge would be meted out this instant. People fall upon each other, beating and clawing. Women start screaming. Policemen raise their batons to lash out.

'Kalida,' I yell, not even aware that I have stepped out of the car, and run towards him. 'Make them stop.'

Kalida moves his head from Arun's shoulder and looks at me uncomprehending, tears mirrored in his coal-black eyes. 'Kalida,' I grip his arm and try to pull him up. 'Make them stop. Say something to them. Tell them about peace.'

Arun releases Kalida and stands up.

'Kalida!' I grab him by his shoulders and shake him. Screams rise in the crowd now as the policemen enter it and a stampede breaks out. Sinking to the doorstep beside Kalida, I begin to sob, 'Kalida, talk to them; talk about peace.'

He rises at last, like a messiah, drawing his small frame up to its full height, tears still streaming down his face, grey hair loose around his shoulders.

'Revenge,' his voice trembles over the violence and descends into its midst, seeping through the cracks. 'Revenge,' he says again, a little more steadily now. Yells get halted in throats, screams get severed in mid-volume, and a hush begins to spread over the crowd. 'So more little girls can die, more mothers can lose their sons, more wives their husbands and more sisters their brothers? The colour of blood, my friends, is not Musalmaan or Hindu or Sikh or Christian. The colour of blood is red. The colour of blood is death. And you saw it today. Blood. Not just Hindu blood, but human blood, a loved one's blood, Indian blood. When will the people of India realize this?' He pauses for a moment, his eyes searching the crowd. 'Are you all Indians?' he asks.

Silence.

'Are you?'

'Yes,' tentative voices reply.

'I tell you today that you are not, because if you were, you would not kill India's children, your own brothers and sisters. No, my brothers, not revenge. Brotherhood. No more blood, no more fights, no more Hindu Musalmaan, but brothers in this the bosom of our mother, our Hindustan. No more blood. No more revenge.'

Peace lasts for a few minutes and then the voice of doom. 'If you want peace, Kalida, tell your Hindu brothers no Shivratri juloos in Islam market, or we Musalmaans will see to it that they regret it.'

Kalida raises his hand. 'I will try, but I want you, my Musalmaan brothers, to promise that there will be no more violence till that time.'

There are grunts of agreement. 'Now go home,' Kalida says, waving his hand at the people. 'Go home peacefully so that these bodies can be taken to the hospital.' Slowly, crumbling at the edges, the mob begins to leave the area. I watch it spread out of the street, a river of bodies flowing out. Eventually, the police jeeps begin to back out of the street along with the press vehicles. Finally, only the ambulance and the people near the bodies remain. Kalida steps up and with the help of three other men, raises the corner of one stretcher and climbs into the back of the waiting ambulance. Shurajit and Bishan help pick up the other, and Arun, the third. The old woman rushes to them, clawing at their arms, trying to pull the stretchers down. Some women pull her away and take her back to the doorstep. I rise and watch a man in a white lab coat close the doors of the ambulance. Slowly, the vehicle goes down the street and disappears around the corner. Suddenly the old woman frees herself from restraining hands and rushes into the empty street, wailing, 'Come back, come back. Don't take my children away.' I stand watching her, and anger fills my being—anger at the old woman's grief, anger at her for having borne a son who perpetuated this. I watch her stand alone in the middle of the street beating her sagging breasts and lamenting her bereaved womb; but I cannot go to her. I cannot console her. I can only stand and watch her; and then slowly, I turn towards the street and, stepping within a foot of her shrivelled form, begin to walk away into the city.

I walk aimlessly for hours, through bustling markets lit up with neon signs, through quiet residential streets with lighted windows showing families sitting together watching television screens, unmindful of the blood seeping just under the skin of the earth. On and on I walk, a hopelessness invading my being. I remember Daddy telling me how after arriving in San Francisco, he wandered up and down the hilly streets of the foreign city for days, sleeping on park benches in the shadows of skyscrapers with the bag of gold coins hidden inside his shirt, and his quilt folded under his

head. He ate from garbage cans outside Chinatown, afraid
to buy food with his stolen gold. Then one day, an old
American lady with grey hair piled on top of her head and
very white, shrivelled skin saw him and took him to the Sikh
temple society at Berkeley. They gave him food there and a
change of clothes and got him employment as a farm worker
in a rice field. It was different there. Even though most of the
other workers were Indians, he felt no fellow feeling. He
worked alone, never exchanging stories about his life with
the others, never sharing their nostalgia for home. In fact, in
the evenings, after work, his eyes still pricking from the
husks he had separated from kernels of rice, he would follow
the shrill sirens of foghorns and disappear inside the wet
nimbus of fog rising out of the waters around the city. Some
days he would stand for hours, staring at the automobiles
running back and forth on the suspended driveways of the
Golden Gate bridge, on others, he would ride the cable car
up and down Nob Hill, wondering if his heart would leap
out of his body along with his breath when the carriage went
down the steep incline. Some evenings he would peer at the
lighted balloons of bay windows and listen to lilting sounds
of music and happy laughter and be amazed at it, for in all
his years, he had never heard such uninhibited laughter. It
was so different there, he was sure that his life, prior to this
foreign place, would cease to exist in space and he would be
able to begin another life.

Then one day, news that India was finally free came to
the farm and along with that came news of the finality of
Partition. That evening, sitting away from the other workers,
drinking beer and celebrating freedom from British rule,
Daddy saw emotions run wild among the Indian workers.
All of a sudden, a young Sikh, Beant Singh, stood up and in
a drunken fit, fell upon Rahematullah, a Muslim worker,
blaming him for the Partition. Soon, the other workers were
upon the Musalmaan. Daddy sat alone, watching the men
beat up Rahematullah. He saw the man's face become a
bloody mound of flesh as blow fell upon blow and he went
down, his arms raised before his face to ward them off.

Daddy saw his Muslim blood and he saw his own father stuffing his entrails back into his belly. He saw Gajji's decapitated body riding the tonga, and suddenly, he too was upon the prone figure, beating it, kicking it, smashing its face with his feet. And then he ran. He ran back to the streets. That night, lying on a bench in the park, he looked up at the sky and saw a star dislodge and begin to fall deep, deep into the blackness of space, and he knew that nothing had changed—not the world, not the people, not he— nothing except the corner of the pit that housed his life; a pit so deep that no living matter could crawl out of it.

I look up at the sky so brilliant, the stars so steady. No star falls out, because I know that the one that fell was the one Daddy saw and that is still orbiting somewhere in the darkness, its death inevitable. Once a star begins to die, who can save it?

I know now that Daddy cannot be rescued, not even by the all-forgiving waters of the Ganga. I know he seeks his atonement and that his liberation from interminable penance lies in a miracle that, perhaps, only Kalida can perform.

I'm not sure how long I walk, but I suddenly see fluorescent lights and a red and white sign reading 'Palace Hotel'. I climb up the short drive and pull open the glass door. I walk up to the reception desk and ask for Scott Ferrier's room.

The receptionist looks at me from head to toe, noting my untidy hair pulled free from the braid, my green silk salwar-kameez with streaks of grime, my street-blackened bare feet, and hesitates for a moment before dialling a number on her phone.

'Mr Ferrier, there's a young lady down here who wants to see you,' I hear her say, and then she turns to me and asks me my name in Hindi.

'Simran,' I say. 'Simran Mehta.'

She repeats it into the phone and a moment later tells me to wait. 'Mr Ferrier will be down in a minute.'

I stand by the reception desk, looking aimlessly around. Except for a man in a white and red bellhop's jacket, the foyer is empty, and then suddenly there is Scott, hurrying towards me, his face lit up with joy. His beaming manner is so at odds at this time, I almost turn around to go back out again.

'Simi,' he says, looking around hurriedly. 'What a surprise!' He draws me into his arms and whispers, 'What are you doing here? Is it safe?' Then, seeing the receptionist looking at us with interest, he steers me towards the elevator. 'Come, let's go up to my room,' he says. 'You're so cold. Why aren't you wearing something warm?'

Once in his room, he sits on the bed holding me close. 'Something happened, right? Tell me what happened, Simi. Where's Arun? What are you doing here by yourself? Are you all right?'

Suddenly, such a trembling takes over my body that my teeth begin to chatter. 'God, you're freezing,' he says. 'Here, let me.' He draws me down on the bed and pulls the blanket over me, tucking it under my chin, but the trembling continues, shaking the bed as though with tremors from a terrible malaise. Scott slips into bed with me and pulls me into his arms, lending me the warmth of his body. His hand slips under my shirt and begins to rub my back. He places his lips against mine and stills the chattering teeth with his tongue, all the while pressing himself close, transferring his warmth to me. Slowly his hand comes around between us and his fingertips, now no longer brisk, rise over the mound of my breast and circle my nipple through the fabric of my bra. His tongue shoots past my teeth, delving deep into my mouth to shoo the cold away. His hands begin to pull my shirt up around my neck and then reach down to untie the cord of my salwar. Putting me down on the bed again, he removes his clothes and takes me in his arms once more, pressing himself against me. I can feel the outer layers of my skin tingle with his warmth, but the blood inside me is so cold, I can feel myself tremble deep within. Reaching behind me, Scott unsnaps my bra and pulls it off. His lips begin to move over my breasts now, holding the stone-cold nipples in the hot cove of his mouth before sucking on them. 'I need to be warmed on the inside,' I want to tell him and, as though he has read my silent plea, he hooks his thumbs in the waistband of my panties and slides them off. Scott begins to caress me, with his hands first and then with his tongue. His gentleness gives way to an urgent probing. I can feel his burning restiveness before he slips inside me, and I let myself be penetrated with his warmth. Slowly, as though straightening out the limbs of a collapsible doll, I relax each muscle. Suddenly, Scott withdraws and slips out of bed. Instinctively, I draw my legs close together to contain the heat he has left behind, but he returns a moment later and takes me back in his arms. He separates my legs with his own, and I feel a cold sheath inside me. I cry then, feeling so bereft, so cold, so deprived of the warmth he had promised for a moment.

Later, I lie awake, listening to him breathe evenly. Slipping out of bed, I lift the cover to look for my clothes. He opens his eyes. 'What are you doing?'

'I'm going back.'

'To Jhakher?'

I nod.

He looks at me for a moment, his eyes searching my face. 'What happened, Simi? What are you doing here?'

I shake my head. 'It doesn't matter now. I've got to get back. Daddy's ashes are there.'

'Arun told me he managed to get them. When are you going to scatter them?'

'Very soon now. Perhaps today. I've got to talk to Arun.'

'Why did you come to town?'

'There was a shooting. I came with the others.'

'See, I told you it's hopeless,' he says triumphantly, sitting up. 'These people are bent upon destroying themselves. There's nothing you can do. As soon as you take care of your father's ashes, I'll get our tickets for home.'

I let him talk while I dress, then I turn around and say, 'You go home, Scott. I can't. I'm sorry. Thanks for taking care of me.' I move towards the door.

'Wait a minute.' He bounds out of bed and pulls on a

pair of boxer shorts. 'What do you mean, you can't? I thought the deal was you were only going to stay till you scattered the ashes?'

I don't say a word. I don't want to tell him how Daddy's soul will probably never find peace, that there seems to be no redemption for him. I don't want to tell him how the idea of abandoning him here to suffer interminably, chills my heart. I don't want to tell him that Kalida's organization seems Daddy's only hope, that I am the only link to that hope—his hope in death, as he had called me. Scott wouldn't understand. Ever since he came to India, our lives have diverged. Somehow, he just doesn't seem to understand any more. It is as if he hears my words, but they are foreign and unfathomable. I wonder how that has happened. Or perhaps, our language was always alien; we just never talked to each other before.

'You're crazy,' he says. 'This country has really fucked your mind.'

I open the door.

'Wait,' he says. 'Just tell me one thing. Did you or did you not promise me that you'll leave once you've scattered the ashes?'

'I didn't promise anything.'

'I can't believe this.' He walks back into the room distractedly, going to stand at the windows with his back to me. 'I quit my job and come thousands of miles to rescue the woman I love, and she tells me she doesn't want to be rescued. Shit,' he says, moving the curtain aside with an angry hand. A three-quarter moon peeps out from the folds.

I just stand there at the door, not saying anything, feeling grateful for the guilt that engulfs me.

'Do you still love me?' Scott asks.

I'm glad his back is to me because I don't want the coldness in me to negate the pain his face will surely show when I tell him what I must. But he turns around slowly, letting the curtain fall back into place, hiding the face of the moon.

'Do you, Simi?'

'Yes,' I say quietly. 'I'll always love you. I always have. But I don't think I'm in love with you. Perhaps I never was. We were so comfortable with each other, like Siamese twins joined at the hip, never imagining life without each other, manipulating our moves to accommodate the other. But we seem to have been severed now. Perhaps Daddy's death did it, or perhaps, India. I don't know. I only know that I can see you standing across from me now and that length between us is widening. I'm sorry, Scott. I'll always love you. The part of me that shared blood cells with you will always remain with you. But there's a whole new me that you don't know, that I didn't even know existed.'

'It's not you. It's this damned country. Don't you see how it's changing you?'

'Yes. This country is changing me. It's making me realize who I really am,'

'It's not. It's imposing itself upon you. It's messing you up. You've been overwhelmed by everything that's happened. You'll get over it. Believe me. You just need to distance yourself. You need to come back home.'

'This is my home, Scott, just like it was Daddy's.'

'So, that's it. It's not you. It's not this country. It's your father. I can't believe you're letting a dead man come between us.' And suddenly, his face looks stricken. 'I'm sorry. I'm sorry, Simi. I didn't mean to say that. It's just that I'm ... I think you're making a big mistake.'

'I've got to stay, Scott,' I say, reaching for the knob behind me. 'I'm sorry I put you through so much. You've been a real friend. Goodbye, Scott. Promise me you'll go back to the US.' I turn around and pull the door open.

'Hold on.' I turn to face him. He leaps across the room in a panic. 'You're saying it's over between us?'

I nod. 'I'm sorry,' I say, looking at him steadily. He looks back at me, his eyes searching mine like a child trying to figure out a problem.

'Goodbye, Scott,' I say again, softly.

'I love you, Simi.' His voice sounds confused, as though surprised by the survival of a love no longer reciprocated. I want to put my arms around him then and tell him about the obligations of love, the debts that one must pay. But then I recall the crushing weight of those debts and seek only to protect him. 'Go back to the US, Scott,' I say, turning away from him towards the open door.

'How will you go back?' he asks from behind me.

'I'll take a cab or something,' I say without looking at him.

'I'll call Arun.'

'No. Don't. I don't want to disturb him at this time. I can go on my own.'

'Are you out of your mind? It's the middle of the night. Don't put yourself in more danger than you are already. Hold on, I'm calling him.'

I step inside and close the door again. Scott pulls out his telephone book from the nightstand and thumbs through the pages. '27365,' he says the number aloud before dialling it. 'Arun? Scott,' I hear him say. And then, 'Yes, she's here.' He replaces the receiver, and without looking at me, tells me Arun is on his way. He sits with his head in his hands, his shoulders slumped, weary.

I lean against the wall and slide down to sit by the door, looking away from him. I can't go to him. The comfort in my arms is ruinous.

'I wish you would forget this whole India thing,' he says after a while. 'You're not cut out for it. Why can't you just come back with me? You don't have to marry me if you don't want to. Just come back home. You can donate money to the cause from the US. You can even adopt a child from India. You don't have to be here to help. Remember when we were in school and you wanted to sponsor a child in Ethiopia and we had no extra money, so I took that job delivering newspapers? Remember, how we used to sit bundled together in my Beetle and drive around town at 5 a.m., swinging newspapers out of the window into people's frontyards?

'We never sent the money.'

'No, we still owe some starved child seventy cents a day.

That's how many days—let me see . . . How long has it been
since sophomore year? Seven years? That's three hundred
and sixty-five days a year, into seven. How much is that?'
He pulls out a drawer and gets a pencil.

'2135 days,' I say before he can calculate on the paper.
I was always better than him at math.

'2135 into seventy cents makes it 16145 cents. That's
$161.45. So, we still owe that child one hundred and sixty-
one dollars and forty-five cents. Let's go back and send that
money. Come on, Simi. You don't belong here. You belong
in my red Bug painted in giant black polka dots.'

'You don't even have that car any more.'

'Ladybird Bug or black Honda Accord, what difference
does it make as long as it's my car? And I need you sitting
beside me on the passenger seat.' I can't bear the pleading
note in his voice.

'Delivering newspapers?' I say on a false laugh, trying to
swallow the lump in my throat. I know if I cry now he will
log each tear as a debt he owes.

He laughs back half-heartedly. 'If you want, I can pick
up that job again. I need a job anyway.'

'Scott, don't, please.'

He looks down at his hand placed palm down on the
blue faux velvet bedspread, following the shape of the
fingers all the way to the flowered self-pattern in the fabric.
'I'll call the airline tomorrow,' he says quietly to his hand.

I lean my head back against the wall and close my eyes.

The phone rings, jolting us both. Scott's fingers hover
over the receiver for a second before he picks it up. 'We'll be
down in a minute, thank you,' he says. Then, still not
looking at me, he says, 'Arun's here.'

I get up, wanting to go to Scott one last time, to look
into his eyes just to make sure the aquarelle in them is still
intact. But Scott gets up suddenly and with long strides,
hurries towards the bathroom. 'Please close the door behind
you,' he says over his shoulder. His voice sounds strained. I
haven't seen Scott cry since the time he got his first chin hair.
I remember it was during a summer vacation. One morning

he walked into my house with his chin held high, strutting like a proud peacock, displaying a tiny, fine hair growing out of a corner of his chin like a dropped eyelash. He called me a baby, boasting about how much of a grown-up he was, especially since my androgynous form at that time seemed to show no signs of maturing into womanhood. I remember I was so jealous I couldn't bear it. So that afternoon when he napped on the lounger in the backyard, I armed myself with my mother's eyebrow tweezers and yanked his burgeoning manhood out. Scott woke up, yowling in pain. I brandished the tweezers in front of his eyes, letting him see the symbol of his manhood ruthlessly uprooted. He cried then, not loud sobs, but quiet tears running down his cheeks, his lips trembling at the corners as if to contain the pain of having lost all.

I let myself out, shutting the door behind me soundlessly, and walk to the elevator.

Arun is standing by the reception desk, his face a study in wrath. He takes my hand and rushes me out of the hotel.

'Are you crazy?' he whispers to me through clenched teeth. 'Don't we have enough on our hands to worry about without having you slip off to meet your lover?'

I let him pull me along to the side of the hotel where his motorcycle is parked in the shadow of a wall.

'I told you I would bring Scott to Jhakher when it was safe. Couldn't you wait till then?'

'I'm sorry,' I say quietly. 'I didn't mean to worry you.'

'You know, Kalida has sent Bishan and Shurajit into Amritgarh looking for you. They're probably still out there wandering the streets. Tomorrow I would have had to go to the police again.'

'I'm sorry,' I say again.

He grunts and kick-starts his motorcycle. I wait for him to get on before straddling the seat behind him.

The wind is cold and painful as it lashes against my face, my bare arms and my hands. I shiver and draw closer to his back, letting him buffer most of its punishment. My hands holding the sides of the seat soon numb and my shivering becomes uncontrollable. Arun stops the motorcycle on the side of the road and takes off his jacket.

'Here. Haven't you been here long enough to know nights get really chilly? Why didn't you borrow something from Scott?'

'I don't want your jacket,' I say, tears pricking my eyes more from his words than the wind.

'You'd better take it. Believe me, no one has the time to look after you if you get pneumonia.'

I grab the jacket and slip it on angrily, thrusting my arms into the warmth of the sleeves. He watches me struggle with the zipper in front with my numb fingers before brushing my hands aside and zipping it.

Silently, he kicks the engine on again and I get on, gripping the sides of the seat to keep from falling as he turns sharply round the corners. From time to time I bring up my fisted hands and blow into them to reawaken their life. At an even stretch of road, I feel Arun's hand as cold as mine on my hand on the seat. Slowly his fingers pry mine open and, bringing my hand to the pocket of his pants, he slips it in. Then he does the same with the other. I stretch my fingers and lay them flat against his thighs. Through the thin material of his pockets, I can feel his muscles contract for a moment as though his body is rejecting the foreign objects placed against the skin, then his blood changes course and detours through the vessels of my palms. And for the first time that evening, a warmth begins to flow through my body. I lay my cheek on his back and let the tears flow, soaking his shirt and scalding his back, paying him back in kind.

The compound is dark as we drive up the path, but as we reach the courtyard, a light in Kalida's room approaches the door, and he walks out, turning on the switch in the front room. He is still wearing the clothes stained with the little girl's blood.

I get off the bike and bend to touch his feet.

'Are you all right?' he asks raising me by the shoulders.

I nod. 'I'm sorry. I didn't mean to cause you so much worry.'

He nods. 'Tell Bishan and Shurajit,' he calls out to Arun before turning to go back inside. I watch him walk into his room, and in a moment, the light is extinguished.

I turn towards Arun, but he is already kicking the engine of his motorcycle alive.

'Thanks,' I say to him over the din. 'For everything.' He swings his leg over the machine and kicks back the break. I cross my arms over my belly and grip my elbows. 'Oh, wait a minute.' I wave a hand before his face. He puts his feet on the ground and pushes the motorbike to park again.

I unzip the jacket and take it off.

'Thanks,' I say, handing it to him. He takes the jacket and pulls it on before releasing the break again and driving off, leaving a plume of smoke in his wake. Slowly I walk into the house and spread two mattresses on the floor for Shurajit and Bishan before sitting down by the desk, waiting for them.

Just as the sun begins to peek over the trees, I hear them trudging up the path, their feet dragging as if they have walked all night, which they probably have.

I run out to greet them. Their tired faces light up on seeing me safely back. I grab them both by the waist and we sway together in a group hug. Kalida, coming out from his room, smiles at our reunion. 'Today we start work for the Shivratri procession,' he says.

Our smiles wan immediately. We detach ourselves from each other and begin preparing for the day.

chapter fourteen

For the next couple of weeks, people come and go in the commune. Kalida arranges a meeting of leaders from both factions, Muslim and Hindu. I am allowed to sit in for some of the negotiations. The Muslims seem to have a valid claim: every year the Hindus organize a procession for Shivratri which goes through all the main markets except Islam Market where most of the Muslim stores and a masjid are located. But this year the Hindus are insistent on leading the procession right through this bazaar, passing in front of the masjid before proceeding to a Shiva temple located in the next market. The Muslims want to know why.

The Hindu leaders insist that the couple of Hindu stores in Islam Market have always felt left out of the festivities, and this year, the juloos committee has decided to include them. 'It should have been done many years ago, but we were remiss,' one of the leaders says.

'But they can join the procession. Why does the procession have to go to them?' one Muslim leader wants to know.

'The holy procession makes the surroundings auspicious,' another Hindu replies. 'The owners of those stores have as much right to God's grace as any other Hindu.'

'But that is a Musalmaan section and we want Allah's grace there, not Shiva's.'

'But those two stores are not Musalmaan.'

'Then we'll have to do something about that. Maybe those stores shouldn't be there.'

I can see nostrils flare and eyes narrow. Voices begin to rise and postures become belligerent.

'That road is a thoroughfare. It is not the private property of your minority. It belongs to all the people of Amritgarh,' the Hindu leader insists.

'But we as a minority, have rights, too. It is the duty of the government to uphold the rights of minorities and to protect them. Now we ask you, Kalida, to take our cause to the government and have an order passed against this procession.'

I can see how all this just goes around in circles over and over again. Finally, Kalida is able to make the leaders agree on a compromise—that the procession will go through a portion of Islam Market, but instead of passing before the mosque, it will veer off into a street behind it to emerge again onto the main road a few kilometres past the masjid.

I am jubilated at seeing a potentially volatile situation diffused so successfully. Gratitude for Kalida and hope for Daddy swells in my heart.

Despite the promises of the leaders, Kalida continues rigorous preparations for Shivratri.

'Do you still foresee danger in the situation?' I ask him.

'Behind the disguise of religion, treachery smiles,' he says. 'I hope it will not live up to its nature this time. But we have to be prepared. We will distribute handouts professing unity and tolerance, but I'm sure the Hindu leaders will spread their own word, telling the community to unite under the banner of the procession and protect their religion. To hate is easier than to love and tolerate.'

Kalida prepares a speech that he hopes he will not have to use. 'We will only be present to diffuse any potential danger,' he says. 'We will spread around the stores and talk to the people to keep them from reacting adversely. That is all we will do, unless . . .' he does not complete the sentence. We prepare for the procession as though for a verdict. The evening before the procession, Bishan and I complete the printing of all material to be used the following day. 'I have to go to Amritgarh to arrange for vehicles for tomorrow,' he says. 'Will you clean up here, sister?'

'Of course.' I take a rag from the corner and begin mopping the machine's sweat. After I'm done, I bring the broom from the kitchen and begin sweeping the room. Discarded paper, swabs of inky cotton, dust balls, all come together in a pile near the machine. I poke the spiky grass of the broom under the machine to woo any stray dirt there. When I pull the broom out, a corner of a sheet of paper peeps out. Gripping it with my fingertips I pull it out. It is an A4-size white sheet, not at all creased, but old dust-balls cling to its corners like fuzz. I start to crumple it to add it to the growing pile of dirt when I realize that it looks like nothing Bishan and I have printed for the forthcoming occasion. Faintly curious, I brush off the dirt with my hand and, squatting on my haunches, begin to read.

AN OPEN LETTER TO THE PEOPLE OF SIND

Ever since the formation of Pakistan, the people of Sind have been battling an oppression that is both external and internal. On the one hand, the Government of Pakistan, consisting of a Punjabi majority, has repeatedly ignored Sind's distinct identity, thus suppressing the spirit of the Sindhi people, and on the other, the rampant feudalist designs of government-backed landlords has created a society where people suffer like slaves.

Even the Colonial Raj recognized the individual superiority of Sind and in 1851, declared Sind as the only state with its own language—Sindhi. Sind, dear brothers and sisters, is not a part of Pakistan. It is separate, distinct, superior. Its language is not just one of the languages of Pakistan. It is an expression of the people. It is a medium of freedom.

This is a call to all freedom lovers of Sind to rise and declare a war on all oppression. This is a call to our brothers and sisters to openly condemn dehumanizing slavery. This is a call to unsuppressed spirits to break loose from the stifling bounds of a government that itself is a puppet of foreign powers.

*Rise, people of Sind. We are with you every step
of the way, sharing every wound in the battle, every
drop of blood lost and, finally, every victory.*

Jiye Sind Zindabad.

I flop on the floor, the pile of dirt at my feet scattering every
which way. I know this has been printed by CCPH. In fact,
I do not doubt that it has been printed in the belly of our
very own machine. The typeface is familiar, the ink is the
one I have fed to the machine so often, the formation of
letters the very ones in our typesetter. How could this have
been printed without my knowledge? I have been present at
every printing session, working alongside Bishan all along.
When was this printed, and why?

Suddenly I remember. I remember the night I heard the
machine rumble and the following morning Kalida mentioning
that Bishan had worked on it during the night. He must have
been printing these out, and somehow, one of them slipped
under the machine, lost to his sight. Snatches of conversation
I had with Bishan and Shurajit begin to flash in my mind:
'Kalida will return from Kashmir if everything goes as
planned.' 'Bishan is waiting for the time he will not need a
passport to go to Pakistan.' And I remember Kalida's closed
expression when he told me he didn't want me helping
Bishan at night, and Bishan's anger at Shurajit for insinuating
there was business other than that of peace in Kashmir. I
remember, too, that this work was done just a few days
before Kalida's visit to Kashmir. Kalida must have delivered
this and who knows what else, to the terrorists of Sind.
Then, with painful clarity, I remember the news of the
children killed in a school-bus bombing in Karachi. My hand
flies to cover my mouth as I realize the implications: Kalida
is helping the cause of terrorism in Pakistan. And fast on the
heels of this thought comes denial. No, I tell myself. That is
not possible. Not Kalida, not the man who only a few days
ago sat with a dead child in his lap, crying like he had lost
his own. Not the man who stood before a riotous crowd and
promised unconditional peace. Not the man who was my

hope for Daddy's redemption. But then, hadn't he said, the second principle is violence—first violence, then peace? Oh my God. I am numb as realization dawns on me. This can't be true. This can't be true.

'Didi,' I hear Shurajit's voice outside the room. I get up hurriedly, desperately looking around for some place to hide the letter. Finally, I fold it over and over again till it is as little as a square on a chessboard, and slip it inside my bra.

'Didi,' I hear him call again. I grab the broom and begin sweeping. 'I'm here, Shurajit. I'm cleaning this place. Bishan has gone into town to arrange for a vehicle.'

'I know,' he says entering. 'Dinner is ready. I could use some help serving it.'

'Sure,' I say, gathering the dirt back into a small pile and scooping it up on a piece of cardboard to deposit it in the trash can outside. 'Let me wash my hands and I'll join you in the kitchen.'

I hurry through the meal, hardly eating anything myself, avoiding everyone's eyes.

'What is the matter?' Kalida asks me. 'Are you worried about the procession? Do not worry, ma, Thakur mongol korbey.' I nod, not looking at him, not wanting to see the face of hypocrisy. I help Shurajit clean up and lay extra mattresses on the floor for the activists who will stay the night. Then bidding everyone good night, I go into my room, closing the door behind me and switching off the light.

For hours I sit on the mattress, repeating words from the letter in my mind like a mantra. Rise and declare war. We are with you in every step, in every wound, in every drop of blood lost, in every victory. In my head, I see newspaper reports about riots in Sind, and the Pakistan government's suspicion of a 'foreign hand'. Kalida's hand. The hand of all the members of CCPH and other organizations like it, murderers hiding behind masks of liberators, instigators of violence, robbers of peace. I lie down on the mattress and close my eyes, inviting Daddy inside my head. I want to hear him again. I want to hear him tell me again how keepers of religion sowed seeds of hatred in his unsuspecting heart and how he was banished to Nanowal. How Nanowal went up in flames and how he changed from an innocent, trusting child into a hostile persecutor, from victim to frenzied killer.

Amjad and Daddy attended a Muslim League rally one afternoon. Late that night, Amjad woke Daddy up. 'Come with me,' he whispered. 'I want to show you something.' He was carrying an unlit kerosene lamp in one hand and a rope in the other.

Tiptoeing in their bare feet, they went down the three flights of stairs to the dry well in the backyard. Pushing away the wooden cover of the well, Amjad made an opening large enough for him to slip in. Then pulling out a box of matches from the pocket of his pajamas, he lit the lamp and, tying its wire handle to one end of the rope, handed it to Daddy. 'Lower it into the well gently,' he instructed. Together they watched its formless, flickering light descend into the dark depths of the well, illuminating the dank inside like a ghostly dungeon. When the lantern hit the bed with a soft thud, Amjad pulled the rope up a couple of feet, and taking the end from Daddy, placed it under a large stone.

'Come on,' he said, climbing over the edge, 'Let's go in.' His feet groping for notches in the wall, he began to descend into the well. Daddy followed suit, his bare toes gripping the rough stones exposed in the notches below and his fingers curling around the stones above. Finally, he heard Amjad jump off to land in the soggy bottom with a squelch. He looked down to see in the light of the lantern that swung gently near his head, his friend bending over a large chest on the floor of the well. As Daddy alighted, Amjad snapped open the bolts of the chest and swung the lid back. Ornaments of gold and silver glittered in the chest along with silver utensils. There were also a number of leather bags, their corners tightly bound with string. Whistling under his breath, Daddy bent and reached for a bag. It was heavier than he expected and, as he pulled it out of the chest, he heard a dull tinkle of coins packed closely together.

'Did your father steal these?' Daddy asked Amjad.

'No, these are Ammi's,' Amjad said, pointing to the

ornaments. 'And these,' he poked a finger at a bound bag, 'are full of gold and silver coins that Abu has saved. Abu has hidden these to keep them safe from the Hindus when they come to loot our home.'

Daddy nodded fearfully, thinking that perhaps, Amjad and he ought to hide their kites in the well, too.

After staring at the treasure for a few moments longer, Amjad closed the lid of the chest and shot the bolts home. Then together, Amjad following Daddy, they climbed up the well, pulled out the lamp and tiptoed back into the house to their rooms and fell asleep, dreading the Hindus.

A few days after that, Amjad and his father were turned away from the mosque by the kazi. 'You have a kafir living in your house,' he told them. 'Turn him out, or you will be excommunicated.'

Returning back home, Amjad's father sent his sons upstairs and told his wife about the incident.

'No, never. He is my son,' she screamed. 'I will not turn him out.'

'I am not asking you to turn him out, begum. I am only saying that maybe it will be better if we send him away for a while, at least till this ill wind blows over.'

'But where can we send him? He is an orphan.'

'Maybe to his aunt's?'

'Never. She is no aunt. She will treat him worse than a servant. How can I bear that? He is my son. Don't you understand that? I love him like I do Amjad.'

'Yes, begum. He is my son, too. But they might harm him here.'

'Who?'

'The Muslim League. They want Musalmaans to unite against their Hindu brothers.'

'Allah.' Amjad's mother could say no more. She, too, had felt the tension in the air. In the marketplace, the Hindu women had started avoiding even cursory conversation with their Muslim neighbours. Shops were becoming exclusively Hindu or Muslim.

'But not to his aunt's house. Anywhere but there.'

'I'll see,' Amjad's father promised.

One evening he called Daddy to him. 'Manohar beta, I want you to go to Nanowal,' he told him.

'Where's Nanowal?' Amjad's mother asked, her hand pressed against her heart. The moment she had feared for months seemed to have arrived.

'It's a village near the Yamuna.'

'Why Nanowal?'

'Manohar's father is there.'

'My father?' Daddy had stopped wondering about his father's whereabouts a long time ago. Sometimes, he lay in his bed, reminiscing about life in his village when his whole family had been together, but he never imagined he would see any of them again.

'I have been making inquiries. A friend of mine has relatives in Nanowal. They used to live in your village till the plague drove them away to Nanowal. They knew your father.'

'But my father went to the Himalayas.'

'Yes, maybe for a while. But beta, we cannot all discern Allah. Your father returned. But he is to be revered for trying to achieve that goal. He is better than all of us who only live on accepting His presence, making no effort to reach Him. You will be safe with your father. I will write a letter to him so that he can receive you at the railway station.'

That day Amjad's mother went to the Pir and got an amulet to ensure Daddy's safety. 'How can I be sure he will return to me unharmed?' she asked the Pir. 'These are such troubled times.'

The Pir gave her another amulet similar to the first. 'Put this at the bottom of a trunk. Open it every day after you read the fatiya. If the stone in the amulet remains intact, your son will come back to you unharmed. If the stone vanishes, understand that he is no more.'

She brought the amulets home, holding them secure against her breast. The following morning, after reading the first namaz, she went up to Daddy's room and, while he

slept, quietly tied one amulet around his neck. 'What . . .?'
Daddy mumbled.

'Sh,' she whispered, kissing his forehead. 'Allah will
protect you. Promise me you won't remove this amulet.'
Daddy nodded his head, acknowledging the shield in his
dream state. She placed the other amulet in a piece of red
velvet and slipped it at the bottom of a wooden chest
containing old clothes and Daddy's quilt.

Three days before Daddy's journey, Amjad and Daddy
began to grind glass. They had wandered around garbage
dumps for days, collecting bottles. Now they put those
bottles in a large iron jar and began crushing them into
powder to coat the yarn Daddy would take along for his
kites with him to Nanowal. For two days they hammered
and ground in alternating shifts. Finally, when all that
remained of the bottles was glittering white sand at the
bottom of the pot, they borrowed an old linen dupatta from
Amjad's mother and sieved the glass, collecting the filtered
diamond dust on a newspaper. Then Amjad lit a small fire
in the frontyard and cooked a broth of flour, sago seeds,
water, and the sap of a gum tree. After hours of boiling,
when the broth was thick and sticky, Daddy and Amjad
twined yards of nine strands together and dipped the yarn in
the pot to prepare it for its glass armour. Drawing it out of
the pot on the end of a stick, they walked to the street and
strung it between two lamp posts, tying up the two ends to
stretch it taut. While Daddy coated the yarn with glass
powder, Amjad fine-edged it, running it inside a rag held
between the tips of his index finger and thumb. For a whole
day the yarn was left thus to dry. When Amjad's mother
finished packing all the clothes she had made for Daddy and
two of Amjad's best shirts in a tin trunk she had received in
her dowry, Daddy and Amjad rolled the yarn on a spool and
slipped it into the side of the trunk. Then they decided which
kites Daddy should take with him. Amjad offered him his
two favourite ones, a large red kite with a yellow feathery
tail to impress his opponents, and a small black tailless one
for tough battles. 'Take them,' he advised. 'What if there is

no kite maker in Nanowal?' Daddy took the kites and placed them on top of his clothes in the trunk. 'If I win any kites with these, Amjad, they're yours,' Daddy promised.

By the time the tonga arrived for the railway station, Amjad's mother had tied four rotis, spicy cabbage—his favourite vegetable, a raw onion, and two pieces of his absolute favourite sweetmeat, barfi, in a handkerchief. 'Eat it when you get hungry,' she said, holding him against her bosom.

'Don't come running back to us,' Amjad joked with Daddy on the way to the station. 'Finally, I will be the only son again. Ami will spoil me now as she used to before you stole her love.'

The railway station seemed like the site of a festival celebration. There were people everywhere—crowding tea stalls, haggling with hawkers, squatting among piles of tin trunks and rolled up bedding. As Amjad's father made his way towards a train, Daddy gripped a corner of his loose shirt, afraid that he might lose him in the crowd. The train destined for Nanowal was fast filling up. Tripping over pieces of luggage on the floor of the train and elbowing his way through passengers, Amjad's father located an empty berth. Before anyone else could claim it, he placed Daddy's trunk on it.

'This berth is taken, bhaisaab,' said a woman sitting on the seat across with a baby on her lap. 'My husband has just stepped out to fetch some water.' Her neck and arms were adorned with so many gold ornaments, Daddy wondered how she bore the weight.

'Sister, my son is travelling alone to Nanowal. Surely your husband will not be using the entire berth? My son will only take one corner of it.' The woman looked around, searching for her husband. But not wishing to argue with a strange man, she acquiesced.

Amjad's father lifted the trunk and tried to slide it under the seat, but there was no space; in fact, the entire floor was covered with various pieces of luggage. The woman's feet rested on a large tin trunk.

'Is all this your luggage?' he asked the lady.

'Yes, we are leaving Lahore. I mean, not for good. We'll come back after ... There are so many rumours.'

'Yes, sister, the times are not good. Allah be with you.'

Amjad's father put Daddy's trunk in one corner of the berth beside the window and settled Daddy in. 'Are you going to Nanowal?' he asked the woman.

'Yes. We have to catch another train from there.'

'Could you please alert my son when the train gets there? He might miss the station,' he requested the woman. 'He is travelling alone.'

The woman looked around once again before nodding.

Amjad's father gave Daddy two rupees. 'Use it carefully,' he said, swallowing hard. 'Respect your father. Pay him our regards.' Then kissing him on the forehead, he bid him farewell. Clutching the handkerchief of food and the money in his lap, Daddy watched Amjad and his father get off the train. A few seconds later, there was a tap on his window and Amjad's face peered at him through the dirt-smeared windowpane. Daddy raised one hand, the money still clutched tightly in his fist, and placed it on the pane. He tried to smile but his lips could only manage a trembling lift at the corners. Amjad's face was all crumpled up and his eyes were watery. He put his hand against Daddy's on the pane, his palm open, fingers spread as though imprinting the lines of his fate against Daddy's curled fist. As the train whistled its intention, Amjad's father put his arm around his son's shoulders and drew him away from the tracks. Helplessly, Daddy watched the distance grow between them, his throat hurting from the tears that were knotted there.

The woman across from him was standing now, looking around frantically. She put the baby against her shoulder and it started to cry. Her gold necklaces must have scratched its cheek. His own tears forgotten, Daddy watched her walk to the end of the bogie, straining her burdened neck to distinguish between bobbing heads.

'I told you not to leave the luggage.' A balding man in a white kurta riding high over his fat stomach materialized out of the crowd. Thick gold chains shone around his wrists and at the open neck of his kurta.

They both walked back to their seats, the baby still wailing. Seeing Daddy on his berth, the man stopped short. 'This is my seat,' he told Daddy. 'You can't sit here.' He looked accusingly at his wife. 'Didn't you tell him?' The wife nodded, looking away from Daddy.

'Well, you have to get up.' He reached forward and grabbed Daddy's trunk. 'Go find another place.'

Daddy got up and took his trunk from the man. For a moment he just stood there, his feet fitting awkwardly between two large trunks.

'Go on. I'm sure there's a seat on that side.'

'Let him be, please. We can fit him here. He's only a boy.'

'But he's a Musalmaan.' The man's voice was distrustful as he identified Daddy's salwar-kurta made so lovingly by Amjad's mother on the Singer sewing machine she had received in her dowry.

'He's only a boy,' the wife repeated. 'What can he do?'

The man sat down on the berth, grudgingly allowing Daddy to sit again. The woman settled the wailing baby in her lap and lifting one end of her kameez, directed her bare breast towards its expectant mouth. Then, covering its head with her sheer dupatta, she leaned her head back.

Nanowal was a day and a night's course from Lahore. A few hours into the journey, the woman opened a large basket and passed a platter with cooked cauliflower on rotis and two pieces of mango pickle to her husband. She gestured to Daddy with her chin, but Daddy shook his head and opened his own handkerchief. Licking the last of the spicy vegetable from his fingers, the man filled a glass from a bottle of water and, taking a couple of sips, gargled and got up to spit it out of Daddy's window, spraying Daddy's arm with spittled drops. Then coming back to his seat, the man pulled out a pillow from his luggage and lay down on the berth, his feet almost resting on Daddy's legs. Daddy wiped his arm on his shirt and squeezed as far into the corner as he could, wishing Amjad was with him so that together they could push the man off the berth and sit on it, their legs spread wide.

As the racing scenery in the train window dimmed before his eyes, Daddy's head sank on his trunk and he slept. Hours later, a gentle touch on his shoulder awakened him. He opened his eyes to see the gold bedecked lady standing over him, her baby ogling him with eyes lined thickly with kohl. It took Daddy a moment to realize the train had stopped. He looked around and saw that people were dragging their luggage to the exits of the train. The berths were empty and the floor below him was bare. 'Nanowal has arrived. You have to get off here, don't you?' the woman said and hurried towards her husband's receding back. Daddy jumped up and, grabbing his trunk, headed towards the exit.

He stood on the platform, searching the crowds around him, wondering if his father would recognize him. He tried to recall what his father looked like, but except for a dull golden kulla in his once white turban and a dirty grey stubble on his sunken cheeks, he couldn't recall anything else about his appearance. A sudden fear gripped his heart. What if neither of them recognized each other and his father left the station without him? His eyes darted from one turbaned head to another, but no one seemed to be looking for a fourteen-year-old boy. The platform started to empty as passengers began to leave for their destinations. Daddy's fear mounted to his eyes.

'Are you waiting for someone, son?' A young man in a vest full of holes stood beside him.

Daddy rubbed the tears out of his eyes with the balls of his hands. 'Yes. My father was supposed to meet me.'

'What's your father's name? Do you have his address?'

Daddy nodded and, pulling out the neatly-folded piece of paper, read his father's address to him.

'Oh, you are Bajrangi's son? I can take you to his house. My tonga is outside.'

Daddy checked the two rupees he had slipped in his

pocket and nodded.

'Everyone in Nanowal knows Bajrangi. He is a man of God. Last year my four-year-old daughter was dying of a fever and Bajrangi cured her with just one dose of medicine he made himself. You are his son? I didn't know he had a family. Where do you live?'

'In Lahore.'

'With relatives?'

'With Abu and Ammi and Amjad, my brother.'

'A Musalmaan family? Are you a Musalmaan? Is Bajrangi a Musalmaan? No, he couldn't be. I have seen pictures of Ram and Sita in his house, but I have also seen a Quran. Are you a Musalmaan?'

'I'm his son.'

They climbed onto the tonga, sitting side by side on the driver's seat. The town of Nanowal had just awakened to the soft light of the early morning sun. It seemed no different from Lahore. People stood in queues at public taps, shopkeepers sprinkled water before their shops, women sat outside their houses, fanning the smoke from angeethis.

'Does Bajrangi know you are coming?'

'Abu wrote him a letter.'

'He mustn't have received it.'

The white door of Bajrangi's house was shut when they got there, but the tonga driver got off and pushed it open. 'He's not at home,' he declared. 'He has probably gone to pick some more of those miracle herbs. He'll be back soon. Why don't you go inside and wait for him?'

Daddy nodded and pulled out his two rupees.

'No, don't worry about it. I can't take money from Bajrangi's son.'

Daddy put the money back in his pocket and pulled his trunk off the tonga. Pushing the door wider, he stepped inside the small room. The mud-baked walls were whitewashed. Except for a wooden cot with a bright white sheet on it and a large tin trunk in one corner, there was no other furniture in the room. Against a wall were some dishes standing neatly in a row and in the other corner was a folded mat. The walls of the room were covered with pictures of various Hindu gods and lying on one end of the bed was an open book that Daddy recognized as the Holy Quran. He stepped forward and touched it, his fingers tracing the fine writing lovingly, knowing that Ammi was probably reading her second namaz right then.

Daddy sat down on the edge of the bed, his hands folded between his legs, his head sunk between his shoulders, waiting for his father. He wondered why he hadn't come to the station to receive him. Perhaps he didn't want to see him. After all, since he'd returned from yogic life, he hadn't even contacted his family. But Daddy felt no anger towards his father. He only felt a dull ache of rejection in his heart.

After a while, he began to feel hungry. He stood up to see if there was any food in the dishes sitting so neatly against the wall. They were all filled with water. He lifted one jar and drank out of it, swallowing loudly. As he bent to put the jar back, he heard a footstep and turned around to see a thin old man hallowed by the sunlight filling the open door. He couldn't see his face very well because most of it was covered with a long, white beard. His kurta-pajama was sparkling white as was the turban on his head. They stood looking at each other across the length of the room in total silence.

'I'm Manohar,' Daddy said softly.

'Achha. How have you been, son?'

'Well.'

The old man moved out of the sun towards the cot. 'Come, sit down.' He motioned Daddy to sit beside him. 'I went back to Lahore once, to your aunt's house. She told me you had run away.'

Daddy nodded. 'I live with my friend Amjad and his parents. Why didn't you come to get me at the railway station?'

'I didn't know you were coming.'

'Abu, my friend's father, wrote a letter to you.'

The old man pulled a postcard out of his pocket. It was folded in the middle. 'This?' he asked.

Daddy nodded.

'The postman left it under my door yesterday. I was going to have him read it to me today.'

Daddy nodded again. 'Can I stay with you for a while?'

'Yes, for a while. I'm a wandering man, son. I don't know how long I will be here. Tomorrow, I might decide to go away to another land—maybe to Burma, or Jarman, or even Amreeka.'

'I can go with you,' Daddy said.

'We'll see,' he said, getting up. 'Stay here. I'll be back. I'll get us some food from Satyan Halwai's shop.'

Daddy fell into the patterns of his father's life as easily as if he had followed them every day of his own. Every morning he accompanied his father when he went to bathe in the Yamuna. On the way back they ate at Satyan Halwai's. His father never seemed to pay any money to the shopkeeper, nor to anyone else for that matter. Daddy was puzzled. One day, he asked him.

'They won't take money from me even if I try to give it to them,' his father said, and the subject was closed.

After their breakfast, Daddy's father opened the door of his house and a stream of people came all day to have their minor ills cured. Daddy ground herbs for his father, who poured some water in the cup of his hand and, muttering a mantra, sprinkled it on the herbs. Everyone received the same medicine, whether it was for a fever or a festering wound. Daddy recalled the magistrate with the infected leg and finally understood his fast recovery. No money exchanged hands. Maybe that was why his father never owed any money, because no one owed him any. To Daddy, this seemed like the ideal life. He saw himself in a new vocation— that of a herb doctor. One day Daddy asked his father what the miraculous herb was.

'It's not so much the herb,' his father replied. 'It's the water. Tomorrow I will show you the power of the water.'

He took him to the river the next morning and pointing to the centre of the current, told him how he had acquired the panacea.

'I have Varuna, the god of the oceans, under control. Any water that I bless with his power, becomes therapeutic. See those waves in the centre? The Ganga flows with greater force in the Himalayas and it is icy cold. For forty nights, I went to the river and stood in it till dawn. Little fish ate up the soles of my feet. Even my mantra has not been able to cure my wounds completely. On the thirty-ninth night, the water began to scare me. It took the shape of a fearful sea monster ready to devour me. I almost gave up the quest, but somehow I gathered enough courage to continue. At dawn, Varuna appeared out of the water, resplendent in his glory, one hand holding a gada and the other raised to offer boons. My tenacity and devotion pleased him. He blessed me with his power and whispered a mantra to me. "Use it only for the good of man," he advised. So that is what I do. I pour some water in the cup of my hand and ask Varuna to bless it; then I mix it with herbs and make medicine. They think the power is in the herbs. Sometimes, I wish I could sprinkle the water on this land to cure its ills.'

Two years passed. Two of the happiest years of Daddy's life. The routine of his father's life brought a permanence into Daddy's displaced world. His unconditional caring for the people of Nanowal taught Daddy a love he had never experienced. He got to know all his father's patients well and suffered their ailments with them, mixing herbs under his father's direction with a sincere desire for their quick recovery. He felt he belonged—not just to a father, but also to the people who lived safe, ordinary lives around him. These people accepted him into the fold of their existence as if he were an essential ingredient. For example, there was their neighbour, old Masi, who smuggled freshly churned butter in a little silver bowl out of her daughter-in-law's kitchen for Daddy and fed him with her own hands, balling the butter between her fingers. Afterwards, she wiped the tell-tale corners of his mouth with her pallu and called him her very own Manohar. And there was the beautiful Kaanan who lived directly across the street, a sixteen-year-old who had skin as white and smooth as the butter Masi fed him,

and hair the colour of mud after a rain shower. There were
rumours that her grandfather had been a sahib. Daddy sat
on the doorstep of his house, waiting for hours just to get a
glimpse of her walk by on some errand or other. He watched
the taut mounds of her young breasts thrust against the
bodice of her shirt and her long, brown braid knock against
first one buttock then the other as she walked, and a
tightness quivered in his groin. Sometimes he played toddler
games with her three-year-old sister, Bimla, hoping that
Kaanan would emerge from the house and join them. There
weren't too many boys his age on his street except for
Premnath, who wore thick glasses and was always muttering
some mathematical equation under his breath as if repeating
a sacred mantra. Games with him always amounted to a
square root or a fraction to the power of fifty-three or some
such outlandish odd number. Then there was Sheikhu with
whom Daddy sat for hours at street corners, listening to him
relate stories from popular Hindi films, ogling over pictures
of film actresses that Sheikhu always seemed to carry under
his shirt. Sometimes he tried to involve Premnath and
Sheikhu in kite flying, but for the most part, his finely-coated
yarn and Amjad's kites lay at the bottom of his tin trunk
carefully stacked away for the time he might need them
again. Just like his love for Amjad and his family. He missed
them sometimes, but he never talked about going back.

One morning, laying out the herbs for the day, Daddy
and his father heard the sounds of loud slogans. 'Le ke
rehenge, Pakistan (We will acquire Pakistan). Pakistan
zindabad (Long live Pakistan)!' For days they had been
noticing members of the Muslim League carrying weapons in
their hands, roaming the streets with shoulders thrown back
in anticipation of some future victory.

Daddy and his father hurried out of the house to watch
a large mob armed with staffs, knives and hatchets. Some of
the men were carrying green flags with a sickle moon and a
lone star. Even as they watched, the mob swelled. Suddenly,
a shout of 'Kafirs!' rang out and some men rushed towards
a cloth merchant's shop. People started screaming and minutes

later, Banwari, the merchant, stumbled out, blood gushing
from a fat stub that had been his arm. Behind him customers
rushed out, tongues of flame at their heels. Within moments,
the shop was ablaze. Shouting slogans, the mob turned away
seeking its next prey, while the armless man collapsed on the
ground before his burning shop, his fading eyes clinging to
the flames.

Daddy's father pulled his son away and rushed him back
into the house. 'Stay here. Don't go out. And lock the door,'
he instructed Daddy and slipped out, shutting the door
behind him. For a long while, Daddy stood just inside the
door, trembling. Then he heard war-like yells outside.
Throwing his weight against the door, he shot the bolt home
and waited. When no shoulders pressed against his door and
no voices ordered him to open up, he rushed to the cot and
pushed it over till it blocked the door. Then seizing the staff
from the corner, he squeezed behind the large trunk and lay
crouched on his hands and knees on the floor.

Outside he heard the crackle of houses as their burning
structures crumbled like the bones of corpses on pyres. He
heard the screams of women and the insane laughter of men.
Scared children wailed loudly for their mothers and amidst
the shouts for help, he heard another sound—'Kafir'. Kafir.
Daddy's being filled with that sound.

Miraculously, Daddy's house was never touched. Perhaps
in some recess of its mind, the crazed Muslim population of
Nanowal still remembered that Daddy's father was a man of
God—not a Hindu god or a Muslim god, but a man of that
one God. But Daddy was afraid. All day he lay crouched on
the floor, his ears alert to the sounds outside. Finally, when
all that remained in the air were hopeless wails and lost
cries, he crept out from behind the trunk and tiptoed to the
door, the staff clutched tightly in his hand. Moving the cot
a little, he bent his head and put his eye to a crack. Smoke
rose out of silent houses like grey souls departing from dead
bodies. Little flames still spluttered like last breaths in some
houses. The road before them lay like a grotesque patchwork
quilt of bodies, exhibiting a pajama-clad leg here, a bangled

arm there. And among them was Bimla, the little girl from across the street, still wearing the flowered pink dress of the day before, sitting on the road, her little palm wiping the blood from her mother's cold face. Near them lay Kaanan with her brown braid around her neck like a noose. Her salwar lay tangled around her ankles and her shirt was hiked up over her thighs, exposing dark brown pubic hairs simmering with embers of blood. Screams rose in Daddy's throat, but he couldn't look away. He had to see it all. Crouched at the door, his eye glued to the crack, he tried to pick out Prem, Sheikhu, Masi, a white turban and a long white beard, but the crack was too narrow. Then an old woman he had never seen before walked into view. She was completely naked; her legs were smeared with blood as though she had been wading for hours through a ruddy lake; her thin grey hair was wild around her sagging breasts and her head was thrown back as she looked towards the sky, searching as though for the first star.

Even as Daddy looked, a man in a dark salwar-kurta, his face covered with a corner of his turban cloth, appeared and stood before Bimla. For a moment he looked up and down the street, then whisked the child off the ground and pressing her face to his shoulder, hurried away.

Hours passed. When a round-faced, silver moon rose behind the darkly distorted shapes of houses, Daddy slid to the floor, resting his forehead against the door. The staff he had been clutching in his hand fell to the floor with a loud clatter. Then he heard it. An almost inaudible knock on the door. He froze, holding the air in his lungs. The knock was repeated, loudly this time. Groping desperately for the staff, Daddy raised himself to his knees and pressed his eye to the crack again. In the light of the moon, he saw a form dressed in white, standing close to the door.

'Who is it?' he whispered.

'Sh. It is I, your father. Be quiet.'

'I thought they must have got you,' Daddy said, pushing the cot away and opening the door. He rushed towards his father, finally giving in to the sobs that had racked his body

quietly all day. For the first time in a decade, his father took
him in his arms and rocked him like he used to when he was
a baby.

'Quiet, son. Everything is going to be all right. We are
going to leave this town. Come,' he said picking up the staff
from the floor. 'I have stolen a truck. We will drive to the
ghat and take a boat out of this insanity.'

They slipped out of the house and tiptoed to the truck
parked at the corner, stepping over prone bodies. A horrifying
stench of blood and burning rose from the dark streets.
Suppressing his sobs and an acute desire to vomit, Daddy
climbed into the truck. The engine was still running. They
drove out of the street keeping the headlights off, crushing
bodies under ruthless wheels.

As they turned the corner of the street, a small group of
men appeared. Brandishing lances and staffs, some men
blocked their way. A couple of them held up flaming
torches.

'Who are you? Are you a kafir or a Musalmaan?'

There was silence.

A man thrust a torch at the windshield to see their faces.
'It's Bajrangi,' he said, 'and his son.'

'Saala, kafir. Kill him,' someone shouted. Daddy's father
jumped out of the truck, holding his staff.

'Let us go,' he said. 'We mean you no harm.'

'Maaro! Maaro!' they shouted.

Daddy slid between the seat and the dashboard. They
thrust their lances through the open door, the windows. The
first jab sliced his scalp just over his ear. Thrusting his fist
in his mouth, Daddy bit down on his scream. Each jab
piercing his scalp after that was only another dull bite on his
knuckles. Blood poured down his temples, his forehead, into
his eyes, blinding him. He felt the heat of a blaze as the truck
was torched. Sightlessly, Daddy scrambled out of his hiding
place and jumped off the truck. Rubbing the blood out of his
eyes, he looked around. The men were gone. In the light of
the blaze he saw his father struggling to get up from the
ground. His stomach had been carved and the innards had

fallen out. The last Daddy remembered was his father picking up his innards from the street and stuffing them back in the gaping hole of his belly. Pulling off his turban and attempting to tie it around his stomach to hold the innards in, he kept repeating, 'It'll be all right, son. It'll be all right.'

Hours later, a Musalmaan found Daddy moaning in pain on the street. Reading the tattooed name 'Amjad' on his arm, he assumed his religion and rushed him to a medical centre.

On the day Mahatma Gandhi visited Nanowal to walk through the riot-shocked streets, to weep with bereaved families, to talk to jihad-crazed Muslims, a postman visited the hospital Daddy was in.

'Are you Manohar Das Sethi?'

Daddy nodded.

'I have a packet for you from Delhi.' He handed him a brown envelope closed with an impressive seal.

'I also have a packet for Bajrang Das Sethi.'

'He's dead,' Daddy said simply.

'I know. I will take this to the office and have it sent back to Delhi.'

He turned around sharply as if he were being watched by some invisible military commander and marched out of the hospital.

Daddy broke open the seal and tore the brown envelope. Inside was a little black book with the Imperial Coat of Arms on it. PASSPORT, it said in large golden letters. On the first page was the picture he had sat for in the studio in Nanowal. The light blue curtains on the studio walls formed a white background in the picture from which his scrubbed face with oil-slicked hair sprung out like a bewildered flower. His lips were stretched in surprise because the smile he had been asked to fix on them had been forgotten when the skinny bow-legged photographer in khaki jodhpurs had disappeared inside a black head mask behind the three-legged contraption, and a white sun on top of a flash-pole had spit fire for an instant. His name and address in Nanowal appeared on the page along with his signature, which he had carefully penned on the form, smiling proudly at his father who could only affix his thumb print alongside the artful signature of Rai Bahadur Jagganath who had to verify his occupation and reason for his visit to foreign countries as a holy man. The rest of the pages in the book were blank. Now he would never be able to fill them with visits to Burma, Japan, Jarman, Amreeka.

He slipped the little book inside his shirt, trying to recall the warmth of his father's embrace. 'Everything will be all right,' his father had said.

'No,' he said to the passport. 'No, nothing will ever be all right again,' shaking the tears out of his eyes in rage. By the time he left the hospital and went back to Lahore, his tears had seeped into his rage and made it inflammable. The murder of Gajji was the only spark it needed to ignite, distorting the rest of his life into one big burn scar.

And I weep. I weep for my father. I weep for his life. I weep for the death that evolved from his life. I weep for the violence that tore him from his life. I weep for him. I weep for the guilt he carried through his life unto death. I weep for him for he was a victim not only of one act of terrorism but of all acts ever perpetrated; for each act multiplied his crime and pronounced him a victim of his own guilt over and over again. And he's dead. My father is dead. Deep sobs roll through my body. I am bereaved. I am orphaned. My father is no more.

I cry till late into the night, till my tears dry up, leaving only their salinity burning my lids. I feel empty, not only of my grief but also of Daddy. I have purged him. I have absolved him. I have delivered him like a newborn babe, pure and innocent.

chapter fifteen

I get up and open the window of my room. Cool, fresh air fills my lungs. Far in the east I can see the first vermilion streaks of dawn. Knowing Kalida wakes up around this time, I turn hurriedly towards the room and pick up Fatima's cotton satchel from the corner. Extracting the brown bag from it, I empty out all the clothes and take out the four hundred-rupee bills lying rolled at the bottom of it. Opening the knot that holds Scott's ring, I add the money in the corner of the green dupatta and re-knot it. Then I tie the fabric around my neck securely. Throwing the burkha over one arm and holding the brown bag in the other, I pick up the rubber flip-flops and open the door of my room slowly. For a moment I stand watching the muffled figures on the floor in the front room. Relieved at their stillness, I shut the door and pick my way between mattresses till I reach the front door. It creaks as I open it. My shoulders tense. I hold my breath for a few seconds, waiting for a curious movement, a shift of position, but there's nothing. Quickly, I slip out of the hut, shutting the door gently behind me.

I tiptoe to the grove, then break into a run down the path, donning the burkha on the way. In a few minutes I am at the outer edge of the fields. The peanut man has not arrived yet. I wonder what time it is. Putting my slippers on the ground, I slip my feet in them and quickly, with yards of black material swishing in and around my legs, I begin to walk in the direction of Amritgarh. Traffic is almost non-

existent on the highway. Once in a while a vehicle hurtles by
at breakneck speed. I think about asking for a ride but
decide against it. I walk for about thirty minutes before I
begin to see the dim lights of a roadside restaurant. Urged on
by the light, I quicken my steps. A beat-up truck is standing
at the corner of the road near the restaurant, and an old man
with a dirty rag tied around his balding head is sitting at one
of the aluminium tables, drinking tea out of a tall, glass
tumbler. 'Bhaijaan,' I say going up to him, 'what time is it?'
He looks me up and down and staring right into the cobweb
lace over my eyes says, 'Sister, I don't have a watch, but I
think it is close to 5 a.m.' I nod and turn to go inside the
restaurant where I can see a man sitting beside a fire,
mopping his brow with the front of his shirt, revealing a
protruding belly button circled with dark hair. 'Do you have
a phone?' I ask him. He shakes his head with a total lack of
surprise as though I have asked him about an item on the
menu.

As I walk back outside, wondering how long it will take
me to walk to Amritgarh, the old man says, 'It is early for
a woman to be out on the road by herself.'

I walk up to him again. 'Bhaijaan,' I say, bringing a
tearfulness to my voice. 'My daughter is very sick. I have left
her at home with my sister. I want to find a telephone so
that I can call a doctor.' He looks at me with such suspicion,
I'm afraid he has seen through my disguise.

'Telephoon?' he says. 'Telephoon a daktar? Don't you
have a hakim in Jhakher who can take care of your daughter?'
I suddenly realize my mistake. How could I have been so
stupid? People don't call doctors here, let alone telephone
them. 'I am from Dilli, Bhaijaan. I am only visiting my sister
in Jhakher. The hakim has already seen my daughter, but he
has given up. In Dilli we always go to a doctor. I have such
faith in them, and in Dilli you can call a doctor on the
telephone at any time. I am not used to the ways of the
village.'

I don't think he believes me, but he doesn't ask any more
questions. Instead, he offers to give me a ride in his truck to

Amritgarh. 'I know a very good daktar there. But it is early, and his clinic will be closed. I can leave you there. I think his house is right behind the clinic. Maybe you can ask him to open the clinic early for you.'

'Shukriya bhaijaan,' I thank him and, sitting down, wait for him to finish his tea.

He gulps down the rest of it and gets up. 'Come,' he says, moving towards his truck. I follow him and watch him swing into the driver's seat. I reach up and, opening the door on the other side, attempt to climb up on the high foothold. My burkha keeps coming in the way. Finally, pulling it over my knees, I climb up. With numerous grunts and groans, the truck's ignition catches and we begin to move. 'What's wrong with your daughter?' the man asks.

'She's been running a very high fever and trembling as if someone is shaking her bones.'

'Malaria,' he declares. 'It is malaria. A bad disease. Once it gets you, it doesn't let go. Again and again it returns, even after it has been cured. You should have given her quinine. Didn't the hakim know?'

'We gave her quinine, but to no effect.'

'Tsk,' he says and thankfully lapses into silence.

Amritgarh is hovering on the edge of wakefulness. Most of the stores are closed. Only the milk and bread shops are serving their first customers. The old man turns a corner where a man is waving incense sticks and mumbling a prayer before the open shutter of his chemist shop.

'The daktar is in this street,' the old man tells me. 'Yes, there. See that sign?' I look at the small board hanging on a door: Dr Mahesh Kathuria, MBBS, London, it reads. 'I cannot read,' the man continues, 'but I think that is his office. He is good, because I have seen sick people all the way out on the street waiting to be seen by him. I think his house is behind the office. See that gate? Yes, that is his house.'

'Shukriya, bhaijaan,' I say again and jump off the truck. I step under the sign and wait for him to make a U-turn to drive back onto the main street, but he just sits in his truck

watching me. 'Shukriya,' I call out to him again, but he
gestures to me to open the narrow, wrought iron gate and
knock on the door. I have no choice but to do that. I lift the
snap on the gate and step into a small yard. When I look
back, I see the man still watching me. Sighing exasperatedly,
I ring the bell on the wooden door. I have to ring three times
before a man in a white undershirt and loose pajamas with
its cord hanging between his legs, opens the door. 'Yes, what
is it?' he says, putting on thick, black-rimmed glasses and
peering at me through sleep-filled eyes.

'Please,' I say softly in English. 'I need your help.'

'Are you a patient?' he asks. 'I don't open the clinic till
8 a.m. Come back in two hours.'

I look behind me and see the truck still standing directly
in front of the gate.

'No, I'm not sick. Please, could I just use your phone?
It's an emergency.'

He looks at my burkha-clad figure, then at my netted
eyes, and begins to shake his head. 'Please,' I say. 'Please. It's
a matter of life and death.'

'I don't have STD,' he says.

'STD? What . . . what's STD?'

He looks at me strangely for a minute before explaining,
'You can only make local calls from my phone.'

'Yes. Yes, that's what I want to do. I have to call a
friend right here in Amritgarh.'

'Wait a minute,' he says stepping into the house and
pulling the door shut behind him. I stand looking at the
closed door, then back at the truck, wondering what to do.
The doctor returns a few minutes later with a key in his
hand and steps out of his house, once again closing the door
behind him. 'Come with me.' He walks out of the yard into
the street and opens his clinic. I wait outside till he switches
on the light. Then, waving at the old man in the truck, I go
inside the clinic. I hear the grunts of the truck's engine then,
and with a heavy grinding, I hear it drive off.

'What's the number?' the doctor asks me, fitting a tiny
key in the brass lock on the rotary dial of a red telephone.

I close my eyes for a moment to remember the number Scott read out aloud that night at the Palace Hotel. '27365,' I say.

He holds the receiver out to me and dials the number. I take the receiver from his hand and bring it to my ear as it begins to ring. It rings and rings. Let it be the right number, I plead quietly. Please, let it be the right number. And then it stops ringing.

'Hello?' a woman answers.

'Is this ... Is Arun there?' I ask hesitantly in Hindi, certain that it is the wrong number, panicking, wondering what to do if it is.

'Arun? Yes, hold on. Let me check if he is awake. Who's calling?'

'I ... I'm a friend of his. Please, could I speak with him? It's very important.'

'Hold on.' I hear the receiver clatter on a table and her voice calling Arun. Why had I imagined that Arun lived alone? I wonder who answered the phone—a sister, a mother, a wife?

'Hello?' Arun's voice sounds in my ear.

'Arun?'

'Yes. Who is this?'

'Arun, this is Simi—Simran Mehta.'

'Simran? Is everything all right? Where are you calling from?'

'Amritgarh.'

'What are you doing here at this hour? Is everything all right? Who else is with you?'

'I'm alone.'

'What? What are you doing here alone? How did you get here?'

'Arun, listen. I really need to talk to you. Can you come and get me?'

'What's the matter? Where are you?'

'I'm at a doctor's office.'

'Doctor's office? Simran, what's the matter? Why are you at a doctor's? And why isn't anybody with you?'

'Arun, listen to me, please. I'm okay. I'm here only to use the phone. Please, can you come and get me? I have to talk to you.'

'Tell me where you are.'

'I'm at Dr Kathuria's office. It's at . . .' I look around at the doctor and ask him his address.

'The corner of Rajendra Bagh and Main Road, next to Khanna Chemists,' he tells me.

I repeat the location to Arun.

'Okay, I know where that is. Can you stay there for about fifteen minutes?'

I turn around again to the doctor. 'Can I please stay here for fifteen minutes? My friend is coming to get me.' The doctor looks at his wristwatch and gives me a beleaguered look before nodding grudgingly.

'Yes,' I say into the receiver. 'I'll be here. Please hurry.'

I sit down on a patient's bench, facing the doctor in his expensive swivel chair. He looks incongruous sitting in the black leather in his undershirt and pajamas with his hands clutched between his legs, swaying gently from side to side. I look around at the certificates on the wall, the posters showing children with beatific smiles, and instruction charts listing the essential food groups. There's a large square-faced black and white clock ticking away loudly. The time it shows is 5:36. When I finish reading everything on the wall, I turn my eyes to the desk. There's a stethoscope on the glass-topped table with its limbs twisted awkwardly. Under the glass I can see upside-down pictures of a family with two adolescent boys, a teenage girl and an overweight wife. There's a small metal cylinder filled with various pens and pencils. It has MedCare written on it in gold letters. A silver cylinder is filled with cotton balls. In one corner is a stack of steno pads and beside that is a miniature Eiffel tower with a heavy bottom, probably a paperweight. I look up again at the clock: 5:41.

'I'm really very grateful to you for letting me use your phone and letting me stay. I'm sure my friend will be here soon. I'm sorry to cause you so much inconvenience.'

He continues sitting with his hands pressed between his legs, swaying this way and that. At last we hear the drone of a motorcycle. I get up and move towards the entrance to watch Arun come to a stop outside. I turn around and, thanking the doctor again, walk out quickly. Behind me, the light goes out and I hear Dr Kathuria close the door of his clinic.

'What's the matter?' Arun says, pulling off his helmet. 'Why are you here?' His hair is tousled, anxious around his head.

'Can you take me to Haridwar?'

'What? Now?'

'Please, Arun. I must go there. I want to lay him to rest in the Ganga.' I hold the bag of ashes up.

His eyes narrow at me.

'Arun, please. Can you take me?'

'Of course,' he says. 'But can you wait? You pulled me out of bed. I'm a little disoriented. It's a four-hour ride to Haridwar. I'll have to make arrangements. Can we go tomorrow? The Shivratri procession ...'

'Fine.' I cut him off. 'If you don't want to take me, I'll catch a bus. Can you at least give me a ride to the bus station?'

'What's the hurry, Simran? I said I'll take you. Surely you can wait a few hours.'

I shake my head and start walking away towards the end of the street. 'I'll get a cab or something,' I say over my shoulder.

He grabs my arm from behind. 'What's the matter? Why are you in such a hurry?'

I try to shake his hand off. 'I've got to go.' Tears begin to fill my eyes. I thought I had expended the pain. He draws me into his arms. 'Sh,' he whispers. 'Something's the matter. I can tell. Tell me about it?'

I shake my head against his shoulder. 'He ... Daddy ... All his life he suffered ... wasted.'

'Come,' Arun says drawing me towards his motorcycle. 'Let's go someplace where we can talk.'

'Get on.' He pulls his helmet back on again and kick-starts the motorcycle. I yank my burkha over my knees and climb on behind him, gripping the bottom of his seat with one hand and holding the bag with the other in front of me on the seat between us. We drive in and out of empty streets for a while before he slows down in front of a neat, two-storey house at the end of a street.

'Where are we?'

'My home.'

For some crazy reason my heart begins to thump then.

'Come on,' he says, wheeling his bike up the driveway and parking it behind the white car he had brought to the jail the day of my release. He walks to a door and turns the key.

'Who else lives with you?' I have to ask him.

'My parents and my younger sister.'

'Oh.'

He leads me into a room and turns on a switch. Four glass tulips held together on a brass ring hanging from the ceiling explode with light that scatters all over the room, reflected in tiny round mirrors woven into embroidered elephants on cushions and wall hangings. Right under the chandelier is a brass coffee table with a glass top on which three princely mirror-work elephants complete the motif of the room.

'How beautiful,' I say instinctively.

'The elephants owe their presence to my sister, and the mirror-work to my mother,' he says, the lines of his face softening indulgently. 'So?' he gestures to me to advance into the room. 'Tell me what happened. Why are you in Amritgarh alone so early in the morning?'

'I want to go to Haridwar,' I say, placing the bag carefully on a sofa and untying the strings of the burkha to pull it off.

'Yes. You told me that. But why have you suddenly decided that? What happened?'

'I just have to go. Will you take me?'

'Tell me what the matter is, Simran.'

I look at him, at his face. It looks different in this realm of mirror-work and elephants, this world created by his loved ones. He looks more involved in this world than in any I have seen him.

I turn my back to him and dig inside the front of my shirt to pull out the folded piece of paper. 'Here, read this.'

He smoothes out the paper with a hand and begins to read. I watch his face for an expression of shock, possibly even anger, but there is none. The density is back in his face—a face that has already ingested too much of life.

'Where did you find this?' he asks quietly.

'Under our printing machine. And I know it was printed on our machine. I also know Kalida went to Kashmir, not to talk about peace to the militant groups there, but to deliver these letters and God knows what else, to his accomplices so they could be taken to Sind. He's a terrorist. CCPH is a terrorist organization.'

'It's only a letter, Simran. You can't label an organization "terrorist", simply because of a letter.'

'Simply because of a letter?' Don't you realize what it means?' I ask him. 'Don't you realize that Kalida is instigating terrorism in Pakistan?'

'What makes you think that?'

'It says so clearly in the letter. "Rise and declare war. We are with you, sharing every wound and every drop of blood lost." If that isn't a call for violence, what is?'

'It's nothing, Simran. Forget it. Come. Let me take you back to Jhakher for the procession. Then, later, I'll drive you to Haridwar.'

'How can you say it's nothing? The people in Pakistan are killing each other as a result of this and other propaganda like this, and you say it's nothing. Those school children died in Karachi.'

'Domestic terrorism in Pakistan is Pakistan's problem.'

'How can you say that when it's being supported by organizations from this country? Besides, terrorism is terrorism no matter who perpetrates it.'

'It isn't as simple as that, Simran.' He sits down.

'Nothing in India is. Haven't you realized that by now? Nothing here can be perceived as just black or white. There are always justifying shades of grey.'

'Nothing justifies hurting innocent people.' I turn towards the door, unwilling to listen to his generalizations. He gets up hurriedly and grabs my arm. 'No. Wait a minute. You have to hear me out now.'

I pull my arm out of his grasp but turn and sit beside him on the edge of the sofa. 'You've lived with Kalida for months now. Do you really think he's a terrorist?' he asks. 'Do you think he can be a cold-blooded killer of innocent children?' His eyes look at me compellingly. I don't respond, but I wait for him to continue, to persuade me, to make me believe the evidence is lying.

'Kalida is one of the most respected peace activists of this country,' Arun says. The government fears him for his ability to lead people, and the people trust him with their lives. Everyone believes that if any organization can bring some kind of coherence to all this chaos, it is Kalida's CCPH; and if any one person can bring peace among the communities here, it is Kalida.'

'Then how do you explain this?' I gesture towards the letter lying face up on the sofa beside him.

He leans his head back on the sofa and takes a deep breath. 'You have to have lived through the Partition to understand this.' He suddenly turns his head and looks at me. 'But then, maybe, you will understand—because of your father.' He's quiet for a while, looking at me, trying to gauge my depths. Then he begins speaking slowly, as though making sure I hear each word. 'A lot of people in this country, especially people in the regions of Punjab and Bengal, the two states that were split to create Pakistan, have never forgiven Pakistan for coming into existence. Many of them lost loved ones, and many still have loved ones living across the border. These people continue to believe that the division is temporary, and that sooner or later, the two countries will be one again. A lot of others believe in this unity for the sake of peace—a natural solution to this unnatural state of terror. And then there are some who believe they can hasten this process.'

'How?'

'Kalida was a Naxalite,' he says. 'That was a cause whose justification was its end. Violence was a necessary means. For Kalida, war is a necessary means—to peace. In your book that probably makes him a terrorist, but in some other books, he's a patriot, a hero fighting for a cause.'

'But the incitement of terrorist organizations in Pakistan to perpetrate violence. How is that helping the cause of peace in India? Or unity, or even war for that matter?' I question.

'It's weakening Pakistan's stability, destroying it from the inside. And, if Pakistan-backed terrorism keeps escalating in India, very soon, war will seem like the only answer. War, justified by the need for national security. Even the world community will understand that. But the climate has to be right—in both countries.

'I can't believe you can talk about war as though it is a desirable thing. People die in wars, Arun. Nations are destroyed.'

'Ironically, war also has a way of uniting people as has no other calamity.'

'So CCPH is consciously helping create this climate. So, Kalida is not just a terrorist, he's also a warmonger. I can't believe you can sit here and defend him.' I look at him in disbelief. 'I want to know where the law is in all of this. How is the CCPH able to operate undetected?'

'I'm sure the law, as you say, is already aware, but chooses to look the other way, because it, too, realizes that this, perhaps, is the only solution. In fact, I won't be surprised if Kalida has connections with RAW, and CCPH is a protected organization.'

Suddenly, a horrifying thought invades my mind. 'Is Kalida ... is CCPH responsible for some of the incidents here in India, too?'

He looks at me and away.

'Answer me, Arun. The communal riots after the Babri

Masjid incident, Janki Das, Sultana's house ... was CCPH party to that in some way?'

'I don't know,' he says in a barely audible voice.

I grope behind me for the arm of the sofa and, lowering myself on its edge, sit looking at an elephant on the cushion across from me. The mirrors held within embroidered circles in the elephant's feet have begun to crack, making it look as if he is crumbling under his own weight. Or perhaps, someone has rested too heavily against him. I get up and press the broken glass with my fingertips. My skin pricks only mildly, but when I draw my hand away, a tiny shard like a diamond shaving is sticking to the tip of my finger.

I stand looking at the piece of glass on my fingertip. 'Did you know about this when you took me to Jhakher that first time?'

He nods. 'Please don't misinterpret his motives, Simran. No matter what the means, ultimately, his cause is peace. And the work CCPH does for peace and harmony is not just a cover. It's the very essence of the organization. You've seen that for yourself.'

'Are you involved, too?' I ask softly.

He comes to me and takes my hand in his own, looking at me despairingly.

'Simran, I know how this must sound to someone like you.'

I snatch my hand away from his. 'Are you involved?' I ask him again.

'I'm a member of CCPH,' he says, 'but ...'

I don't wait to hear any more. I grab Daddy's ashes and my burkha from the sofa and run out of Arun's house.

'Simran,' I hear him call after me, then I hear his footsteps. I begin to run faster. His footsteps go back towards the house again, but I keep running, struggling to slip on the burkha with one hand. I can't seem to find the sleeves of the unwieldy garment.

I hear the motorcycle being revved up. Throwing the burkha on the road, I look up and down the street for a place to hide. Around the corner I see a cab stand with a driver cleaning the windscreen of his car with a rag. 'Bus stand,' I yell to him even before I reach him and, wrenching open the door of the cab, jump in. Thankfully, the cab driver senses my urgency and, without even wasting time by lowering the meter, gets in behind the wheel. I see the motorcycle around the corner as the driver starts his car. 'Hurry,' I tell him.

He shifts into gear and steps on the accelerator. We hurtle onto the street only inches from the oncoming motorcycle. I see Arun pull his brakes and swerve precariously, his foot landing on the road to steady the machine. The cab driver yells an obscenity at him through the window and drives past.

Soon we leave the side streets behind and hit the main section of town where the city of Amritgarh is preparing for Shivratri. People are hanging colourful streamers across the roads. Storekeepers are stringing plastic tulips with tiny bulb hearts on their roofs. Sweetmeat stores and gift stores and toy stores are extending their boundaries to lay their wares on tables outside.

'I'll have to take a longer route, saab,' the driver informs me. 'Through side streets. The main road is blocked for the procession.'

'Fine,' I say. 'Just hurry.'

I can see the dented petroleum drums serving as roadblocks up ahead. The driver veers off into a narrow residential street and comes to a halt. The street is packed with vehicles, all re-routed by the procession. Children, celebrating a holiday from school, run around in and out of houses, dangerously close to the bone-crushing wheels. Slowly, with drivers yelling invectives at each other and honking incessantly, the traffic heaves forward. We are almost at the end of the street when I begin to hear distinct sounds of drums and metal clappers over the din. As we approach the intersection of two perpendicular streets, the sounds get louder and are now accompanied by tuneless singing and chanting. I look through my window towards the main road and see red flags bobbing over a large crop of heads. I can see some of the processionists—a group of sadhus with matted hair, holding tridents. Some of them are wearing only loincloths and others are completely naked, their bodies smeared with ashes. As we grind to a halt behind the grimy, out-of-shape bumper of a truck, I see a group of women following the sadhus. They are dressed in simple, housewifely clothes, walking along merrily, chanting hymns and clapping two-foot long, flat iron bars, keeping a mindful eye on the children who accompany them with great alacrity. Then comes a float of a temple on wheels, holding aloft the black, swollen phallus of a Shivalinga. A pot-bellied, bald priest wearing only a thin linen dhoti, is doling out prasad from a large platter and charanamrita from a shiny brass jar. Behind the float is a jeep fitted with large speakers on its front ends, blasting out the voice of a man dressed in an ochre silk kurta, standing beside the driver. Even from this distance, I can see three bright red parallel lines stretch right across his wide forehead from temple to temple. He is singing into a hand-held microphone, leading the chorus. Around the jeep I see half a dozen men in dirty kurta-pajamas, with keg-shaped wooden drums mounted with hide on both sides, hanging from their necks. They are beating thin, curved sticks on the hides with an amazing agility of wrists. Skimming the edges of the procession, I see a handful of stray policemen twirling their batons aimlessly. I wonder where the members of the CCPH are positioned.

Sitting in the cab, looking out its window, I see group after group of people spill into the wide aperture of the intersection like slides on a projector screen. And all the time, the rhythm of drums beats like the heart of the procession.

The traffic before us begins to unsnarl a little, and my cab grinds forward in first gear, covering the distance of the intersection, hiding the procession from my view again, but its drumming pulse continues to sound steadily. Once again we come to an intersection and once again I see frames of it in the aperture: sadhus striding arrogantly on, disdaining the material world with their naked bodies, housewives full of religious verve and blindfolded fanaticism, children energized with festival spirit, the phallus of Shiva aroused and erect, brazenly exposed to all eyes young and old, Hindu and Muslim, the loudspeaker calling all who are devout to join the procession. We drive through innumerable streets, losing several of the other vehicles to intermittent destinations. Finally, we come to a dead stop. In front of us, blocking off the rest of the street, is another barricade of petroleum drums.

The driver looks back at me. 'We'll have to wait here, saab,' he says. 'The procession will come up that street from Islam Market and pass through here. Then the road in front of the masjid will be clear and I will take you down the main road.'

I look at the street before us, realizing this is the street that had been the bone of contention for the Hindu and Muslim leaders; the street they had compromised on. 'How long do you think it will take?' I ask.

'Twenty to thirty minutes.'

'How far is the bus stand?'

'It is just on the other side of Islam Market. Two minutes.'

'Can I walk there from here?'

'Yes, but I will take you.'

'All right,' I say, peering through the windowpane at the empty street leading out of Islam Market, attuned now to the sound of drums and the drone of an amplified voice. Suddenly the phut-phut of a motorcycle overwhelms the sounds of the procession. I'm not taken unawares. At the back of my mind I have been expecting to hear this all along. But I'm not ready to deal with Arun. I know his betrayal has lodged itself in my heart deeper than I'm ready to acknowledge just yet. Perhaps later, after Haridwar, after Daddy, I will unfold my heart and examine the wound and treat it, or perhaps I will die from it. But not now, not yet.

'I want to get off here,' I tell the driver and pay him hurriedly from the money I have tied in the corner of the dupatta. Grabbing the brown bag with Daddy's ashes, I step out of the cab and run into the empty street. The drumbeats

and the chanting in the main road are deafening now.
Wondering how far away the procession is, I rush towards
the intersection of the main road. Even as I emerge into the
centre of Islam Market, I am jostled by the first of the
processionists. I clutch the bag tightly, holding it against my
chest, and run head on into the procession. I elbow my way
through naked men covered with ashes, holding aloft tridents
and shouting 'Jai Shiv Shankar.' I want to break through
their ranks and proceed down the rest of Islam Market
towards the masjid and from there to the main road towards
the bus station. Behind me the sound of singing and drums
rises to a crescendo and suddenly stops. Its abrupt absence
sucks a vacuum into my mind. I turn around slowly and
look down the length of the procession. It seems to have
come to a dead stop. I see the sadhus with matted locks and
men in saffron kurtas. I see the open jeep with the
loudspeakers and drummers, but I see no women. I see no
children.

'My Hindu brothers,' the voice from the speakers booms
again. 'To show these Musalmaans that we Hindus have
every right to go anywhere in this, our land, the land of the
Hindu, the procession will now proceed in front of the
masjid as was initially planned.'

I stand paralysed. A deathly hush falls over the area for
a moment and no one moves. Then, several store shutters on
either side of us rattle shut. Cheers of 'Jai Shiv Shankar'
erupt from the procession and the first steps are directed
towards the masjid. A trident-bearing sadhu pushes me aside
and moves forward. Others begin to follow.

Suddenly I see a familiar figure step onto the street in
front of the procession, clutching the corner of his dhoti in
one hand, the other inert against his stomach, his grey hair
hanging loose, flowing around his shoulders. For a moment,
relief and gratitude infuse my body at the sight of Kalida.
Then, memories of his betrayal invade.

'No.' I see him walk up to the head of the procession
and hold his arm up as if he intends to keep the crowd at
bay single-handedly. 'Stop.' The cheers cease only for a
moment before they are repeated with doubled vigour.

Sadhus in twos and threes begin to trickle out of the procession, moving towards the narrow road leading to the masjid. 'Stop,' Kalida says again. 'Kailash Chand,' he calls loudly to the Hindu leader, the head of the procession committee. 'Stop them. We had an agreement.'

The sadhus keep going past him. 'Kailash Chand,' Kalida calls again. 'Stop them.' I peer through the crowd, trying to spot the man who sat beside Kalida and the Muslim leader, Inayat Ali, in Jhakher and swore a compromise in the name of peace, but I can't see him anywhere. When I look back at Kalida, he is being pushed aside by the sadhus. 'Stop,' he says, pressing against the tridents. 'If any Hindu crosses over to this road, he will have to cross over my body first—my body, a brahmin's body.' I watch in horror as Kalida lies down on the ground before the crowd at the entrance to the masjid road.

For a moment, steps halt, then a naked man with long dreadlocks and a trident of ash drawn on his forehead from the tip of his nose all the way up into his hairline, steps deliberately on the prone form and proceeds towards the masjid. Suddenly there are others, all stepping on Kalida's body, rushing into the road before the masjid. 'Kalida,' I scream, trying to elbow my way through to the front of the procession to where his body lies trampled on the ground. Sounds of 'Jai Bhole Nath' rise from the speakers and the crowd goes berserk, gushing into the road like lava from an erupting volcano. Then I hear screams near the masjid. Peering through the shifting tide of bodies, I see Muslim youth pour out of the masjid waving staffs and swords, hitting out at the processionists as they come. Terrified now, I begin to push backwards through the crowd, seeking escape. And then, the earth explodes.

There are clouds of dust swirling over me. My eyelids feel heavy as if they are layered with that dust. I can't seem to breathe through my nose. My nasal passages feel stuffed, as though something has been pushed up my nostrils. I suck in air through my mouth. My throat feels raw and prickly and my lips are dry. When I lick them, my tongue comes away with a tasteless, gritty powder. In my head, or perhaps around me, I hear screams—disjointed, as though playbacks on a tape recorder. Amidst them I hear a lone voice repeating over and over and over, 'Uda dia, masjid uda dia?' I can't comprehend the words, but some instinct makes me turn my head in the direction of the masjid. Beyond the eddies of dust, I see a haphazard mass of grey smoke rise from within the confines of crumbling bricks and refract against a sky that seems so porous and so low I feel I can touch it just by stretching my arm. I try to raise my hand to it, but there's pain in my fingers. My knuckles seem to be clenched tight as though in a trap. Moving my arm slowly, I bend it at the elbow and bring my hand up to look. It is sticky with blood, the fingers gripping something tightly: the rolled top of a bag, it sides limp and torn, bottomless. Consciousness spasms, and I scramble up hurriedly to sit on my haunches. In a frenzy I begin to scoop Daddy's ashes from the ground into my lap—the ashes and the soil and the debris and bits of bone and flesh.

They find me like that—the ambulance crew—my lap full of violence.

When next I open my eyes, I see Arun looking down at me.

'Hi,' he says, smiling. I smile back because he is smiling so unguardedly, I forget he was ever an enigma.

'How do you feel?' he asks, running a feather-light knuckle down my cheek.

'Fine,' I say. 'Just fine.'

'Good. The doctor says you're fine, too. Just a few nicks and cuts from flying debris, but other than that, you're just fine.' He smiles some more, and then suddenly his eyes fill with tears. Memory returns, pawing at my mind like a stray dog whose loyalty I have won by constantly assuaging its hunger. 'Kalida?' I ask him urgently.

He shakes his head, his face crumbling. He stands before me sobbing unashamedly. I let him cry. After a while I sit up and draw his head down to my shoulder.

There are vehicles parked all along the side of the main road around the peanut stand, almost blocking off the entrance to

the narrow path that leads to the compound in Jhakher
where Kalida's body has been brought for last rites. The
courtyard before the hut is full of people dressed in white.
When I step out of the shadow of trees with Arun, a whisper
pervades the air. Everyone turns around to look at me. A
woman in a white sari with very short grey hair gets up and,
picking her way through the sitting forms, comes to me to
take me in an embrace. 'We've been waiting for you,' she
says and leads me to the front room. Kalida has been laid on
the floor. A sheet of the purest white covers his body all the
way up to his neck. His hair is combed back from his
forehead and down under his head to lie spread out on his
shoulders in soft grey curls, almost mingling with the hair of
his beard. I never noticed he had curls in his hair, or that the
furrows etched parallel in his high forehead were exactly
three in number, running like a caste mark from temple to
temple, or that his eyelids, delicate, almost parchment thin,
were of a very old man's. I look at the lines on his face, a
fine network like a fisherman's weave, trapping all that was
deeply felt—life, love, sorrow, the sun, air ... I place a
fingertip between his eyebrows—so cold, quiet now,
unprovoked, but somehow vital. There is the essence of an
energy remaining under the surface of Kalida's mortality.
His face glows as if a sun is growing within him. Peace, I
think, the last principle. No. This is too vivid. It is like the
afterglow of an ecstasy, or a sudden flowering of an epiphany.
In that instant, I am filled with such envy for Kalida, I lay
my head on his chest and breathe in his death smell.

*

The metropolis of Washington DC is suffering winter's
treachery again. It is almost spring, yet the wind chill
temperature is close to freezing. I step into BWI airport
wrapped in a thin grey, rayon blanket loaned to me by the
airline. Refusing to let Arun buy me clothes, I had borrowed
a dress from Elaine Johnson at the Consulate for the journey.

She also helped retrieve my passport and arrange for my ticket back home.

Not having any luggage to claim, I am walking away from baggage claim towards the exits marked TAXICABS, when, behind me, I hear someone call my name. I turn around. Scott is standing a few feet from me, the aquarelle in his eyes brilliant, iridescent.

'Arun called me,' he says, quietly. 'He told me you were travelling without warm clothes.' He holds out a familiar black wintercoat, its sleeve holes dark and inviting like the inside of a womb. But I hesitate.

'It's your coat, Simi,' Scott says. 'Don't worry, I'm not offering you mine.'

I pull off the blanket and slip my arms into the sleeves tentatively. Scott smoothes it over my shoulders and offers me a ride home.

I don't go to my own house. I can't, just yet. Instead, I ask Scott to take me to his condo. Sitting snuggled in a thick blanket, drinking a blend of warm milk and Kalhua, I listen drowsily to the commercials on television. Scott has turned it on to watch the CBS evening news. Setting my cup on the table, I cushion my head on the arm of the sofa and close my eyes. Dan Rather's voice floats over, pronouncing lullabies from all over the world. 'And now an update on the bombing in the city of Amritgarh in India,' I hear him say. My eyes fly open.

Scott flips the channel hurriedly. 'I'm sorry,' he says. 'I had no idea.'

'It's okay,' I say. 'Turn it back on. I want to hear.' He punches channel nine again.

'. . . is still a mystery,' Dan Rather is saying. On the screen I see a clip of the masjid looking already like an ancient ruin, a confluence of histories, an embrace of souls.

One time I remember I asked Daddy if he missed India. 'Like a lover,' he said, holding a hand over his heart as if to contain the broken pieces within.

I remember the radiance on Kalida's face. How blind I have been. I saw Daddy suffer all his life and assumed it was his guilt that consumed him. When all along, what he was really suffering from was the epiphany of love. It was the love affair he couldn't get over. I gave his pain reasons and devised solutions, essential principles of cause and effect. How was I to know that in such love, no principle follows its given course, or any course at all? That in such love, there are no principles, only a random beginning and an unprincipled end. Or perhaps, not even that. Perhaps in such a love affair, there is only a continuum—from Daddy's heartbreak to Kalida's consummation. That is why Daddy didn't let me annihilate his pain in the obliterating waters of the Ganga, but chose instead, to mingle with the soil of India, bloodied though it might be.

Realizing at last that I have delivered his soul not to peace, not to penance, but to ecstasy, I pull out my right hand from within the blanket. It is bandaged from the wrist to the tips of my fingers, but I know that under the stark sterility, my blood has erased the imprint of Daddy's teardrop. I wonder if the drops of blood I spilled on the soil of India would extract any promises of their own. I shut my eyelids, and let the distance between time zones converge behind my eyes.